Honeymoon Phase

PRAISE FOR THE NOVELS OF AMY DAWS

"I dare you not to fall in love with the Mountain Men Matchmaker series!"

—Lucy Score, #1 *New York Times* bestselling author, on *Honeymoon Phase*

"Deliciously funny and spicy."

—Elsie Silver, #1 *New York Times* bestselling author, on *Seven Year Itch*

"A hilariously fresh and spicy rom-com that I couldn't put down!"

—Meghan Quinn, *New York Times* bestselling author, on *Nine Month Contract*

Dear Reader,

You have officially entered mountain man territory!

Check out the other hilarious and emotional love stories in the Mountain Men Matchmaker series by Amy Daws, starting with *Nine Month Contract* (Wyatt's story) and *Seven Year Itch* (Calder's story), available now from Canary Street Press.

And look out for their CEO brother Max's single dad boss/nanny love story, *Last on the List*, available now in all formats!

If you want more sexy rom-coms with humor and heart, check out the other stand-alone stories in the Wait With Me series by Amy Daws, releasing in print in 2026 from Canary Street Press, and available now in ebook and audio!

ALSO BY AMY DAWS

The Mountain Men Matchmaker series

Nine Month Contract
Seven Year Itch

The Wait With Me series

Wait With Me
Next In Line
One Moment Please
Take A Number
Last on the List

The Harris Brothers series

Challenge
Endurance
Keeper
Surrender
Dominate

The Harris Brothers spin-off stand-alones

Payback
Blindsided
Replay
Sweeper
Strength

For additional books by Amy Daws, visit her website, amydawsauthor.com. For exclusive news on upcoming releases and updates on all your favorite characters, sign up for her newsletter at amydawsauthor.com/newsletter.

Honeymoon Phase

AMY DAWS

CANARY STREET PRESS

Recycling programs for this product may not exist in your area.

ISBN-13: 978-1-335-49843-4
ISBN-13: 978-1-335-00111-5 (Hardcover)

Honeymoon Phase

Copyright © 2025 by Amy Daws

All rights reserved. No part of this book may be used or reproduced in any manner whatsoever without written permission.

Without limiting the exclusive rights of any author, contributor or the publisher of this publication, any unauthorized use of this publication to train generative artificial intelligence (AI) technologies is expressly prohibited. Harlequin also exercises their rights under Article 4(3) of the Digital Single Market Directive 2019/790 and expressly reserve this publication from the text and data mining exception.

This is a work of fiction. Names, characters, places, and incidents are either the product of the author's imagination or are used fictitiously. Any resemblance to actual persons, living or dead, businesses, companies, events or locales is entirely coincidental.

For questions and comments about the quality of this book, please contact us at CustomerService@Harlequin.com.

TM is a trademark of Harlequin Enterprises ULC.

Canary Street Press
22 Adelaide St. West, 41st Floor
Toronto, Ontario M5H 4E3, Canada
CanaryStPress.com

HarperCollins Publishers
Macken House, 39/40 Mayor Street Upper,
Dublin 1, D01 C9W8, Ireland
www.HarperCollins.com

Printed in Lithuania.

To all those a part of the Dead Dad Club.
We can do hard things.

Prologue

FACT OR FICTION?
Marriage of convenience is a thing.

Dear Ms. Addison Monroe or more affectionately known as "Roe,"

It has come to my attention, as your closest rugged, bearded male confidant, that you are in need of a husband to take over your father's lumber supply company. While I in no way support the antiquated mindset of your ancestors who created the trust stipulation that forces you to marry, I realize that we cannot always pick our family and desperate times call for desperate measures.

I too am in a desperate situation. All my brothers are now wife'd up and everyone in my family is giving me "the look" like I'm next.

I don't want to be next.

I will do anything not to be next.

I want to live on my mountain with my pet rooster and be free until I'm old and gray.

It seems you want a similar situation; therefore, I think we should wed.

Please reply with your answer at your earliest convenience.

Your friend,
Luke Fletcher

Chapter 1

FACT OR FICTION?
My brothers and I all fell for the same girl.

Luke

10 Years Earlier

"No woman is better than this," my brother Calder says, standing at the lookout point of Fletcher Mountain. He's flanked by pine trees as his eyes move from me to my brother Wyatt on my right.

He looks up behind us at our three cabins nestled perfectly in their prospective locations all at various levels of construction. It's a beautiful sight seeing our homes beside each other atop a Colorado mountain. A fucking dream some might say.

Wyatt bought this peak outside of Boulder just a year ago. At the time, the only existing structure was a dilapidated red barn with an outhouse. Our dad thought he was crazy for moving up here and living in the mice-infested apartment above the barn. But Wyatt made it work. He always craved a life outside of town. He doesn't people real well.

But he was onto something, because we all realized quickly that there's something magical about his mountain. It's like an instant anxiety reducer when you're here. Which meant that when Wyatt offered me and Calder a plot of land to build our own places next to him, we jumped at the chance.

Now the three of us brothers reside in a full-blown compound-living situation that many people think we're crazy for. But it works for us. We carpool the thirty minutes into Boulder every day and work construction for our father. We get drinks together after work and even make the occasional meals together. Monthly poker nights, weekly barhopping excursions. We're each other's best friends, which sometimes feels bigger than family. We fight, yes, but we work through it. And for the most part, we get along. Some might say we're the closest brothers they'd ever seen.

Hard to believe we were beating the ever-loving shit out of each other less than twelve hours ago.

All because of a girl.

My swollen eye stings as I shake out my fist, wishing I could erase the memories of everything that went down last night. Wyatt's lip is still covered in dried blood from my cracked knuckle and his busted lip. Calder's cheekbone is red and swollen and I know there's a wicked bruise developing on his back from Wyatt ramming him into the bar. We've been in some brawls together before, but we were usually teaming up against other guys . . . not each other.

Judy, the owner of The Mercantile where we were at last night, threw us all out and called our dad. It was like we were a group of rowdy teenagers, not three grown men in our twenties. But I was instantly thrust back into my childhood when my dad pulled up and dragged all three of us up the mountain to give us a lecture that made us feel an inch fucking tall. And we're all well over six foot.

It wasn't one of our proudest moments.

And I'd love to place blame on the woman who came between us . . . but deep down, I know we are the ones responsible for this.

The three of us made a bet over a girl and that bet blew up in our faces, ending with a husband we never knew about and a nail-biting paternity test involving all of us.

If I never see Robyn Whitaker and her "husband" again for the rest of my life, it will be too damn soon. Those two took their fucked-up relationship back to Colorado Springs with their baby on the way and I tried not to spit on their car on their way out of town. The shame I have over that relationship is something I can't even look my father or mother in the eye about.

"Let's make a pact to never fall in love," I add, my eyes sweeping down the mountain vista to land on the small rural community of Jamestown. It rests at the bottom of Fletcher Mountain and it's a place I intend to call home for the rest of my life, even if that means I have to spend the next decade making up to Judy for trashing her bar.

"Seriously," I add, turning to address both of my brothers. "We can do one-night stands or casual fucks or random hookups. We can satisfy our needs however we need to, but we don't do girlfriends. Ever. We sure as hell don't do wives. All relationships do is bring trouble. Hell, look how it turned out for Max."

Wyatt and Calder both jerk their heads back, not laughing at my glib tone, but taking it seriously, which I appreciate. As the youngest of four boys, I tend to let the older brothers do the dictating, but I want to be heard right now. Our oldest brother Max's story is a messy one. He lives in Boulder and is successful in business, and a great dad to his daughter, Everly. But losing his college girlfriend and the mother of his daughter to another woman wasn't easy on him. It's been years since he was divorced and he's still a stiff, controlling pain in the ass. And I get it. No amount of time can heal that level of trauma.

That situation, plus our mess with all three of us secretly fucking the same woman behind each other's backs, makes it painfully obvious that the Fletcher brothers are not suited for true love. Our parents' happy marriage did not translate into our DNA. Letting a woman in is a recipe for disaster. Who needs that mess in their lives?

I step closer to my brothers, capturing their full attention when I grip each of them by a shoulder. "We have this peak. We have our homes. We have our father's business. We're best friends who live the dream up here . . . or we used to, before we let Robyn get between us. Nothing in life is more important than us. Right?"

"Damn right," Wyatt growls in his deep timbre.

"Hell yes," Calder confirms, grabbing my shoulder back.

I smile the first smile I have in the past few months of the shit show that was my love life with the woman who moved into the barn apartment and caused this conflict with my brothers. It feels good. Healing. Like we're getting back to who we used to be and can finally see the forest through the trees.

"You boys done with this bullshit now?" our dad's voice barks from nearby and all three of us turn our heads to look at him.

I straighten and move to stand in a line to silently voice my apology alongside my brothers for ripping our family apart, not to mention our father's business.

"Good," he huffs back before offering a tight smile. "Maybe you can come see your niece, then."

"Seriously?" I ask, stepping away from my brothers to move toward my dad as hope blooms in my chest. My brothers both look just as excited as I do. It's been months since we've seen Everly. Max cut off our contact with her when this Robyn thing all blew up and rumors started circulating around Boulder. And no matter how many times I texted asking if I could just talk to the little tyke on the phone, he refused. Said we needed to get our life together before we could be uncles again.

Honestly, Everly is probably my number one reason to never let a woman into my life again. She isn't even ten years old, but she's got us all wrapped around her tiny finger. She's an important part of our lives, and I'm ashamed I let this Robyn stuff allow me to lose sight of that.

"We're not here for a long time. We're here for a good time," my dad says with a wink. "Let's go spoil our Evie-girl."

And with that, we all hightail it off the peak and down to Boulder where romantic love can be a thing of the past and our niece can resume being the one and only love of our lives.

Chapter 2

FACT OR FICTION?
My niece has bigger balls than I do.

Luke

Present Day

My brothers are lying assholes. Sellouts. Traitorous jerks. You know those people who say one thing and do another? That's those three fuckers.

Ten years ago, we stood on this mountain and made a pact to be she-man woman haters until we were old and gray. But the image I'm looking at right now is the exact opposite of that. I'm staring at disgusting rural mountain suburbia. It's like our rustic mountain setting is being gentrified. This scene of my brothers and their new lady friends looks like it could be out of *Alternative Amish Life* magazine or some bullshit.

How the mighty have fallen.

Wyatt walks over to his wife of five months, Trista, and holds his hands out to take their eight-month-old baby, Stevie. They're on the front porch of Calder's cabin while Calder stands there in all his tattooed, bearded, obnoxious glory. He has his fucking pet cat strapped to his chest in a baby carrier while his hand is stuffed down his girlfriend Dakota's back pocket, groping her ass as they all sip on lemonade and cool down after they've just moved Dakota permanently onto Fletcher Mountain.

Sellouts.

Then there's Max standing up there with his wife, Cozy.

They've been married for years now and Cozy and Dakota are best friends, so they were all too happy to drive the thirty-odd minutes up from Boulder and help Dakota get settled in. Their two kids are loving all this too. Even though Everly's at college, she's still smiling and slurping down refreshments with Ethan like this is the best day of her life because Dakota's auntie status is more official now.

All three of my brothers are coupled up even though a decade ago, we stood right on this lookout point and made a pact. A pact that we held strong but they somehow forgot about the moment these three women came into their lives.

Heavy sigh.

Max gets a free pass since he wasn't a part of this pact. He's Mr. Corporate and lives a very different life in Boulder, but I thought after his divorce, he'd be anti-woman as well.

Though I can't deny that Cozy was perfect for both Max and Everly. She fit right into that family, even getting along with Max's ex and her wife. One big happy modern family. And we've had eight years enjoying their wild son, Ethan, too because of that love. Ethan is a menace you can't help but love.

And I guess Wyatt gets a free pass also because his situation with Trista last year was complicated. Hired surrogate turned lover? That was never going to end well. That miserable fucker needed Trista or he was going to brood himself into an early grave.

But Calder falling for Dakota? That seems intentional. Like he was pointing at me and saying the last one in love is a rotten egg. That's Calder's style too. Probably didn't even want to fall in love but since Wyatt did, he just followed suit so he wouldn't be left behind.

Now there's just me. The baby of the family left to fend for myself on this mountain all on my own. Our brotherly late-night drinking sessions have turned into late-night diaper runs or Calder making sex eyes at Dakota so blatantly that I have to leave his cabin mid-beer.

It's depressing.

And the worst part is . . . I've sacrificed a lot for the pact. More than my entire family even realizes.

Everly bounds over to me, her blond ponytail swinging with the backdrop of the giant U-Haul parked behind her. "What are you doing over here all by yourself, Uncle Luke? Don't you want some lemonade? We moved a shitload of boxes today."

I roll my eyes and turn away from the mountain breeders to drop down onto the bench Calder made after our dad died a few years ago. It has his infamous saying etched on it, "We're not here for a long time, we're here for a good time," and I can't help but think the shit happening behind me doesn't look like a good time.

"I hate being a third wheel," I mumble under my breath. "Or seventh wheel I should say."

Everly huffs out a laugh as she joins me on the bench. She tucks her long legs under her chin and eyes me thoughtfully. "I was thinking it's high time we change that. I'm a pretty decent matchmaker you know."

"Yeah right." I tug my baseball cap low on my face to conceal my brooding.

"I'm serious." She pokes my shoulder and scoots closer to me. "You know it was me who finagled the single room in Mexico for Uncle Calder and Dakota, right?"

My eyes bug out of my head as I turn to look at my niece, who looks far less innocent than she did moments ago. "He was pissed about that."

"Oh please." Everly waves me off. "He wasn't pissed. He was in love. He just needed enough one-on-one time with Dakota to realize it."

I twist my hat around so it's backward, tucking back my

shaggy hair behind my ears with it. I want to be sure I can see my niece clearly right now because I'm having trouble believing the words tumbling out of her mouth.

She hits me with a lascivious smirk. "And you know I was the one who found Trista, right?"

I frown and shake my head. "Yeah, but just to be a surrogate for Wyatt," I argue, turning to face my evil-looking niece head-on. "You can't take credit for them falling in love."

"I knew she'd be perfect for him. Why else do you think he rejected all the other surrogate applicants he spoke to at that agency? He was looking for love, not a surrogate. He just couldn't admit that to himself. The lies we tell ourselves are so obvious sometimes."

"Bullshit," I laugh and look out at the mountain view, my eyes narrowing as I replay the last year of our lives when I watched both of my brothers fall in love in rapid succession. "You're not that powerful."

"Need I remind you of Dad and Cozy?" she asks coyly. "That was my matchmaker origin story."

"Holy fuck," I deadpan as I recall Everly's wild plot to get me, Calder, and Wyatt to help her with Max and Cozy after they got in an epic fight all those years ago. Everly was like eleven at the time and she parent-trapped them like a boss. My nephew, Ethan, is living proof of how well that worked.

As if on cue, I hear the squawk of my rooster, Rufus, and turn around to see Ethan sprinting up the hill toward my cabin. Usually roosters are the ones to terrorize humans, but not in this case. Evil Ethan always strikes first. Rufus spots the little terror and flies off my porch rail, running toward the forest for cover.

My poor cock.

And I realize that the rooster technically isn't "mine" because Trista was the one to adopt him. He's one of the many random animals that kept appearing in the barn this past year thanks to her ever-growing rescue center.

But Rufus chose me.

A few months back, he decided that my front porch was his home turf instead of the nice chicken coop Wyatt built for them down by the barn. So yeah, me and Ruf-meister are tight. The early morning wake-up calls are brutal, but I've found that I like that damn bird. I even bring him inside for treats in the evenings. Rufus loves tortilla wraps and walnuts and sitting on my lap during TV time. It might be weird to have a pet cock but at least I'm not strapping him to my chest and taking him for walks through the woods like Calder and his cat, Milkshake. Weird fuck.

"I think it's your turn to find love, Uncle Luke." Everly's eyes narrow on me and my skin begins to crawl as she gets that scary look about her that she used to get as a kid right before she got exactly what she wanted. This girl has a freaky way of persuading people to do whatever she tells them. Maybe it's because she has a rich-ass father who has a private plane and multiple houses and wipes his ass with hundred-dollar bills. Or maybe it's because she has three uncles who spoil her rotten any chance we get. Or maybe it's because despite all the privileges she's received in life, she's still the purest, kindest, most positive person I've ever met and you just can't help but want to move mountains for someone like that.

One way or another, the end result is that my niece . . . is a force of nature.

I level my eyes at her. "You really are an evil genius, aren't you?"

"I prefer to call myself a 'mastermind.'" She waggles her brows and gets a wild look in her gaze. "Now, come on. What's your type? Give me something to work with. I think I know but I want to hear what you have to say."

I shake my head firmly, trying to muster up the strength

to say no to my niece. "Don't add me to your matchmaking schemes."

"Why not?"

My lips thin as my heart thumps with an ache I've been trying to ignore for the past several years. "Because it's pointless."

"Why?"

Because I'm the greatest hypocrite of them all.

I inhale a heavy breath as I allow myself to say the next words out loud for the first time. "Because the woman I want doesn't want me back."

The quiet sounds of nature are deafening during the silence that spreads between me and Everly. My niece's voice is soft when she asks, "How long have you been in love with Addison Monroe?"

"How do you know it's her?" I balk defensively.

"Because you brought her to Mexico for Wyatt and Trista's wedding and stared at her like a lost puppy the entire time."

I pull my hat forward to cover my face, feeling like a complete schmuck. It's extremely humbling having your college-aged niece read you with so little effort. And yet, here I sit on a mountain surrounded by pines . . . pining for a girl I can never have. I am pathetic.

"I wasn't sure of your feelings until the end of the trip, or I would have tried to force you two into the same room as well." Everly purses her lips like she's disappointed in herself, which is fucking ridiculous.

I swallow the knot in my throat, attempting to regain control of this conversation. "Let's talk about when you're flying back to Ireland for college. I'm going to miss you something fierce again. This summer went way too fast."

"Stop trying to change the subject." Everly scowls back at me.

"I don't want to have this conversation with you," I groan, feeling the weight of the world on my shoulders.

"Why not?"

"Because Addison is getting married, so none of it matters." I drop the truth on my niece just to get her to realize this isn't a conversation that will have a happy ending. Not for me anyways.

Everly sucks a sharp breath as she presses her hand to her chest. "To who?"

"I don't know. But when Roe puts her mind to something, she gets it done." I roll out my shoulders, feeling tense over just saying the nickname I pegged her with shortly after we met. I think it was a defense mechanism to put her in the friends-only zone. *Addison* is too feminine. Too intimate. *Roe* is tough. Ballsy. It's a derivative of her last name of Monroe, like what we do with guys Calder and I play intermural hockey with. It helps put her staunchly in the bro category where she belongs, so no one gets hurt.

But the way my body reacts when I think about her is very un-bro-like. And she's not even standing in front of me right now to inspire such indecent thoughts.

"I need more details, Luke," Everly snaps, losing patience with my less-than-stellar storytelling.

I exhale heavily. Maybe if I tell someone the full situation, I'll stop feeling like my head is about to explode. Maybe I'll stop looking at my brothers in love with murder in my heart. Maybe I'll stop moping on this bench every night. Maybe I'll stop stressing out over what one of my closest friends is attempting to do with her life.

"Roe told me when we were in Mexico for Wyatt and Trista's wedding a few months ago that she has to get married before the end of the year or her father is going to sell the lumberyard."

"Say what?" Everly exclaims, her voice taking on a raspy tone.

I grip the back of my neck and shrug. "Her dad is old-school and refuses to pass it on to her if she's on her own. The requirement is built into the trust that her great-grandfather created for the business. No single person can take over the company. So now she's trying to find some random dude to marry her so she can take full ownership."

The Cheshire cat smile that spreads across Everly's face is terrifying. "This is perfect," she peals, clapping her hands excitedly.

"How is this perfect?" I ask, gaping at my niece, who I consider myself very close to, but she seems far too happy over my less-than-ideal situation.

Everly has always felt more like a little sister than a niece. I'm thirty-three years old, so fourteen years older than her is obviously a big age gap, but Max had Everly when I was barely a teenager myself, so I feel like I grew up with her at the kids table. And we've always had this easy way of talking. Regular texts and phone calls even when she went away to Ireland for college. Actually, especially when she went away for college. I was worried sick every day of something happening to her. If she didn't text me back within an hour, my blood pressure would start to rise with every passing minute. Everly knows that about me too, so she does a good job keeping up with communication. She's really the only one who knows how much my head races to bad places if the people I care about are unreachable.

It's why I call my mom all the time too. Calder calls me a momma's boy for it, but it's not a bad thing to worry about our widowed mother. She's all alone now and God knows what could happen to her every day. She used to have my dad looking out for her, but now she has no one. I hate thinking of her in that big house all alone. I can't help but stress over the people in my life, especially the women.

Luckily Everly tolerates my need for communication fairly well. I miss her. And I've missed her words of wisdom. I don't know how the fuck she does it, but she really does give good advice. She has since she was young. Unexpected answers that feel pure and honest and untainted by the darkness of the world. It's no wonder she's a self-proclaimed matchmaker. She's good at peopling.

Unlike Wyatt, who grunts more than speaks, and Calder, who's constantly pushing people's buttons. Or Max, who always wants to control every situation he comes into contact with.

Everly, on the other hand, has this uncanny ability to make people say yes to things they wouldn't normally say yes to and somehow thank her for it when it's all said and done. In some ways, I've missed her scheming. Being so far away from her this past year while she was abroad for school has sucked, but I'm proud of her for branching out. My niece is braver than all four of us Fletcher brothers put together. Maybe I need to channel some of Everly's bravery in my own life to help me get over Roe.

"I couldn't have written this better myself." Everly rips me out of my inner musings as she begins tapping her fingers on her chin, clearly deep in some sort of plotting mode. "The universe is basically handing you this love story. You can be her husband!"

"No, I can't."

"Why not?"

"Because Roe doesn't want me. She doesn't even want to be married. She doesn't want love. Ever. She's anti-love. Anti-kids. Anti-anything traditional. Has been since the moment I met her, making it damn near impossible for me to confess even if I wanted to."

"Why is she anti-love?" Everly asks, her brows pinched together in confusion. Her innocent, naive heart knows no different than love and happily-ever-afters.

"That's just how she is," I reply, refusing to give Everly any more because some heavy shit happened to Roe when she was younger, and I would never betray her confidence by blabbing about her trauma to my niece. "I just know that whoever Roe finds to marry, it's strictly going to be a contractual business arrangement. They'll stay married for a year until she can fulfill the trust fund's requirements and then she can take ownership of the lumberyard. After that it's divorce court and 'peace out, sucker.' She's already got a prenup written up."

"So, you can be the sucker," Everly chirps, her body vibrating with urgency. "You two are friends so this makes perfect sense. Volunteer to be her husband."

"I can't do that, kid."

"Why not?"

"Because I already have," I snap, and my voice echoes down the mountain like a fucking siren call. Holding my breath, I turn around to see if my brothers heard and exhale with relief when they all still seem engrossed in their domestic infatuations. I don't want to hear my brothers' take on my situation, especially when they all seem so happy and in love. I don't need an audience for my failure.

"I wrote her a letter a few months ago and she rejected me. She wants a stranger. She has literally been going on dates with random guys on Tinder to try to find someone. That's why I got desperate and wrote her that stupid fucking letter that she laughed at. It's all fucking nonsense, and I told her that but she's so bullheaded, I can't get her to listen. I'm worried sick about her." I yank off my hat and slice my hands through my hair, hating how heavy this subject makes me feel.

"You're worried because you love her," Everly says quietly. "Not like a friend. Like a wife."

My lips thin as my niece pegs me better than even my own brothers have. It's embarrassing how long I've been harboring these feelings. Roe's made it incredibly clear where she stands when it comes to relationships and I've tried to respect that. I've tried to let these feelings go.

But I just . . .

I love her.

And I hate myself for it.

It didn't hit me all at once either. It was a slow, comfortable build. Like a great steady hike in the mountains where the ascent is gradual enough that I earn every step, but easy enough I can maintain my pace for miles. So I climb and I climb and I climb and don't even realize I reach the top until I look out and see the stunning view that is my friend and realize . . . holy fuck, this is what I've been missing.

It's her.

And when I realized that, I felt both annoyed at myself, for making that pact with my brothers after we all had our hearts broken, and terrified because the woman I loved could never love me back. This was setting up to be even worse than the Robyn situation I found myself in.

I had hoped that inviting Roe to my brother's wedding in Mexico could be my opportunity to possibly push past her hard outer shell. We'd see each other outside of Boulder. We'd lie by the pool or walk on the beach and dance to some music. I even hoped she'd connect with Trista, who I think is a lot like Roe in the sense that neither of them come from traditional families. I wanted her to see a different type of family. I wanted to show her that some people are worth taking a chance on. I wanted to also break the pact I was in with my brothers because they both have obviously moved on from that. Maybe it was my turn now too.

Then on night two, she dropped the bomb on me.

Told me she's looking for a marriage of convenience.

Not love. Not soulmates. Not a happily-ever-after.

Just a simple contract.

So, we slept in our separate rooms in the villa, behaving like friends because that's all we were and that was all we'd ever be.

And after we got back, I lost my ever-loving mind and wrote her that letter, trying to save her from her dire circumstances, to which she rejected me like I was a joke.

Now I'm preparing for my friend, who I'm in love with . . . to marry another man.

"If you love her then you have to go for it, Luke," Everly says, sounding desperate.

"I already tried once."

"You didn't try hard enough!" Everly urges, her blue eyes wide and excited. "We have to help her see. We need to spell it out for her. We can go deeper than a letter. Maybe we can write up a pros and cons list of all the reasons a friend would make a perfect fake husband. Things that will make her see that choosing you is so much better than choosing a stranger."

"What if I have too much pride for that, Evie-girl?"

"Love is stronger than pride." Everly grabs my arms and forces me to look at her, her blue eyes bright with determination. "Best-case scenario, she falls in love with you back. Worst-case scenario . . . she doesn't, and you've at least helped a friend out and kept her safe. But then you'll know and can finally move on with your life."

I pull my hat off and rake my hands through my hair, agonized over this place I find myself in. A few years ago, I never even wanted a girlfriend. Now I'm supposed to try to marry one of my closest friends as a manipulative way to get her to fall in love with me?

Jesus, I'm pathetic.

Then again, watching Roe marry a stranger sounds too painful to watch. Not to mention dangerous as fuck.

Maybe Everly is right. Maybe I could even convince myself that I'm simply encouraging my friend to marry me for her protection. That's what a friend would do, not stand aside and leave her to face potential danger. I can't let her do this with just anyone when I'm obviously the safer choice. I can help her with her situation and ensure her happiness and safety at the same time. That's definitely what a friend would do.

And if in the end, she doesn't share my feelings, I'll accept that as her choice and let her do what's best for her. Even though it will probably kill me.

"Let's say she agrees to marry me this time. What then?" I ask, pushing the heaviness away from my chest as I pose this question to my college-aged niece.

Everly smiles victoriously. "Then the real fun begins, and we figure out how to make your wife fall in love with you."

Chapter 3

FACT OR FICTION?
Old men make good husbands.

Addison

"Marry me, Chuck," I holler, throwing my hands out and kneeling before the forklift as the man old enough to be my father, and who was complaining of gout earlier this morning, climbs into the driver's seat.

He barks out a wet cough and shakes his head, his face full of so many wrinkles, you could turn it into a maze. "I'm going to say no for a fourth time. I'm sorry, darling. You know I hate breaking your heart."

I buzz my lips and stand to prop my hands on my hips. "Where's Bullhead? He hasn't said no to me this week yet."

"But he said no last week. Why do you think his answer will change?"

I shrug. "He's older than you, so I'm banking on him being a little senile."

Chuck eyes me with zero humor on his face. "I've said this before, but I'll say it again. You ain't gonna find any man in this lumberyard willing to say yes to you because everyone here knows your daddy. And if I walked up to your daddy and told him I'm marrying his twenty-eight-year-old daughter, I'd be watching a two-by-four break my nose and finding myself canned before the blood dried."

"But I'm a lumberyard heiress, Chuck!" I stomp my foot dramatically. "I can buy you a new nose."

"I'll stick with the honker I got." The forklift beeps a loud noise as he backs up away from me and with a growl, I turn on my heel and make my way back into the building center.

I pause as I stare at our signage etched across the glass door.

MONROE LUMBER AND BUILDING CENTER: FAMILY OWNED SINCE 1903

Apparently, that means fuck all to my father because he went and had to *fall in love*. Gross.

I stomp inside the building and make my way to the office in the back. It used to be my father's throne, so it's not much in terms of decor. Just a cheap veneer desk and filing cabinets covered in sawdust and cast-off office chairs that have seen better days. But the view of the lumberyard with the Front Range behind it is one that I've gotten used to and don't feel like surrendering if it's up to me.

And apparently, it is up to me. Me and my future unsuspecting husband. My phone buzzes in my back pocket and I pull it out to see my dad's face on the screen like he knew I was thinking about him.

"What do you want, Old Man River?" I snipe into the line as I drop down onto my desk chair.

"Well, someone's in a mood," my father drawls. "You too busy for your old man?"

"Chuck turned me down again," I grumble, propping my Converse platforms up on the desk.

"What about Bullhead?"

"I think he's hiding from me." I squint as I look out the window to see if his truck is here. I don't even know why they call him Bullhead. That's just been his name for as long as I can remember.

"He's still got a few brain cells left, then." My father clears his throat, and I can hear the drizzle of fresh coffee brewing in the background. "How many proposals have you done this week, then?"

"Just Chuck so far, but it's only Monday."

He pauses to take a loud sip, and I can picture his long gray mustache damp and stained from his regular coffees. "You know this is for the best, Addie May."

"Bullshit," I reply for the hundredth time. "I'm not giving up."

My dad and I have been having the same fight for the past six months since he dropped the massive bomb on me that he was moving to Florida with his new girlfriend and planning to sell the lumberyard to an interested buyer who'd put in a huge offer. Our family-run business for over a century is going to be sold off to some outsider.

Gross indeed.

"Your day-to-day life won't change. You'll still stay on as sales manager and have a stake in the business just like I will, but you won't be the primary owner. It's too much for one person to take on and you'll still make plenty of money."

"I don't care about money," I argue.

"Someday you will."

I lick my lips and drop my head back on my chair. "If I was a boy, we wouldn't be having this conversation." I wince as an image of my little brother flashes into my eyes.

My dad tsks. "The trust says nothing about gender, and you damn well know it."

"So you say," I murmur petulantly.

"Damn it anyways, Addie," my dad growls into the phone and I wince. I don't love poking him like this but until he concedes, I'm afraid that's just what our relationship is. I want this nightmare to be over. He continues with a more forceful tone, "The trust states that no single *person*, not man, not woman, no PERSON can own the lumberyard. My grandfather was old-fashioned but not sexist. Whether you were a boy or a girl, you're not qualified to inherit the business until you're married for a minimum of one year. I wouldn't have been able to take it over from my dad if I hadn't married your mom."

"Don't bring her up." A thickness forms in my throat at the mention of her and I wince at the sound of my teeth grinding in my ears.

He sighs. "I'm just saying. It's not about a business partner. It's about a life partner. Owning a company on your own is a lot of work and having that emotional support at home is important. That's why the trust says you have to reside with your partner, not just be married. Making a house a home and all that."

"You didn't have any of that after *she* left." I wince because we're talking about her again and I hate it. "You managed just fine."

"You were my home," he states firmly. "You're the one who gave me this potbelly with all that damn bread you kept making."

"Exactly." I slap my hand on the desk, sending sawdust particles everywhere. "I cooked and I managed to work at the yard. You know I can run this place with my eyes closed. Please just let me do this on my own. Let's hire a lawyer and change some shit around in that crusty old trust."

"Not gonna happen, Addie. I don't want that stress for you. It's too much for one person to bear."

Silence grows between us, and I lower my phone, stopping myself from arguing with him more.

He thinks I'm messing around with this husband quest, but he's dead wrong. I will find someone and fulfill the requirements of that trust. It's time I stop teasing the lumberyard guys and get serious since it's clear my dad isn't changing his mind.

My dad isn't a bad man. Stubborn, yes, but I know he's just trying to protect me, which is crazy because he raised me on his own like a feral animal in this lumberyard. I remember sleeping in his office on nights he'd have to wait for a late delivery or coming in with him at the ass crack of dawn to fulfill an order and having to take the city bus to school. I have been illegally driving the forklift since the age of fifteen. Hell, I was fourteen when I had my first beer with my dad and his cronies. I remember being smashed between him, Chuck, and Bullhead in a single cab pickup as we barreled down a gravel road while they made me hold a case of Budweiser on my lap and hand them fresh ones every time they tossed their empties out the window. I was scared out of my mind the cops would catch us, but I never told them about that because they'd make fun of me and call me "soft."

I wasn't soft.

I just hated littering and still to this day stop my vehicle if I see trash on the side of the road. We get one freaking world, you know? Find a damn trash can, people.

And I know some people of Boulder judged my father harshly for how they saw him raise me. But I'm grateful for my upbringing. The shit my dad and I went through together bonded us in a way that means I will forgive him for this bullshit trust he's refusing to revise, because I'm tough and self-sufficient and worked my way through some dark shit at a young age. And I have the calluses on my hands to prove it.

Which means I will not go down without a fight over this business trust stipulation. Even if that means getting my ass married, which is something I never planned to do.

I just didn't realize how hard it would be to actually find a guy. Apparently no one wants to sign a prenup stating they'll marry me, live with me for a year, and divorce me while receiving absolutely nothing in exchange. Weird, right?

Only that's not true. I did have an offer. But it's not one I could ever say yes to.

"How's Edith?" I ask, pulling my phone back up to my ear and attempting to show some semblance of humanity to the man who gave me everything I have in life except this lumberyard.

"She's good. She's at her weekly bridge club. I'm nursing a sunburn from shuffleboard yesterday."

I snort as I fight back a laugh. My dad sounds happy, despite our drama over the family business, and I guess that makes me happy. I never saw him date a woman after my mom left. Never even looked at one. Until Edith.

Now the old goat is slathering himself with aloe vera and happy as a clam in that retirement village they moved to. Though it's more of an early retirement village as he's just newly sixty. But the way he just up and decided to retire early is still an adjustment. Life is weird how it can change on a dime.

"Still can't get used to you living in Florida. I never thought I'd see the day you left Boulder."

"Me neither, Addie. But you'd be amazed at what one might endure for the love of a good woman. Hey, maybe that's your problem. Maybe you should be trying to marry a woman."

"Is that allowed?" I stand and walk over to the window with a furrow to my brow. "I mean, I don't really know a lot of women, but that does open up my prospects a bit."

"Addison, it's called a joke—" he pauses for a second before adding "—unless you're coming out to me in which case I owe some money to Bullhead."

I roll my eyes and make a noise in the back of my throat. "Keep your money, Old Man. I'm strictly dickly."

Long, heavy pause.

"I could have lived my whole life without hearing those words come out of my daughter's mouth."

"I've heard ten times worse come out of Bullhead's mouth!"

Dad harrumphs. "Yeah, he's burned too many brain cells I'm afraid."

"But seriously though, I'm open to same-sex marriage for this trust issue to be resolved. How did you hit on Edith? What was your move?"

"Goodbye, Addie May. I'll see you in October for the Man of the Mountain competition. You're still doing the awards presentation, right?"

"Does a bear shit in the woods?" I deadpan.

Another heavy pause. "It's moments like this that I recognize how much I failed as a father."

We hang up and I walk over to the bulletin board on the wall by the window where the Man of the Mountain flyer is pinned. The top text above the logo is "Sponsored by Monroe Lumber and Building Center." At the bottom of the flyer, it reads "All Proceeds to Go to the Fallen Angels Family Center," a charity that supports families and victims of drunk drivers.

My throat tightens as I rub my finger along our business logo. This event is huge for the yard every year and raises a shit ton of money for this charity. What if the new owners my dad wants to sell to don't sponsor this every year? What if the charity has come to depend on this donation and struggles without it? Has my dad put any of that in writing?

Damn, I need a husband. Or a wife! They started offering the women's division with Man of the Mountain a few years ago on a different weekend and you bet your ass I signed up as fast as I could.

I then proceeded to get my ass kicked by real-life lumberjills that work in the mills or reside in logging towns. I was delusional to think working in a lumberyard prepared me to go up against lumberjills. The truth is, I'm a bougie Boulder-born "softie" compared to those beasts, but it was a fun experience to at least try and fail at.

Now I just show up and present the medals to the winners

and a check to the charity at the closing ceremonies. A much easier gig that my dad pawned off on me years ago the moment his knees started struggling to climb those stage steps.

And he just wants to sell that family tradition right out from under me.

It's too bad I've never made friends with any of the ladies I competed against or maybe I could ask one of them to be my fake partner for a year until I inherit this company. But honestly, the lumberjill squad scares me. And what would I even say? "Hi, my name's Addison. I'm not a lesbian but would you consider being my friend and maybe marrying me and living with me for a year so I can inherit my family's lumberyard and then divorce you?"

I roll my eyes. Women are way too smart to say yes to that. Men are simpler creatures. I've really only had guy friends . . . or at least . . . guy friends of my dad's since the lumberyard was basically our whole life. I host a meal for the guys at least once a week at the yard here without my dad around. That's friendship, right? Or does it not count if they're my employees? Are they just tolerating me because I'm the owner's daughter?

Luke Fletcher is my only friend outside the lumberyard and he's definitely not my dad's friend. My dad can't stand Luke. He mean mugs him every time he comes in. It's comical really. I think the old man assumed it was a romantic thing developing between me and Luke, so that's why he went into the "I own several guns and know how to use them" mode, but that's all for nothing. Luke and I are just friends.

I don't really even know how our friendship happened. One day he was one of the burly bearded brothers who came in to pick up building supplies for Fletcher Brothers Construction, and the next day he was just . . . a part of my life.

We grab drinks or lunch together pretty regularly since we both work in Boulder. I even have him over to my apartment for dinner quite a bit. Cooking is a passion of mine but it's not fun doing it for just one person, so I like having Luke over. Chuck and Bullhead don't have the refined palates that some of my more daring dishes require.

Luke, on the other hand, loves everything I make.

I haven't cooked for him in a couple months now because we're sort of in a fight? I'm not sure. I just know we haven't spoken much since he offered to marry me after we were in Mexico for his brother's wedding. The whole thing was awkward as fuck. I thought he was messing with me, and it turns out he was serious I guess? I'm not sure because he's avoiding me like an asshole.

And hell, I miss him. He's usually such a safe space for me. I can be "soft" with him, and he never teases me for it, because he only knows me that way. I never hide that part of myself from him.

Unlike my dad and his friends, who I've had to act tough for most of my young adult life. I remember getting my period at work and asking if I could run to the store for something and my dad barked at me to get back to work because we were way behind. I didn't have the courage to tell him what my real problem was, so I just balled up toilet paper and got back on the forklift.

The horror I felt when I got off the chair and saw that I'd leaked on the seat haunts me to this day. I snuck back into the lumberyard after hours to clean up my mess so none of the guys would see it the next day. That kind of secrecy gets tiring.

And with Luke, it doesn't even exist. Hell, one time I randomly told him on the phone that I was crabby because I had my period and he brought me chocolate when he came to pick up an order. Who taught him how to do that for a woman? His mom? That's impressive because she had four boys, so it's not like she had any reason to discuss it. Or maybe it was his niece that he's super close to. All I know is he's going to make a great husband to someone someday. Just not me.

My eyes catch sight of movement out in the lumberyard, and I step in front of the window to get a better look.

My heart rate quickens because it's Luke Fletcher out there talking to Bullhead as if I conjured him here with my thoughts. Dang, he looks good. Has he gotten more buff since our trip?

When I first met the Fletcher brothers, I could barely tell them apart. They're all well-over-six-foot, bearded, and built bros who must share a closet as well as a mountaintop because I rarely see them in anything but plaids and jeans, even in the thick of summer.

But Luke has a slightly leaner build to his frame than the others. That was very clear in Mexico when the guys were all shirtless in the pool. All of them are extremely fit for thirty- and even fortysomething-year-old men. But Luke's muscles are way more defined. I could see every ridge of his abs and the deep V of his hips that disappeared into those low-slung boardshorts. The genetics in that family are out of this world.

Luke moves differently too. His gait is quicker and more purposeful. Probably from being the youngest of four boys and always running to catch up. *I remember what it felt like to have a little brother chase after me.*

My throat feels tight as that thought conjures up a memory I don't want to explore, so I grab my phone and make my way through the building center to head outside.

The August sun is blazing as I beeline across the hot pavement, straight for my buddy. He hasn't picked up an order here in weeks, usually sending his brother Calder instead. I'm about to give him a piece of my mind about that. Luke's head turns as if he can sense my approach, and when we lock eyes, I instantly feel lighter.

"Hey, shithead!" I bellow as I barrel right into him, giving him a hard shove in the gut that pushes all the air from his lungs.

He laughs and shakes his head, stumbling back and pressing his hand to his hat in that shy way he has about him. He squints and shoots me a smile. "Hey, Roe."

"Long time no see." I prop my hands on my hips and glance over to Bullhead, who's writing something down in a clipboard. "I can take over, Bullhead."

"Okay, boss lady," Bullhead says, tucking his pencil behind his ear before passing off Luke's order form to me. He waves his goodbye and takes off and I turn back to my friend, noticing he seems to be avoiding eye contact with me.

"What brings you in today?" I ask, glancing down at the sheet but not really giving a shit about it.

"Oh, we need some decking quotes for a new smart house we're bidding out," Luke replies, walking over to a large stack of uncapped composite decking we just got in. It uses a lot of recycled plastics in it, so it's always something his brother Wyatt goes for with all the green developing the Fletcher Brothers started doing the past few years.

"Why didn't you call me?" I ask, blocking the sun from my eyes as I squint up at him. Luke is a solid six foot two and I'm maybe five-six in my platform shoes, so he's definitely got the height advantage on me.

"Wyatt wanted me to come see what you had on hand."

"Cool, cool," I reply, wondering why it feels so fucking awkward with my friend right now. "We can get you set up for sure."

"Thanks," Luke replies, stuffing his hands into his pockets.

"So how have you been?" I ask, sitting down on a stack of two-by-sixes that wobble under my weight.

"Good, you?" Luke replies automatically as he moves over and steadies the wood.

"Can't complain." I shrug dismissively. "It's weird not having my dad around here every day."

"I bet." Luke glances back at the building center. "Nice for me though. I don't have to worry about a rifle being pointed through that window right there."

I laugh as I recall the time I stood right here with Luke, and we saw my dad holding his hunting gun in the window. He wasn't aiming it at us, just showing it off and making his feelings known.

"He's all talk."

"So you keep telling me." Luke yanks his baseball hat off his head and runs his fingers through his sandy-brown hair that's longer than I've ever seen it. It curls out at the bottom when he puts his cap back on and I have a strange urge to run my fingers through it. Not that I would ever act on that urge.

My God that would be awkward.

There was a moment in Mexico, however, where I thought Luke was wanting to cross our friendship boundaries. He had this look in his eyes when we got to the villa and realized we had to share a two-bed suite that made me so fucking nervous.

It's not that I don't find Luke attractive. I'd have to be dense as hell not to notice.

It's just that I could never cross that line with him because I like him too much. I'm not a relationship girlie and I never will be, so to sleep with someone I consider a friend would be the quickest way to lose said friend. Same goes for marrying said friend.

Thankfully, Luke never acted on anything. In fact, after I unloaded to him about my husband hunt plan, he told me he planned to never get married as well. Which is why I was so taken off guard by that letter he wrote me. I still don't really know if he was serious about that or just joking. Going MIA with me for nearly two months makes me wonder.

"You doing okay without your dad around though? Seriously?" Luke stares at me with a concerned look in his eyes that feels like a warm hug.

I shrug and wrinkle my nose, trying not to reveal just how much it's been affecting me. "He's happy so that's all that matters."

Luke's brown eyes search mine. "You matter."

Damn him. He always sees right through me.

"Hey, why don't you come over for dinner tomorrow night?" I ask, trying to get the focus off me. "I haven't cooked anything decent in ages."

Luke's brows lift with interest. "What's on the menu?"

"Whatever you like. I'm running to the store tonight so you can place your request."

"Oh shit . . . that's an offer I can't refuse." He crosses his arms over his chest, his corded muscles on full display as he pinches his chin in thought. "Your Alfredo is amazing. Your salmon is amazing. Oh . . . that bang bang shrimp you made one time still makes me drool randomly."

I laugh and shake my head, letting the food compliments roll over me in a way that heals my soul. I love cooking for people and hearing how much they enjoy it. It's an act-of-service thing that scratches a part of my brain and gives me validation on some fundamental level.

"Is it too hot for your jambalaya?" Luke asks, glancing up at the sun. "That's basically a soup, right?"

"It's more of a stew or a one-pot dish, but who gives a fuck. Fact or fiction . . . soup is my favorite food group?"

"That is a fact," Luke replies with a warm smile.

I smile back at him, feeling better than I have since my dad flew out to Florida over a month ago. "Seven 'o clock work for you?"

"I'll bring the beer."

"My man." I slap my hands on my thighs, grateful that it feels like the old Luke is back. Hopefully he's done being mad at me over this whole husband hunt thing. We're too good of friends to let a potential fake marriage come between us.

"Come on into the AC and we can talk about what you guys need to order."

"Sounds good," he says, and I feel myself grinning as I lead the way back to my office. This smile right here is why I'll do whatever it takes to keep Luke in my life . . .

. . . because no one makes me feel as good as him.

Not even soup.

Chapter 4

FACT OR FICTION?
Lumberjacks make good husbands.

Luke

The first time I met Roe was at the lumberyard. She was driving a forklift and pulling down a stack of two-by-fours and loading them onto a trailer for a customer who was basically catcalling her the whole time. He and the guy with him both chuckled and stared at her ass while telling her to "take her time" as she climbed up into the equipment.

I wanted to bash their heads in.

But it was unnecessary because Roe had it covered. She drove the forklift over to the lumber the guys were picking up, forked it onto her machine, and deposited it on top of the man's truck cab instead of in the bed of the truck. The guy yelled and screamed for her to stop because the wood was scratching his brand-new truck. Boards dropped off the top one by one, denting his hood and cracking his windshield, even ripping off one of his side mirrors.

He screamed at her that she was a dumb bitch, and he wanted to see her boss and she just sat in her forklift and smiled gleefully before she replied, "I am the boss."

The man and his buddy sobered right up and asked who would pay for the damages and she said, "Probably our company insurance, but we won't pay nearly as much as your offspring who have to walk around this earth with a perverted misogynistic asshole's DNA in their veins. Can I get you anything else today?"

I'd never been more turned on.

Which was an odd reaction, I'll admit. I wasn't sure it made me better or worse than the asshole with the trashed truck. She helped me next, and I watched her silently as she loaded up my order and she didn't even spare me a glance.

When I went inside to pay her, I heard myself asking her out for drinks. I thought she'd laugh in my face and run me out of there with her forklift.

But she didn't.

She handed me my receipt and asked me when and where.

I didn't intend for it to be a date. I'm not a guy who "dates" per se. But I'd be lying if I said I wasn't hoping to fuck her afterward. She's a beautiful woman and her terrifying vibe was a weird, unexpected turn-on for me.

But then she showed up to the bar and we started talking. She rambled about her sourdough yeast she named Mildred and asked me about my favorite kinds of foods. We discussed work and our parents, and it was the easiest conversation I've ever had with a woman. I realized within an hour that I didn't want to stop talking to her. Ever. And if I had sex with her . . . the talking would stop.

So . . . I friend-zoned myself for the first time in my entire life.

Our friendship was good for several years. Solid. Comforting. Then my dad died, and it got weird. She pulled away and didn't come to the funeral and that killed me. I told myself I was done with her, that not showing up was an inexcusable thing a friend would never do.

But suddenly, I found myself back at her place and we were eating dinner in her living room like nothing happened. I'd expected her to apologize, to ask me how I was doing. But it was as if she had no clue what grief felt like—or she understood it all too well—and nothing was said. I knew from the very limited things she'd told me about her childhood that it hadn't been easy. So, I had to make a choice. Forgive her for not caring for me "how I'd wanted" or hold a grudge and lose her friendship forever. Forgiving her had been the better option.

Plus, *I missed her.*

Somewhere along the way I realized that I loved her too much to stay mad at her and that was a terrifying realization I was trying not to focus on too much at the time.

I make my way up the exterior staircase to Roe's apartment. She has a one bedroom in a small quadplex that ain't much to look at. I always wondered why she doesn't buy something nicer because surely she makes decent money with the cost of lumber these days, but Boulder real estate is out of control. And Roe really is a no-frills kind of girl. I think she'd put a bed in that lumberyard office if she could. She doesn't want for much.

Except a husband apparently.

I touch my pocket, feeling the folded-up pros and cons list Everly made me print out for tonight. It's fucking embarrassing. I helped her write it up after three whiskeys and she added in some dramatic language that I will admit made me laugh. Going for the comedy angle was smart. Roe doesn't like to do deep talk, so this really did feel like it could work.

But the closer I got to Roe's place, the more I worried that the whole thing could come off as desperate.

How did I let my niece talk me into this? It's like Everly is still that eleven-year-old girl playing with her dolls, but this time, it's actual humans she's playing with. Me in particular. And apparently the rest of my entire family.

Mastermind indeed.

Roe is going to laugh in my face if she reads this, but Everly is going to kick my ass if I don't give it to her. Which woman am I more afraid of?

I lift my hand to knock on the door and in mere seconds it

swings open and I struggle to catch my breath at the sight of my friend.

I had the same reaction yesterday in the lumberyard because it's been a couple months since I've laid eyes on her. Yesterday, she was dressed in her standard work overalls, tank top, and sneakers. Today she's soft and homey-looking. Like she's ready to curl up on the couch and watch TV.

I hoped this pull she had on me would be less intense after some time apart, but it isn't. It's alive and well and possibly worse than ever with this offer in my pocket.

"What up, loser?" Roe cajoles with a big smile that hits me right in the gut. She's got a towel flipped over her shoulder and is stirring what smells like a batch of brownies. "Get your ass in here, I'm dying of thirst."

She turns on her heel, leaving her door open and I can't even stop myself from letting my eyes drift down her backside. She's got an ass that looks like she does squats for a living . . . which I suppose she does. Her top half is smaller and more petite, but the weight of her bottom . . . it fucking haunts me.

"Nice to see you too, Roe," I murmur, trying to regain control of my thoughts.

I follow her through the small hallway and hang a right into her kitchen. It's surprisingly large for such a small space. I would have laid out this property with a galley-style kitchen to give more square footage to the bedroom and bathroom, but I think this was the selling point for Roe. The girl loves to cook.

"It's been ages since you've come by," she calls over her shoulder as she tips her bowl into a glass baking dish, using a spatula to scrape out the chocolate batter.

"I know." I rub at the heaviness I feel in my chest. "If you recall, our last conversation here was me telling you that going on Grindr to find a husband was not a good idea."

"Oh, that's right." Roe bites her lip and shoots me a coy

smile. "I upgraded to asking Chuck, Bullhead, and the guys at the yard if that makes you feel any better."

"Oh yes, I feel great about that," I huff, dropping down onto a stool at her small kitchen island while she opens her oven and puts the brownies inside. "I want to talk to you about your husband hunt, actually."

"Luke," she groans my name, and it sounds unintentionally sexual. She sets her bowl inside the sink and turns on her heel to look me in the eyes. "Can we have a beer before you start giving me the third degree again? I've missed you."

She has no idea how much those three little words mean to me. I've missed her too. A lot. My eyes do a quick sweep of her body, refamiliarizing myself with all her curves. Roe is a stocky little thing with muscles that put many grown men to shame. Round shoulders, noticeable triceps, and quads that I have caught myself ogling more times than I should. And her ass. My God. Working in the lumberyard most of her life has developed her body in ways that should be a crime against humanity. Though I think some of these muscles are thanks to the recreational women's rugby she played for several years in her early twenties. Either way, she's a beast. The limited times I've had my hands on her have taught me that she could kick my ass in a wrestling match. And it'd be the best ass-kicking of my entire life.

But it wasn't her looks that I fell for first. It was who she is at her core. She chooses essence over appearance. Tonight, she's dressed in pale green spandex shorts and a matching high-neck tank top. The little sliver of her olive skin at the waistband peeks out showing that she's fit, but she still eats. The perfect blend of soft and hard. Like a wild river carving its own path through a manicured garden. She's got a faint sign of makeup that's probably from the day before, knowing her, and a smile that could cheer me up after the worst of days.

Her long black hair is folded up into a clip and her hazel eyes make me forget what I was even mad at her for.

"I missed you too," I say, sounding a bit breathless and fighting the urge to walk over and wrap her in a giant bear hug.

"I hope you also missed some spice because I may have overdone it on this batch of jambalaya."

Shaking myself out of my stupor, I look down to crack open a bottle of beer and hold it up to her. With a smirk, she pads over in her bare feet and hoists herself up onto the counter beside me. She waits for me to crack mine before clinking our bottles together and taking a sip.

"What's new on Fletcher Mountain? What's happening? Tell me all the things."

My brows lift, trying to decide where to start. "Well, Dakota moved into Calder's cabin."

"That didn't take long," Roe laughs and shakes her head while taking another long sip. "I could see it in Mexico."

I offer a tight smile wishing my Mexico trip turned out a bit more like Calder's. "It's a whole different mood on the peak now. Very . . . domestic."

"Yuck."

"Yeah, yuck," I huff and drink nearly half the contents of my beer before wiping my sweaty palms on my jeans. "Dakota's cool though. And Stevie is getting so big. Going to be one soon, which is wild to me."

"Has Everly gone back to Dublin yet?"

"Not yet. Two more weeks."

She nods thoughtfully. "You're going to miss her."

"I know," I reply heavily. "I'm trying not to think about it too much."

"At least you have Stevie nearby. And Evil Ethan still visits the mountain, I'm sure."

"Oh yeah he does." This makes me smile as I fumble with

the label on my beer bottle. She has a nickname for my nephew just based on the number of conversations we've had about my family. I like that she knew them before we went to Mexico. And when we were there together, just as I expected, she fit in with everyone so easily. How does she not see how good we could be? I shake my head and focus back on our conversation. "Stevie giggles for everyone except Ethan. She is *not* a fan of that little terror."

"Oh my God, that's funny."

"I know. I think he's just too wild and unpredictable for her. Of course, he's mortally offended and tries way too hard. It's only making it worse for the poor lil guy."

"Does she laugh for you?"

"Easily," I reply with a smile. "I was babysitting for Wyatt and Trista last week and I had her full-on belly laughing with Rufus. I know how to get him riled up and she loves the sounds he makes. I have a video if you want to see."

"Um, yes!"

I pull out my phone and Roe leans in close as I play the video of Stevie and my rooster. The scent of her wafts over me so I close my eyes and inhale more deeply. Eucalyptus and green tea. I know that's what it is because her lotion is always out on the counter in her bathroom. She made me use it on my hands once when she saw how dry and chapped they were from working outside in the cold. I hated eventually washing my hands after that application because I liked having her scent on me.

God, I'm so fucked.

"What's new with your domestic situation?" I ask, unable to stop the words from tumbling out of my mouth. Roe gives me a dubious look and I hold my hands up defensively. "I'm just wondering if I need to be shopping for a wedding gift for you."

"I wish." She buzzes her lips as she hops back down off the counter to go check her pot on the stove. "The husband hunt continues. But I had a great idea last night when I couldn't sleep."

"Oh, what's that?"

"Man of the Mountain," she exclaims, wagging her brows at me.

"What are you talking about?"

"I'm talking about lumberjacks, Luke!" She scurries back over to me and perches on the open stool, legs spread wide in that laid-back rough and tumble swagger she has about her. "Think about it. They're simple creatures who work long hours and make shit money, so getting free rent for a year just to marry me on paper would be a no-brainer for them. I've been around enough to know they barely even come home. They're usually out in logger towns for two to three weeks a month."

"So, then what? You're just going to live with one of them for one week a month? Here?" I look around like a second bedroom is going to materialize any second.

"Yeah." She shrugs and glances into her living room. "I know it's only one bedroom, but I can take the couch. It's not like my insomnia lets me sleep much anyways. It still counts as living together but we'd barely have to live together. Isn't this great?"

She shoves me playfully, almost knocking me off my stool. The girl seriously doesn't know her own strength. I shake my head, still processing everything she just said. "So, for one week a month, you're going to let a stranger come stay here with you?"

She rolls her eyes. "You're making it sound worse than it is."

"I really don't think I am," I reply, shocked that this idea feels even worse than her online dating for a husband.

"Maybe he won't be a stranger." She gets a coy look in her eyes and walks back into the kitchen.

I shoot daggers into her back. "What is that supposed to mean?"

"Just that I've maybe hooked up with a couple lumberjacks that I've met at this competition in the past, so I might as well marry one I can possibly reap some fringe benefits from. After so many weeks out in the forest, it turns out they are *very* grateful in the bedroom."

My hand tightens around my beer bottle so hard I think it could break in my hand. I knew Roe did casual sex. Hell, so do I, so I'm not judging. We're young, unattached people. Sex is normal. I'm not trying to be a dick about this.

But we haven't really spoken about our conquests to each other. We've sort of tiptoed around it in all the years we've been friends. We exist in this safe space where our intimate lives cease to cross over each other. Hearing about her fucking lumberjacks does not feel like a safe place for me. I feel very unsafe!

"Is there one in particular you want to reconnect with?" I ask, knowing I will probably hate the answer to this question.

"Not necessarily. I mean, I know a lot of them from all the years we've sponsored it. But we don't exactly exchange numbers." She winks at me, and I feel a sudden urge to punch a wall. Or a tree. Or a logger.

I swallow the knot in my throat and pitch my voice to be casual, as heat crawls up my neck. "You find one to fuck every year?"

"No," she laughs and wrinkles her nose. "My game isn't that good. But the loggers are kind of perfect. They're only in town for the competition so it's an easy no-strings sort of thing."

"Last year?"

"Last year what?"

"Did you hook up with someone last year?" The year that I finally started admitting my feelings for you because I realized my brothers and I were no longer on the same anti-woman page.

She frowns and pinches her face as she thinks. "I don't think so."

"The year before that?"

Her face twists with amusement. "Maybe. I'm not sure."

"Seems like something you should remember, isn't it?" My tone is clipped, and my mouth is dry, so I guzzle the rest of my beer and waste no time cracking open another.

"When was the last time you slept with someone?" she asks, eyeing me with a challenging glint.

I lick my lips and shrug, not really wanting to answer this question but knowing I have to because I got so damn nosey with her. "It's been a while. Usually my brothers and I would go out in Denver together and it was easier when we wing-manned each other, but since they've all wife'd up, things are different."

"Dry spell," Roe peals and strolls over to prop her elbows on the counter across from me. She rests her chin on her knuckles and gazes deeply into my eyes before she presses her finger between my brows. "Maybe that's why you seem so grumpy."

"I'm not grumpy," I huff and lean away from her to drink more beer. Beer is my only friend right now. Beer will save me from this sweet hell I find myself in.

"Then stop scowling." She turns around to start dishing up our food. "I think this lumberjack plan is genius. And if I find someone I can hook up with during this whole stupid yearlong cohabitation, that's a double bonus. Casual sex with my husband sounds just crazy enough to work. Bring on the loggers!"

She draws out the last sentence in a growly singsongy voice, so I down the rest of my second beer and reach for number three. I'm going to have to crash on Roe's couch or call my brothers for a ride home tonight at this rate.

We sit side by side at the counter eating and my mind races so much I barely taste the food. I know I'm eating it though, because the spice is causing my forehead to dampen with sweat. No wonder Roe only ever sees me as a friend. She's used to hulked-out lumberjacks in the bedroom. They probably wouldn't even react to spicy food. I am weak compared to them. A mere mortal.

She begins sharing her animated tales of proposing to Bullhead and Chuck the past few weeks, but I barely hear her. I begin cataloging every woman I've ever slept with and wondering how I was able to win them over so easily. The nice guy thing has always just kind of worked for me, but Roe seems completely oblivious to my charms.

Was it having my brothers as wingmen that helped? Do I not have game? Surely I've hooked up with women without them being in the room.

Right?

Fuck.

Is that what I've been missing with Roe? I need a wingman?

I polish off the last of my beer and stare at my plate, realizing I've stress-eaten two bowls of jambalaya and at least four slices of Roe's homemade sourdough. Normally I wax lyrical about how her bread is so life-changing, but my taste buds still don't seem to be firing at all cylinders.

I'm a mess.

"I bagged up a loaf for you to take home," Roe says, cutting into my mental freak-out.

I turn my head and find her smiling softly at me, and I swear that smile makes me feel like I'm the only man in the world. Why does she do that? Why does she look at me like that? It fucks with my head, and it makes me want to shove that bread off the counter, spread her legs wide and devour every square inch of her instead. At least until she forgets any lumberjacks who ever touched her.

I'm positive Addison Monroe tastes better than bread.

I bet her lumberjacks aren't "grateful" for her bread like I am. They probably don't even eat it. They probably eat bark and nuts and live game they kill after they've fucked it because they're so desperate for sex out there in the woods, they'd fuck anything.

They could fuck and kill Roe too.

They have access to a plethora of sharp objects and all the skill sets required to cut up a body into small enough pieces that no one could ever identify it.

Jesus I'm getting dark.

I'm buried so deep in my thoughts that I don't even realize I've said my next sentence out loud until Roe asks, "What was that?"

I blink to find we're standing side by side at the sink washing dishes. I don't even remember walking over here, but my hands are currently wrist deep in soapy water.

Licking my lips, I repeat what I just said while staring at my hands, "Marry me."

"Not this again." She elbows me and the warmth of her skin on mine causes a riot of goose bumps to move up my arm.

"I'm serious this time." I turn to stare at her, grabbing a towel to wipe my hands dry. I've aborted my mission of trying to get my friend to fall in love with me. Now I'm simply trying to prevent her from getting murdered or raped or assaulted.

Fuck.

I'm losing it. I'm going off the rails here and need her to say yes to this or I don't know what I'll do.

She frowns up at me, her long dark lashes fanning her cheeks as she blinks rapidly. I chuck the towel to the counter and reach into my pocket to pull out the list that Everly doctored up for me. It's crumpled and I feel like a seventh grader passing a note to a cute girl in class just like I did with the stupid letter I gave her, but fuck it, it's now or never.

My best friend's life is at stake.

A nonappreciative-for-Roe's-bread lumberjack, with all the necessary skills to dismember a body, could be the one she chooses . . . and he could then kill her, hide the bits of her body anywhere, and then—

"Luke, what's going—"

"I've thought this through," I murmur and as she begins to unfold the paper, I feel sweat collecting on the back of my neck. "I'll be outside. Let me know when you're ready to discuss."

Chapter 5

FACT OR FICTION?
Best friends make good husbands.

Addison

"*Let me know when you're ready to discuss,*" Luke says before turning on his heel and walking out to my front deck like he's conducting a damn business meeting and not hitting me with his second marriage proposal in only a few months.

"Shit, shit shit," I hiss under my breath, irritation crawling up my back. We just got past the last marriage proposal and things were finally starting to feel normal again between the two of us. Why does he keep doing this to me?

My hand shakes as I hold up the white printer paper, terrified of what I'll find inside. Another awkward letter. I thought the last one he gave me in my office at the lumberyard was a joke and I started laughing instantly.

It wasn't until he hightailed it out of there that I realized he was serious. I know it was mean to laugh, but it's what I do when I'm uncomfortable. But marry Luke? *Let him see all my flaws up close and personal?* My God, if I wanted that, then I'd want a real marriage. But that's not what I want.

The idea of marrying my closest guy friend makes me uncomfortable. Stir-crazy. Unsettled. All the not comfy feelings I can think of. We'd cross a boundary that can never be uncrossed, and he could discover that he can't stand me and then simply . . .

Leave me.

Which is why I'd rather marry a stranger, so that after a year, when no deep and meaningful friendship has been formed, we simply part ways. I've told Luke this. What the hell is he having trouble comprehending about that? Doesn't he like just being my friend? Isn't that easier? God, when he walked into my apartment tonight, I wanted to hug the shit out of him. He's like . . . my favorite person in the world and that's saying a lot because I don't like most people. But he makes me feel at ease. Watching him sweat while eating my jambalaya was the highlight of my night—even if he was quieter than normal—and now that's all out the window.

With a deep growl, I unfold the paper to see what he's written and get this shit over with. My brows furrow when I notice it's not a letter but a pros and cons list.

Okay . . . that's different.

Pros & Cons to Marrying Your Friend

Pros:

- I have my own job and am part owner of my own company. I neither want nor need your lumberyard dynasty and recognize the general badassery of you being the sole owner of a business in a male-dominated industry. Slay, Queen.

- I own a large cabin we can cohabitate in with spectacular views and a spare bedroom you can sleep in, so this marriage will remain one of convenience and not one of nakedness.

- I put the toilet seat down . . . no exceptions.

- I am a food enthusiast and whilst I do not possess the abilities to make the international delicacies you excel at, I vow to clean up after every meal and give you a five-star rating. I will also happily run to the store for missing ingredients that inevitably pop up with culinary experiments.

- You'd be safe from all the creeps out there.
- And most importantly, I am your friend. If you can't marry your friend, who can you marry?

Cons:

- I have a big cock. He roosts on my front porch and sometimes comes inside my cabin. His name is Rufus, and he crows at 6:04 a.m. every day. If he shows any cock-like aggression towards you, I will move him back to the barn. You will be my number one hen.
- Moving to Fletcher Mountain means a small commute to Boulder for work every day but you can join the Fletcher Brother carpool. Wyatt is a stickler about our carbon footprint.
- Your father hates me. No good workaround for that reality I'm afraid.
- I have brothers who are my neighbors. They are obnoxious and nosy and will most likely be pains in our asses. You've been warned.

With all this said, I believe with perseverance we can work through these difficulties and form a happy, platonic union. Let us merge our families at your earliest convenience so you can fulfill the feminist destiny you were born to achieve.

Your friend,
Luke Fletcher

Okay, I'm not laughing this time. Not laughing at all. Not . . . laughing . . . A nervous giggle bubbles up my throat and I slap my hand over my mouth to try to hide it. *Fuck! Stop laughing, Addison.* You're going to push him away again and he's the only man in the world who seems to be able to tolerate you these days.

Get your shit together, Monroe!

I blow out a slow breath and attempt to look at this list more critically. He wants me to move onto Fletcher Mountain for a year? Is he unhinged? I've only been up there, like, twice in my life. And didn't he tell me once they can get snowed in for days up there? I won't survive that kind of isolation. What would we even do for days together? I'm a tomboy for the most part but I can't do off-grid. I need groceries and snow removal and signs of life around me.

But if I said yes to this and we lived here, I know for a fact Luke wouldn't take my bedroom and let me have the couch. He's too noble and shit. Damn him.

Rereading the list, I snicker at the big cock comment. Luke is a good writer. Not something I would have suspected of a burly mountain man. Then again, he has cinnamon roll energy. He's sweet and sensitive and gooey on the inside. No wonder he's good at expressing himself.

Ugh, no heart eyes happening. This is Luke we're talking about. He's annoying! He's obviously a bad listener if he's proposing to me twice now. He's being an overprotective pain in my ass.

But God, imagine having someone to cook for every single night. That would be so much fun. I could maybe even do food for his brothers and Dakota and Trista. They were so much fun at the wedding in Mexico. I could do a street taco theme night to bring us back to our trip. I could make everyone a weekly fresh loaf of sourdough. I guess that mountain compound is a bit of civilization now that Dakota and Trista are living up there, so I wouldn't be completely isolated. Hell, if a baby can survive up there, surely I can too.

Shit . . . stop this, Addison. You're not marrying Luke. This is not smart.

You need to marry a lumberjack. Someone dumb who smokes weed all day and you can't hurt with your weird closed-off, messed-up heart. You know this. Luke is just too nice for his own good.

"Be strong, be strong, be strong," I whisper to myself as I make my way outside to join Luke so we can discuss this.

He's pacing across the wooden decking, and the warm late summer air does little to cool the anxiety I feel swirling in my gut over letting him down for a second time. But I'm not letting him down. He's not professing his feelings for me, he's just . . . being Luke. A golden retriever people pleaser who would sacrifice a year of his life if I say yes to this. I can't do this to him. I can't do this to him. And what if he met someone in that year? I couldn't stop him from getting together with the love of his life. *God, that would be hell.*

His head jerks toward me as I stand awkwardly in the doorframe. I hold the paper up, trying not to notice how the twilight sun casts a warm glow on his bronze skin. "This was . . . really something."

"Something good or something bad?" Luke tilts his head, trying to read me like we're playing poker.

"It's funny. Were you really good at writing in school?" I ask as I walk over to the railing and lean on it for support.

"I don't know." He shrugs, looking highly annoyed at my sidetracked thoughts.

I need to lay it out there for him. Tell him it's a firm no and we need to stop discussing this, but first I ask, "Can you tell me why you care so much?" I turn to look at him, my eyes raking over his face for some sign of the feelings that I thought he was showing me in Mexico. If this is about wanting to be more than friends, then that's even more reason we shouldn't be considering this.

"I'd do anything for you, Roe," he replies, his eyes dark and piercing on me as he adds, "You're my best friend."

My breath escapes my lungs at those words he just said so easily, and without being able to stop it, my chin begins to wobble. I turn to look away so he doesn't see the overwhelming emotion that hits me with that declaration. He's never called me his best friend before. Only one other person in my life has called me that, and the memory of that hits me like a ton of bricks.

Luke steps closer to me, and I feel the heat of his arm brush against mine, sending a riot of goose bumps up my back. "I'd rather you saddle yourself with me for a year than put yourself at risk with a stranger, Roe. I will lose my mind worrying about you."

"This is too much to ask though," I reply, all humor draining from my face. "It's a whole year. And what do you get out of it? I know you said in your first letter that your family is on your ass, but that's not enough of a reason to marry me, is it?"

"The comfort of knowing you're safe and I don't have to text you every two hours to make sure a logger hasn't ax-murdered you seems like a pretty good reason to me."

I shake my head and glance down at the list, terrified that I could be holding the worst—or best—idea ever.

"Let me put it to you this way," he says, turning my attention back to him. "Would you help me if I needed it?"

"I don't know if I'd marry you," I reply with a laugh.

He bobs his head from side to side. "Well, I always have been nicer than you. Fact or fiction?"

He repeats the phrase that I only ever use with him, causing me to smile. I shove him playfully, my hand lingering on his abs for a moment before I whisper, "Fact."

"Then that's all this is. I'm just trying to be your best friend. You should let me."

I jut my chin out, shaking it adamantly. "The fact that you called me your best friend means we shouldn't do this."

"Why?"

"Because I can't lose you, Luke," my voice breaks at the end as I have to blink rapidly to fight back the unexpected tears threatening to spill. "My dad has already hightailed it out of Boulder. Chuck and Bullhead barely tolerate me at the yard. You're the only guy who actually likes me in this town and I need you. I need you around. I need us to be good. I've missed you these past couple of months and I worry this could ruin everything. If you marry me, and live with me, you're going to get sick of me."

And want to leave too.

I turn away to hide the tears welling in my eyes and sigh when Luke's big arms wrap around me. He rests his chin on my head and squeezes me for a moment, not saying anything, just giving me a minute to pull myself together.

I hate change. And this "best friend" of mine keeps trying to push me into a situation that terrifies the shit out of me. I know he cares about me, and he wants to protect me, but I want to protect him too. And the only way I know how to do that is by saying no to this proposal.

I press my face into his chest and wrap my arms around his waist, hugging his strong hard body back with everything I have. "I hate my dad for putting me in this position so much."

"No, you don't," he says, rubbing the back of my neck. His fingers tangle in the hairs falling out of my clip as I feel his chest rise against my face and he inhales deeply. "Your dad hates *me*. But *you* don't hate your dad."

"I hate that you know me so well," I murmur into his shirt.

"No, you don't."

"No, I don't," I sigh heavily. "You're my best friend too, you asshole."

He shakes with silent laughter that just makes me squeeze him harder. After a long pause I pull back and look up at him, nodding with a renewed sense of determination. His brows lift as I say, "If I can't find anyone at Man of the Mountain that feels safe, then I'll take you up on your offer. But only as my last resort."

I smile up at him and can't help but notice the tight set of his jaw. It's not what Luke wants. But it's what's best for both of us.

I hug him one more time. "Thank you, Luke. Thank you for offering. It means a lot that you care so much." I stand on my tiptoes and press a kiss to his spikey cheek before shoving him away from me in that playful way we have with each other. "Let's go back inside. I've got ice cream to go with the brownies that I bet are still warm."

"Right behind you," he replies flatly, and I do my best not to look back at him because I'm not sure I'd like what I'd see.

I fear I could have broken my best friend's heart.

Chapter 6

FACT OR FICTION?
Google can teach you anything.

Everly

Operation Turn My Uncle into a Lumberjack So He Can Marry His Best Friend and Force Her to Fall in Love With Him is in full effect!

When Luke texted me a week ago telling me the only way he can marry his best friend is if he can figure out how to become a lumberjack, I'm pretty sure he was joking.

But I responded with . . . *bet*.

You see, I have a doctorate in good ol' Google and where there's a will, there's a way. My education is obvious when you look at what I did for my uncle Wyatt. I learned more than I'll ever need to know about gestational and traditional surrogacy and now I have an adorable cousin and new auntie to show for it. I also used Google to brush up on my rusty Spanish skills to help get Uncle Calder sacked up in a one-bedroom palapa in Mexico. So really, figuring out how to turn Uncle Luke into a lumberjack is par for the course in my matchmaking endeavors.

I've learned a lot about lumberjacking the past few days and have now come up with a foolproof plan that even my lovable uncle can't screw up. Which is how I find myself back on Fletcher Mountain one week before I fly back to Dublin, watching my uncle stare at the mound of logger supplies spread out on his front porch.

"This is a bad idea," Luke says, picking up a pair of boots with spikes that look like lethal weapons.

"No, it's not," I state, pushing Rufus out of my way. He clucks and flaps his wings like I drop-kicked him instead of gently scooting him out of the way. *So dramatic.* That rooster is always getting into everything and we're on a tight deadline right now. "This was your idea, Luke, and I think it's important that you follow your instincts. Don't bitch out on me now."

Luke's eyes lift from the logger gear to me. "I'm not bitching out. I'm just wondering what happens if this actually works and I get her to marry me after all this?"

"That's phase two. This is phase one. Just stay focused. I've done some research on the Man of the Mountain and I think you've got a shot at not sucking at everything."

"Well, with an endorsement like that, I'll be unstoppable," Luke deadpans as he squats down beside me and picks up a throwing axe in need of some sharpening. Maybe purchasing some of this gear secondhand was a bad life choice. I bet if I ask my dad he can upgrade Luke's gear and throw his company logo on a flannel shirt to be his sponsor. Then at least we can look the part, even if Luke doesn't quite have the skills to pull this all off.

"I watched the Lumberjack World Championships on YouTube this week and it's intense."

"I did the same." Luke pinches the bridge of his nose. "We're in way over our heads."

"No we're not!" I argue, looking around for the rope thing that I ordered to go along with the spiked boots. "Look around, Luke! You and Calder and Wyatt used to be city boys until you moved up here. Now you're proper mountain men who've been chopping your own wood for years. Lumberjacks are really just mountain men's hotter cousins."

"Nice, Everly," Luke grumbles.

"Well . . . I watched a lot of footage this week." I swallow the attraction blossoming in my chest right now because I didn't realize how hot professional lumberjacks were. "I'm talking hours," I whisper, feeling my cheeks flush with heat. "I'm really bummed I'll be back in Ireland and unable to attend this event."

"Gross, Evie. Just stop." Luke holds his hand in front of me. "I don't need to hear about my niece lusting after lumberjacks. I got enough of that shit from Roe, thank you."

"Sorry." I shake my head from side to side. "They're just so agile."

"That's it, I'm out—" Luke stands up and I rise, grabbing his arm to yank him back to the task at hand.

"Relax, okay. This Boulder event is small and doesn't use any power tools so at least our risk of dying goes way down."

"That's a relief," Luke scoffs, propping his hands on his hips.

"Except for the speed pole climbing. I think you could seriously die from that. Or paralyze yourself, because I can't find anywhere for you to practice that. How many weeks do we have until the competition?"

"Six." Luke swallows hard and I do the same.

I nod, deep in thought. "You'll be fine. Some of these other activities aren't so bad. Chopping will be easy for you. You guys do that up here already. Axe throwing is literally a date night activity now, so if you suck at that, there's no hope for you. Boom running could be tricky, so you'll definitely need to work on that. You have to sprint over a series of linked, floating logs from one dock to another and back, as logs begin to spin out of control. Good chance you get wet but at least you won't be dead.

"Then there's the two-person bucking saw competition where you have to pull the saw through a twenty-inch white pine log. You have to sever a complete wood cookie off the end of the log faster than the other teams. You get randomly assigned another contestant as a teammate for that but you need to practice which is why—"

"She called us," a voice bellows from the distance and I look past Luke to find Calder and Wyatt walking up the gravel lane toward us.

"You told them?" Luke hisses, shooting me a lethal stare like I totally betrayed him.

"I'm going back to Ireland next week and you need help training," I exclaim, using a band around my wrist to tie my hair up. "And I'm not going to be here for the competition so you're going to need all the support you can get."

Luke steps closer and whispers, "How much do they know?"

"We know you're doing this because of Addison Monroe," Calder drawls, flopping down on the front step and stretching out his legs like he's trying to get a suntan through his denim. "I knew you've had the hots for the lumberyard chick for years. Just didn't know you had the balls to marry her. Fake marry her? Honestly I'm still confused with what's going on exactly." Calder picks up the long rope that's supposed to be used for the pole climb.

Luke turns to glare at me and I hold my hands up defensively. "Oh please. You already told them she was looking for a husband. Why hide it now? Plus, you know how hard it is to keep secrets in the Fletcher family."

Luke pinches the bridge of his nose. "This is humiliating."

"Calder and Wyatt are the only ones who know. I told them they can't tell Dakota and Trista or Grandma because if they do they'll mess up phase two."

"What is phase two?" Luke groans, looking like he's about to vomit.

"I'd like to know too," Calder says, raising his hand. "Keeping secrets from Dakota makes me really nervous. That woman can see right through me."

"Yeah, Trista will kill me too," Wyatt interjects as he leans on the deck railing.

"Hey, who do you think is scarier? Dakota or Trista?" Calder asks, looking thoughtful.

"Good question," Luke answers, weighing in. "My knee jerk is Trista 'cause her cowboy boots look like they could kick Wyatt's ass real good. But Dakota was super scary that day we brought the shelves to her T-shirt shop."

"Right!" Calder says excitedly like he wants his girl to win this competition. "She gets these freaky veins in her forehead when she yells. They kind of look like rabbit ears with horns. I worry about brain aneurisms."

"You guys haven't seen Trista try to pen up her pig when he's not wanting to come in," Wyatt says with a grave look. "She makes these weird noises that aren't words, just a slur of letters . . . like she's speaking in tongues. She kind of sounded like that when she gave birth to Stevie too. Don't ever tell her this, but I hate thinking about it."

"All the more reason Dakota and I should never have children," Calder says with a shudder.

"I think Mom could be a contender for scariest as well," Luke adds with a tightness to his jaw. "She is so small but you know she can inflict weird pain with her boney fingers. Remember as kids how she'd reach into the back seat and pinch us when we were fighting?"

Calder and Wyatt both nod in silent agreement.

"Guys, tighten up!" I clap my hands to get them to focus on me. "We need to stay on track. It's important to keep the fact that you know this is a marriage of convenience a secret from Addison and the ladies because otherwise, Luke will have no reason to fake it with her. And it's going to be those faking moments I strategically set up that will make Addison stop seeing him as the lovable best friend and start seeing him as a man she wants to spend the rest of her life with."

"And go to Bone Town with," Calder says with a wave of his

hand. He holds his fist up to Luke, silently asking him to pound it and Luke hesitates a moment before giving in. Wyatt chuckles under his beard and I slap my hand over my face in horror.

I am working with a bunch of apes. My uncles are knuckle-dragging morons who are lucky I'm here or otherwise they wouldn't even be able to form complete sentences.

"Calder, I need you to take this seriously," I state, feeling some forehead veins of my own pop out. "And if you can't then I will kindly ask you to get the heck out of here so we can get to work."

"Cool your jets, Ev," Calder huffs, looking hurt. "I'm in, okay? I just have to fuck with Luke because . . . well . . . he's Luke and it's kind of just what we've always done."

Luke rolls his eyes, clearly used to this sort of treatment while I have to inhale deeply to lower my heart rate before I punch my lovable uncles in the face. *Maybe I should try the Grandma pinching thing.*

Shaking my head, I take a few steps down the deck to breathe in the fresh mountain air, trying to walk off some of this pressure I'm feeling. It's self-induced pressure, but pressure all the same.

When I decided to go away for college, I made a promise to myself to find love for all three of my uncles and I'm two for three, yet for some wacky reason, number three seems a hell of a lot more complicated than one and two. And number one involved a pregnancy! How is this more complicated than that?

Either way, I have to do this. I can't leave Luke all on his own. He's . . . Luke. He's the best. And I can tell he's going to be devastated if Addison marries someone else, so we have to stay focused here. We have to succeed at this. And that means calling in reinforcements in the form of bearded, brawny, unruly uncles.

I smile as I glance at all three of them ribbing on each other. As much as they're pains in my ass, I love the heck out of them.

They were devastated over my decision to leave Colorado, which only motivated me further to help them find their own happily-ever-afters. They've created this incredible compound up here on Fletcher Mountain and they need to share this with someone other than me and Ethan.

Plus, humblebrag moment? I have a knack for matchmaking. I got my dad and Cozy together when I was only eleven. I knew they were in love with each other and it has been a privilege watching their love deepen throughout the years. My mom is also crazy happy with her wife. I'm surrounded by the GOATs of love which is probably why my own love life is such a mess. I have high standards for good reason. I expect good communication, grand gestures, perfect dates. Romance! I want the man I bring to meet my dad someday to be a Prince Charming. Not some college asshole who wears a gold cross on a chain and calls me "Stretch" in his thick Irish accent.

As if.

And while my three uncles might not look like Disney princes, I know they deserve love. And I'd feel so much better living my life so far away knowing that someone is here to take care of them.

I just wish I knew about this marriage plan Addison had earlier in the summer. I got so distracted with helping Calder start up his furniture business that I didn't make enough time for Luke.

Luckily my uncles will do anything I ask of them, so I will depend on them to help me out with this match since I'll be thousands of miles away.

"Okay, Everly, we're listening." Uncle Wyatt leans against the wooden pillar, arms crossed, scowl back in place. "Tell us what we need to do."

I nod and clap my hands together, swiveling on my heel to dig into my backpack. "I found a lumberjack workout regimen.

It's a lot of cardio, Luke, in addition to some skills training. But I think you're already in pretty good shape, right?"

"I guess so," Luke huffs and nervously plucks the paper out of my hand. His brows twitch when he sees the list. "That many miles a day?"

"Like I said . . . it's intense." I grab another sheet out of my bag and hand it to Calder. "This is a diagram on how to suspend the booms. I thought you could set up some floating logs in the creek out back for him to practice. There's one area I know that gets pretty deep so it seems doable, don't you think?"

Calder stares at the sheet and nods. "I can handle this."

"And, Uncle Wyatt, I need you to stop chopping wood at your place for a while. Luke needs to take over and I'm hoping you can help him with his form. Speed chopping is crazy fast, and Luke is going to need all the fallen timber he can get for practice."

Wyatt exhales heavily. "You got it, kid."

"What will you be doing while we're working Luke to within an inch of his life?" Calder asks, staring up at me with a smirk. "Sipping lemonade and bossing us around?"

"I'm going to work on finding some poles for Luke to practice climb. That competition scares me the most."

"Everly, is this really going to work?" Luke asks, staring dubiously back at me. "How is me becoming a lumberjack going to get Roe to fall for me, exactly?"

"Because it shows her that you'd do anything to help her. And you're putting yourself front and center to prove it. It's a grand gesture, Luke. One that you need in order for her to take your proposal seriously. And since a lumberjack is what she said she wants, we'll give her exactly what she wants so she has no reason to say no!"

Calder shakes his head and laughs. "This is so desperate."

"I have two words for you," Luke growls, dropping the spiked boots onto the ground. Calder stares back at him curiously before Luke says, "PowerPoint."

"How the fuck do you know about that?" Calder asks, standing up to face Luke and losing all humor on his face.

"It backed up on our company iCloud account, you moron." Luke's shoulders shake with silent laughter. "I knew you were a freak, but Dakota . . ."

Calder lunges for a cackling Luke, and Wyatt steps between them, pressing a hand to each of their chests, not saying a word, just eyeing them both into submission.

"What PowerPoint?" I ask Luke, frowning curiously. "Not the one that you guys made to try to talk me out of going to Dublin, right?"

"No, not that one," Luke replies, looking sheepish. "Fat lot of good that did. You're leaving again in a week."

Luke's somber mood is contagious and before I know it, I'm gazing at three giant, bearded, pouting mountain men all pissed at me for preparing to fly across the ocean again.

"Come on, guys," I say with a soft smile. "We made it through the first year of me being away okay."

"Yeah, but I just got used to having you around again," Calder mumbles, staring down at his boots. "I need your help with my furniture business. I don't know what I'm doing on Instagram."

"Stevie's going to really miss you," Wyatt adds with his lips turned down, using his daughter as a scapegoat instead of his goat like he did the first time I left.

"I'm going to miss you guys too." I feel my chin begin to wobble as I look at the state of them all hunched and depressed. This summer has been incredible. I helped Uncle Calder launch his custom furniture brand and move his first serious girlfriend into his cabin. I loved on my cousin and got to watch Wyatt be an incredible dad and husband. Luke and I had countless deep conversations on Grandpa's bench at the lookout point.

I'm going to miss those most of all, I fear.

Tears prick my eyes as I glance out at the view of Fletcher Mountain. Fall is coming and it's going to look so beautiful. I never seem to get enough time up here. I owe some of my best childhood memories to this peak and my three crazy uncles. The influence they've had on me and my life? It's insurmountable.

They deserve these happily-ever-afters. Only one more to go and my work here is done, and I feel like I can finally start living my own life to the fullest.

"Alright, enough mushy talk," I sniff loudly and swipe at my damp cheeks. "I only have one more week with you guys, so let's work together to kick Luke's ass and turn him into a lumberjack so he can marry his girl!"

"I like the sound of that," Calder says with a light shove to Luke.

The corner of Luke's mouth tugs up into a shy grin. If Addison doesn't see how wonderful and special my uncle is by the end of this . . . *I will fly back from Dublin and end her.*

Until then, I need to get my ass back to the life I'm creating over there. I struggled adjusting to Ireland my first year and spent many nights alone and completely out of my element, but things were looking up just before summer break . . . so long as that gold chain–wearing Irish boy gives me a wide berth.

Chapter 7

FACT OR FICTION?
I like dead people.

Addison

Me: Drinks after work tonight? We can go out or I can come up the mountain if you want.

Luke: Sorry, swamped with work.

Me: It's been a month of this. What is your brother doing to you?

Luke: Since Calder is working on his furniture stuff more now and not for the company, I have to pick up the slack. Sorry.

Me: I thought you said you were my best friend. Fact or fiction?

Luke: Fact. BFF4L

Me: Best friends see each other more than once every couple months.

Luke: Don't worry, I'm coming to Man of the Mountain, so I'll see you there. Let's hang after.

Me: That's still three weeks away! You already know you're busy for the next three weeks?

Luke: Yes, but after that I'm wide open. I'll be around so much you'll get sick of me, I promise.

Me: Fine.

I sigh heavily and thunk my phone onto the dashboard of my SUV, irritated at my so-called best friend for the third time in a month. For a whole month he's been too busy to hang out. For a whole month he's been slow to answer my texts. If I didn't know any better, I'd say he's pissed I didn't accept his second marriage proposal, which is ridiculous because he should be grateful I'm not taking him up on his offer. I'm a lot to handle.

And living with Luke for a whole year? What would that even be like? I'd drive him nuts with my messy sourdough baking and the amount of dishes I go through when I cook. Plus, I don't sleep at night because of my insomnia, I mix my colors with my whites and leave cups of water on every end table I can find. Marrying me would for sure ruin our friendship. Mankind is lucky I never plan to marry anyone for real.

Not that suitors are lining up with offers.

The foulmouthed daughter of the local lumberyard isn't exactly the kind of girl guys are dying to take home to meet their parents. Not to mention I'd have to be in a relationship first for that to even be an option. I've never even had a boyfriend—which was fully by choice!

I'm good on my own. Great, even!

I slide out of my car and stretch for a minute, adjusting my sports bra and shorts before I walk through the familiar wrought iron gate that leads into Blue Mountain Cemetery. This cemetery is a quiet little jewel outside of Boulder that I run through on a weekly basis. It has a great view of the Boulder Flatirons and big green space on the other side. And it has some seriously cool old headstones that I love to check out.

Some people might see it as maudlin or outright rude for me to exercise in a cemetery, but I love dead people. I like to read everyone's names and imagine what their lives were like. The number of women I spot buried next to two or more husbands will never stop impressing me.

You go, girl.

Plus, it's the only place I can go to find a true sense of solitude. So many hikers and joggers hit the mountain trails and it turns into a contrived circus. Cemeteries are perfect for someone who doesn't want to be found. It's this quiet suspension of reality where I can just exist in something bigger than me. I like feeling inconsequential, and nothing makes me more aware of that feeling than being surrounded by the dead.

I slow my pace and check my watch, noting that I've clocked two miles and am on the final stretch of my familiar path. There's a hidden section over a small hill that has a giant weeping willow with a bench where I love to end my runs, so I make my way over there.

Sweaty and out of breath, I lower myself onto the bench under the tree. The cool concrete bites through my leggings as I sit back and admire the view, my chest heaving as my eyes drop to the nearby black headstone that reads:

AARON MICHEL MONROE
BROTHER–SON–BEST FRIEND
2002–2010

"Hey, little bro," I croak as a gust of wind blows the long wispy branches all around me. I look up and smile, feeling like my little brother is saying hi right back.

"Boy has it been a hell of a week," I add with a huff, stretching my arms out on the bench as I make myself comfortable.

I pause as I look up at the Flatirons in the distance, frowning as I realize my mind is noisier than usual after a run. Most of the time, I talk to my brother about a whole lot of nothing. Today though . . . there's a heaviness in me that even a good sweat didn't ease. But I guess if there's any good place to unload the burdens of the brain . . . it's with the dead. As it turns out, dead brothers are great listeners.

I've contemplated death enough to know that you can make it whatever you need it to be. And right now, I don't imagine my brother eternally stuck at eight years old. I imagine him old enough to drink and relate to the unhinged shit in our family. He sees it all from his place in the sky, right?

"Actually, it's been a hell of a year," I correct, chewing my lip and flashing to images of dropping my dad off at the airport. "Dad has really thrown me for a loop with this marriage bullshit. Acting like having a husband will fix everything, like he's shown such a great example marriage. Him and Mom were a fucking joke, right?" I exhale heavily and drag my forearm over the sweat on my brow. "The fact that Dad watched Mom walk out on us after you died and he can still look me in the eyes and tell me I have to be married to inherit the lumberyard is ludicrous. Totally ludicrous. That's why I'm not taking any of this seriously. I'm going to find a random guy at the lumberjack competition and ask him to marry me. And Dad knows! He knows I'm out there looking for randoms. He doesn't seem to care. All he cares about is a marriage license I guess. So if I manage to pull the trigger with someone and show him proof that I'm married, then the yard is mine and there's not a damn thing he can do about it."

I bark out a dry laugh at the ridiculousness of all of this but my mind is suddenly steamrolled into another subject. "And then Luke! You know Luke. I've told you about him. He's being all weird and protective . . . telling me it's not a good idea for me to marry a lumberjack. Like I haven't been around enough mill guys to know exactly what they're like."

I sniff and wipe at the sweat collecting on my upper lip and then raise my voice to hear myself over the locusts. "He wants to marry me instead . . . just temporarily of course. Can you believe that? Boy is out of his mind and now seemingly punishing me for saving us both a hell of a lot of torment."

I drop my elbows to my knees and rest my face in my hands, feeling the weight of the world on my shoulders. I like being alone, but sometimes it's exhausting. Sometimes this sense of fight I have against everything, and everyone, feels draining. At least when Dad was still living here in Boulder, I could fight with him about it and get things off my chest. Now I just feel this clock ticking and if I don't do something drastic, my whole life is going to change. Suddenly I won't be my own boss. I'll be working for someone else. Fuck that. I've given way too much of myself to the yard to let some outsider come in and try to manage me.

I stand up off the bench and kneel next to Aaron's headstone, tracing the dates with my finger, wishing like hell my brother was here to talk back. I wonder what he would look like right now? I bet he'd be tall like Dad. Dark hair like mine. But his eyes were always so piercing blue where mine are more of a dull hazel.

"Not a day goes by where I don't wonder what it would be like if you were still here, little bro. We'd be running the yard together, fighting over who's going to take over the company. Wouldn't that be great? I'd much rather fight with you than the old man. I miss fighting with you."

I blink at tears welling in my eyes. "I used to get so annoyed at you trying to follow me around everywhere. I almost hit you with the Weed eater that one time because I didn't know you were right behind me. My little shadow." I expel a garbled laugh and lick my lips, trying to remember those hugs he gave me. Boney arms wrapped tightly around my waist. His little face smashed into my stomach. "Damn it I didn't know how good I had it," I cry out, my voice cracking as hot tears spill freely down my skin. "I hate that I didn't know, Aaron. I'm sorry I didn't know. I'm sorry I didn't see you."

Snot dribbles down my nose and I jerk away from the headstone. I'm blubbering like a mother who just buried her child, not a sister who lost her brother fifteen years ago.

I come here so often, and never cry. Ever. I talk to Aaron almost every single week and rarely shed one tear. God, grief is such a motherfucker sometimes. It sneaks up when you least expect it.

I swallow the painful knot in my throat, anger replacing heartache. This whole marriage thing is putting so much pressure on me, I'm a mess. I hate this. I hate not having control of my own life. It's bullshit. My father raised me to care about that damn business and just like that, he's trying to rip it out from under me.

But I refuse to go down without a fight.

I wipe my nose on the back of my hand and stand, my joints sore from the run, but it's a good pain. It reminds me that I'm still alive and I'm going to keep moving until I get exactly what I want. If not for me, then for my little brother.

"Because you don't have the opportunity to fight. This is for you, little bro."

Chapter 8

FACT OR FICTION?
Lumberjacking is a family affair.

Luke

"You got this, Luke!" Dakota cheers from where she stands by the creek that runs down the backside of our property.

Trista moves to join Dakota, with Stevie propped on her hip. "You ready to watch your Uncle Lukey eat shit?" Trista coos, pointing her daughter's tiny little hand toward me.

"Just be careful, Luke." My mom stands beside them holding her phone up to the scene. I know that on the other end of that phone is Everly's face watching this spectacle from her university in Dublin.

She's been doing weekly check-in calls with me to make sure I'm sticking to my workout regime. The little shithead is a ballbuster, that's for sure. She set up my whole family with a strict training schedule where everyone helped me out in their own ways, and I have been run ragged for weeks now.

Wyatt collected piles of fallen wood for me to chop, Calder has been practicing the boom runs with me, even getting himself on the logs to help coach me along. Max found his way up the peak to work on axe throwing with me, though I suspect that was because Ethan thought he could toss some blades as well.

Rufus was nowhere to be seen during those sessions, thank God.

Even my mom got involved by bringing meals up for us to eat between trainings. She never used to like driving up the peak without my dad, but she's become braver since Stevie was born. Not willing to miss a minute of her new granddaughter's life. Winter will probably be a different story, but it's been nice seeing her up here more. She's becoming a part of our day-to-day lives since Dad has passed and I love it.

"I hope he gets wet." Evil Ethan snickers and covers his mouth like the eight-year-old asshole he is.

Max shoves Ethan so hard, he almost falls over while Cozy just shrugs at her son. "You asked for that."

"Hurry up, Luke! I have plans tonight," Everly yells through the phone.

I frown and glance down at my smartwatch. It's 9 p.m. in Dublin right now. What the fuck kind of plans does Everly have that don't start until 9 p.m.? "What are your plans tonight?" I yell toward the phone.

"Luke. Focus," Max barks at me with a frown. "It's not just Everly that has other shit to do today."

I cut my oldest brother a look. Maybe he should be more concerned about his daughter's plans. And besides, it wasn't my idea for everyone to come up here and watch me make an ass of myself. Everly was the one to start the irritating group chat this morning and now here they all are to watch me do my final practice run for Man of the Mountain.

This is the last obstacle of the day and if I can nail this, maybe I'll finally be ready for the competition.

Calder stands on the other side of the bank, pointing his phone at me. He's been threatening to post my failures on his business page because he's certain they could go viral and help him sell some furniture.

The fucker.

I point to him and yell over the rush of the stream, "If I make it on the first try, you're buying beers at the Mercantile after this. Got it?"

"Easy money," Calder huffs, readying his camera.

I take a deep breath in as I stare at the row of three logs anchored into the stream in front of me before twisting my hat backward and tucking my loose hair behind my ears. My shoulders ache from the strenuous workouts. I've grown muscles in places I didn't know I could grow muscles. And other than a couple of videos of me eating shit on the floating logs, the mocking from my brothers has been minimal. Now is the time to show them all this hard work has been worth it.

With a deep breath, I jump onto the first log, moving my feet quickly with short fast steps. My arms fling out, swinging in opposite directions of my legs to help maintain my balance. My pulse quickens as I hit the second log, and it starts spinning under my feet so I adjust my steps to re-center my weight over the booms.

I hear Max's voice the loudest, cheering me on as I fly over the third and fourth log, almost slipping off right at the end before I take a flying leap and crash directly into Calder who catches me with a loud harrumph.

"Holy fuck you did it!" Calder wraps his arm around me and points me toward my family. "The fucker actually finally did it!"

Everyone cheers except Ethan, who seems strangely committed to my demise. We walk over to join them and I accept several pats on the back and a big thumbs-up from Everly before she hangs up. I slip out of my water shoes and wipe my feet off on a towel before stepping back into my work boots.

"Who's coming to the Merc with us?" Calder asks, slapping me on the back.

"You boys go on without me. I'm going to go lay Stevie down for a nap," Trista says, shooting me a warm smile. "Amazing work, Luke. I'm seriously impressed."

"I'm going to go help Trista." My mom stretches her hands out to take a drowsy-looking Stevie before glancing over her shoulder at me. "Nice job, Luke. Can't wait to see how the competition goes for you in a couple weeks."

"I thoroughly enjoyed that, but I'll let you boys go do your victory drinks alone," Dakota says with a wave. Calder steps in front of her and presses an indecent kiss on her in front of all of us. Ethan makes a puking sound, and Max gives him another shove.

"We have to go too, but nice work, Luke," Max tuts in his business voice. "I don't know how you'll fair against the pros, but at least you won't embarrass the Fletcher name."

"Thanks, I think?"

Wyatt gives me a hearty shove, offering me a silent congratulations. "I'm going to go kiss my girls goodbye and then I'm in for those drinks."

"Really?" I reply, my eyes wide. Wyatt rarely has time for drinks anymore, taking his dad role very seriously. Calder looks equally surprised.

"Stop looking so shocked."

An hour later, the three of us are seated in the warm and cozy vintage-vibe bar of the Mercantile, our rural mountain town watering hole. The only spot you can go in Jamestown for food and drink. It's located damn near at the end of our lane, just across the highway. The building used to be an old general store, but has been converted into a bar, restaurant, and grocery spot. It's good for us to get essentials without having to drive in to Boulder. And in the winter months, when the snow is heavy and my brothers and I are feeling trapped, the Merc is just a snowmobile drive away.

"You look like shit," Judy the owner squawks as she strides over to me and my brothers.

"Everything in my body hurts," I groan as I shift in the hard wooden chair.

"How come?" she asks, crossing her tiny arms over her chest. Judy is maybe a hundred pounds soaking wet, and no one knows her age because she'll never reveal it. She's one of those people who could be eighty but looks sixty. All I know is, she hasn't aged a day since we moved out here and she loves it when we tell her that.

"This dumbass is competing in Man of the Mountain," Calder says, calling me out with a teasing smirk.

"You what?" Judy cuts me a look.

"Our boy Lukey here fancies himself a lumberjack."

"I really wish I could lift my arms above my waist to punch you in the nose right now," I reply flatly.

Judy frowns. "You're barely a mountain man though."

This sobers me right up as I stare accusingly at Judy.

"How do you figure?" Wyatt drawls, his voice rough from lack of use.

Her nose wrinkles. "You're all Boulder transplants. Once a city boy, always a city boy."

Wyatt's brows furrow.

"Judy, I'm hurt," Calder exclaims, pressing his hand to his chest. "We've lived on that mountain for over a decade. How can you think this of us?"

"That's how I know you're a transplant." Judy points right at him. "A real mountain man wouldn't give a flying fuck what anyone thinks. You guys want your usuals?"

We all nod, trying to hide the devastation written on our faces. Judy pauses and chucks me under the chin. "Don't look so glum. You wear that flannel well. And your beard came in eventually."

She walks away and I self-consciously press my hand to my chin, combing my fingers through the extra length. I haven't shaved in a month, thinking that if I let my beard grow a little longer before the competition, maybe I won't stick out like a sore thumb. Judy is making me doubt that.

Calder breaks the silence. "Does anyone else feel like they were just kicked in the balls by a spiked boot?"

Wyatt and I both raise our hands.

"Judy just hurt my feelings," Wyatt mumbles, his lower lip sticking out.

Calder points to Wyatt. "I didn't even know you had feelings!"

"I'm in way over my head." I sigh heavily, cradling my face in my hands. "I'm barely a mountain man and now I'm trying to add lumberjack to my résumé like it's so fucking easy."

"Shut up." Calder whacks my forearms, knocking my face out of my hands. "We've come too damn far for you to start doubting yourself now. You're competing in this event if I have to drag your ass there myself."

"And let's not forget the real reason you're doing all of this," Wyatt says as he passes out the beers Judy just delivered. "All this for a girl."

Wyatt holds his beer up to me and the small smirk on his face looks so much like our father it hurts to look at him. I clink his glass and then Calder's before taking a fortifying sip. It's been quite the month.

Calder wipes beer foam off his mustache before asking, "Be honest, you've had it bad for Addison since the day you met her."

I tilt my head, considering that for a moment. "I don't know if that's true. I mean I was obviously attracted to her, but in case you fuckers forgot, we had a pact to never fall in love again after Robyn."

Both my brothers bristle at the mention of her name. She is not someone any of us like to talk about. In fact, it's our most humiliating memory to date. I've worked really hard to make sure Addison has never heard about that story, because I'm certain she'd look at me different. How I slept with the same woman my brothers slept with at the same time is beyond me. I was in some sort of fucking trance. I swear Robyn Whitaker is a witch.

"Wyatt fell for someone first," Calder says, pointing at him like a child.

Wyatt shrugs. "Falling for the mother of my child was the best thing that ever happened to me." His eyes soften as he blinks down into his beer.

"Dakota forced me to fall in love with her, so you can yell at her, not me," Calder mutters and I cut him an accusing look. "She did! I'm no match for a woman who hates me. It's like catnip. I go crazy trying to win them over. We'd been doing foreplay for seven long years. You and Addison have to be approaching that amount of time, too. But it still seems crazy to jump right into marriage. Are you sure you're ready for that?"

They both stare at me expectantly as I wince and quickly bring my beer to my lips. "Isn't it kind of the dream to marry your best friend?"

"I suppose so," Wyatt answers honestly. "But if she doesn't feel the same way, it's also a real quick way to getting hurt."

I nod slowly, absorbing his words. "I resisted her for a long time . . . mostly because of our pact. Told myself I liked our solo mountain life and I knew sleeping with her once would never be enough. Then I told myself I wasn't good enough for her and she deserved better."

"And now?" Wyatt asks, watching me thoughtfully.

"Now it feels like if I don't give it everything I've got, I could lose her to someone else and will spend the rest of my life regretting it."

I swallow the knot in my throat and look up at the grave, knowing looks they both share with me. They're taking me seriously for once, which I appreciate. As the youngest of four boys, it's real hard for my brothers to ever look at me like a man and not the annoying little brother who's always messing everything up. But I've seen them in their darkest hours with Dakota and Trista. And I know damn well they'd go to any length to win them back if there was a chance of losing them.

Even if it meant becoming a fucking lumberjack.

I lick my lips and add, "And I'm tired of not knowing what we could be. And if that means I have to compete in a competition I'm completely unqualified for, then so be it. Her hope was to find a husband at Man of the Mountain . . . this is me tossing my name into the hat. If I need to pretend to be a lumberjack to get her to *see me* as more than a friend, then so be it."

The corner of Wyatt's mouth tugs up into a smile before taking another sip. "And that is why we're here to help. We see you, Luke."

"And if she doesn't see you after this, then she doesn't deserve you," Calder tuts defensively. "And we'll buy our lumber supplies elsewhere."

I smile as Judy brings our food over and we tuck into it like starved animals. It feels good. Like the old days. And as happy as I am for my brothers who have found the loves of their lives, I've missed when it was just the three of us on that mountain. We'd carpool into Boulder, work all day for our dad, grab drinks after work, and then head back up the peak. Wash, rinse, repeat. It was a good life. A simple life.

But things keep changing on us ever since Dad passed. First Wyatt started getting stir-crazy and talking about wanting to become a father. Then Calder started huffing about not wanting to work for the family business anymore and doing his own thing instead. Now he only works with me and Wyatt a couple days a week so he can devote more time to the custom furniture line that he works on in his shop behind his cabin. Wyatt and I had to hire some extra crew which means Wyatt is often on the jobsites managing them while I'm back at the Fletcher Brothers Construction shop sending out proposals and doing the bookwork.

We're all working separate jobs instead of building shit together side by side. It's good work and we're all happy because we're doing what we love and what we're best at, but we're not as close as we once were. Our annual bonding trip that started after the whole Robyn thing hasn't happened in two years now. Ever since Trista moved up onto the mountain, it's been a thing of the past. So in many ways, this lumberjack training has brought us back together again, which is a fringe benefit.

Our dad would be proud.

Hard to believe it's been three years now since he passed.

I feel myself tense up as the memories of the day he died needle to the front of my mind. I regret so many of the decisions I made that day. What I did wasn't enough. *I* wasn't enough. I failed him and I failed my mother and my brothers, and now he's gone. And no matter what anyone says, I will carry that guilt and shame with me until I'm cold in the ground with him.

With that heavy thought, I hold my beer up one more time and eye my brothers seriously. "We're not here for a long time, we're here for a good time."

"Hell yes," Calder confirms while Wyatt nods and joins me in a drink.

A sense of pride overwhelms me at the three of us. We've come so far in the past decade. We've become men, fathers, husbands, boyfriends, goat daddies, cat daddies, and cock daddies. It's my turn to step up to the plate and do something that scares the shit out of me. And apparently that starts with a lumberjack competition.

Chapter 9

FACT OR FICTION?
My best friend is hot.

Addison

Man of the Mountain should be renamed Man *Meat* of the Mountain because as I look around at the endless lumberjacks sauntering around Boulder City Park with contestant numbers stuck to their flannels, I feel a hunger that I have never felt before. Maybe it's because I'm on a husband hunt and considering the potential for fringe benefits. *God it's clearly been way too long since I've been laid.* Or maybe it's because I'm pushing thirty and my hormones are surging, but my God, I want them all. Tall, short, wide, narrow, beards, and no beards . . . there are all types of rustic bros walking around for me to propose to. All I have to do is find one willing to give up a year of his life.

Easy pickings.

I scan the crowd for Ivan Morin. He's a lumberjack from Nova Scotia that I saw on the docket and remembered hooking up with a few years back. He was good in bed, and I recall him loving weed more than anything, so I feel like a temporary marriage would be no big deal to him if I manage to find him.

"Addie May," a familiar male voice croaks from behind me and I turn on my heel to see my dad walking toward me.

"Hey, Dad!" I walk over to his giant six-foot-four frame. I cross my arms and smile as we stand in front of each other awkwardly.

We've never really been a hugging family. You don't really hug someone you see every damn day, but since he's moved to

Florida, it feels weird to run into him. Like I should shake his hand or something, but that's weird too.

I turn my attention to Edith and give her a wobbly smile as she grips my dad's arm. They both look tan, wrinkled, and happy. And on some level, that makes me happy. On another level, I hate them both for finding each other and putting me in this situation.

"Nice to see you, Addison," Edith says, stepping forward and pushing a strand of my dark hair off my shoulder. It's very maternal and I feel myself shiver away from the touch. Edith never had children of her own and every time I see her, I get the sense that she'd like that type of relationship with me, but she's barking up the wrong tree.

It's not that I don't like Edith, I just have no desire for a mother figure in my life. Ever.

"Nice to see you too," I force through clenched teeth as I step away from her so she can't quite reach me.

My dad frowns down at my T-shirt exposed under my open flannel, "'Split me like a good girl'?" A look of disgust mars his face. "Really, Addie? A company T-shirt would have sufficed."

I shrug. "It's punny."

Edith covers her lips to hide her snickering. I knew I liked her for a reason. I open my mouth to defend my fashion choice, but my dad doesn't seem like he cares anymore as his eyes move past me, his whole face dropping into a deep scowl. I turn around and my lips part when I see who he's glaring at.

It's three of the four Fletcher brothers making their way across the grass toward us. You'd think they'd blend in amongst the sea of flannel here today, yet somehow, they don't. Their tall, broad frames and trim beards command attention. And I swear, people move back to clear a path for them, their jaws dropping as they ogle the fresh meat. I move my gaze from the older two and feel my brows furrow when I notice that Luke has a contestant number across his chest. *What the hell?*

They make their way over to us and I feel my thoughts racing in confusion over the number and Luke's overall general appearance. He looks . . . different. Did he get more muscular in the past month and a half since I've seen him? His hair got longer, that's for sure. It's sticking out from under his backward hat and his light brown beard is fuller and longer than I've ever seen it, aging him in a deliciously masculine way even with the boyish backward hat on.

My best friend looks . . . fucking hot.

What is going on here?

Luke's eyes land on me and the smile on his face does something to my insides that it should never do. Is that butterflies? I don't get butterflies for Luke. I get warm and cozy flies, maybe some pesky gnats because I'm not blind. But never butterflies.

This is so weird.

"Hey, Roe," Luke says, coming to stand in front of me. He pulls his hat off and runs his fingers through his tousled hair and I feel myself want to run my hands through them too. Like super bad.

Dad clears his throat loudly from behind me and I feel myself jump at his greeting. "Hello, Fletcher boys," he gruffs, stepping past me to reach his hand out to shake Wyatt's and then Calder's. "It's been a while."

"Luke," my dad grumbles but doesn't reach his hand out to shake.

"Hello, Mr. Monroe, nice to see you again." Luke stuffs his hands into his pockets and stares down at the ground.

My dad tuts his obvious irritation and I have to fight back a laugh. He is such a dick to Luke and all nice and cordial with

Wyatt and Calder. It's seriously messed up. He's not even trying to hide it.

"How's Florida treating you?" Wyatt asks, and I half hear them catching up with each other. The Fletcher family and Monroe Lumber have worked together for years. My dad even helped Wyatt out after their dad passed and Wyatt suddenly found himself in charge of . . . well . . . everything.

At least Wyatt didn't have to get married to take over their family business.

Luke's eyes move from my dad to my shirt, and he scowls. "Really?"

"It's punny! God, what's with everyone today?" I reach out and poke at the sticker on Luke's hard chest. "Why are you wearing a contestant number?"

"Because I'm competing," Luke replies with a casual shrug while pushing the sleeves up on his forearms and revealing more veins than is decent for a public setting.

"Why didn't you tell me that?" I direct this question to his brothers, who both shake their heads. "Are you guys competing too?"

"We're just here to check out the competition." Calder elbows Luke firmly. "Should be interesting."

"Speaking of which, we should go find some seats. We've got a big group coming. We'll see you around, Mr. Monroe." Wyatt shakes my dad's hand again before he and Calder make their way over to some bleachers set up by the chopping exhibit.

"We should go sit too, John." Edith grabs my dad's arm, pulling his focus from Luke back to her.

"I'll save you a seat next to me, Ads," my dad says with a weak wave, offering nothing but a sneer to Luke.

"Florida definitely hasn't warmed him up to me," Luke says as he watches my dad and his girlfriend walk away.

"What is going on with you?" I ask, giving him a light shove.

"What do you mean?"

"Why are you acting like it's totally normal for you to compete today? You've never shown any interest in lumberjack stuff before. In fact, I think you had some choice words for lumberjacks at my house several weeks back."

Luke shrugs dismissively. "Things can change."

"Why not tell me though?" My brows furrow as I stare up at him. "Why keep it a secret?"

Luke's eyes narrow ever so slightly as his gaze moves from my eyes to my mouth and then back to my eyes. His lashes are impossibly long, and I feel mesmerized by them for a moment before he says, "You said you were looking for a lumberjack husband."

"Yeah?" His brows quirk, and I burst out laughing. "That's what you're doing? Competing to be my fake husband?"

The humor drains from his face slightly as the muscle in his jaw thumps under his beard. "Nothing about this is fake."

My mind reels with the serious look in his eyes. "Is this why you've been too busy to hang out this past month? Have you been . . ." I glance down at his arms that are putting in a really good shift inside that flannel. I reach up and squeeze his bicep, my insides clenching at the sheer bulk of it. "Have you been training for this?"

"And what if I was?" he asks, taking a step closer to me and causing me to lean back from his intense body heat.

"Then I'd say you're absolutely crazy, man," I reply with a laugh, letting go of his arm and stepping away for some much-needed air. Surely, he didn't do all this for me. He must have had an interest in this stuff before I ever brought it up.

Right?

"It's not crazy to want to be there for a friend." Luke's voice is curt and businesslike, but when his eyes drop back down to my shirt, they twitch with something I can't quite decipher. When he looks back up at me, the corner of his mouth tugs back into a smile. "And I guess I'm hoping third time's the charm."

Luke begins walking backward away from me, turning on his heel with that swift swagger of his and my eyes blatantly drop to his ass as he goes.

What in the actual fuck is happening?

Chapter 10

FACT OR FICTION?
Lumberjacks can fuck right off.

Luke

Split me like a good girl is on repeat in my head as I grip my axe and set up for the wood chopping competition taking place in a few minutes. I glance down the line of twenty other lumberjack contestants standing in front of their stumps. We're to cut through a two-foot-wide tree truck section starting on one side and then switch over to the other side until it's cut fully in half. My research showed that good lumberjacks can get this task done in under a minute. In my practice sessions, I never beat ninety seconds.

I guess there's a first time for everything.

And with the simmering irritation I feel over Roe and her shirt and the fact that some of these lumberjacks have possibly split her like a good girl . . . I have a feeling I could crush this competition.

"Woo-hoo, Luke!" a voice calls from the distance and I look up to see my sister-in-law Cozy cheering for me. She's next to Max and the rest of my family who are currently occupying two full rows of bleachers. There's Max and Cozy sitting by each other with Ethan standing on his seat, then Calder, Dakota, my mom, Wyatt, Trista, and little Stevie. My insides damn near melt when I catch sight of Stevie dressed in a flannel shirt with a matching stocking cap.

God, if I could pull a win out on my first competition, that would give me all the momentum I need to take me through the rest of the day.

Let's fucking go.

My eyes scan the crowd for Roe and when I see her sitting beside her dad, I feel every muscle in my body come to life. She smiles and waves at me as I prop my axe on the ground. Without hesitation, I hold her eyes as I spit into both of my palms before rubbing them together to show her how serious I am. Within seconds, she's no longer smiling.

She looks bothered.

Good.

That makes two of us.

"Addison!" The lumberjack next to me yells her name, tearing our eyes apart. I look over to see him waving enthusiastically.

"Ivan?" I hear Roe call back from the crowd.

Who the fuck is Ivan?

He smiles and props his axe on his shoulder, looking way too at ease for my liking. My eyes flick between them as they seem to be having a silent conversation and the hairs on the back of my neck begin to prickle as I examine him more closely. He has a good fifty pounds on me and a nose that could hunt for fucking truffles it's so big. This can't be her type . . . right?

The announcer begins the countdown and I snap my head back to my wood, feeling distracted and irritated and wondering what the fuck my best friend has done with a guy like that. The buzzer goes off, and I have a delayed reaction before I lift my axe and swing sideways into my log, the sharp crack of steel meeting wood ringing out over and over as twenty split pieces tumble to the ground. I rear back and swing again, my mind bursting with thoughts that are about anything but this fucking wood I'm working over.

What *is* Roe's type? I don't know because we've never discussed it. Probably a safe bet it's not me. Which means she'll have to fall for my personality before anything else. I might as well give up now.

My adrenaline surges when I notice both guys on either side of me have switched sides of their logs after what feels like no time. They start chopping into the fresh side to meet the weakened middle and I begin to panic.

Fuck, I'm behind. I'm way the fuck behind.

I swing harder, my movements becoming erratic and uneven as the soft patter of wood chunks fling into my face hitting my clear goggles.

Finally, I reach the center of the log and rush over to the other side to begin and it's in that moment I realize Big Nose Ivan next to me is done. I swing and swing, desperate to not come in last, my brain splintering harder than the wood as I struggle to keep my pace, my muscles burning as the smell of freshly chopped pine overwhelms me.

By the time my log finally breaks off and lands with a heavy thud to the ground, I am gassed out. Hunched with my hands propped on my knees, I look over, fighting for my life as Big Nose stands there looking barely out of breath.

The announcer begins reading off the standings, Big Nose in first and me in last. With a growl, I kick my foot out to knock over the bottom half of my log. This kind of fit could rival Evil Ethan.

My eyes find Calder standing at the water table, so I make my way over, ready to hear all the shit he's about to talk.

"Well, that sucked ass," Calder says with a laugh.

"No shit." I yank my hat off and shove my damp hair off my forehead as the palms of my hands ache from how hard I squeezed the axe. I take a cup from the table and drink it before throwing the rest on my face. "I feel like that whole heat lasted ten seconds."

Calder tips his head and scratches his beard. "Guy next to

you finished in fifty-five seconds. I was timing it. Who the hell is he? I saw him waving at Addison."

"Think his name is Ivan," I grind through clenched teeth and look over my shoulder to find him talking to my best friend. Of course he is.

"They look friendly."

I crack my neck while shaking my head. "Yep."

"This is worse than I thought." Wyatt's deep voice breaks through my inner torment.

I glower over at them. The way he's leaning into her makes me suspect that Big Nose has seen her naked. I consider how hard I'd have to swing my fist to break Big Nose's nose. Is it easier to break a big nose or harder?

Calder gives me a light shove. "We need to change tactics."

I eye him curiously. "What did you have in mind?"

Competition number two is the axe throwing event and I feel relatively confident, which is probably delusional of me. But precision is the name of the game here as competitors throw a double-bit axe as close to the center of a target as possible from a set distance away. It was one of the easiest tasks to practice with Max and Ethan on the mountain, but after getting my ass kicked on the first event, I realize that the training I did is likely no match for the years of log work these bros have on me.

Which is why after a quick convo with Calder, we decided that my side game has to be stronger than everyone else's. They're all here to win a competition. *I'm here to win my future wife.*

Two contestants compete against each other until one is left standing. My first enemy is some guy who looks at least a decade younger than me. I walk over to him, my eyes laser focused on Roe as she flirts with a couple of flannel fucks.

"Hey, there," the kid says to me, tipping back his corny trapper hat that looks like it's made for a toddler.

"Where you from, man?" I ask as he stretches and checks the blade on his axe.

"Denver."

"Nice . . . right in our backyard."

"Yeah."

I narrow my eyes, trying to focus on him and not my best friend. "How good are you at this event?"

The kid smiles. "Pretty fucking good."

I wince at that response. "How much for you to throw this heat?"

"Huh?" He frowns back at me.

"You heard me. How much?"

"Forget it."

"Come on . . . everyone has a price." I tilt my head and eye him head to toe. He screams . . . *I saw this on the internet and obsessively taught myself how to do it but have no idea how to operate a real tool.* "I own a construction company with my brothers . . . I'm sure there's something you need done in Denver. We're a quick drive over. Name your project."

The guy's brows furrow as the scorekeeper prepares the board. "You any good at custom shelving? I have this gaming setup that's a mess and a whole vision board for how I want to lay it all out in my apartment to look sick."

I smile gleefully. "Oh, I got you covered."

The kid keeps his promise and throws the match, doing a good job making it look convincing. I introduce him to Calder afterward and I see the kid showing Calder photos on his phone for the shelving unit he wants created. I feel bad making this my brother's problem but it was his idea to try to figure out other ways to win this competition.

Wyatt watches the other heats and determines I can beat everyone except maybe Ivan and sure enough, I make it all the way to final two.

And the fact that Addison couldn't keep her eyes off me through the entire competition is all the fuel I need to finish this competition.

Now I'm in the championship round against none other than Big Nose.

Damn it anyways.

I can't bring myself to try to bribe him out of a fair match because one way or another, he knows Addison, and I do not want this getting back to her. He was talking to her the whole time during my matches, so I'm lucky I landed the axe on the damn bull's-eye at all.

"Hot one out here, eh?" Ivan asks with a loud sniff, his accent bleeding through.

"Yeah sure," I murmur, barely giving him my attention as I twist my hat backward.

I grip my axe and focus hard on the bull's-eye. I'm five throws away from sending this guy back to whatever Canadian city he hiked out of, so I can't let him get in my head right now.

The match begins and we both stand side by side and toss at the same time. First toss we both hit a direct bull's-eye, his a little high, mine a little low. Five points each. We toss again, both of us nailing the center right on target. We do it three more times, each of us hitting bull's-eyes every time.

I glance over to Max, my eyes wide with disbelief because in all the practicing we did together, I never hit five in a row. I'm on fucking fire. Between that and the crowd roaring all around me, and the feeling of Roe's eyes on us the whole time, the pressure is on.

We switch lanes and have to toss another five times in the opposite bull's-eye and we both land bull's-eyes again.

"Kill him, Uncle Lukey!" Ethan yells and I hear the whole crowd laugh at the small boy with such vicious words.

I smile and release my axe, wincing when I see that for the first time, I didn't hit the bull's-eye. I hit the three ring. "Fuck,"

I murmur under my breath, gripping my hat to my head in horror as I look over and see that Big Nose nailed his bull's-eye.

We have one more toss to go and even if we both hit bull's-eyes, I'll lose. And with how Ivan is tossing, the odds are good he's going to nail it.

"Redemption," I call out and the scorekeeper moves toward us holding her hand up to pause the play of game as she walks up to the boards.

"Player has called redemption." She points to the green dots on the upper right and upper left side of the board, outside of the target ring. "If player hits redemption circle, the match will go into sudden death one-throw playoff."

The crowd cheers loudly, clearly enjoying the fact that I've upped the stakes. We've got a real nail-biter at Man of the Mountain today, I guess.

"Good luck, eh?" Ivan says as he holds his axe out to me to tap.

"Thanks," I mumble, and twist my hat around to face forward, glaring at him under my bill as we clink our blades together.

I glance over at Addison, who gives me a hearty thumbs-up but then I look back over my shoulder and see Big Nose waving back at her. Is she tossing those thumbs to me or this fucker? Goddamn it, who's her fucking friend here?

"You got this, Luke!" she calls out as I hold my axe up and her voice feels like a wave of comfort rolling through my body. God, I have it bad for her. When did it get this bad? Where was I? Was I a willing participant or did fate just say fuck it . . . you can't figure it out yourself, we're going to force this on you?

Ivan gets his blade off first, landing smack-dab in the center. Another perfect bull's-eye. The crowd goes wild as they wait for me to throw. My pulse thumps in my ears and with a deep breath, I toss my axe and wince when it thunks into the upper right corner. It's close, but I can't tell if it's touching the green for sure.

The crowd goes quiet as the scorekeeper walks up to my bull's-eye and inspects it, even pulling a flashlight out of her fucking pocket to shine on the blade for a better look. After what feels like an eternity, she turns around and makes a zero signal with her fingers, indicating I did not hit the green dot, and the crowd goes fucking wild.

I smack the top of my hat, yanking it down over my face. "Fuck," I growl under my breath, kicking my boot into the ground and wondering why the fuck my own damn town is cheering for this outsider.

"Heyo . . . good try, man." Ivan holds his fist out to me, and I bump it, feeling my skin crawl as we connect.

I skulk my way over to my family, ready to hear them lay into me about fucking up, but Addison steps into my path, draping her scent all over me. "Shit, you were so close to winning that one!"

"I know," I huff, my whole body vibrating with irritation.

"You still did really good though," she says, falling into step with me.

"Not good enough," I bark, wincing at the ache in my shoulder as I try to move past her.

"What's with you?" Addison reaches out and grabs my arm, forcing me to turn around to face her. "Why are you taking this so seriously?"

"You know why," I bite, narrowing my eyes on her.

"Seriously, Luke. You don't need to do this. I know Ivan from a few years back. We've been catching up and he's unattached, so—"

"That's not how today is going to go." I lick my lips and step into her space, my body radiating protectiveness as I fight the urge to wrap my hands around her waist and claim her as mine in front of everyone here so fuckers like Ivan back the hell off. "If I win this shit today, you're marrying me, not him. Got it?"

Her jaw juts out as confusion shifts to rage in her stormy hazel eyes. "What the hell has gotten into you?"

I stare down at her lips, swallowing the knot in my throat as I wonder for the hundredth time what that soft mouth might taste like. "Just being a good *friend*."

The two lines between her forehead deepen as she pouts her reply, "And that requires you to bark orders at me?"

"Maybe once in a while, you need to be told what to do." I pin her with a scolding look before I lift my chin and turn to walk away, feeling her eyes on me as I move. I have no idea what she's thinking. Nor do I want to. I just have to get through the next four competitions to get this Ivan fucker out of the game.

Chapter 11

FACT OR FICTION?
My best friend has lost his mind.

Addison

I watch with my brows furrowed as Luke readies himself with the other lumberjacks for the boom running part of the competition. The contestants all change into shorts, tank tops, and water shoes to prepare for the event that requires them to run across a row of eight booms that float across the length of the small pond in the park. They have to make their way across them, round a barrel on the other side, and then run back.

Most usually make it all the way across and back without getting wet, so it just comes down to the best time. But I think Luke could use a dip in the cold water right now because this competition has him way too heated up.

Maybe once in a while, you need to be told what to do.

I squirm in my seat, offering a tight smile to my dad as I squeeze my thighs together and try to stop myself from feeling excited by the way Luke spoke to me. I've just never seen this side to him before. The dominant, self-assured, angry side.

What the fuck is wrong with me that I like it so much?

I am sick. I should not be turned on by a man telling me what to do. Even if that man is my best friend. Especially if that man is my best friend!

A best friend with godlike muscles that were *so not there* five weeks ago. And when he turned to face me after one of his axe throws, I swear I could see a solid six-pack through his sweat-soaked shirt. Would he mind if I lifted said shirt to count them? With my tongue?

My God, it's clearly been way too long since I've had sex.

My eyes snap to the right when I see Luke come out from the changing area. He's ditched his hat and his shaggy hair is blowing in the breeze as he stretches and talks to his brother Wyatt. I wonder what they're talking about. It's probably incredibly narcissistic to think they're talking about me, but I'm just trying to figure out why Luke decided to do all of this. Is it just to marry me? Is my life really that important to him? I know he thinks it's unsafe of me to marry a logger, but I've known Ivan for years, so he's clearly an exception. I think Ivan and Luke might actually get along if Luke gave him a chance.

Either way, this is my decision and I will not let hot, brooding, bossy Luke change my course of action. In fact, now I'm even more determined to find a lumberjack who doesn't have the last name of Fletcher. All the Fletcher brothers seem a bit unhinged today. I swear I saw Calder trip one of the contestants earlier. Like . . . on purpose, stuck his foot out and tripped the guy, then pointed to a little girl standing on the other side like she was the one to do it.

There must be something in the air up on Fletcher Mountain and I'm going to stay far the hell away from it.

"So what were you saying earlier about your dad's lumber supply business?" Ivan asks, appearing out of nowhere beside me, and I smile and turn around to talk to him while the first contestant prepares to run across the row of floating logs.

"Oh, just that he's retiring from the business and looking to sell or pass along to me."

Ivan sniffs loudly as he looks down at me. "You'd take over the whole building center? How would you manage that?"

"What do you mean?"

"I mean . . . surely you wouldn't talk directly to the mills and stuff. You have a guy on staff for that I assume."

"Yeah. Me."

"Right," Ivan replies with a laugh to which I stare back at him, not joining in. He frowns. "Like you negotiate the rates and buys and everything?"

"Yes . . . why are you saying it like that's a big deal? You knew I worked for my dad."

"I thought you were the receptionist. Or maybe did the bookwork for the company. Payables, receivables, that kind of stuff."

"Why did you figure that?" I ask, staring up at him and wondering what the hell we talked about when I hooked up with him four years ago. Obviously we didn't talk enough.

"I've just never met a woman who knows the difference between pine and oak, let alone one that talks to the sawmills directly."

"Then you don't know Roe at all," Luke's voice interjects from behind and I turn around to see him standing a foot away from me with a murderous look in his eyes. "Monroe Lumber would be nothing without her and that was true even before her dad retired."

His words fill my heart with something really intense and I almost smile. Almost.

The thing that stops me from smiling at my best friend is the fact that Luke's hands have somehow snaked around my waist in a weird, claiming sort of way as he shoots daggers at Ivan.

"What are you doing?" I hiss through clenched teeth as I fight the surging desire that's coursing through my body at his very intimate and foreign touch.

"Just coming over for a good luck kiss," Luke says loudly, looking directly at Ivan.

"A what?" I ask, not following what's going on, so I turn around in Luke's arms, my eyes flying wide when his big paws slide dangerously low on my back. I grip the chest of his tank top, balling the fabric in my fists. "What the fuck are you doing, Fletcher?"

A slow, dopey smile spreads across his face as he looks down at me. "You heard me, snookums."

Snookums?

Now he's gone too far.

"We'll be right back," I state through clenched teeth to Ivan as I grab Luke by the shirt and drag him behind me. We make our way over to the long row of porta-potties and I do my best to ignore the rancid smell as I give my friend here a hard shove in the chest. "What the fuck is going on?" I ask as soon as we're concealed from the crowd.

"That guy is a creep, Roe," he says, pointing his finger back to the place we just vacated. His exposed arms reveal a serious farmer's tan and I have to stop myself from admiring Luke's corded arm muscles.

"He's perfectly fine," I balk and prop my hands on my hips.

"Everything he just said to you was misogynistic bullshit."

"So what." I shrug and feel my body tensing up. "I hear that shit all the time."

"Not from me," Luke replies, his eyes intense, and I swallow the knot in my throat because I know he's right.

From day one I never got a single sexist vibe from Luke. Or any of the Fletcher brothers for that matter. And the fact that Luke asked me out for drinks and didn't try to sleep with me proves that point even further. He's one of the good ones. *Normally.*

"Luckily, I don't need Ivan to be perfect for a one-week-a-month marriage," I reply, crossing my arms over my chest. "I just need him to sign a little contract and go live his life as usual."

"After he moves in with you," Luke growls and begins pacing in front of me, murmuring expletives under his breath.

He slices his hand through his wild hair and I find it really irritating how good that floppy hair looks on him. He looks good in pretty much anything though. Even in his dorky little water shoes. Damn him.

"I don't know what's gotten into you today, but you need to chill the fuck out because I'm going to do what I came here to do and no man—well-meaning or not—is going to stop me." I lick my lips and pause before adding, "And if you keep pushing me like this, then you're no better than that walking embodiment of toxic masculinity Ivan out there."

Luke stops pacing and stares back at me like he's been shot and I have a moment of hesitation, wondering if I went too far. I know Luke is a good guy, but whatever kind of tactic he's using right now to get me to fake marry him instead of Ivan or anyone else is too much. This is my life and my decision and no man is going to get in my way.

"Try not to drown out there," I snipe as I brush his shoulder to storm past him, desperate to get some space from his wounded eyes. Luke is clearly going through something that has very little to do with me, and the less I know about it the better. I pause and turn on my heel to add, "And if you ever call me *snookums* in public again, I will knee you in the nut sack."

He rolls his eyes and I walk away to find my seat with my dad and Edith. My brows are stuck in a constant state of furrowing as I sulk through the next thirty minutes.

However, the entire time I watch the event, I can't seem to shake the memory of Luke's hands on my body. Luke and I don't touch like *that*. Ever. We shove and hit. Or I should say, *I* shove and hit. Luke just kind of takes it from me. He takes a lot from me, come to think of it. And he never complains.

But today he seems to have found his voice with me and it's bothering me how much I seem to like that side to him. His assertive voice is hot.

Unfortunately, that macho bravado doesn't help him in the booms. He comes in third and is seated in fifth place in the overall lineup of twenty lumberjacks with only two more events to go. Ivan took first, making it look far too easy for a man his size, but I can't even bring myself to cheer for him. I'm irritated by his remarks earlier and not really sure why I defended him to Luke. Ivan deserves a knee to the nut sack as well.

As I look up at the scoreboard, I realize that it will take a miracle for Luke to win best overall. Ivan would need to bomb the next two events to even give Luke a chance and I really don't see that happening.

We make our way over to the bucking saw competition and I cringe when I look at the board and see that Luke's paired up with none other than Ivan, who seems to really have his hackles up around Luke. This should be interesting.

The announcer explains that the bucking saw event has two men using a two-person bucking saw to pull through a twenty-inch white pine log. They have to sever a complete wood cookie off the end of the log faster than the other teams who are all lined up to go at the same time as well. I realize that even if Luke and Ivan take first place, it will only further improve Ivan's standing, which does nothing for Luke.

Luke and Ivan glower at each other as they stand across a three-foot-long cross saw, neither of them taking their eyes off each other as the announcer reads off the teams all ready to roll right alongside them. They begin a countdown and the two ready themselves, eyes on each other as they bend over and grip their saw. Luke's muscles are glistening in the October heat and it's such a sight, I can't even be bothered to look at Ivan.

The buzzer goes off and I swear to God, I blink and they've sawed their cookie clean off, crushing through the timber in barely three cuts. The other teams are still sawing away as both Luke and Ivan continue holding on to the long blade, the metal bowing in the center as they both refuse to let go, yanking on the handle to force their teammate to stumble.

Finally, the scorekeeper comes over to announce them as winners and they release their saw handles, both walking away and refusing to celebrate their victory. Luke's eyes find mine and are pools of molten lava as he glares up at me.

"What is wrong with that boy?" my dad husks from beside me.

I inhale deeply, my heart rate thundering at his intense eye contact. "I wish I knew, Old Man."

Chapter 12

FACT OR FICTION?
I'm probably going to die today.

Luke

"Okay, folks, the final event of the day is the ninety-foot speed climb. This is the big event everyone has been waiting for. Climbers will scale a ninety-foot cedar spar pole using steel-core climbing rope, spurs, and lots of grit. Once they reach the top, athletes will descend at rapid speed, tapping their spurs inside designated sections on the pole as they make their way back down to earth at a staggering speed to stop the clock."

Wyatt, Calder, Max, and myself all stand shoulder to shoulder, arms crossed, staring up at the ninety-foot pole suspended upright by ropes and cranes as we watch lumberjack after lumberjack fly up the pole and practically fall down to the bottom. There's a bell at the top contestants have to ring and a large crash pad at the base that catches them when they drop the last ten to twenty feet or so. A few of them have come down a bit faster than they intended and there's been some limping off to the nearby medic tent, which has only stoked my anxiety. A uniformed EMT is currently on the mat, assessing one of the competitors on the mat now, casting an ominous glow on the entire event.

"This pole is at least four times longer than what you practiced on at our jobsite," Calder says, swallowing nervously as he squints up to the top of the pole.

"Yeah," I reply with a huff. "Everly texted me and said I should probably just forfeit this event."

Max nods seriously. "That's a good idea."

"I'm not forfeiting," I state firmly.

"Why?" Max asks, moving to stand in front of me. "It's not like you're going to win the competition. That Ivan guy has it all but won."

"I don't give a fuck," I reply with a growl. "I'm finishing this shit today."

Wyatt scratches his beard and shakes his head. "This isn't smart, Luke."

"It's climbing a fucking pole. How hard can it be?" I tut, bending over to adjust my spiked boots. I grab my gloves and rope up off the ground and try to get myself mentally ready.

Calder sputters out a laugh. "Come on, man. These guys are moving crazy fast. This isn't worth getting paralyzed over."

Max opens his mouth to agree with Calder but looks past me as a cold hand grabs my shoulder, twisting me around. "Luke, can I speak to you for a second?"

With a frown, I slide my gloves on and allow Roe to pull me off to the side, out of earshot of my brothers. She licks her lips, her eyes moving from the pole to me and back to the pole before she says, "Don't do this event."

"Why?" I snap, my shoulders tensing defensively.

"Because you're not going to win."

"Thanks for the vote of confidence, friend."

Her jaw is tight with her frustrated scowl. "I don't want you to die."

"I'll be fine." I huff as I slide my gloves on and give her a pat on the shoulder before making my way back over to the event.

"No you won't," she growls and jogs around to stop in front of me. She presses her tiny hands flat to my chest and uses all her might to walk me backward away from the warm-up area. I see my brothers all watching us curiously, Calder laughing like usual. She thrusts her finger up at my face, drawing my attention back down to her. "I know you signed up for this competition today as some sort of proposal scheme but this needs to be done now. I won't marry anyone, okay?"

I laugh and shake my head. "You'd rather lose your family legacy than marry me? Real nice, Roe."

"I'd rather lose the lumberyard than watch my best friend plummet to his death, yes." She wraps her arms around her body, refusing to make eye contact with me as she rubs her lips together nervously.

"God, you're so stubborn sometimes." I laugh.

"You're determined to climb up a ninety-foot pole. Now come on," she adds, her voice cracking at the end as her face shifts from anger to worry. "Admit defeat and just be done with this. Let's go get a beer and be friends again. I hate fighting with you."

I tilt my head, staring down at the woman who's occupied way too many of my thoughts these past few months. Hell, these past few years. I haven't been the same man since the day I met her. Whether that's a good thing or a bad thing, I know that it has more to do with her than me and I hate that.

This competition may have started as a way for me to get her to see me but now it's a way for me to see myself. As more than just the youngest Fletcher brother, as more than just a friend in love with his friend. For so long, I've watched on as my brothers have succeeded in all they do. And it's not that I'm jealous, but I've pushed myself harder than I've ever pushed myself before and considering the odds against me, I've proven that I'm capable of more. I want to finish what I started here.

I want to see myself as the man I want to be. A man who finishes things. A man who doesn't let everyone down and maybe just once saves the day.

"This isn't just about you, Addison," I state, staring down at her, my jaw taut with determination. "Maybe it started that way, but that's not all this is anymore. I'm finishing this fucking competition today and if you choose to marry Big Nose Ivan, then I won't get in your way."

She opens her mouth to say something but instead just squeals a noise of anger as she turns on her heel to stomp away. A better man wouldn't stare at her ass as she walks off. I am not that man.

Maybe I'm more like Ivan than I thought.

Or maybe I'm just obsessed with my best friend.

Either way, I need to get my head in the game because I'd prefer to be able to walk myself out of this city park when everything is all said and done today.

The announcer calls my name up to the ninety-foot pole and I stop by my brothers to grab my rope, ignoring their looks of concern and refusing to glance out into the audience at my mother and the rest of the family. This isn't about anyone but me. If I stay focused I can do this. I can accomplish this goal.

I walk up to the pole that Ivan has just completed his run on. He's looking past me and when I look over my shoulder to see him watching Addison . . . again, I can't help but say, "That's my future wife you're gaping at, so I'd appreciate it if you look the fuck away."

Big Nose frowns and stares back at me. "Shit. I didn't know you two are engaged."

I adjust my rope and nod. "We're not . . . but we will be."

Without another word, Ivan steps aside and I wrap my rope around, kicking out my feet as I prepare to climb what feels like a football field's worth of wood.

The announcer does a countdown and when the buzzer goes off, I launch myself upward, driving the spikes on the insides of my boots into the cedar pole and using my arms and legs in a coordinated motion to make my way up the wooden beam. I feel good at first, steady and strong, but as I continue the climb, my quads begin screaming in agony, my forearm veins looking like they're going to pop with the effort of heaving my ass up this goddamn pole.

"Damn Everly for not finding a ninety-foot pole for me to practice this on," I huff, my lungs screaming as I continue to climb. I feel the pole swaying in the wind the higher I get and my entire body starts shaking, which makes my coordinated motions even more difficult. I look up at the bell and it still looks so fucking far away. I feel like I've been climbing for hours. Why isn't it closer?

I glance down and that's when my entire body seizes up. "Oh fuck, I really shouldn't have done that." I press my forehead into the wood, wondering how everyone already looks like tiny ants when I'm only halfway up this fucking pole.

I wonder what it would take to get a rescue team up here and help me down? Fuck, they can't do that. I have to figure this out myself. Which means I have two choices: continue climbing and risk freaking out at the top and being unable to come down. Or bitch out and start descending now and embarrass myself in front of my town and my family.

As I fight to catch my breath, I hear my damn niece's voice in my head. *If you love her then you have to go for it, Luke. Love is stronger than pride.*

I inhale a deep breath and glance down again, spotting my brothers all down there staring up at me. Damn they worked so hard to help me get here today. I can't give up now.

As I dig deep for the strength to move my foot up, it's then that I hear my dad's voice creeps in my head. *"Get your ass up that pole, Luke. We don't have all day."*

That brings a smile to my face. I miss his voice. I miss his presence. God, what I wouldn't give to hear what he thinks of all this. Before I know it, my body is moving again and I'm climbing, up, up, and up. I don't know how long it takes. Time sort of moves strangely when you're suspended a hundred feet in the air and all you can hear is the deafening wind. But when I ring that bell, my adrenaline spikes and I start skating down that pole faster than I could have ever imagined. My gloves squeeze hard on the rope to hold tension as my feet move impossibly fast in and out of the pole. The crowd cheers loudly and I feel victory on the tips of my fingers when suddenly, my spike misses a notch.

My heart jumps into my throat and I feel myself falling, sliding down the fucking pole, my chin scraping against the rough wood as I go, unable to stop my descent. I'm like a fucking car crash happening in slow motion but everything is a blur.

I'm airborne for what feels like a whole goddamn minute before my back strikes something hard. My body convulses when all the wind gets knocked out of me and I fight to catch my breath, my whole body seizing up in a desperate attempt to save my own fucking life.

Murmured voices are loud all around me and I blink up, seeing only the blue Colorado sky and by the time my body finally stops torturing me and lets me take a full breath in, my vision is clouded by the view of my brothers' bearded faces.

"Holy fuck, Luke, are you okay?" Calder asks, grabbing my face and yanking it toward him.

"Ow," I cry, my body contorting weirdly on the mat below me. This mat looked a lot softer when the other competitors landed on it.

"You skidded down half the pole, Luke. What the fuck were you thinking?"

"Didn't do that on purpose," I croak, feeling every muscle in my body weep in agony.

"Is anything broken?" Wyatt's deep voice cuts in.

I wince and shake my head. "Don't think so."

"God, you're an idiot," Calder says with a laugh.

"Was I fast?"

"No, not at all," Calder replies, laughing some more.

"Really?" I squint to look up at all my brothers' faces to confirm that Calder isn't fucking with me.

Max injects an opinion next. "You were fast when you fell maybe, but the climb took ages. Some of the audience got bored and went home. Mom took Ethan to get a pretzel."

"Seriously."

"But it got interesting when you dropped at the end," Calder says, looking down at me with wide, eager eyes. "Did you mean to do that?"

"No, I didn't. Why, did it look intentional?"

"No, not at all," Wyatt replies curly. "You fell like a rock."

"My chin hurts."

"Yeah, you're bleeding pretty good," Max eyes it nervously, looking like he could puke at the sight of it. "The EMT is coming over now. Can you feel your legs?"

I wiggle my legs and nod. "Yeah, I can."

"Good," Calder huffs. "I really don't want to have to come back and work for Wyatt again."

Wyatt cuts Calder a menacing look and suddenly my brothers are all shoved out of the way and a small hand whacks me hard on the chest that was just deprived of oxygen for a few seconds.

"Are you happy, you fucking idiot?"

My brows furrow. "Not especially. I think I'm bleeding."

"You deserve to bleed!" Addison roars, and her face appears over mine, the veins in her forehead protruding in a really angry way. "You were the slowest, most boring climber of the day and then you decided to scare the shit out of everyone right at the end."

"Yeah . . . I didn't mean to do that part," I groan, feeling an ache in my back.

"Of course you didn't," Addison snarls and stares up at the pole, clearly fuming. "You don't know what you're doing."

"But I did it." I smile and when she looks down at me, she does not smile back. She is *mad* mad.

"You lost. Badly. You won't even place in the top ten so it wasn't even worth it."

I sigh heavily and wince as I touch my chin and see blood on my glove. "Can we talk about this later? I think I might need stitches."

"No, we can't talk about this later, Luke. We will talk about it now because if I marry you, you can't be a moron like this, okay?"

"Huh?" I blink up at her. Am I concussed, or did she really just say she was going to marry me?

"I mean it . . . if we do this, you need to at least try to compromise on some stuff or we're never going to survive a year of this."

"What are you talking about?"

"Marry me, you asshole." She scowls down at me like she didn't just say the four most magical words I've ever heard.

I swallow the knot in my throat . . . and I think I swallow some blood before I reply, "But I lost."

"Trust me, I know," she sighs heavily and pinches the bridge of her nose. "Marry me anyways because . . ." A soft look sweeps across her face as she looks down at my body that I really hope isn't mangled but since I still haven't been able to see anything but faces and sky, I have no idea. "Marry me because you're my best friend and I need you."

I open my mouth, but am unable to say anything because a pair of EMTs come over with a stretcher and move Addison out of the way. "What is that for?" I ask, staring at the yellow board.

"It's protocol for anyone who falls more than twenty feet,"

one guys says as he begins tucking the board under half of my body. "We need to ensure there's no spinal injuries."

"Oh shiiit," I groan as the men manhandle me onto the stretcher, strapping my forehead and body down and making it impossible for me to move in any way. They stand up to haul me away and my mind is reeling with everything that just happened. How bad am I hurt? Where is my family? Where is Addison?

Finally I find my voice and yell, "Wait, wait, wait a second. Roe? Roe, are you here?"

I call out her name and after a few seconds she appears above me out of nowhere, her black hair fanning her cheeks, her eyes full of concern. "What? What is it?"

I smile up at her and she frowns. "Yes."

"Yes what?"

"Yes, I'll marry you." I hit her with the most dazzling smile and have a moment of wondering if all my teeth are in place.

She rolls her eyes. "Fine, but you better not be paralyzed. If I have to wipe your ass on the toilet, I'm going to ask for alimony after our divorce."

My body shakes with laughter and then I wince, everything hurting all at once. And as the two guys carry me away from my future bride I think . . . having her wipe my ass sounds like a decent way to spend the rest of my life.

Chapter 13

FACT OR FICTION?
I want a . . . mustache ride?

Addison

"Oh my God, what is that on your face?" I burst out laughing as I climb into Luke's truck outside the lumberyard on a sunny Friday afternoon.

"Does it look stupid?" my best friend asks, glancing at himself in the rearview mirror. He runs his fingers over the hair on his upper lip. "I can shave it off if you think it's awful."

I turn in my seat to fully take it in as Luke pulls out of the lot, self-consciously touching his face now that I've literally pointed and laughed at him. I wasn't trying to be a bitch, I was just . . . not expecting this on a man only thirty-three years old. I'm used to old man mustaches like my dad's or the yard guys. Those mustaches are stained by coffee and frozen with snot in the cold winter months. Or I guess I've seen those weird swirly hipster mustaches on some bartenders in town, or the obvious creepy pornstaches.

But on Luke? This mustache? I squint as I take in the sight of him again. I hate to admit it, but I think it's working for him. It's got this rustic, effortless quality to it. Thick and sloped downward on his upper lip with a little bit of playful character to it. It's giving confident, mature, masculine. His beard did that too, but this makes Luke stand out a bit from his brothers. A little . . . originality. A thirty-three-year-old has to be confident to rock a 'stache, right?

"I'm not mad at it," I state with my voice rising in pitch

dramatically. My eyes drop to his square jaw where he has four stitches etched into the front of his chin. "I've just never seen your chin before so it took a second to adjust."

"They had to shave my chin in the ER and asked if I wanted to keep the 'stache. I was a little loopy on muscle relaxers when I said yes but it's growing on me." He rubs his face and a flush of color darkens his cheeks as I blatantly inspect him.

I smile and then frown as I continue my ogling, only to balk at what he's wearing. "You're dressed up," I state accusingly as I take in his tan slacks, white shirt, and brown dress shoes.

"Well, we have an appointment to get married," he says, adjusting his collar.

"I know, but it's not real," I reply with a frown.

"I know, but we're going to see your dad afterward, so I want to look respectable," he says, cutting me a look. "Plus I wasn't sure if we'd need to take pictures or something."

"Well, shit," I exclaim, glancing down at my work jeans and dirty Converse. "Why didn't I think of that?"

"You look great." Luke waggles his brows playfully and I shove him in the shoulder.

"Go to my house, I need to change."

With a heavy sigh, Luke turns on the next road and makes his way to my side of town. When he pulls up in front of my building, he says, "Our appointment with the clerk is in twenty minutes, so you better hurry."

"I'll be freaky fast!" I call out as I hop out of his truck and run up the steps to my apartment, already knowing what I'm going to wear because I was cataloging my whole wardrobe on the way here. I have the perfect outfit that was a bit of an impulse purchase last year after I became obsessed with Caitlin Clark. She's a former Iowa Hawkeye basketball player who wore this stunning Prada outfit to the WNBA draft. I found a dupe of it and bought it without having a single place to wear it because

I still had to have it. And weirdly, I feel like it's been waiting for this occasion.

It's a white satin blazer with a matching miniskirt and underneath I have this loose, cropped rhinestone top. It's a little sexy with a little class—a combo I enjoy on the rare occasions I have to get dressed up. Since I hate wearing heels, I finish the ensemble with my black platform Converse that don't look like they've been worn around a lumberyard all day. Taking a few minutes in the bathroom, I add a bit of mascara and blush and spray myself with some perfume before unclipping my hair and rifling my fingers through it, then I finally rush out the door and back into Luke's truck.

I buckle up and yank the mirror down to add a touch of lip gloss. "What are you waiting for?" I ask, when I notice he still hasn't pulled away from my building.

I turn and find him staring slack-jawed at me. "You just had that outfit lying around?"

"Do you think it's too much for the clerk's office?" I glance down at my exposed legs that probably would have looked ten times better with some shimmery lotion.

"No, it's not too much. It's perfect. You look . . ." Luke clears his throat and I glance up to see him blinking rapidly. "You look beautiful, Roe."

My chin trembles at that very sweet, very heartfelt compliment. "I was just trying to rise to your level, man. You clean up good, Fletcher."

One perk to Luke losing his beard? I can see him blush. And that boy is flaming red as he puts the truck in Drive and makes his way to the clerk's office to marry me. Who knew I had to marry my best friend to get him to stop being mad at me? What a sap.

Ten minutes later, Luke is pulling into a parking spot of the county clerk building and he holds a finger up to me as he hops out of the vehicle, rushing over to my side of the vehicle to open my door.

What a move.

He holds his hand out to me to help me out of his truck, his eyes dropping to my legs briefly before flashing back up to my face. Now I feel like my cheeks are suddenly really hot too. This whole moment reminds me of Mexico all over again. We're like two weirdos not used to seeing each other in nonwork clothes and forgetting how to behave like civilized adults.

As we walk the tall flight of concrete steps up into the old building, Luke asks, "So are you going to keep your apartment, then?"

"Yes, I'm going to keep my apartment. Why? What do you mean?"

Luke opens the door to the building and steps back. "I mean, paying rent for a whole year at a place you're not living in seems like a waste, no?"

"I guess so," I reply, considering that thought. "I don't really want to lose it though."

"Maybe you can sublease?"

"Yeah, maybe," I reply as we make our way through security.

We probably should have sat down and ironed out some of the specifics of this arrangement beyond the prenup, which I emailed him after he got home from the ER. I paid a lawyer a pretty penny to draw up a contract that basically says we leave with what we came into the marriage with, so whomever I marry can't retroactively decide he wants half the lumberyard.

Not that I'd worry about Luke ever doing that. But when I was trying to find guys on Tinder to marry . . . hell yes, I needed a legal, binding contract. I need to protect my family legacy as well as myself.

We follow the signs to the clerk's office and check in for our appointment, not even able to sit down before being called to the desk to fill out the paperwork. Colorado is a self-solemnizing state, meaning we don't need witnesses or a judge or an officiant of any sort to get legally married. In my research, I actually discovered that Colorado is the easiest state to get married quickly in. We just fill out some paperwork, show our IDs, pay the thirty-dollar marriage certificate fee, sign our names, and that's that. We are man and wife.

"Will you be changing your name?" the clerk asks me, her tone flat. "If so, I can get you those forms as well."

"Oh . . . um . . ." I look to Luke with wide eyes. "I forgot about this."

He shakes his head. "You don't need to mess with that, do you?"

"Yeah, I don't think so. You don't care, right?"

"Why would I?" Luke asks and I feel weirdly rejected, but obviously that's the right answer. He's already signed my pre-drafted prenup and we're going to dissolve the marriage in a year, so no need to go through the headache of a name change just to change it back.

"Keeping my name," I reply to the clerk.

"Okay, then I just need you two to sign here."

I feel Luke's eyes on me as I sign first and then I watch him nervously as he signs next.

"Would you like me to notarize this today?"

"Um . . . yes?" I state with a frown. "Why wouldn't we."

"Well, you have thirty-five days to file your marriage license if you want to wait."

"We don't want to wait," Luke says immediately, taking the words right out of my mouth.

"Great. I'll head to the back to get this notarized, then. It will be just a moment."

"We need you to notarize this as well please," I say, handing over the prenup.

She eyes it and compares Luke's signature before nodding. "I'll be right back."

She disappears and Luke and I stand at the counter all dressed up in the drab county clerk's office.

"It's wild we're actually doing this," I state, trying to fill the silence.

"My family is going to lose it." Luke blinks back his disbelief.

"Are you sure you want to keep the secret from all of them?" I ask as I think about our text exchange from yesterday. "The fact that this is just a temporary thing is kind of a big secret to keep. And you're already so close with your family."

Luke's jaw goes tight as he shakes his head. "If I tell my mom this isn't real she will make it her life's mission to figure out how to make it real."

"Oh shit."

"Yeah, and my niece is a self-proclaimed matchmaker so she can't be trusted either."

"Yikes."

"We're better off faking it with them or they'll just make our lives miserable."

I swallow the knot in my throat. "You're really not doing a good job selling Fletcher Mountain right now."

Luke's brown eyes snap up to meet mine and he reaches out to grab my hand in reassurance. "Oh, don't worry, Roe. You'll love it up there. Fletcher Mountain . . ." He pauses for a moment before adding, "It feels like finding a secret that the whole world should know about, but you're the only lucky one."

I smile as he begins rattling off all the things he loves about living up there with his brothers and I try to focus on the fact that this is just for a year. I can do anything for a year. Even maybe, possibly, make friends with his brothers' significant others.

I just hope everyone doesn't hate me when Luke and I have to end this in a year. That is yet another thing I didn't consider.

But the lumberyard is the rest of my life. I have to do this. I just hope Luke will help me manage the fallout with his family that'll come when our one year is up.

Alternatively, they might be relieved I'm out of Luke's way so he can find his true soulmate.

That thought causes a pit to form in my stomach, but I'm distracted when the clerk returns, waving the papers in the air excitedly before sliding them across the counter to us.

She smiles. "Forgive me but I never get to do this part." She clears her throat dramatically. "Luke Fletcher and Addison Monroe . . . I now pronounce you husband and wife."

I smile and feel that happiness deep in my bones. I know I wanted a stranger, I know I wanted this to feel like a business deal and detached. But there's something really special about how my best friend would do all this for me. And right now, I can't recall a single reason why I was so determined *not* to accept Luke's proposals. He really is one of the good ones, and that song is playing on repeat in my head as I smile up at him like a goof.

"You can now kiss your bride."

"What was that?" I ask, turning my ear toward the woman and she yanks me out of eye-fucking my best friend.

"You can now kiss your bride!" The woman stares at us expectantly and we both hesitate. Shit. I forgot about this part too. God, what the fuck is wrong with me?

"We don't have to." Luke smiles politely at the clerk. "She's weird about PDA."

"No, it's fine," I exclaim and Luke's head swings around to stare at me in surprise. I'm a little surprised too, but I've never really minded touching Luke. He's different. He's safe. But kissing him? The idea of it has me spiraling. Best friends aren't supposed to kiss . . . then again, platonic best friends don't usually get married either. And above my little physical touch hesitations, I feel overwhelmed with gratitude. I'm grateful for my friend and this moment and the future he just helped me lock in and I want to show him that. We're adults here. It's no big deal to give your friend a quick kiss of appreciation. Right?

I step closer to Luke with a smile. "We should. This is it. We finally did it!" I laugh awkwardly and my hands tremble as I reach up and cup his face, my fingers tingling against the light stubble of his freshly shaven jaw.

His brows furrow down at me, his eyes searching mine for something I'm not sure of. I bite my lip, realizing I've never noticed the gold flecks Luke has in his eyes before. I always thought they were just chocolate brown, but they're not. They're brown with honey mixed in. They're captivating. His lips aren't bad either. At least his lower lip. His upper is hard to see under the hot guy 'stache, but that lower one. It looks good. Very kissable.

I inhale sharply when Luke steps in closer to me, his hands finding my waist, and I get that same feeling I had at the lumberjack competition when he held me in front of Ivan. As mad as I was at him for that, I can't deny how it felt. Luke makes me feel good. Respected . . . and maybe even a little bit naughty when he's looking at me the way he is right now.

Before I lose my nerve, I stand up on my tiptoes and lift my lips to my best friend's, fusing our mouths together in what I expect to be a platonic, no-heat, chaste type of kiss. The kind of kiss you give to your grandma, if you're the kind of family who kisses their grandma on the lips. I'm certainly not. I would definitely never kiss my grandma the way I'm kissing Luke.

A noise vibrates in his chest and I feel him angle his head to the side to meet my lips more fully.

I'm kissing my friend for the first time in all the years I've known him.

I've kissed Luke on the cheek a good number of times.

Countless hugs, shoves, hits, and maybe even an occasional brief snuggle.

But never anything like this.

I inhale a trembling breath as his lips part and move ever so slightly against mine, timid but present. Firm, but gentle. So very Luke. A perfect blend of good and bad. Happy and mad. Comforting and infuriating. I meet his energy and move my lips with his as my hands roam off his face and back into his hair. My fingers widen as I comb through his shaggy length, feeling my body arch so we're flush against each other.

I want more but I also know this is Luke. My friend. The man who's doing me a massive favor by marrying me so I can take over my dad's company. He should most definitely not be a man whose lips are making me wonder what a mustache ride might actually feel like.

That horrific intrusive thought has my brain flashing back to reality like an explosion and I quickly yank away, untwining my hands from Luke's hair to cover my mouth in pure shock, my lips tingling at the loss of him.

Luke blinks back at me, lips parted, eyes burning with a look that I have never seen before. A look that has me squeezing my thighs together and biting my lip so hard, I could cry.

"That'll do it," the clerk says, her head propped on her hand as she stares starry-eyed at us. "You two are going to be very happy, I can tell."

I burst out into nervous laughter and Luke joins me, both of us flustered and avoiding eye contact as we turn away from each other, because what the actual fucking fuck was that?

The lady slides all of our papers into a folder and we walk out of there with a notarized prenup, a marriage license, and one more stop to make. Hopefully we can keep our hands to ourselves at this stop or we both might be in very big trouble.

Chapter 14

FACT OR FICTION?
The only thing worse than one mustache is two.

Luke

Jesus fuck, what was that?

I lick my lips and swear I can still taste Addison's lip gloss as we drive out to her dad's house just a few miles outside of Boulder in a rural area.

Am I dreaming or did Addison want that kiss as well? I thought it was going to be hard work to get her to admit her feelings for me but after one little kiss, I'm feeling a lot more optimistic about this plan Everly and I cooked up together. Roe's pupils were dilated after that kiss. Her breasts were heaving under that tiny, cropped top. My head hurts from how hard she gripped my hair.

And I want her to do it again.

I want her to do it for the rest of our lives.

The craziest part is, that kiss was nothing. It was a brush of the lips. No tongue, no inappropriate hand movements. It was a sweet, tender brush of our lips under fluorescent lighting and a perfect stranger observing it.

And it lit our whole bodies on fire.

She felt it. She had to have felt it. No way am I in this alone.

And the way she can't even look at me now? My best friend is bothered as hell and she has no idea just how much more I plan to bother her the moment she moves onto my mountain.

I smile smugly as we pull into her dad's property. It's a decent-sized lot with a large machine shed that shows a couple ATVs and a run-down truck. I've never been out here before, but Addison told me about her upbringing, and she painted a fairly accurate picture. The property is pretty basic and the house is nice but possibly in need of some updates. It looks like the type of place a single man who owns a successful lumberyard would live in if he didn't have time to manage it all on his own.

"You might want to wipe that smile off of your face before we go inside because my dad is probably going to kill you," Addison deadpans from the passenger seat. Her tan, sculpted legs on full display in that satin skirt are not making my life any easier.

I attempt to frown as I slide out of the truck and make my way over to her door to open it again. "I'm not scared of your dad, Roe."

"Since when?" She huffs out a laugh as she grabs the handle to help herself down out of the truck.

"Since we got that piece of paper about twenty minutes ago that says you're mine," I reply honestly.

"I'm yours?" Addison stares up at me, her eyes lit with something I can't quite decipher. Is she offended by my words, or intrigued?

I shrug. "In a sense. And really, what's he going to do? Kill his daughter's husband?"

"Husband." Addison flinches and covers her mouth as she grins girlishly. "That's so weird. You're my husband, Luke."

My brows lift, loving the sound of that. "You're my wife, Roe."

"Weird!" Addison covers her ears and shakes her head. "I don't feel grown-up enough to be a wife."

"Oh please, you make bread from scratch and run an entire fucking lumberyard of dudes like it's nothing. You're ultimate wifey material."

Addison's cheeks flush with my words as we make our way

up the front steps, but she pauses at the door and hits me with a serious look. "Just let me do the talking, okay? And whatever you do, don't catch yourself alone with him."

My head jerks back but I nod woodenly. "You're the boss."

The corner of her mouth quirks into a grin. "A boss and a wife. Maybe being married isn't so bad after all." She knocks on the door and lets herself inside before calling out, "Dad, it's me. You in here?"

"In the kitchen," his voice barks back.

Addison reaches behind to grab my hand and pull me closer to her. Her palms are sweaty, revealing that she's perhaps not as brave as she thinks she is. I stare at our hands clasped together, loving the sight of them. Hers is tough from her work at the yard, but it's still small and feminine. I like how it looks inside mine. Her hand would look really nice with a ring on it. I should get her a ring. Something that's very her so she can't be all weird and act like it's unnecessary.

My fantasizing about Addison's hands comes to a crashing halt when I look up and see her dad at the kitchen table with a slew of guns in disrepair all around him and various types of gun-cleaning products next to a silo of Miller Lite.

We came at a bad time.

"Hey, Addie May," John says with a big smile until he sees me come in behind her. He frowns down at our hands clasped together and I try to yank mine free but Addison has a sweaty steel-trap grip on me.

"Dad . . . Luke and I have some news," Addison says excitedly as she pulls me forward to stand beside her. She grips my arms and glances over at John's girlfriend, Edith, who's standing by the kitchen sink. "Luke and I just got married!"

Edith gasps and claps her hands instantly, jumping up and down. "Congratulations, Addison!"

"Thanks, Edith," Addison exclaims and turns back to her

dad. She slides the extra copy of the marriage license we purchased across the table . . .

. . . beside the guns.

"Here's the proof."

John refuses to look at the piece of paper, choosing instead to lean back in his seat and grab his giant beer. He shoots me a menacing look and I suddenly really regret the mustache decision because I didn't think about the fact that Addison's dad has a mustache. And now I feel like a fucking dick sitting here with a cheap knockoff version of his mustache telling him I just married his daughter, when he most likely knows it was just so she could take over the company he's trying to sell.

John downs the rest of his beer and crushes his can in his hand before standing up. The loud scrape of the chair on the floor is deafening as he points a finger toward the front door. "You. Outside."

"Dad, now listen." Addison steps forward with her hands held up. "It's my choice who I marry and—"

John cuts Addison a look and, just like that, she stops talking.

I really need to learn that look.

Licking my lips I nod and offer her a tight smile before turning on my heel and making my way out the door, hearing the loud thud of his boots following close behind me.

Whatever you do, don't catch yourself alone with him.

God, I really am screwed. This is the fucking pole climb happening all over again. Why do I keep putting myself in these situations? I'm a fucking masochist.

I step out onto the front porch and turn on my heel, watching warily as Addison's dad stomps to the far end, pacing and opening his mouth to speak but then closing it after deciding otherwise. He's a tall man, decent-sized belly. Not overly muscular, but something tells me he could still kick my ass even without his armory of guns.

Finally he stops pacing and props his hands on his hips. "Did you not think it proper to ask my permission to marry my daughter before you actually married her?"

My brows lift as I consider that fact. Under normal circumstances, yeah, I probably would have asked, but these weren't normal circumstances. And he knows that. So I hit him back with the only thing I can think of. "Since it was your daughter who asked me to marry her, I guess I thought that tradition didn't really apply here."

John huffs out a noise of indignation. "Of course she asked you. That still don't make this right."

He begins pacing again, his boots loud on the worn-down deck. I really don't want this man to hate me for the next year of this marriage. In fact, it'd be nice if I could get him on my side. If I am to win over his daughter in the end, I'd rather we be . . . I don't know . . . friends maybe.

He reminds me a lot of my own dad. Tall, blue-collar, unrefined. And overprotective to a fault. Not completely dissimilar to me.

I clear my throat and step forward, holding my hands out in surrender. "All due respect, sir . . . Addison is a big girl and is perfectly capable of making up her own mind on who she marries. And what business she can operate on her own," I add, standing up a bit taller because I'm speaking for her just as much for myself, and something about that makes me feel braver. "She's a very capable woman."

"She don't know what she's in for," John tuts, eyeing me through his furrowed brows.

I shake my head and wince. "I disagree with that."

"You don't know what you're in for!" He points back to the house. "She's a fucking lot."

I fight back a laugh. "I'm aware."

"And you might think this marriage is just a piece of paper

to help her get what she wants, but you need to know something, Luke Fletcher. You listening to me?"

"I'm listening."

He inhales deeply through his nose, shaking his head at the house before saying, "She was scared shitless when you were climbing that pole last week. Damn near had a panic attack watching you make an ass of yourself up there when you know you had no business doing that." He barks out a wet cough and shakes his head in disgust. "So whether you two are just friends or truly married, this shit is real on some level, she cares about you for some reason I can't figure out. Which means if you break her heart, I swear to Christ, I will grab my side-by-side shotgun and rain so much buckshot in your ass you won't be able to shit right for the rest of your life. You got me, boy?"

I blink back my shock, struggling to maintain eye contact, because what John has just said to me means more than he'll ever know. He's given me hope I wasn't a hundred percent sure I had before now.

Addison cares about me.

My best friend maybe even loves me. But whether it's as more than a friend remains to be seen I guess.

"I understand you, sir." I lick my lips and inhale deeply before adding, "And I may not have asked for your permission, but I'd like you to know that eventually I'd like your blessing and I hope with time, I'll inspire you to give it to me." John huffs out a noise of disbelief so I add for good measure, "But until that day you can rest assured that I'll make it my life's mission to make your daughter happy."

John nods slowly and I feel my shoulder straighten a bit more in his presence. I don't know if it's because of the lumberjack competition or because I just married my best friend or because of that kiss that I wholeheartedly didn't expect, but I don't feel as afraid of him as I once did. He's just a man as am I. And while having him on my side would help, Addison's opinion of me is really the only one that matters.

"Edith, if I wait any longer, there might not be anything left of Luke!" Addison yells from inside the house and her footsteps grow louder as she stomps through the house and swings open the front door with all the grace of a lumberyard chick. Her eyes find mine instantly and she looks me up and down, the two lines in her forehead deep as ever. "You're alive?"

The corner of my mouth lifts. "I'm alive."

"You don't need any more stitches." She squints as she inspects my face.

"Naw, I'm all set." I shoot her a wink and she exhales heavily as Edith walks outside to join us.

"Can we take you two to supper tonight to celebrate your happy union?" Edith asks, wrapping her arm around John like she's used to his bullheaded ways. "We head back to Florida tomorrow, and I would just hate not to have commemorated this day with you both in some small way."

"Sorry, Edith, we can't," Addison says, glancing back at me with clenched teeth. "I have a ton of packing to do."

"Oh, so you're moving in together?" John gruffs, eyeing us both seriously.

"Well, yes. That is what married couples do, right?" Addison volleys back.

John tilts his head and eyes me warily. "And it's a requirement of the business trust."

"Oh, is it?" Addison replies coyly, walking over to me to hold my hand. She nuzzles into me, and I know it's all for show, but my damn heart still starts racing at her close proximity. "I didn't recall that, but no matter because I'm moving into Luke's place up on Fletcher Mountain."

"You're what?" John roars, his eyes wide.

Addison swallows. "Yep. It's bigger than my place and I think it'll be just perfect for us." She grins up at me and hesitates before pulling me down to give me an awkward kiss on the cheek.

There are a few seconds of heavy silence before John buckles over, his booming laugh dry and exaggerated as the deep wrinkles around his eyes crinkle on top of each other.

Addison props her hand on her hip, clearly agitated by this reaction. "I don't know what's so funny about that."

John holds his finger up, still laughing and I can't decide what's more terrifying, him laughing or him cleaning out his guns. It's a toss-up really.

He finally recovers control of himself, wiping at his damp eyes. "Nothing funny at all. I can't wait to hear how you like mountain living in the dead of winter."

"I'm going to like it just fine," Addison scoffs and grabs my arm to pull me down the steps. "Come on, Luke. Let's go."

"One more thing," John says, stopping us in our tracks. We turn around and the mirth in his eyes looks damn right menacing. "We need to have a wedding. A proper one."

"We already did that," Addison says with a nervous laugh. "I left the marriage certificate on the table for you to see for yourself."

"But I wasn't there." He holds his hands up and shakes his head.

Addison frowns at me and I frown back, not sure where her father is going with all of this. "Dad, it was a spur-of-the-moment thing."

"I understand that. Young love is unexpected in so many ways." He loses all humor on his face. "And in a year, you can inherit the lumberyard just like you wanted. What serendipitous timing."

"Exactly," Addison says, wrapping her hands around my arm and laying her head on my shoulder.

"But I feel cheated."

"Cheated how?" She looks up to me like somehow I know what the fuck her disturbed father is up to.

John shrugs and wrinkles his nose. "I didn't get to walk my little princess down the aisle."

"Princess?" Addison scoffs. "You've never called me a princess in your entire life."

"Well, I've never seen you so . . . in love before." He smiles and tilts his head as he points at me and her. "It's softened you."

Addison's face tightens as she glares up at her dad. The two look like a couple of bulls getting ready to charge each other and I glance at Edith, who's just as freaked out as I am.

"I want to see you in a fluffy white dress, Addie May. I want to take you by the arm and give you away in the traditional sense. You're my only daughter after all. I feel cheated that I didn't get to experience that moment."

Addison lets go of me, her shoulders slumped in defeat. "So what are you saying?"

"I'm saying I want a wedding. A proper one. I'll pay for everything, don't you worry about the cost, I know how damn frugal you are. But it needs to be done up right. With a preacher and people in the chairs. I want to see Bullhead spin you around on a dance floor and I want this man here . . . Luke . . . to look me in the eyes and ask me for my daughter's hand in marriage."

My throat feels like sandpaper as Addison's father steps close so we're toe to toe, and he eyes me so hard I feel like I could disappear into the earth right here, right now.

"Fine," Addison chimes in and both of our heads swerve to look at her.

"Fine?" I ask, my eyes bugging out of my face.

"You're bluffing," Addison's dad responds with a laugh.

"Name the date." She quirks a brow and eyes him with the fire of a thousand suns.

John's smile is positively gleeful as he rubs his hands together, deep in plotting mode. "I'll be back in December. A nice Colorado winter wedding before the New Year sounds perfect." He crosses his arms with a smug look on his face. "You can plan a wedding in a couple of months, can't you, princess?"

Addison steps up to her dad, her hands on her hips, her chin jutting upward as she enunciates very clearly, "Looking forward to it, Old Man."

And with that, my wife grabs my arm and drags me away with her terrifying father shooting daggers at me while we go.

But at least they aren't buckshot.

Chapter 15

FACT OR FICTION?
Fletcher Mountain is doing too much.

Addison

It's Sunday morning and my stomach swirls with anxiety as we drive Luke's truck up the winding gravel lane leading to the top of Fletcher Mountain. Autumn is in full effect as it's nearly the end of October, so it feels like I'm driving straight into a damn Hallmark movie as a kaleidoscope of burgundy, gold, and yellow leaves blanket the ground while we weave through the thick forestry.

The air is cool and carries hints of incoming snow. Snow in Boulder is always a possibility in the fall and the spring, but I expect it's even worse up here as our elevation climbs with each winding turn.

"So is winter really brutal up here like my dad said?" I ask, biting my lip and glancing up at the large green pines clinging to the hills.

"We have a tractor for snow removal parked in the Morton building behind my place, but when it's really bad we have to wait until the private plow company we pay for can carve us out."

My eyes widen with that bit of information. "How long do you usually have to wait it out?"

Luke shrugs. "Depends on the storm. We had four days up here with no power last year."

"Four days!" My hands tighten on my seat belt. "How did you not freeze?"

"All of our cabins have woodburning fireplaces, so it's not the heat we worry about. It's our refrigerators and phones and stuff that are a problem, but we have generators for those."

"Oh my God," I groan and pinch the bridge of my nose. "Maybe moving up here is a bad idea."

"Little late to back out now." Luke laughs and glances into the bed of his truck where nearly my whole life is packed up.

Okay, obviously not my whole life. I spent all of Friday night and Saturday packing up what I thought I might need for the next year, choosing to leave all of my big furniture behind as Luke has all of those types of things. So really, I just needed my clothes and my kitchen supplies.

Either way, I'm not giving up my apartment just yet. Who knows how this thing with Luke is going to go. It might be nice to have a space that I can get away to if living with him ever becomes . . . too much. *That is if I'm not snowed in with him.*

Good God.

The thought of being trapped with Luke didn't bother me so much until I was a fool and decided it would be a good idea to kiss him on our wedding day. What was I thinking? Friends don't kiss friends on the lips. Friends give each other shit and bail each other out of jail. They don't . . . smooch. They don't run their fingers through thick, silky hair. They don't almost lift their leg and wrap it around said friend's hip . . . or try to count whether there's a six- or eight-pack under said best friend's shirt.

All those muscles under my fingertips.

My body hums with memories of that embrace that I've been struggling to forget. It was tender and intimate and managed to light up an arousal in me that even my vibrator couldn't satiate on Saturday night. And you bet your ass I dedicated plenty of time to "kneading the dough" if you know what I mean. Who knows how easy it will be to have alone time when I'll be living with my guy best friend for the next twelve months.

Luke and I haven't exactly talked about what our love lives will be like during this marriage of convenience, but I think it goes without saying, we won't be sleeping with other people while we're together. Not if his whole family thinks this marriage is real.

Plus, if word ever got back to my dad that Luke was sleeping around on me, he wouldn't just come for Luke. He'd burn down Fletcher Mountain just to dance on its ashes.

I frown as the idea of Luke with another woman needles something deep inside me. Thinking of him with other girls never bothered me before, but now, it definitely does. I guess that sheet of paper we paid thirty dollars for does something to my mental disposition. Hopefully in a year, that won't be a thing, and we can go back to being just regular old Luke and Addison and forget about that time we had to kiss in front of a clerk at the county courthouse.

Either way, I have to live with him to make this seem real to everyone. And I need to show my dad that I'm really doing this or he'll use it as an excuse to sell the yard out from under me. That old man of mine doesn't seem to have any faith that I can do it on my own, which just makes me want to prove him wrong even more.

Luke drives past the red barn and my head jerks when I see his sister-in-law Trista standing outside filling a bucket out of a spicket. She waves and then frowns as her eyes move to the back of the truck.

"Have you still not told your family about us yet?"

Luke makes a noise in his throat.

"Luke!"

"What?"

"What are you waiting for?"

He grumbles and yanks his hat off, running a frustrated hand through his shaggy hair. "I just don't want to hear it from them."

"Hear what?"

"Just . . . everything." He cuts me a grave look. "You're going to learn real quick that my family is never short of opinions. I'll tell them, I swear. Obviously they're going to notice you moving in today so it'll come out today. Probably."

I frown, puzzled over his resistance to sharing the news after he was the one so adamant about us getting married in the first place. I found it better to rip it off like a Band-Aid with my dad, though him making me plan a damn formal wedding feels like he's inflicting a punishment on me for figuring out how to get around this stupid business trust. But he's the one who forced this on me. Desperate times call for desperate measures.

We drive past Wyatt's and Calder's cabins, and as Luke backs his truck up to the front door of his cute cedar-sided house that I've only been in a couple times, I see an SUV barreling toward us at a terrifying speed.

Luke jumps out of the car, concern etched all over his face as he makes his way over while the vehicle skids to a stop, kicking up gravel and dust all over him.

"Lucas William Fletcher!" a voice screams and I move to the front of the truck to see Luke's mom standing there.

"Mom, what's wrong?" Luke asks, his voice full of fear.

"Tell me it isn't true."

"What?"

"Tell me it's some sort of sick prank."

"What's a sick prank?"

"Did you get *married* and not tell me?" she screeches so loud, it echoes off the mountainside.

My jaw drops and I fight the urge to run and hide as I watch Luke stand before her, all six foot two of him, hunched with head hanging low as his five-foot-nothing mom tears him a new asshole.

"I couldn't believe my ears when John Monroe called me on the phone this morning to discuss the particulars of this big wedding."

"John called you?" Luke asks and cuts me a wary look as my hands form fists at my side. Of course my dad called her. He's going to do everything in his power to make this as painful as possible for the two of us.

Movement draws my eyes down the hill and I spot Calder and Dakota standing out on their front porch watching the show. Trista is making her way up the lane from the barn as well and, sure enough, Wyatt emerges from his cabin, baby in tow.

News sure travels fast on Fletcher Mountain.

"You bet your ass John called me and it should have been *you!*" She jabs her finger into Luke's chest, her short blond bob falling into her face with the aggressive movement. Johanna is small, but has some weight to her, so you know she's capable of wielding that finger with purpose. "I raised you better than this, Lucas. To elope and not even tell me is unforgivable. I'm heartbroken. If your father were here right now, I would make him kick your sorry ass!"

My heart lurches at the stricken look on Luke's face at the mention of his dad and before I know it, my feet are moving toward both of them, my heart pounding in my chest. "I'm sorry, Johanna. I'm afraid this is all my fault," I say, tucking my hair behind my ears to try to take some of the rage off of Luke and put it on me.

Johanna's stormy eyes turn to me and soften instantly. "Honey, this isn't about you. You are positively lovely. I could tell that from our time with you in Mexico."

"Thank you," I state, sparing a glance at Luke.

"Which is how I know you deserve so much better than a son who doesn't tell his own mother when he got married." She cuts a menacing look back to her son.

Luke grips the back of his neck and stares up at the sky. "Jesus, Mom, it's been like three days."

"I don't give a shit!" she exclaims, stomping her Dr. Scholl's shoe into the gravel. "I should have been the first one you called. John said you came to the house to see him on Friday. Did you forget where your family home was?"

Luke winces and yanks his hat off, running his fingers through his hair as he murmurs, "No."

"We were going to surprise you," I sputter out, my body tense with anxiety as I grab Luke's palm with one hand and wrap my other around his arm as a sign of unity. "It was my idea," I continue, my brain wracking itself for what to say next. "We were going to surprise your whole family. Tell you when we were all together."

Johanna's rage turns to confusion. "Is that right?"

"Absolutely," I reply firmly, forcing a toothy smile back at her. "We just had to tell my dad earlier because he was heading back to Florida."

"I see," Johanna tuts, crossing her arms over her chest, her chin dropping as her lips curl down.

"This is so exciting, you guys," Trista exclaims, coming up around the car and standing beside Johanna. She wraps her arm around Luke's mom and begins rubbing her back in a soothing, comforting motion. "Isn't this great, Jo? You were just saying how worried you were for Luke to be all alone up here. This is so amazing. Congratulations!"

"Did you guys seriously get married?" Dakota squeals from their deck before grabbing Calder and dragging him up the hill toward us.

Wyatt joins in too and, before I know it, the entire Fletcher family is wrapping me up in a big hug and offering me and Luke their congratulations. Luke receives several pats on his back from his brothers and I begin to see the reason why Luke wanted to keep this all a secret from them.

They are a lot.

But he's the one who chose to live up here with them all on the mountain. He's the one who volunteered his home for us to live in. This was all his idea, as a matter of fact. And it took three proposals to get us here. Did he not realize how hard this might be?

"Calder, go to our cabin and grab that prosecco in the fridge," Dakota says, whacking her boyfriend's tattoo-covered arm with a sense of urgency.

"What's prosecco?"

Dakota rolls her eyes. "The champagne."

"Oh . . . what do I bring for cups?"

She winces and then shrugs. "The red Solo cups are fine."

"So bad for the environment," Wyatt growls under his breath as Calder turns to do as his lady told him.

Trista comes in close, her eyes sparkling with excitement. "Let's see the ring!"

"Oh, um . . ." I hesitate before Luke interjects.

"It's coming still." Luke smiles awkwardly at me and glances down at my empty hand. "Like I said before, this was all really impulsive and spur-of-the-moment so there's a lot we still have to figure out."

"Impulsive is fun!" Dakota smiles, showing me all her teeth. "I could totally tell you two had the hots for each other in Mexico."

"Oh, is that right?" I giggle woodenly, my eyes flashing nervously to Luke.

"This boy is smitten with you," Trista adds, grabbing Luke's arm playfully. "You snagged a good one here. Heart of gold."

"Definitely," I say around a laugh as Calder appears, popping the cork and sending it flying down the mountain.

"You're going to go find that," Wyatt drawls and Calder rolls his eyes.

Dakota pours everyone some bubbles and as she tries to pass a cup to Johanna, she holds her hand up to refuse. "None for me, thanks."

"Are you sure?" Dakota asks with a frown.

"You kids go ahead and celebrate. I should be getting home." She turns to make her way back to her car and Luke follows her, worry all over his face.

"I'm really sorry for not telling you sooner, Mom," he drawls, looking like a lost puppy begging for a home. "It's been such a whirlwind. We're getting Roe moved into my place right now. We haven't had a moment to breathe."

She glances at the truck bed full of my belongings and offers him a weak smile. "Congratulations to you both."

She turns to leave and Luke stands there looking completely destroyed. The sight of him devastated over hurting his mom is killing me to witness so I step forward, red Solo cup in hand and say, "Johanna?"

"Yes, dear?"

I swallow the knot in my throat, feeling all the Fletcher family eyes burning into me. "Um . . . Luke and I are planning a proper ceremony we want to do in a couple of months. My dad really wants to walk me down the aisle and everything."

"Yes, he mentioned that. That's so nice," she says, opening her car door and holding the frame like she needs to get going.

"Yeah, um . . . I don't know anything about wedding planning so I was wondering if you'd . . ." I lick my lips nervously, my hands sweaty around my cup as I cast a terrified glance to Luke. "Would you maybe help me with everything?"

Johanna stares back at me, her eyes as wide as saucers. "You want me to help you plan your wedding?"

"Only if you want to," I rush out, terrified that maybe she

hates the idea. "I'm just not really a girlie girl and have no idea where to start, but I could probably hire a professional if you're too busy or—"

My voice is cut off as Johanna eliminates the space between us and crushes me in a big, giant hug, her arms trembling around me.

I hold my breath as my entire body tenses in her embrace and I stand there with my arms out, plastic cup in hand, refusing to hug her back.

It's nothing personal really. I have the same trouble accepting affection from Edith. It's just . . . one of my quirks. I'm not big on physical affection, especially when it comes to women. *Raise your hand if you have mommy issues!*

"I'd love to, sweetie," she murmurs into my hair before pulling away, her eyes red rimmed as she smiles, looking genuinely happy for the first time since she came up here today. "This is going to be so much fun! You leave it all to me."

"Thanks, Johanna," I murmur through a forced smile.

"Call me Mom or Jo. Whatever feels right." She chucks me under the chin and squeals before hugging me one more time. When she lets go, she cuts a menacing look to Luke, still obviously not ready to let him off the hook. But he looks mildly relieved when she turns around and says, "Pour me some of that champagne, Dakota!"

"You got it, Jo," Dakota calls back and does as she's told.

Luke sidesteps to wrap his arm around me. "I owe you big for that one, Roe," he murmurs into my hair before pressing his lips to my temple.

A flush of heat spreads through me as he stands there, holding me like it's the most normal thing in the world. And strangely, it does feel normal. Luke feels good to me. Comforting. A stark contrast to how I felt with Johanna's affection. What the hell does that even mean?

"It's the least I can do," I croak quietly, and we both exhale a heavy breath and sip champagne on the mountaintop with his family, celebrating our happy union.

And it is happy . . . so far. This marriage is what I wanted to get the lumberyard, which is the bigger thing that I wanted. I can handle this Fletcher family. I can handle a little wedding planning with Luke's mother. It'll be a piece of cake. Wedding cake, that is.

Chapter 16

FACT OR FICTION?
That's a big cock.

Addison

Luke's cabin is nice. Ten times nicer than my place. Nicer than any single male deserves honestly.

It's a modern, cozy mountain chalet vibe with rustic natural wood touches all over. The main floor is an open layout with the kitchen and dining area on the right when you walk in and a sunken living area on the left. The walls on either side of the stone fireplace are framed with freshly chopped wood stacked all the way up to the ceiling, confirming what Luke said about staying warm in the winter.

Natural light pours in the front windows that provide stunning views of the mountainside and the small community of Jamestown down below. I went to the Mercantile once with Luke years ago now but haven't been back since. I imagine we'll be going more often now that we're living together.

God, that's so weird to say.

I'm moving in with Luke. I've never had a roommate in my whole life. I lived with my dad until I was twenty years old and went straight from his place to my one-bedroom apartment that I still have today. Hopefully living with my dad prepared me at least somewhat for this situation I'm walking into.

Off the kitchen and living area is a short hallway with two bedrooms directly across from each other and a bathroom at the end of the hall. Luckily, Luke's room has its own attached bath, so the hallway will be all mine. I know we're friends and everything and apparently now husband and wife, but sharing a bathroom with Luke Fletcher was certainly not on my bingo card this year. I'm not ready to see his mustache whiskers in the sink or worry about him walking in after I've pooped.

Come to think of it, I'm going to start pooping at the lumberyard. I can hold it until then and it will be best for our friendship to keep that side of me a mystery. There's really only so much those toilet sprays can disguise.

I glance around my bedroom, which is starting to look semidecent now. The queen bed already had bedding, but I threw one of my fuzzy blankets on top, then stuffed the closet to within an inch of its life and filled the small dresser in here with my unmentionables. Luke's brothers helped haul all my stuff inside, but they put the boxes marked bedroom into Luke's room so we had to move them across the hall after they left.

Acting like Luke's real wife for the next year is going to be a serious challenge. I'm starting to see how this will benefit Luke though, which, as his best friend, I'm totally on board for. Who knows how they'll react in twelve months once we're done. Perhaps he'll play the broken heart card, and they'll leave him be for a while after.

At least we're both clear on our opposition to marriage.

Marriage . . . a real marriage . . . is just never something I want in life. I've been this way since I was a teenager. I like control too much. I like to make my own decisions. I don't want to factor another person into my day, which is why this whole marriage clause in the family trust is so damn ironic.

Not to mention my parents' marriage was never one to admire, so if there's even a remote chance I could turn out like them . . . hard pass.

But acting like Luke's wife won't be that hard. Really a wife is just a friend, and Luke and I do the friendship thing pretty well, so it'll be fine. As long as I don't have to kiss him in front of everyone, we'll manage.

I lick my lips as that kiss from the clerk's office rushes to the forefront of my mind. The way his hands squeezed at my waist, I swear to God I can still feel him pressed—

"How's it going in here?" Luke asks, yanking me out of my traitorous thoughts as he stands in my doorway, looking around the bedroom.

His hand is hanging from the top of the frame and the casual lean of his body is making those dirty thoughts I was just having feel really hard to push away. "Um . . . I'm good. I think I'm pretty much done in here and ready to move into the kitchen."

"Perfect. Trista just dropped off some food for us if you're hungry."

"She did?" I ask, my stomach instantly rumbling at that mention.

"Yeah, come on." He taps my doorframe and continues down the hall toward the kitchen.

I blow out a long breath, calming myself before I emerge, pausing in front of his bedroom door and taking in his large king bed. It's covered in a soft gray comforter and perfectly made. I wonder if Luke made that because I was coming over or if he's a wake-up-and-make-your-bed kind of guy. I guess I'll find out soon enough. And he'll find out I'm a never-make-my-bed kind of girl.

I make my way out into the kitchen just as Luke dishes up something that looks like a pasta dish into a couple of bowls. I sit down at the kitchen island beside him and salivate when I smell pesto.

"God, I'm starving."

"Me too and I haven't been working nearly as hard as you have."

We both go to town on some yummy bow tie noodles and

while we eat, my eyes wander around his kitchen with envy for the tenth time since I got here today. I've been in Luke's house before but this is the first time I've been in it and looked at it as mine . . . for the next year at least.

He has a full chef's-style kitchen with black cabinets, white marble countertops and light wood accents throughout. We're seated at the island that holds three brown leather barstools, but my eyes zero in on the most important part . . . a double oven.

Let me say that one more time . . .

A double oven.

I am officially aroused.

"Where should I put my KitchenAid mixer?" I ask, scooping another bite into my mouth.

"Oh, actually . . . I think I have a cupboard for that." Luke stands and moves around the island to the lower unit cupboard by the sink and my eyes go wide when he opens it.

"Does that thing pop up?"

"Yep. I think it's literally meant for one of those things. There's an outlet inside too."

"Oh my God!" I exclaim excitedly. "Why did you install one of those if you don't even bake?"

"The cabinets in here were yanked out of a remodel we did ages ago," he says, turning to lean on the counter as he splays his hands out wide looking positively indecent with that mustache, backward hat, and bare feet. "The marble countertops are recycled too. I designed the kitchen around the castoffs from that house because they were still in pretty good shape and I was on a limited budget."

"Holy shit, this whole kitchen is recycled?" I gape at the appliances that still look nice. "Who on earth would gut my dream kitchen?"

"Someone loaded," he replies with a huff, rejoining me at the counter. "At least I found them all a loving home."

"Yes, you did." I open my mouth to take another bite but gasp when I remember something I really should have got out of the box as soon as we arrived.

Abandoning my food, I scurry around the island and grab the box up off the floor that contains my most prized possession. "Okay, I have someone very special for you to meet," I say as I pull back the cardboard to grab a glass jar with a lid. "This is Mildred."

Luke rolls his eyes. "You've already introduced me to your sourdough starter, Roe."

"I know but now that you're roommates with her, I think you need to give her a proper greeting."

"What the hell is that supposed to mean?"

I shrug and blink coyly back at him. "Maybe give her a sniff or something."

Luke fights back a smile, clearly thinking I've lost it, but does as I say, popping the sealed lid off and bringing the glass to his nose, twitching his mustache as he inhales deeply. "She smells of rich ferment."

My jaw drops as I fight back a smile. "Are you flirting with me, Fletcher?"

"I'm flirting with Mildred." He winks and the sight of him looking at me like that while clutching my precious dough does a weird thing to my insides, so I quickly grab her out of his hands to put her in the fridge before she gets so excited, she bubbles up and I have to make bread all night long.

"Do you guys have well water here?" I ask as I open the fridge door.

"Actually it's natural spring water from the creek that runs out back."

"Holy shit." I clutch Mildred to my bosom. "Mildred is going to thrive on that."

Luke laughs and shakes his head. "You are off your rocker."

"This was your idea, pal." I can't wipe the smile off my face as I continue unpacking my stuff, feeling more excited with every passing minute. I should have fake married Luke ages ago just to get my hands on this sweet kitchen.

Golden light streams in on my face from the dining room window and I walk over to admire the view. "This won't suck to come home to every day."

"Yeah, it never gets old either." Luke joins me, standing right beside me, our shoulders brushing as we take in the sweeping vista. "I remember when we were building Wyatt's cabin and I had to drive back to my apartment in Boulder, I swear I could feel my soul being sucked out of my body the closer I got to town." He sniffs and shakes his head at his memory. "It just feels so much calmer up here. Like you can forget life's problems down there."

I nod in agreement and turn my gaze from the view to Luke. He's wearing a classic blue flannel and his eyes are soft and a sleepy-looking. He looks so cozy and safe. Like I could just wrap my arms around him and lie down with him all night.

That erratic thought causes a knot to form in my throat as I jerk my head back and try to fix my brain. This is just my friend Luke. Not my cuddle buddy, not a guy I should be fantasizing about kissing. Just . . . Luke.

A soft tapping comes from the front door and I frown as I look over to it.

"That's just Rufus." Luke walks over to open the door and my eyes widen when I see a chicken march through the door.

"Your rooster comes inside?" I ask, remembering that name from his pros and cons marriage proposal.

Luke bends over and pets the brown and auburn feathers on his body. "Yeah . . . he usually comes inside at this time of night for a snack. You don't mind, do you?"

I cross my arms and smile. "Oh, this I have to see."

I watch in fascination as Luke's rooster follows him into the kitchen, sticking close to his feet as he gets some tortilla shells out of the fridge and pulls half a piece off before moving over to the cupboard to retrieve a small ramekin dish. He digs into another cupboard for some crushed walnuts and then gestures for me to follow him into the living room.

I sit on his camel-colored leather sofa as Luke adds some more logs to the fire and stretches out on the rug, lying on his side as Rufus the Rooster comes over, clucking up a storm in anticipation.

Luke tears the tortilla into tiny pieces and puts them in the small dish, holding it out for the bird, and Rufus pecks at the ramekin, jerking his head back to get the food down his sharp beak. Luke smiles up at me like a kid on Christmas morning. "It's cool, right?"

"It's something," I reply with a laugh, tucking my legs under my chin.

"Did you ever have any pets?" he asks, taking his hat off and setting it on the floor to run his hand through his hair. The fire backlights his wavy strands making him look like he's posing for some sort of farm life magazine.

I hesitate before answering his question, my knee-jerk response wanting to be no. But there's something about this moment and this night and, hell, this week, that makes me want to tell the truth.

"I had a dog as a kid," I croak, my voice quiet.

"What was its name?" Luke asks, adding more tortilla shreds to the bowl.

"Backpack." I swallow down the tightness in my throat.

"Backpack." Luke laughs and looks up at me. "How'd you come up with that?"

My cheeks flush with anxiety as I answer, "My little brother named him."

Luke loses all humor on his face as he holds my gaze for a long, quiet moment. He knows my brother died in a car accident years ago, but that's the extent of what he knows and honestly, it's more than most people know. I told him about it one night because he asked, and there's something about Luke that really makes me not want to hide from him.

I slide down off the couch and sit crisscross, reaching out to run my hand over Rufus's tall tail. "Aaron had just started kindergarten, so he was pretty into backpacks I guess."

Luke chuckles but that sympathy in his eyes is still there, holding me without touching me. "It's a cool name for a dog."

"Yeah . . ." I feel a pressure in my chest build as I say the next part. "He died in the car accident too."

Silence grows between us, and I look up to make sure Luke heard me. He did. His eyes are intent on me as he lets me process the words I just shared.

"I'm sorry, Roe," he says softly, abandoning his bowl and reaching out to lay his hand on top of mine.

"Me too." I feel my eyes burn with incoming tears. "We buried my brother with Backpack's collar."

"I'm sure they found each other on the other side," Luke says, his voice full of comfort.

I shoot him a watery smile. Luke always feels like comfort to me, which is unfair because he has the loss of his dad to work through as well. He doesn't talk about his dad much either. Or maybe he does but just not to me. I wouldn't blame him after the way I behaved during that time in his life.

I guess both of us have some death traumas we're still unpacking in our own ways. Maybe we never will unpack them fully. Maybe death is just something you have to learn to carry with you all the time and you can never truly unload the sadness of it.

He eyes me with arched brows. "Fact or fiction. Aaron was a little stud."

"Oh, that's a fact," I reply with a garbled laugh, grateful for the levity. I turn to face Luke, my hands gesticulating with pride because I never talk about my brother, and it feels good. "He would make me approve all his outfits before school every day and would take ages gelling his hair. He missed the bus so many times because he was in the bathroom primping."

"Really?" Luke laughs and the crinkles in his eyes give me butterflies. "I'm sure your dad loved that."

"It made him crazy. Said he couldn't wait until I got my license so I could drive Aaron to school." My voice drops at the end as I realize Aaron didn't live long enough for that to happen.

God, life is such a fucking bitch.

Rufus bocks, ripping me out of my quiet turmoil. "Ugh, I feel like I've aged a decade this past week." I groan and stretch my legs out and wiggle my toes. "So many big life changes. Marriage, moving, wedding planning."

Luke watches me thoughtfully for a moment before replying, "And don't forget about the lumberjack competition."

"How could I forget that?" I smile and reach out to touch his chin. "Your chin is looking way better."

He reaches up to trace the same area, our fingers brushing as I pull my hand away. "I hope I have a cool battle scar as a keepsake."

"You certainly surprised the hell out of me that day."

He laughs and shakes his head. "Just wait till you see me next year."

"You're going to do it again?"

"Fuck yeah I am," Luke chirps, his eyes narrowing with determination. "I need to put that Ivan fucker in his place."

I giggle and cover my face, not sure why I like the idea of

Luke being jealous of Ivan so much. It's not a normal reaction a friend has with another friend, but it still feels good. I like knowing he cares.

Luke looks up at me, the crinkles around his eyes deepening as he smiles. "I know it's only day one . . . but I like having you here."

I tilt my head and look around the room, taking in the warm, cozy feel. "I think I'm going to like it here." We're silent for a moment before I add, "But there is no way in hell I'm joining that Fletcher family carpool spreadsheet you texted me."

"What?"

"You guys leave for Boulder every day at six thirty in the morning!"

"Yeah, so?"

"It's a no from me."

Luke hops up from the floor and wipes his hands off on his jeans, Rufus squawking at the quick change of position. "Wyatt is going to be pissed at you."

"Why?"

"Because Fletcher Mountain is an eco-friendly peak. Did you peep the solar panels when you got here? You're increasing our carbon footprint and he is not going to be pleased."

"Well, you're my husband," I snap up at him.

"Yeah . . . and?"

"And you should stick up for me like I did for you today with your mom," I exclaim, glowering up at him with all the rage I can muster when deep down I friggin' love this kid.

Luke watches me for a moment, a strange look in his eyes that I can't quite read. He takes a beat and lowers himself down onto the sofa so he's no longer towering over me. "That was really cool what you did for my mom today, by the way."

"It was nothing." I reply, looking away so I don't say out loud, *I didn't do it for her. I did it for you.*

"No, it was something." He makes a noise in the back of his throat and adds, "I fucked up and you saved the day and made her really happy. Thank you for doing that."

I offer him a weak smile. "I'm going to need help planning this dang wedding anyways."

He chuckles softly. "Yeah, your dad knew exactly what he was doing with that request."

"He's evil." I growl, my hands balling up into fists. "But at least we'll have a couple months to get used to faking this marriage thing so by the time I have to walk down the aisle to you in a puffy white dress, we can make it look halfway convincing."

Luke's eyes tighten ever so slightly before he nods and bends over to pick up Rufus. "I'm going to put this guy back outside and then probably crash. Back to the real world tomorrow."

"Ugh, work. I hate Mondays." I reach my hand out for Luke to help me up and as he does, in one fluid motion, I pull him in for a big bear hug, squeezing his waist and burying my face in his chest. Rufus clucks loudly at my sudden close proximity and I think I feel the peck of his beak in my hair.

"What's this for?" Luke asks as he wraps his free arm around me and rests his chin on my head.

I squeeze tighter and inhale his scent of sandalwood and lavender. It's rugged and soft. Just like Luke. "Thank you just isn't enough."

I pull away and his hand lingers on my back, his eyes warm on mine as he looks down at me. "Sleep well, wife."

That label has my contented smile growing. "Good night, husband."

And the two of us part ways to head to our separate bedrooms for some much-needed space to wrap our brains around what the next year of our life is going to look like.

Lord help us.

Chapter 17

FACT OR FICTION?
Phase two is going to be a bitch.

Luke

On Monday morning at 6:04 a.m., I wake to the familiar crescendoed cry of Rufus crowing over all of Fletcher Mountain . . . from my front porch. I yawn and stretch, my muscles screaming from one of a myriad of things I've done to it in the past week:

- Man of the Mountain competition
- Man of the Mountain medical emergency
- Clenching my entire body while I waited for the six-foot-tall local lumberyard owner to run me off his property with a shotgun
- Clenching my entire body while I waited for my mom to grab me by the ear and kick my ass
- Moving my new fake/not fake wife into my cabin only shortly after said mountain activities
- Fighting off a raging boner I had pretty much the entire night as I dreamed of a dark-haired beauty sleeping only ten feet away from me

But the honeymoon is already over so I clomp my ass into my bathroom for a cold shower and to prepare myself for another fun-filled day at Fletcher Brothers Construction.

It'll be good to lose myself in work for a bit. I need to not let thoughts of Addison living with me and the fact that we're married and planning a traditional wedding completely consume my thoughts.

Although, it meant a lot to me when she opened up about her brother last night. That's the side to Roe I love the most. The soft side. Normally, she's this tough, ballsy, outspoken person . . . which I also like. But when she's sensitive and lets her guard down—that's when I really feel like I see her. A perfect dichotomy of sweet and savage unlike anyone I've ever met.

But I have to have an identity outside of her in the next several months or I will drive myself crazy. So work will be good for me.

Plus, I like my job. There's a deep satisfaction I feel bidding out jobs. I enjoy reviewing blueprints from architects and researching the materials and costs to compile a detailed proposal. Wyatt might be the big ideas guy but I'm the one who figures out how to turn those ideas into a reality. The success we've found in our recent smart housing development is due in large part to my work behind the desk. It's good I remember that.

I lace up my work boots and slip my Carhartt coat over my flannel before quietly making my way out of my bedroom, careful not to wake Addison. My thoughts are all in vain though because as soon as I step into the hallway, I nearly barrel right into Roe as she pads barefoot out of the bathroom at the exact same time.

"Shit, sorry," I say, backing up and holding my hands up to try to get out of her way, feeling much too close to her in this tight proximity.

"Good morning," she says around a yawn as she rubs her eyes, her hair in a messy ball on top of her head.

"Good morning," I answer, trying really hard not to check her out in the T-shirt she's in.

"You headed out already?" She squints up at me as her eyes adjust to the sunlight beginning to peek through the windows.

"Yeah. Sorry if I woke you."

She shakes her head and yawns. "You didn't. It was—"

"Rufus," I finish her sentence with a knowing tone. "He's a pain in the ass."

She shrugs. "You warned me."

The corner of my mouth lifts at that. "Did you, um . . . sleep okay otherwise?"

She wrinkles her nose. "Yeah, I slept fine. Oh . . . can you drop these off for me?" She grabs me by the jacket and drags me down the hall into the kitchen where I see two loaves of bread wrapped in clear plastic baggies. "One for Calder and Dakota and one for Trista and Wyatt."

"When did you make these?" I ask, admiring the golden crust.

"Last night."

I blink back at her before reaching out to force her to look up at me in the daylight. "Did you sleep at all?"

"I slept," she exclaims, looking up at me with sleepy eyes, her face bare of her normal makeup. I like seeing her out of her makeup. It feels intimate. "I just wanted to thank them for helping me move and for the food last night. Mildred was super active yesterday, so I started some loaves before we moved and sitting in the heat all day, they rose so well, I got them all out." She smiles softly as her eyes move over my body. "So this is what you wear to work every day, huh?"

I chuckle and shrug. "You've seen me in my work clothes before." I lean in close and waggle my brows. "Spoiler alert. They're not any different from my everyday clothes."

She licks her lips and looks up at my hair. "Never seen your hair wet like this before though." She reaches up and ruffles my damp locks with her fingers, causing my eyes to close as the sensation flows through my entire body.

When I open my eyes, they lower down to her chest. She's wearing a baggy orange Monroe Lumber T-shirt with slouchy socks and I'm guessing a whole lotta nothing underneath. "And this is what you wear to bed every night?"

"Pretty much." She shrugs and crosses her arms over her chest, pushing her breasts upward.

"Were you cooking in my kitchen last night in just this little thing?" I reach out and grip the waist of her shirt, noting the thinness of the fabric.

She pokes her finger into my chest. "It's *my* kitchen now, Fletcher, so you just make way in here, alright?"

Silence grows between us and I have to swallow the knot in my throat as my eyes drop, noticing how hard her nipples are as they poke through the fabric. I can't help but wonder if she might not be wearing panties either. *I bet she wakes up wet in the mornings.*

My cock thickens inside my jeans at the illicit image of her being completely bare in front of me like this. Just a tiny layer of fabric is separating us and all I'd have to do is press her up against the fridge and reach my fingers under her shirt to find out if she's wet.

She releases a shaky breath and I clear my throat and turn my back to her, acting like I'm looking for my phone. "I, um . . . better get going or the carpool is going to leave me."

She shoves the two loaves toward me and murmurs, "Have a good day, Luke," before beelining down the hallway, looking almost as bothered as I feel.

"See you later, Roe," I offer weakly and, when she's out of sight, I adjust the groin of my jeans and attempt to collect myself before gathering the bread and my work bag off the dining room table.

Fucking hell.

My best friend has been here for less than twenty-four hours and I'm getting hard in the kitchen before morning coffee. I better get my shit together or I could scare her the fuck away.

I head out my front door, breathing in the fresh mountain air to try to cleanse away my dirty thoughts. Making my way down the hill, I spot Wyatt and Calder seated on the tailgate of Wyatt's truck waiting for me, work boots swinging back and forth. Shit-eating grins permanently in place.

"Well, well, well . . ." Calder says with a dirty look. "Did you consummate the marriage, baby bro?"

I frown over at him. "How do you know that word?"

He smiles. "It's my word of the day. Fitting, isn't it?"

"Shut the fuck up." I toss the heavy loaves of bread at both of them simultaneously and they catch them against their chests. "Roe made you losers bread as a thank-you for your help."

Calder laughs and shakes his head. "I told you, Wyatt. He didn't close the deal before he married her and now he's got to live with a woman who would rather bake bread than fuck him."

"Can we go please?" I growl, yanking the truck door open.

Wyatt fights back his own smirk as we all pile in. Me in the back because I need a moment alone with my unruly cock. And no, I am not referring to Rufus. No doubt it will start waking me up at six every morning too, knowing what my wife wears to bed.

Fuck.

We drive down the mountain in silence and the smell of sourdough starts filling the car when my phone starts buzzing in my pocket. I pull it out and wince when I see who it is.

"It's Everly, isn't it?" Calder asks with a knowing tone. "No one else calls this early."

I exhale heavily.

"Did you not tell her the news?" Wyatt asks, glancing at me in the rearview mirror.

"I crashed early last night after I called Max."

"That means he told her first and you're about to get your ass reamed." Calder giggles excitedly, turning in his seat to watch the show.

I let out a pained noise before swiping my screen to answer. Everly's bright blue eyes pierce right through me, her long blond hair framing her face like the angel I know she's not.

"Who is with you in the car right now?" she growls, skipping right past a nice, normal hello.

My brothers cut each other a knowing look as I reply, "Just Wyatt and Calder."

"How dare you!" she screams, launching right into her ass chewing. "I had to hear that you and Addison got married from my dad . . . my dad! Even Ethan knew before me. Ethan! I should have been the first one you called, Luke."

"Everly, I'm sorry," I reply, turning my hat backward so she can see my face. "Everything happened so fast."

"So fast you couldn't' even call to tell Grandma?" She presses her hand to her chest, her face stricken with disappointment. "I can get over it. But Grandma? Luke. That is unforgivable."

"I know, okay? I already heard it enough from her, I don't need to hear it from you too. I've had a lot on my mind. This shit is like . . . getting real now."

"I'd say! Grandma said she's planning a wedding?"

For fuck's sake, how long was I asleep? "Yeah, it's something Addison's dad wanted done before the end of the year I guess."

"You better plan it over my Christmas break so I can be there or I will straight-up kill you. I'll use one of those logger supplies and gut you in your sleep."

"Good grief." I roll my eyes and look out at the pine trees, wondering how much it would hurt if I just jumped out of the moving truck right now. "Text me the dates and I'll discuss it with Roe. We won't do it without you."

Everly murmurs some expletives under her breath before asking, "So what's your plan now?"

"I have no idea." I frown and lift my shoulders helplessly. "You told me not to worry about phase two until we were done with phase one."

Everly eyes me speculatively. "How is it living together? What's your sleeping arrangement?"

Calder and Wyatt exchange another look that has my eyes narrowing. It is fucking humiliating doing this in front of all of them. But I suppose I asked for this the moment I let them help train me for the lumberjack competition.

"Addison is set up in the guest room."

"And last night was your first night together?" I nod. "How did it go?" she adds.

"Fine I guess. She was busy unpacking a lot. And she must have been up real late because she had freshly baked bread for the guys this morning."

Everly puzzles over this. "That's kind of weird, isn't it?"

I lift my shoulders. "She's mentioned she doesn't sleep well so I don't know. Maybe it's normal for her."

"Making bread in the middle of the night is only normal if you're hammered drunk."

"She wasn't drunk, Everly," I snap, my body tensing at the accusation.

"I know that. I'm just saying if she's up making bread all hours of the night, it has to be a mental thing." She taps her fingers to her lips, already in plotting mode. "You should try to find relaxing activities to do in the evening with her to help her feel more at ease. Watch a movie or something. Talk to her more maybe?"

"I know how to act around a woman, Ev, especially Roe. We are friends after all." I grumble, my face feeling like it's in a permanent state of scowl because I feel like a kid being told what to do by his mom when he's at sleepaway camp. "And we talked plenty when we ate the food Trista made us and I fed Rufus with her."

My niece perks up at that. "What do you talk about?"

"I'm not going to tell you every conversation I have with her," I growl and pull the phone away.

"Fine, jeez. Stop being so testy. You must not have slept well either."

Hell. I am in hell.

"After talking to Grandma, I decided I think you should definitely be a part of the wedding planning."

"Really?" I ask, cringing because what the fuck do I know about wedding planning?

"Try to contribute some ideas to the wedding that you know Addison would love. Think about her personality and make it all really cute and personal. Plus, these are the moments you get to spend more time with her. You do want to spend more time with her, don't you?"

"Of course I do," I reply honestly and flinch when I realize how true that is. It was fucking hell going to sleep in my big bed all alone while she was just a couple walls away from me, also alone . . . and apparently naked under that T-shirt.

I turn the phone away, horrified at the fact that I just pictured my wife naked while my niece was on the phone with me. That's sick even for Fletcher brothers standards.

"I'm going to text Grandma with some wedding planning ideas I have so just go with it, okay? We're still maintaining the secret from Grandma and the ladies." She pulls out a pink notebook with a furry pen and starts jotting some things down. "Let Addison settle in a bit this week but start thinking about what else you can do outside of wedding planning. This is your time to woo her, Luke. Listen to what her interests are. Try to anticipate her needs. Act like a husband, not a roommate. Set the mood in the cabin. Maybe pick up her favorite coffee on your way home from work one day. Decaf if she has sleep issues."

My brows furrow as I contemplate all of that. "Why are you acting like this is so urgent? We've got a year to do all this, Evs."

Everly shakes her head from side to side. "She has to fall in love with you before the wedding ceremony, Luke."

"Why?" I ask and notice both of my brothers looking at each other with concern.

"Because the moment she walks down the aisle and sees the way you look at her . . . she'll know the truth anyways."

A heaviness grows in my chest over that sobering reality and, somehow, the stakes got as high as that ninety-foot pole I ate shit on.

Everly's voice is thick when she adds, "And you deserve for her to be looking back at you the exact same way."

Chapter 18

FACT OR FICTION?
This lumberyard chick is an Autumn.

Addison

I'm late for work Monday morning because . . . well . . . I didn't realize how friggin' long it would take me to drive from Jamestown to Boulder. It's not a particularly long drive, it's just a hell of a lot longer than the five-minute jaunt I'm used to. I'm definitely going to need to start bringing my computer home in the evenings this winter though because if I get snowed in and can't make it down the peak, I need to be able to at least manage my sales calls.

Thankfully, Chuck and Bullhead have the day-to-day stuff at the yard pretty well-handled. I don't run the forklifts or pull orders down very often these days. Since my dad started spending more time in Florida, I've taken over a lot of what he used to do in terms of sales and ordering. The only thing he hasn't fully let me in on is the meetings he's had with the potential buyers that came out of nowhere. Apparently they're from Colorado Springs and do some level of developing, and they offered him a mountain of money that I can understand looks appealing to him. He's burned-out and ready to cut ties and leave the yard behind.

But I'm not.

And it drives me crazy that he keeps telling me he's saving me from myself. I know my own mind, damn it.

I'm distracted when I pull into the lot and see that all the forklifts are lined up on either side of the building center doors, framing the entrance. White balloons and paper bells hang from the prongs and I can't for the life of me figure out what this could be about. Did I forget about a special event we're throwing? We don't host many events here so who the hell authorized this? Maybe my dad forgot to tell me something before he flew out?

I glance around the yard to see if any of the guys are outside to ask and it's a ghost town, so I hightail my ass inside to see what all the fuss is about.

When I push through the double doors, my jaw drops to the floor when I am greeted by my entire crew of about twenty people inside the showroom, coffee mugs in hand standing beneath a giant banner that says:

CONGRATULATIONS MRS. FLETCHER

"Oh fuck . . . she's here!" Bullhead croaks and hits a button on a dusty old boom box where a loud wedding march song crackles through the shitty speakers. Everyone cheers and holds their mugs up, clapping their hands and offering me their well-wishes.

Chuck appears beside me, gesturing to the crowd and ramping them up even more.

"What is this?" I ask as Chuck walks me back toward the counter where customers pay and I see a large cardboard box and, when I'm close enough to look inside, I see it's a giant sheet cake with my face on it.

I cringe and cover my eyes because it's a horrific picture of me with two middle fingers up and my tongue out. It was taken by my father years ago. I was an unruly teenager at the time and I'm pretty sure all he did was tell me to smile for the camera. This photo has lived on the bulletin board of our break room for close to a decade and I'm 90 percent sure they just plunked that dusty photo right on this beautiful white frosted cake.

Chuck puts two fingers in his mouth and whistles loudly to quiet everyone down. "Shut up so I can say a little something."

Everyone settles down and I feel my cheeks flame red. "What are you doing, Chuck?"

His voice is loud so everyone can hear as he says, "Well, your dad called to tell me the news over the weekend and the guys and I wanted to show you how happy we are for you, Addie May." He barks out a dry laugh and everyone raises their mugs in agreement.

I look around and see that they've got balloons and streamers and cheap bridal shower decorations strewn all over the place. They even set out the potluck table in the break room and there's four crockpots and casserole dishes and what looks like a cheese and meat tray all laid out. "You didn't have to do all this."

"Sure we did, darling." Chuck smiles so big, I can't see his eyes. "Most of us have seen you grow up around here and this was the least we could do to celebrate your news. You're not just your father's daughter. You're ours too."

My eyes start to sting and I lick my lips to stop my chin from trembling. "Thank you."

"We all pooled our money and got you a little something too."

"No," I exclaim, holding my hands out as Bullhead walks up with a giant box wrapped in brown paper. "No gifts. I won't take it."

"Shut up and open your present, damn it," Bullhead croaks before stepping back.

I sigh heavily and roll my eyes, not liking a single minute of this kind of attention, especially when this was all to fulfill a stupid trust fund requirement.

Regardless, I rip into the paper and my jaw drops when I see a familiar logo on the box. "Is this?" I look to Chuck and Bullhead and all the other guys who look like they're positively bursting with excitement.

I drop down to my knees and go nuts ripping off the rest of the paper. "You got me the Challenger Bread Pan?" I squeal as I grip the box in my hands so hard, I could break through the packaging.

"You've only been talking about the damn thing for two years," Bullhead croaks, taking a sip of his coffee mug.

"You guys!" I shake my head and stare down at the three-hundred-dollar black cast-iron bread pan that I've wanted but refused to ever buy because the price is outrageous and I have a perfectly good pan that makes bread just fine.

But this . . . this feels . . . special. I'm overcome!

I glance up at the mostly middle-aged and senior men all staring at me like I'm their kid opening a bicycle on Christmas morning, not their boss who signs their paychecks. My face contorts out of nowhere and without a word, I throw myself into Chuck's arms, hugging him with every shred of emotion I have swelling inside of me. I bury my face in his chest to hide my tears. He smells like gasoline and tobacco and it feels like home. He shakes with silent laughter so I pull away, wiping aggressively at my face.

"You're all a bunch of assholes," I snark, thrusting a finger at the lot of them, and they all chuckle back at me. I clear my throat and nod, staring down at my gift that I can't wait to test out. "And you're all getting fresh loaves of bread next week." They cheer and I sigh heavily before adding a heartfelt "Thank you."

"Monroe Lumber belongs to a Monroe . . . or I guess Fletcher now?" Chuck shrugs and puts his arm around me, his face going serious as he looks out at everyone. "And we're all just real grateful we get to keep calling you boss for the foreseeable future and not some asswipe from Colorado Springs."

The guys all cheer and I let out a garbled laugh.

"Now get back to work, you slackers," Chuck shouts, waving his hands out. "We'll have potluck with the blushing bride at lunchtime."

Everyone grumbles their replies and disperses, leaving me alone to dab at my eyes and inhale a deep breath. I've just about gathered my thoughts when I spot a tiny blonde woman in the corner of the showroom. Is that my . . .

Mother-in-law?

Johanna Fletcher waves enthusiastically and makes her way over to me with a big smile. "I've never seen anyone cry over a bread pan before."

"You saw that?" I cringe and sniff loudly, trying to hide the remnants of my emotional outburst.

"What a testament to how loved you are around here."

I wrinkle my nose and shrug. "Or a testament to how many hints I drop about the things I like."

"That too maybe." Johanna laughs, glancing down at the pan. "You know when Steven was alive, I used to use my granddaughter to drop hints to him about what I wanted for Christmas or my birthday."

I smile at that. "I'm sure that was effective."

"Oh gosh yes. Steven would do anything Everly asked of him. All my boys would too." She laughs and I can't help but see the pain in her eyes with her casual discussion of her late husband.

My brows lift. "I enjoyed getting to know Everly in Mexico. She's so . . . dynamic."

"As are you, dear," she says, setting a binder on the counter between us. "Now, I know this is sudden, but if you want to get this wedding planned before Christmas like your father wants, we have no time to waste."

I force a smile I don't altogether feel. "You know, if you wanted to just take over and do most of it, I would be totally okay with that."

"Well, what about your tastes? Do you have a mood board or a Pinterest board or something I can use for inspiration?"

"A mood board?" I rasp, blinking back my bewilderment. "No. I don't have a mood board."

"Well, what do you like?" Johanna asks, propping her elbow on the counter and smiling excitedly at me. "What are your favorite colors? Favorite flowers? What kind of esthetic do you envision for this special day?"

"Oh gosh . . ." I murmur, wracking my brain because I've literally never thought about this in my entire life. I barely even celebrate my birthday, let alone have an opinion on what I like for a wedding esthetic.

"This is no problem!" Johanna opens her binder and points to the first sheet of paper. "I printed off a little QR code thing you can scan that takes you to a quiz online that you can fill out and that will help guide all of our decisions. Let me know when you have it done and I can take it from there. Oh, also, I've taken the liberty of setting up some dress fitting appointments."

My lips part. "Dress fittings?"

"Yes. The bridal stores in town require appointments. Such a pain, but I managed to snag a time at one this Saturday. We need to move quickly because if they have to order, they'll need several weeks I'm sure. Do you want me to invite the girls? Or do you want to let them know yourself?"

"The girls?"

"Cozy, Trista, Dakota, and whoever else you're close to."

My brows furrow. "Oh . . . like . . . we all try on dresses?"

"No silly, we just watch you try on dresses." She chuckles like I just said the silliest thing in the world. "Unless you want them to be bridesmaids?"

"Um . . . I haven't thought about bridesmaids."

"No problem!" she says, pushing the binder toward me. "It's all in the quiz."

I stare down at the binder, suddenly feeling like I'm back in school and needing to cram for a big test. I never liked school. Hated it in fact. My head is swimming with information overload and we've only just begun.

"Do you mind if we exchange numbers before I head out? That way I can text you with calendar requests?"

"Um . . . sure," I mumble and hand over my phone to watch Luke's mom type in her number and then call my phone.

"Be sure to save that!" She points to the device in my hand and I smile and nod woodenly. "Okay, I have loads to do and you have a lumberyard to run!" She looks around and presses a hand to her chest before staring back at me. "This is very impressive, Addison."

"What is?"

"You. Here." She inhales deeply. "My son sure knows how to pick 'em."

With a wave of her fingers she's off like some sort of fairy godmother-in-law and before I know it, I'm at my desk on a website I've never heard of and several clicks into a wedding quiz from hell and catapulting myself into a full-blown panic attack.

After spending over an hour on this miserable quiz, I'm still only halfway done. Halfway? What the fuck other questions do these people have for me? I want out but now I've come so far and it seems like a waste to click out now. And I bet then I lose my answers. I haven't even got to reception questions yet!

In a fit of rage, I grab my phone and call the only person who deserves this fury.

"Hello?" Luke answers, his voice calm and casual, the complete opposite of my inner psyche.

"What season are you?" I bark into the phone, bypassing pleasantries as I pound away on the keyboard of my computer.

"What?"

"What season are you?" My voice rises as I stand up and step away from the computer like it's about to light on fire.

"I don't know what you're saying."

"I need to know your season so I know what color palette to pick for the wedding," I snipe, pushing my hand into my hair. "I think I'm an Autumn, but if you're a Spring, we're basically fucked according to the quiz."

"According to what quiz?" Luke growls, finally reaching my level of frustration. "Are you having a stroke?"

"No. I'm taking a quiz your mother gave me after she dropped by today with a binder that looks like it contains the codes to the nuclear bombs."

Luke exhales heavily. "Of course this is my mother's doing. I would expect nothing less of Johanna Fletcher. This is where Everly gets it—"

"When did we get engaged?" I ask, cutting him off midsentence.

"Huh?"

"It's customary to send out engagement announcements and we screwed the pooch on that one, but I'm thinking we can send one out retroactively. I need to text your mom to get the name of a good photographer. Shit, what the hell am I going to wear for that kind of photoshoot? I *really* need to know what fucking season you are, Luke. I'm assuming your personal style is rustic, right?"

"Um . . . it is if that's what you want it to be."

"I think I'm classic so we're fucked again, Fletcher. This is a—"

"Go outside," Luke barks forcefully, cutting me off.

"Huh?"

"Go outside," he repeats again. "Get on a forklift and move some shit around."

I frown and glance out the window with confusion. "Why?"

"Because you need to touch some fucking grass, and for you I think that means operating heavy machinery. Get away from the wedding planning shit. I'm on my way back from Denver now and I'm coming to see you. I'll be there in thirty minutes."

"You don't have to come here. You're probably busy. I shouldn't have called."

"Roe."

"Fine, I'm going." I huff and hang up the phone.

He might be right. Just looking out the window at the guys working makes me feel better. But a loud engine would help me relax even further. So I follow Luke's instructions and head out to join the crew, fully intent on kicking Bullhead off his forklift so I can have some sort of weird-ass lumberyard-chick therapy session.

Sounds kind of dirty.

The fresh air is healing and I lose track of time unloading a shipment of plywood that came in from one of our suppliers. I'm snapped back to reality when I hear Bullhead yelling my name, so I pull the noise-canceling headphones off my ears and glance down to where he's waving up at me.

"You have someone in your office, boss!" he shouts and cuts a look over to a couple other guys nearby. "It's loverboy," Bullhead adds and makes a gross hip thrusting action. That is something I really did not need to see on a sixty-year-old man today. He hooks his thumb to the building. "Get off my rig so I can get back to work."

I shut down the engine and slide down off the equipment, giving the guys a wave as I make my way into the building center. My heart rate starts increasing all over again and I wonder if perhaps I should have stayed on the forklift a bit longer, although I don't think my change in blood pressure is because of wedding planning.

It's because my husband is here.

God, that's weird to say.

Luke stands in front of my desk all tall, flannel and adorable with his little mustache and backward hat, but the concern in his eyes when I walk through my office doorway has me feeling guilty for calling him earlier.

"I'm so sorry you had to come here," I say, pulling my jacket and gloves off and flopping them on a nearby chair.

"Don't be," he says, moving over to me and putting his hands on my shoulders. He crouches down in front of me to get a good look at me. "You feeling better?"

"I am," I reply with a sheepish smile. "I got to drive the forklift."

He chuckles and stands up straight, looking down at me with a sexy smirk. "Remind me to show you how to operate the tractor this winter."

My eyes light up. "Hell yes." Seems my husband knows me well.

Of course he does, Roe, he's your best friend. Good God.

He shakes his head and walks over to my desk. "Is this my mom's binder?"

"That's the one." I shudder just looking at it.

He picks it up and slides it under his arm. "I can handle this."

"But how are you going to know if baby's breath is tacky or classic?" I deadpan, then frown when I realize I'm kind of serious.

"Roe." Luke licks his lips and fights away a smile, revealing a dimple that I never noticed before. "It doesn't matter. None of this matters. Whatever we do is just for show. Remember?"

"Oh yeah . . . right . . ." I murmur, my brows furrowing as I look back into the showroom and notice the banner on the ceiling has fallen down on one side. It feels ominous in a strange way. I clear my throat and look back at him. "This isn't real."

I swallow the painful knot in my throat, hating how those words feel on my tongue. After the gift from the yard guys and Luke's mom acting all sweet and caring and now Luke coming here all protective and chivalrous, I guess I'm feeling a bit like . . . all of this feels pretty damn real to me.

"Come here." Luke holds his hands out to me as I walk over to where he pulls me in for a big hug. As our bodies press together, I feel myself instantly start to calm down as my breaths synchronize with his. He doesn't smell like gasoline and chew, but he smells familiar all the same. I swear he's like a weighted blanket that just makes all the noise go away. How the hell does he do that?

He rubs the back of my head and murmurs, "Feel better?"

"Much," I reply with a dopey smile up at him.

"Good, I have something for you." He digs into his pocket and retrieves a small burgundy box with the word *Cartier* etched into the top.

"What the hell is that?" I step back and point at the thing in his hand like it's a mouse.

Luke chuckles softly. "Just open it."

"I don't want to open it." I ball my hands up into fists and press them into my chest.

"Why not?" He looks at me with an amused smirk.

"Because that looks expensive." I stare down at it again. What is with people giving me extravagant gifts today?

"It wasn't that bad." Luke removes the space between us and forces it into my hand. "Just take it."

My hands are shaking as I hold the box in my hand, terrified that I'm going to open it and find some ridiculous three-carat diamond that Luke spent his life savings on because he's freakishly nice and feels guilty for not having a ring on my finger when people ask.

"Luke, I seriously don't want . . ." My voice trails off when I pop it open and see what's inside. "Oh my gosh."

"Do you like it?" Luke hunches down to get a better look at my reaction but I can't be bothered to look at him, because what I have in my hands is way too beautiful to look away from.

"Here, let me help you." He takes the box from me, pulling the ring out of the slot and grabbing my left hand to slide it onto my finger.

"Oh my gosh," I say again because it's just so . . .

"It's cool, right?" Luke says, sounding like a kid in a candy store. "I saw it and totally thought of you. Does the size feel okay? I had to guess but they said we can exchange it if we need to. I picked it up in Denver this morning."

"Luke, it's perfect." I hold my hand up, marveling at the unique piece of art on my finger. I say "art" because it is. It's a smooth white gold metal band that wraps around my finger in the form of curved nail. It has a row of tiny diamonds wrapped around what looks like a nailhead, adding a touch of sparkle that even I can't be mad at. "It's a freaking wrapped nail with diamonds."

The proud twinkle in his eye is unmistakable.

"But Cartier?" I glance at the box still in his hand. "Luke. I'm not a brand girlie and even I know this couldn't have been cheap."

"You're about to own a lumberyard, Roe. You needed something to represent the success you've earned in your life and I think this does that." His brows furrow and a quiet, almost melancholic vibe descends over him as he rubs his thumb over my ring. "If we're going to fake it, we might as well do it right, you know?"

I look up at him as he holds my hand, bowing over me in that tall lanky way he has about him. He holds my eyes captive as he looks from my eyes to my lips and then back to my eyes. He does that a lot. And every time it makes me want to lick my lips in preparation.

But we don't kiss.

We shouldn't kiss.

We're just friends.

Then again, he just put a Cartier ring on my finger.

I lift my chin up just as he jerks back and clears his throat, fully shattering whatever spell we were just under. His voice is deep and reflective when he says, "Roe, I know you think I'm doing you this big favor by marrying you so you can inherit the lumberyard, but I promise you, babe . . . we are in this whole song and dance together, okay? I'm with you until the end."

Babe?

Did he just call me babe?

And did I just get butterflies when he did?

Holy fuck.

He said some other stuff too though. The end? He said something about this ending?

The corner of his mouth lifts as his eyes smolder on mine. "My family is crazy. Your family is crazy. But you and me. We can be good. We can get through all of this as long as we have each other's back. And I will always have your back."

He pulls me in for another hug and presses his lips into my hair. I close my eyes and sink into the comfort of my best friend. Best. Friend. This is a best friend hug, because that's what Luke is.

For a few hours, especially after seeing all the effort my lumberyard family put into celebrating my fake marriage, not to mention my fake mother-in-law and her detailed binder, I'd traversed from fake to almost real. And my ring? Fuck, my best friend knows me well, which is why he got this ring. That's all.

It's not romantic, and I don't do romance.

Which is why I am not disappointed that he didn't kiss me on the lips . . . because . . . we're just friends . . . and friends don't kiss on the lips no matter how good it feels. And even if I ventured into fantasyland momentarily today, Luke did not. We're just friends who happen to be married to each other. No big deal.

Chapter 19

FACT OR FICTION?
Sourdough makes my wife weird.

Luke

"Oh my God, what is that heavenly smell?" Addison exclaims as she comes bursting into my house on Friday night at six o'clock sharp.

Our house.

Not my house.

She came bursting into *our* house.

That small mental correction has me smiling like a lovesick puppy as I watch my wife unlace her Converse shoes and drop all her stuff in a heap by the front door.

We've been living together for almost a week now and I still get so excited at the sight of her coming home to me. Every time it happens, my heart feels like it's going to explode in my chest. And we're not even sleeping with each other.

I shake away those crazy thoughts to answer her question. "Steak and potatoes. The only thing I really know how to make."

Addison cuts me a look of disbelief as she walks over to the oven and opens it up to peek inside. "What are those?"

"Parmesan potatoes. My mom's recipe. They're not too hard. Just some flour and parmesan cheese and butter."

"Looks incredible," she says, turning to the counter to peek at the steaks that are marinating in a dish. "I thought I was supposed to be the one cooking in this marriage of convenience and you were going to do the shopping. What did I do to deserve this?"

"You cooked every night this week, Roe. This is literally the least I can do." I huff out a noise of indignation. "Besides it's nothing special."

She splays her hand out on the counter where I'm chopping up some lettuce for side salads. "Um . . . you put your life on hold for a year to fake marry me so I can inherit my family business. That's pretty damn special, which is why I should do all the cooking."

My brows fold at her response because nothing about this feels fake, except for the fact that she doesn't sleep in my bed. *And I'd really fucking like her to.*

She snatches a cherry tomato out of the container in front of me and asks, "Do I have time to shower quick?"

"Yeah, no problem. I'll throw them on the grill while you're in there."

"Great," she replies rubbing her hand down my arm as she walks past me. "Be right back."

I watch her disappear down the hall and try my hardest not to picture her stripping down to nothing and jumping in that hot shower all alone. Her fingers undoing the braid in her hair as her soft, dark tendrils caress her creamy back—a piece brushing over her hardened nipple in the front.

Fuck. Stop, Luke.

You're wooing her, not trying to hook up with her in the first week. This is a marathon, not a sprint. Although considering Everly thinks I need to close this deal before the wedding, it's more like a half-mile run maybe. Is a mile a marathon? Or a 5K? Fuck if I know, I just know that every time I see her, I want to kiss the ever-loving shit out of her and see what she looks like under those fucking T-shirts she prances around in at night.

I've had to watch her make sourdough bread every goddamn night this week while I stroke my cock.

Wait . . . that's not what I meant.

Rufus.

I mean stroke Rufus.

We've gotten into a habit of her baking bread while I feed Rufus his nightly snack. Addison usually plays music when she does her "stretch and fold" ritual, and I watch her sway her hips in the kitchen so much that Rufus has shit on the floor three times this week and I didn't even notice because I was too busy eye-fucking her.

God, I have it bad.

I think on some level, I wondered if moving Addison in with me could help me get over her. Like, maybe we weren't as compatible as I once thought, and we'd grate on each other's nerves. I know it's only been a week, but we already have a routine together and that seems like a really good early sign.

And if I'm not mistaken, the touching is getting way more frequent. Roe always has been a little handsy with me . . . usually in playful shoves or hits. But lately, it's caresses and rubs or just resting her palm on me when I'm talking to her. The way she touches me before she says good-night is fucking killing me. It gives me hope that maybe she sees me as more than a friend too, but her head hasn't caught up to her heart yet.

God, I could only hope.

She emerges twenty minutes later barefaced with her black hair wet and tied up into a clip. The smell of her lotion is so strong, I have to fight back the urge to wrap her up in my arms and bury my face in her neck. God, I love that eucalyptus smell on her.

I plate our food and pour a couple glasses of red wine and we sit at the dining room table together, on the same side so we can watch the sun set. That's another one of our routines. She loves watching the sunset so we've started eating earlier so we don't miss it.

She takes a bite of steak and moans. "Ugh, so good."

"I'm sure you could have done better."

"Nope," she says, stabbing another bite of steak. "This is perfection. Food always tastes better when you don't have to cook it."

"That's good to know. I was worried you'd be irritated."

"Naw, I love to cook, but it's fun to be surprised."

"So you like surprises?" I ask, still trying to learn as much as I can about my best friend.

She wiggles her ring finger at me as proof and I can't help but smile. She hasn't taken it off since I gave it to her, and the immense pride I feel in that is alarming. I researched a ridiculous amount of time on the internet to find the perfect ring. Something that wasn't too flashy because I know she would have been awkward about that, but I wanted it to be something that matched her essence. The fact that Cartier had the ring in stock and the sample size fit her perfectly was just fate telling me I got it right.

"Any more surprises from my mom this week?" I ask, taking a sip of my wine.

Addison shakes her head. "She just texted me requesting my guest list, which I was able to crank out without having a nervous breakdown."

"Nice," I reply with a laugh. "How many people?"

"Not a lot. My dad, Edith, like six of the guys from the lumberyard plus a few of my dad's clients that he's known for years. So, all together only like fifteen people."

"Okay, that's perfect. That's about my number too. I told my mom we were keeping it small and not inviting the entire town of Boulder to this thing."

"Who is on your list?" she asks, taking a sip of her wine.

"My mom, my brothers and the ladies, Everly, Ethan, Judy who owns the Mercantile in town, and a handful of my mom's friends from Boulder."

"So like thirty people roughly?" she says, doing some quick math. "That's not too scary. Did you finish our quiz?"

"I did. And you'll be happy to learn that I am a Summer."

"Thank God," she replies dramatically, splaying her hands out on the table. "Our color palettes won't clash with each other and ruin our precious photos."

I chuckle softly. "I can show you some of the things I picked out if you want? No big deal if you're not interested though."

"I'd love to see them," she replies with wide eyes. "Let's see what kinds of vibes I can expect for our big day."

"We also need to pick a date," I state, pausing my eating to eye her seriously. "I was thinking the weekend before Christmas could be good because Everly is home by then and we're not completely taking over the holidays."

Addison nods and her eyes widen. "Holy shit, that's like six weeks away."

"Shit, is that too soon? We could do New Year's too."

"No, it's fine," she replies with a casual wave of her hand. "I'll check with the old man to be sure that works for him, but it's okay by me."

"Cool," I murmur while rising from the table to grab my laptop. My heart rate spikes over the fact that she said it's only six weeks away. That means I have only six weeks left to get my wife to fall in love with me.

No pressure.

I pull up the website my mom set up for us and point to the collage of items that populate on the screen. "I tried to answer all the questions with you in mind and it basically created this whole, like, proposal of what the day could look like."

"Your mom called it a mood board!" Addison says, pulling the computer closer to her.

"Does it look okay?" I ask, watching her nervously because this feels like a test.

I went with understated elegance. It's a winter wedding so I highlighted a lot of greenery and spruce decor with rich red florals mixed in. The website said good colors for an Autumn are burgundy, warm oranges, mustard yellows, earthy browns, olive greens, terracotta, teal, and deep golden tones . . . not that I knew what any of those fucking things were before I lost hours of my life on this godforsaken website.

I can see why Roe lost her shit on it.

But it did a nice job putting everything together for me. Lots of candles in glass holders and reception tables with simple white linens and natural winter accents like spruce tips, berries, and pine cones. It suggested a wool suit in charcoal or navy for me, so I snagged a couple options like that, and for her, it showed lots of long-sleeve lace gowns with fur shawls. Not that I have a clue what kind of wedding dress Addison would pick out. Maybe this will help her decide.

"This is beautiful, Luke," she says, smiling as her eyes scan the screen. "The little wooden accents are so cute."

"I thought you'd like those. I mean, I didn't want to be too on the nose with the lumberyard tie-in, but the natural elements look pretty cool. I have no idea how my mom will even accomplish all of this, but she's kinda legendary for getting shit done."

Addison looks up, her eyes fixing on the window as the sun begins to disappear behind the trees. The golden light on her face is stunning as her hazel eyes look lighter than ever.

"Hey, do you think we could have the wedding outside here?" she asks, catching me completely off guard while I'm busy marveling over her beauty.

I jerk my attention to the window. "Here? During winter?"

She shrugs. "A winter wedding up here seems beautiful. On my run yesterday through those trails you showed me out back, it started to snow, and I swear I just stopped to watch it fall for like a whole hour. I was mesmerized by it. I've lived in Colorado my whole life but never really appreciated the mountains like this."

My chest swells with pride over how easily she's adjusting to life up here. Like she was always meant to be here. And call me delusional, but I love that she's put some thought into this. This wedding means more to her than she's ready to admit and I will do whatever I have to to foster that feeling she's embracing inside of her.

For so long, Roe has lived such a minimal and practical life. She loves the lumberyard and her work, but I've never seen her really dream the way I've seen Trista and Dakota dream. Hearing her state so clearly something she simply wants just because she wants it . . . feels good. Like maybe this whole marriage of convenience is healing her in unexpected ways.

"Plus, my dad is paying for this wedding, and I guess I feel guilty renting an expensive venue when this is all just for show."

My eyes close and I pinch the bridge of my nose, really wishing she didn't add that last part. But she's Roe. She is nothing if not practical.

"We could probably figure it out," I reply with a frown and clear my throat, trying to hide my raging disappointment. "We'd need a backup in case there's a storm or something. The barn is bursting at the seams with all of Trista's rescues and we're still a ways out from developing her new rescue center. But thirty people could probably fit in Wyatt's house." I glance out the side window toward his house, and Addison sidles up next to me to look as well. Even if we got snowed in between my house, Calder's, Wyatt's, and the apartment above the barn, we could probably make it work. "And Wyatt has that big angular window that overlooks the mountain so if we stood in front of it, we could feel like we were outside still."

"That sounds perfect." She smiles brightly and grips my

arms. "I mean, I'm never doing this again in my life, so I guess I want it to be kind of . . . memorable. And a mountaintop wedding could certainly be that."

I nod and watch her thoughtfully, trying to discern what is more important to her, budget or beauty. Please God, let it be beauty, because I'll do anything to keep that smile on her face. I clear my throat and add, "I'll talk to him but I'm sure he'll be fine with it."

"Amazing. Now I just have to hope dress shopping goes this well tomorrow." She cringes and takes a sip of her wine. "Cozy, Trista, and Dakota are coming along, so that should help be a bit of a buffer with your mom at least."

"Is my mom really that bad?" I ask, my face grave. "I can talk to her. Ask her to back off."

Addison shakes her head and her shoulders lift slightly. "It's not your mom. It's me. I'm just . . . weird with moms. Ever since my mom left, I just . . . can't seem to connect with women. Edith, bless her heart, tries so hard with me and I'm just such a bitch to her."

"When was the last time you spoke to your mom?" I ask, venturing into new territory, but considering she spoke pretty freely about her brother the other night, maybe that's a sign she's willing to share more.

"I was twenty, so it's been eight years now." She sets her fork down and steeples her hands in front of her. Her lips thin when she adds, "She'd just got out of prison."

I blink back my shock, trying not to let the first words stumble out of my mouth.

"She was the one driving the car when my brother died." She expels the words with a shaky breath, like they'd been cooped up inside of her for way too long.

"Oh God, Roe. I had no idea."

She makes a strange noise in the back of her throat. "He was only eight and she was a grown-ass adult . . ." She takes a long pause as she holds up her glass of wine, staring at it like a wine expert before adding, "with a blood alcohol level of .21 at the time of the accident."

My heart sinks at the last part of her statement and a sickness forms in my stomach. "I'm so sorry."

She nods, her lips pursed tight before she takes a drink of her wine, savoring it like she didn't just drop the biggest bomb on me. "She was supposed to be sober at the time too, so that was a whole thing she lied to us about. I didn't have my first sip of alcohol until I was twenty-two, which I know is nothing to really brag about, but at the time, it felt like a big deal because I thought I was never going to drink."

"I can understand why you'd hesitate after a situation like that," I say, my mind going back in time to clock all the times I noticed Addison taking a cab even after only one or two drinks. She'd always manage my transportation too, sometimes making me crash on her couch even when I'd only had a couple drinks. I didn't really think much about it at the time, but now, it all makes sense.

"For years I looked at alcohol like this big bad thing that took my brother from me. I was obsessed with it. Noticed what everyone around me drank, noticed what my dad and his cronies drank. Counted every beer can they tossed out of their truck windows driving down gravel roads and went back to pick them all up the next day."

She laughs and shakes her head, pushing her plate of food away before turning in her seat to face me. "This is embarrassing, but when I was a kid, I used to think the cops could find my dad's beer cans on the side of the road and DNA test them and trace it back to him. Then he'd go to jail too and I would be an orphan."

"That's not embarrassing." I reach my hand out and rest it on her leg as a small sign of comfort. "That just shows what happened affected you. It should have affected you. It was tragic."

"It clearly affected my dad, but not in a good way," she huffs, rolling her eyes. "I love that man but when I think back to my childhood after Aaron died, it was seriously fucked up."

"I suppose he was just coping in his own way," I offer, not really wanting to defend Addison's dad, but the man lost his son. His baby boy. I know loss firsthand now and can't imagine how it would affect me if I'd lost one of my brothers. Or if Max lost Everly or Ethan.

Fuck. How does a man ever come back from that?

"Yeah, he's not as bad as he used to be, thank goodness. Which is maybe why as I got older, I realized it was crazy of me to obsess over something I'd never even tasted before. So, one day I just started having beers with the guys after work. I think I expected this big, heavy thing to overcome me. I thought I'd get addicted and instantly start craving it. But I didn't. It was just a drink. It wasn't stronger than me and I took pride in that. I resented my mother for letting it be stronger than her."

I nod slowly, thinking back to when I first asked Roe to go out with me for beers. She would have been twenty-three at the time so not drinking long. I bet her mind was fixating on every sip she took.

"Where is your mom now?" I ask, watching her thoughtfully.

"I have no idea," she replies with a laugh. "She got out of jail, came home to get some of her stuff, and I never saw her again. She didn't even say goodbye."

My eyes tighten as I watch Roe curl up into a ball on the chair, looking so young and childlike. I kind of sensed she had some abandonment issues, but this goes even deeper than I realized.

"Ugh, I don't know why I'm telling you all of this." She shakes her hands out and stands up to start clearing the plates.

"Don't do that," I state, grabbing her wrist to stop her movement.

"Don't do what?" She frowns down at me.

"Don't open up and then shut down. You don't have to do that with me. If you want to talk, I'm here to listen. Always."

Her eyes hold mine captive for a long, silent moment and it feels like we're having a full conversation with no words. She's always carried something dark and painful inside of her. I can see it when she's around her dad. She loves him, but there's a pain they share that I've wanted to understand more. But if I pry too hard to open up, she'll just push me away.

Her breath catches before she drops back down into her seat and leans back against the table, gazing into the kitchen with a pensive look in her eye. "Apparently my mom had gotten out on parole for good behavior or something. We had no idea because we never got to visit her in prison. She had to put us on a list to see her and no matter how many times my dad put in a request, she always denied him.

"Anyways, I was still living at home with my dad, and we'd come home together after work one day to find her car, which was stored in one of the machine sheds, parked out in front of the house with the trunk open. My mom appeared on the front step with an armload of her stuff, and I swear it was like seeing a ghost."

My heart lurches as her voice cracks, and I can't help but notice the tremble in her chin as she fights away the emotion bubbling up to the surface.

"It's weird to have this twelve-year-old mental image of your mom and then suddenly you're an adult and seeing her through more mature eyes. I barely recognized her as I had a totally different image built up in my head. My dad told me to stay in the truck and even though I was an adult at the time, I suddenly felt like a kid all over again, so I just listened and sat there totally mute, watching him follow her in and out of the house as she gathered her things. They were fighting and shouting, and he looked so mad at one point, I thought he was going to hit her."

"Fuck," I murmur under my breath, pressing my fist to my mouth as I swallow down the knot in my throat.

"Finally, he stopped following her and just stood on our front step while she got in her car and backed out of the lane. She stopped beside my dad's truck and looked at me through the closed window. It's weird because it made me think of the prison glass I'd always seen people talk to the inmates through on movies and stuff."

Addison licks her lips and chews the bottom one, pointing to her chin as it begins to tremble. "Her chin trembled just like mine does. It was like I was looking in a mirror that aged me twenty years. We have the same dark hair, same hazel eyes and round cheeks. Same wobbly chin that shows all our emotions."

She swipes at some errant tears that fall down her face before adding, "I held my breath, waiting for her to get out of the car to hug me, to beg for forgiveness, to tell me how much she missed me and that she was sorry for lying to us. She wasn't a bad mom before the accident. I have good memories with her. Memories that now all feel like a lie, because if they were real, how could she just drive away and not say anything to me? How could she go eight years without hugging me and still not want to hug me before she left? Even just to say goodbye?"

Addison shudders a breath as she braces her hands on her knees. I stop myself from touching her, because I don't want to pop this bubble she's in right now. She holds so much inside, she's like a dam ready to break at any second. And if she's going to break, I'm right here to catch her.

She clears her throat and wrinkles her nose, steeling herself for the end of the story. "But she didn't get out. She drove off and I never heard from her again. It's been just me and my dad ever since." She pulls her leg up onto the bench and holds her knees to her chest, shaking her head, raw and spent from that emotional confession.

I reach over and wrap my arms around my friend, holding her to me, kissing her on her head as I say, "She missed out." I swallow the pain in my throat and repeat, "She missed out on a whole lot."

Roe nods woodenly and rests her cheek on her knees, looking at me through watery eyes. "I like it here, Luke," she says, pinning me with a sobering look. "I like being with you and I need us to be good and not worry about this falling apart, okay?"

I frown and stare back at her, guilt settling in my gut over the magnitude of her request. It's a simple request a friend should be able to make to a friend.

It's much more complicated when one of the friends is in love with the other. But ultimately, I'd do anything for this girl.

I half smile, reaching out to touch the curved nail wrapped around her finger. "For better or worse, Addison Monroe . . . I got you."

Chapter 20

FACT OR FICTION?
Fireball makes fast friends.

Addison

"Her wedding date is when?" The bridal attendant gapes at Jo, who tells the woman our December date for the second time.

"We can't get in dresses in less than six weeks."

"Then we'll just have to buy something off the rack," Jo responds cheerily. Definitely not ready to call this powerhouse "Mom," but "Jo" suits her nicely to me.

The attendant eyes me up and down. "We may not have her size."

"Ahem," Cozy barks loudly, stepping up to the tiny bridal attendant and eyeing her with the fire of a thousand suns. "Why don't you and I go for a little walk?"

The attendant looks confused as Cozy escorts her away from us, and Dakota and Trista exchange a knowing look before clinking their complimentary champagne flutes together.

"This is fun," Dakota says with a smile, crossing her legs and bouncing her foot excitedly.

"I haven't even tried anything on yet," I state, feeling like a total fish out of water.

She shrugs. "It's already fun."

I frown at that because it seems so easy and natural for these ladies to be pampered in this plush bridal store. I never even went to my high school prom. I just went to the parties afterward. The awkwardness of asking my dad for money for a dress that he'd have to see me in . . . I shuddered at the thought.

As an adult, I've learned how to shop, but I get almost everything online just to avoid the uncomfortable dressing room moments.

Like this moment right here.

Who knows what Cozy is talking to that woman about right now. I take a deep breath in and lower myself onto the open furry white armchair next to Trista. The only way I'm going to survive this is by leaning on the women around me, even if it kills me to do so. "Trista, where did you buy your wedding dress? You looked so beautiful in Mexico."

"Oh, they definitely had to order my size in." She giggles and takes a sip. "These types of places don't carry sample sizes that would fit me."

"Should I be worried?" I ask, biting my lip. "My proportions are odd. I'm all hips and flat chested and my shoulders are super broad. I should have been a linebacker, I swear."

"Those shoulders are going to look beautiful in whatever you pick out." Jo sits down on the armrest of my chair, hitting me with her wide, hopeful eyes. "Luke says you want an outdoor service?"

"Yeah, is that crazy?" I ask, glancing at Dakota and Trista and then back to Johanna. "I don't want to be difficult."

"Not at all," Jo peals back. "It's your special day. You should get exactly what you want. I am already looking at these gorgeous outdoor tents with heaters for a small reception."

"I heard Wyatt talking to Luke this morning about using our house as backup if there's a storm," Trista says, turning my attention to her. "We're totally good with it. I'll put my breast pump parts away and everything."

"Oh, thank you so much," I reply gratefully, amazed at how this is all coming together. Some snow has already fallen the past week up on the peak, dusting everything in a sparkly white blanket. It's not enough to completely cover the ground, but by the wedding, I expect it will be a white wonderland.

"Fletcher Mountain in December is beautiful," Trista says as if reading my thoughts. "It's like existing on a cloud. Last year was the best Christmas of my whole life up there."

"You were also drunk on newborn baby and a brand-new rock on your finger." Dakota laughs knowingly.

"That is true." Trista shoots me a sheepish smile and then glances at my hand. "I see you have some new hardware as well."

I blush as I hold the ring up to my chest, not wanting any more attention on me, but it's pointless because all the ladies squeal and grab my hand for a closer look.

"So unique," Dakota says with a sigh. "Great work, Luke."

I frown as I look down at it. "Yeah, he's good like that, isn't he?"

"All this planning is making me wish I would have done our wedding on the mountain too. But Wyatt wasn't in such a damn hurry."

"I'm glad you guys got married in Mexico," Dakota says, raising her hand. "Or who knows if Calder and I ever would have happened."

"You two would have happened," Johanna adds with a secretive smile. "He's been waiting a long time for you."

Dakota's smile falls as Jo hits her with that stunning remark. "Why do you say that?"

"A mother knows these things." She taps her nose at her future daughter-in-law because the writing seems to be on the wall for Dakota and Calder. I haven't been around them a lot as a couple, but the few times I've seen them this past week on the mountain, they seem ridiculously happy . . . even when they're bickering.

This whole conversation makes me understand even more why Luke was up for helping me with this marriage situation.

The epic love stories he's surrounded by with his family are a lot to live up to.

"Oh, Addison," Jo says, clapping her hands excitedly. "I'm almost done with the invitations already. Do you want to see them or just be surprised? Luke told me you love surprises."

"I do love surprises." I smile softly at the fact that Luke is out there in the streets trying to protect me from all this wedding stuff. He really is such a good friend.

"Very well, then. I shall keep it all to myself for now. Along with all my reception ideas. Oh, this is going to be so hard, but fun!" Jo squeals and walks away to thumb through her binder, clearly deep in planning mode.

"That woman loves a project," Trista says, pointing to her mother-in-law. "Just wait until you give her a grandbaby and you'll really see everything she can do."

The mention of having a child causes a pit to form in my stomach because . . . I never intend to have a baby. I'll never be a mom, or even have a husband . . . not in the real sense anyways. Guilt niggles with that thought because Jo will want Luke to have a baby. To give her more grandchildren. All these women probably want nieces and nephews. And nothing close to that will ever happen between me and Luke.

I'm a total fraud.

Allowing them to plan my wedding, gush over my ring, help with my dress fitting. What am I doing here? This is so wrong of me, isn't it?

Then again, Luke and I *are* legally married. Does the fact that I'm not sleeping with him make our marriage less real? And kids aren't a necessity for all committed couples. There are all sorts of marriages out there, right? By all accounts, things between me and Luke are going well. Maybe there's an argument that could be made for friends getting married and leaving the romance out of it. We're certainly making it work so far. And if that's what I have to tell myself to stop feeling guilty for bringing everyone here today, then so be it.

"Here we are!" Cozy announces her return, appearing before us with a new bridal attendant whose hands are full of dresses as she hangs them up on the nearby rod.

"Which one is the lucky bride?" the new gal asks, already displaying a better attitude than the last one.

I stand and raise my hand while taking a sip of my champagne. The woman crosses her arms and elbows Cozy. "I see exactly what you mean."

"Right?" Cozy confirms. "You could bounce a rhinestone off that ass."

"Excuse me?" I ask, turning around to look at my butt in the nearby mirror.

"Definitely fitted," the attendant confirms. "If that's what she wants. I pulled lots of options. And some incredible faux fur shrugs."

"She's going to look so hot," Dakota confirms.

"Like Snow White on the mountain with that raven hair," Trista adds, pointing at me.

"Did you pull something to showcase her lovely shoulders? The reception will be heated," Johanna asks, walking over to touch my arms and gaze at my reflection in the mirror.

"Can you take off your sweater, Addison?" Cozy asks, tilting her head to look at me. "We're trying to objectify you."

Trista and Dakota sputter out laughing and Johanna cuts them a look. "No more free champagne for those two."

Their faces fall and I take a moment to admire the women in front of me. All uniquely shaped and confident in their own skin, which only makes me feel more self-assured in mine. Perhaps this is what I missed out on my whole life not having girlfriends, a hype squad.

And as I look at Johanna gazing at me in the mirror with contemplative eyes, I wonder if this is what my mom would be like . . . if things were different.

I don't have long to ponder that painful thought because I'm swept up into a dressing room to try on a mountain of dresses with ladies who make me forget about this wedding being fake, because they're all so perfectly real.

"She said yes to the dress!" Dakota calls out to Pearl Street Pub in Boulder as we clink our glasses together in unison.

"Quiet down," I shush her with a giggle while shooting apologetic glances to the other patrons at the bar.

"Sorry." Dakota laughs as she reaches up to tie her blond hair into a ponytail. "I just thought they should know."

"The strangers in the bar that we've never met do not care about my wedding dress status." I eye her skeptically.

"You never know." Dakota tuts before taking a sip of her Moscow mule.

"I'm so glad we're doing this," Cozy says, stumbling over to us as she fists four shots of Fireball she just ordered at the bar. Her short dark hair falls in front of her face and she shakes her head to push it back. "Since we didn't get to throw you a bachelorette party, an impromptu bar crawl on Pearl Street is the next best thing."

"Okay, but why do we have to keep having Fireball?" I ask, sniffing the cinnamon whiskey and wrinkling my nose.

"'Cause it's like a breath mint and it's delicious!" Cozy answers with a gleeful smile.

Trista holds her shot glass up and yells, "To another woman on Fletcher Mountain!"

"Hear! Hear!" Dakota confirms, lifting her glass to her lips and shooting her shot along with the rest of us.

"You guys are starting to make me feel left out." Cozy winces and blows out her cinnamon breath all over us. "I'm going to make Max build us a cabin on Fletcher Mountain."

"Do it!" Dakota slaps her hands on the table. "Max is so rich, it'd be like nothing to him. You guys deserve a mountain getaway house."

"He does have a house in Aspen though," Cozy replies regretfully.

Dakota shoots Trista a flat look. "When she says things like that it makes her really unrelatable."

"Shut up!" Cozy whacks Dakota on the arm and Dakota nearly spills her drink, causing all four of us to erupt in laughter.

I shake my head, sipping my beer at a much slower pace than the rest of these girlies. This is giving Mexico vibes all over again, and these broads couldn't hold their liquor then either.

But I have to admit, I'm having a blast. After I found a dress that literally took my breath away and didn't need a spec of alterations on, we all went to dinner together and afterward, the girls convinced Johanna to take us to Pearl Street and we've been bar hopping ever since.

Jo stuck with us for the first stop, sipping her demure club soda and enjoying the live band, but then I think she could see where the day was headed and got the hell out of Dodge. The last thing she said to us was to be sure to call one of the boys when we needed a ride back up to Fletcher Mountain.

Johanna paused briefly before she hugged me goodbye, almost as if she was waiting for me to be ready for it. And something in that subtle shift in her embrace made me not recoil like I normally would have. I have to hand it to Luke's mom . . . the woman can roll with the punches pretty well. I suppose having four boys would make her pretty used to adapting to all types of situations. And these three women around me have only added more color to the Fletcher family madness.

"Can we give her her gift now?" Trista asks, drumming her hands loudly on the table.

"You guys didn't have to get me a gift."

"You're going to love it." Dakota reaches under the table and pulls out a white bridal bag that I noticed she was carrying around from bar to bar. But I guess I didn't think to ask her what was inside of it.

"I think Luke is going to love it a bit more," Cozy adds with a wink.

I look inside the bag and wince when I see a whole lot of lace and straps. I slam the bag closed and shake my head. "You guys."

"Come on, pull it out!" Trista cheers, shoving the bag at me.

I exhale heavily and pull out the tiny two pieces of lingerie. It's a white lace embroidered set with lots of room for cleavage and ass.

"For your wedding night." Cozy smiles and nudges me with her arm.

"Although technically she already had a wedding night," Dakota corrects.

"You mean you're not a virgin?" Trista sputters out a laugh, her curly chestnut hair looking bigger and bigger with every bar stop

I just shake my head and quietly tuck the tiny slips of fabric away. Imagining wearing that in front of Luke has my cheeks flushing with heat that I really don't need these ladies to call me out on.

He's been texting me all day, checking in to make sure I'm doing okay. I sent him a pic of us and the girls at the last bar and he sent me a couple of beer mugs cheers-ing each other.

Maybe I should send him a pic of this lingerie and see what he has to say to that. That would be too weird, right? He'd think I was a creep. Or a pervert. I know there's been some type of flirting happening between us lately. Even last night after I trauma dumped my mommy issues on him, we had a moment in the kitchen where I was showing him how to prep my bread and I swear to God, I think he was hard while he was doing it.

I mean . . . I'm not judging him for it. I get horned up when I make bread too. But Luke was definitely not just interested in the bread making last night. Not with the way his chocolate-brown eyes raked over me every time my hands touched his to help him with the dough.

The man has great hands.

Large and warm and rough in all the right places.

"I've never worn lingerie for Wyatt," Trista says with a frown. "Maybe I should try it. Spice things up a bit again now that Stevie is older and sleeping through the night."

"Oh please." Dakota rolls her eyes. "You two do not need any help spicing things up. You're going to be pregnant again soon enough."

"No I'm not!" Trista points an accusatory finger at Dakota. "Animal rescue facility first. Then we can talk about baby number two."

"Where are you at with the rescue center, Trista?" Cozy asks, sipping her White Claw.

"Luke is drawing up a proposal for me now." She smiles brightly. "I can't believe I'm really doing it. I'm going to build my own rescue center on Fletcher Mountain or as I like to call it . . . Mount Millie."

Cozy leans over to me and says, "It took the entire family to strong-arm Trista into accepting the plot of land from Wyatt."

"Oh really? How come?" I ask Trista.

"Because I don't need to be saved by a man, damn it!" Trista harrumphs and takes a sip of her drink. "But Wyatt is so damn pushy."

"Calder too," Dakota confirms.

"Max is unreasonable!" Cozy chimes in.

"They always try to white-knight us." Trista narrows her eyes as she tosses her drink straw onto the table. "And even if you have valid reasons for going against what they want for you, they just strong-arm you until you give in."

All three women voice their tones of agreement and then look expectantly at me to join in. I hesitate with how to respond because, honestly, I fully agree with them. Luke white-knighted his way into matrimony with me, being so insistent I marry him and no one else that he learned how to be a lumberjack for me.

That's outrageous!

And sweet as hell.

If I think about it too much, I get tears in my eyes.

But admittedly, as a husband . . . he kind of rocks. "I wish I could join you ladies and tell you that Luke is a pain in my ass but I'm afraid I can't. He's just too amazing."

"Shut up," Dakota groans.

"No really, he is," I reply honestly. "And he's fun. Like last night when I showed him how to stretch and fold sourdough—"

"Is that what the kids are calling it now?" Dakota sputters out a laugh.

My cheeks flame red. "That is not what I meant. You guys know I make bread."

"Oh yeah . . . make bread." Trista begins making lewd hand gestures.

"Did his dough rise to the occasion?" Cozy waggles her eyebrows at me.

"Do you think he tried to pump-her-nickel?" Trista chirps and bursts into a fit of giggles.

"Most definitely," Dakota confirms. "And I bet he's so nice he even announces when he's going to *crumb*."

"Guys, be careful," Cozy interjects, using her firm mom voice. "Too much yeast will ruin it for everyone."

The three women burst out laughing like cackling hens and I can't help but join in. We laugh so hard, I have to wipe tears out of my eyes. "Damn, I thought the guys at the yard were disgusting but you fine ladies are putting them to shame."

"You're welcome," Dakota says with a smile.

"But the truth is," Cozy interjects, hooking her thumb over to me. "Addison has no issues with Luke yet because they're still in the honeymoon phase."

"I must admit I'm still there too a little bit," Dakota says, raising her hand. "Living with Calder is . . ." She shivers at something I do not want to unpack.

"It'll change," Trista says with a serious face. "When real-life bullshit bleeds into your happy Fletcher Mountain love bubble . . ." She sighs heavily. "It really puts a damper on things."

Dakota and Cozy both go quiet, clearly in the know about something going on with Trista that I'm not aware of.

"Everything okay?" I ask, tilting my head and watching the mood shift in Trista, who's normally so happy and upbeat.

"It's fine, I just got a call from my parents the other day and it's really rattled me."

I frown curiously. "Do you not have a good relationship with them?"

"I haven't spoken to them in years. Didn't even know where they lived."

My throat feels dry as I immediately relate to her circumstances, shocked that we have something so traumatic in common. The timing of this discussion is wild because my heart is still recovering from my emotional confession to Luke last night. Discussing my mom's final departure from my life was so not on my bingo card this week. Nor his, I'm sure. The poor guy probably just made bread with me because he felt sorry for me.

But once I started opening up, I couldn't stop. I've lived so much of my adult life wondering what would have changed if only my mom had said goodbye. If only she'd given me one final hug, maybe I wouldn't wince at the touch of other women and live with this uncertainty about what I'd be like as a mother. To know Trista can relate on any level is shocking. Confessing my past with these women, kind as they may be, will take me some time, but I can't help the words that tumble out of my mouth next.

"Can I ask you a question?" I ask, feeling like the beer is giving me a bit of liquid courage. "From everything that I can see, you're an amazing mom and you and Wyatt are perfect for each other."

"What's the question?" Trista eyes me thoughtfully.

"If you had such shitty parents, weren't you terrified of turning out just like them?"

Trista's face scrunches up in disgust. "God no. I'd never be like them because I'll never join a cult for one and—" she huffs out a shaky breath before adding "—I'd kill myself before I let my kid go hungry."

Silence descends over the table as the weight of that last statement resonates with us. Trista's eyes well with tears and I feel my own begin to blur as I stare at her. She's being so open and vulnerable.

God that must feel good.

"I almost turned out like my parents," Dakota interjects with a pensive look. "But I got out of my shitty marriage and didn't let it turn me bitter. Then I found Calder and I can just tell it's right. I'm not ready for marriage or anything, since it feels like I just got divorced. But . . . he's it for me. I can be myself with him and that's what I was missing from before."

Cozy squeezes Dakota's hand and adds with a soft smile, "I think I brought the best out in Max when we met. He needed someone to tell him it was okay to take a breath and I like being that soft space for him."

I smile through watery eyes as I look at the three amazing women standing before me, showing me everything they found in life, despite some of their circumstances. While they might have some complaints about the pushiness of their Fletcher men, I can tell deep down, they know they struck gold.

And so have I with Luke.

As a best friend.

"This is deep talk for a dive bar, you guys," Trista mumbles around a chunk of ice.

Dakota nods aggressively. "Yeah, and this is supposed to be a bachelorette party, not a group therapy session."

"Let's go somewhere we can dance," Cozy begs, her eyes flashing back and forth between all of us.

"It's like four o'clock in the afternoon," I laugh and glance at my phone to confirm the time.

Dakota grabs my hand and pulls me toward the door. "That's never stopped us before."

Chapter 21

FACT OR FICTION?
You may now kiss your wife.

Luke

It's nearing eight o'clock at night when I pull up to Sundown Saloon to find Cozy, Trista, Dakota, and my wife all sitting on the curb outside the bar eating slices of pizza. They look like crew members on one of our building sites, not women who were out shopping for a wedding dress earlier today.

I pull over and slide out of my truck, shaking my head at the sight of them. "What the hell happened to you four?" I ask, my eyes holding on Addison as she winces and continues nibbling on her pizza.

She looks cute. She's dressed in a pair of cropped black jeans, sneakers, and a fitted sweater that shows off her sculpted arms. Her dark hair is tousled over her shoulders like she's been dancing and she wears a smile that seems genuine. That's a good sign after spending the day with my mother.

"Luke!" my sister-in-law squeals around a mouthful of pepperoni. "Luke is here, you guys!" Cozy's face falls. "But you're not my husband. My husband is coming to get me."

"Your husband has been waiting for you for the past fifteen minutes." Max drawls from across the street.

I jerk my head to see my oldest brother standing there, leaning against his vehicle.

"Max is here!" Cozy cheers like this is new information.

"You already knew that," Dakota drawls, hitting her friend

on the arm. "He called to say he was outside and you said you needed five more minutes."

"Oh no, that was a long time ago." Cozy's eyes are wide with horror as she struggles to get up off the curb. I make a move to help but Max beats me to it, jogging across the street to assist his wife. She cringes up at him. "That was before we got pizza. I'm sorry, honey."

Max sighs and shakes his head. "Are you ready now, sugar tits? Ethan is in the car playing *Roblox* and you know how he gets if he plays video games after nine."

"My kid can't see me like this." Cozy groans and presses her head into Max's chest. "I'm a bad mom."

"No you're not." He chuckles and shoots me a pleading look. I just hold my hands up, having no clue how to help him with his situation.

"Can I bring this in the car?" she asks, looking at her half-eaten slice of pizza.

"Whatever you want." Cozy turns on her heel and runs away from her husband to hug all the ladies goodbye, holding extra tight to Addison. "Luke! I love your wife."

"Yeah?"

"I love you too, Cozy."

Addison giggles in her arms before Cozy squeals loudly, "She said yes to the dress!"

I give Max a "better you than me, sucker" look as he finally gets Cozy into the car, and they take off back to their house.

"Hey, Luke?" Addison's voice is coy as she stands up, walking over to me with a strut to her step.

"Yes, babe?" I reply, trying my hardest not to eye-fuck the shit out of her, but I'm having a hard time because I like seeing her so relaxed and happy like this.

She glances over her shoulder and says, "Me and Dakota and Trista want to ride in the bed of the truck home."

My face falls. "No fucking way."

"Come on," she says, tossing her pizza in the nearby trash can as she walks to the back of the truck to open the tailgate. She begins hoisting herself into the back end and says, "It's not that cold out tonight and it'll be so fun."

"No, it won't because you're not doing it," I say firmly as I wrap my arms around her waist and pull her down from the bed. She fights me a little and the way her ass rubs against my groin is making me seriously uncomfortable.

"Luke!" she huffs, propping her hands on her hips to glower at me.

"Yeah, come on, Luke," I hear Trista whine as well from her place on the curb with her pizza.

"Please?" Addison sticks her lower lip out at me and I swear I'd do anything for her when she looks at me with those hazel round eyes and those lush pouty lips.

I sigh heavily. "I'll go around the block one time."

"Woo-hoo!" She jumps into my arms, yanking me down to her level for a hug.

She yells for the other ladies to join her and the two of them amble themselves up off the curb and scurry over to the back of the truck.

I help all three of them into the bed, rolling my eyes at the ridiculousness of them sitting side by side, legs stretched out like they're going on some sort of amusement ride instead of a quick drive in the back of my truck.

I point a finger at my wife. "I'm not going over fifteen miles an hour."

She purses her lips and nods. "Got it, Grandpa."

Trista and Dakota are both passed out in my back seat as I pull up in front of Wyatt's cabin to drop Trista off first. Addison laughs at the sight of my brother carrying Trista into his cabin and Trista waking up to groan, "My boobs hurt. I need to pump."

Wyatt chuckles and looks down at his wife. "I can definitely help you with that, Lucky."

My nose wrinkles as I drive up the lane a little farther to Calder, who's standing on his front porch waiting for his delivery.

"Was my woman well-behaved today?" he asks Addison as he opens the back door and unbuckles a passed-out Dakota.

"Not at all."

"That's how I like her," he gruffs before picking her up and hip checking the door to shut it behind him. "Thanks for bringing her back home."

"No problem." I offer him a wave and pull ahead to my own cabin, slanting a sideways look to the woman seated beside me. "That's a first for both of them, I'll have you know."

"What? Them getting drunk?" Addison eyes me skeptically. "That's not true. I saw them in Mexico."

"You must bring it out of them." I wink playfully.

"It was their idea to go barhopping, I'll have you know. And I'm not even drunk. They're just lightweights."

"Oh please," I state, rolling my eyes as I park my vehicle and rush over to get Addison's door.

"I'm not!" she argues as we make our way into the house. She pauses on the porch and glances to the corner of the deck where Rufus is sleeping. "Does this guy have a snooze button for Sundays?"

"I'm afraid not."

She makes a little noise as she follows me inside, kicking off her shoes and clutching a white bag in her hands as she walks down the hall to her room. She reemerges from her bedroom, stopping me in my tracks in the hallway. "I can't believe you think I'm drunk."

"Why else would you want to ride in the bed of my truck?" I ask, propping myself on the wall.

She shrugs. "Sounded good at the time."

I yank at the bill of my hat, eyeing her skeptically as she pads into the bathroom, leaving the door open as she brushes her teeth.

I lean on the doorway and ask, "So what was in the bag? I can't imagine a wedding dress fits in there."

"Definitely not the wedding dress," she murmurs around her toothbrush before stopping to spit into the sink. She glances at me in the mirror, looking shy for maybe the first time in her entire life. "It's for the wedding night."

My brows lift but she avoids my reaction as she resumes brushing her teeth, bending over the sink to rinse her mouth out.

When she stands back up and wipes the foam off her lips, I watch her carefully as I ask, "Did you buy lingerie, Roe?"

"I didn't buy it," she tuts defensively, her cheeks flaming red as she turns to face me. "It was a gift from our lovely neighbors."

"How thoughtful of them," I murmur, my body humming to life with just the idea of Addison wearing something sexy. Sexy isn't really her style. Don't get me wrong, she always looks sexy, but she doesn't dress sexy.

However, I get hard seeing her in her basic oversize T-shirts she wears to bed, so I fear my bar is pretty low when it comes to this woman.

Addison rolls her eyes at the expression on my face as we both make our way down the hall, lingering outside of each other's prospective rooms. "Obviously they don't know that we've only ever just kissed."

"We haven't kissed," I reply with a self-deprecating huff.

Her jaw drops and she turns on her heel to look at me with righteous indignation. "The hell we didn't!"

"When did we kiss?"

"On our wedding day, you asshole," she snaps, whacking me in the chest before crossing her arms to glower up at me. "How could you forget?"

I roll my eyes. "That doesn't count as a kiss."

"Why not?" The lines between Addison's brows deepen as she chews her lip.

I grip the bill of my hat, pulling it down as I step closer to her. Her back flattens against the wall as I lower my voice and say, "Because it wasn't intentional."

"Oh, so you would have done something different?"

"Hell yes I would have."

"Like what?"

"Trust me, Addison Monroe, when I kiss you with intention, you'll know it."

Her eyes flash with something resembling the look she gave me last night when she was trying to show me how to make her fucking bread. If I didn't know any better, I'd say she wants me to kiss her.

Imagine that.

She inhales a shaky breath as her tongue slides across her ruddy lips. I watch her collarbone as her chest rises and falls, her breaths coming out more labored than before.

Her throat moves as she swallows and her voice is a whisper when she says, "So do it."

My eyes lift to hers. Pupils dilated. Lips parted. Cheeks flushed. I shake my head slowly from side to side, my body screaming at me for my reply. "No way, you've been drinking."

"I'm not drunk," she snaps, arousal being changed to rage as she eyes me with a defiant look. "I have the tolerance of a lumberyard worker."

"You sure about that?" I take a step back and rake my eyes over her whole body. "Hold your hands out to your sides."

A cute smile spreads across her face as she does what I say.

"Touch your nose with your right hand."

She moves her left hand and then quickly shakes her head as she moves her right, giggling when she realizes she almost fucked up the first exercise.

I purse my lips and glare at her. "Stand on one foot."

She does, quirking a brow at me and waiting for the next command.

"Now hop three times."

She hops three times, stumbling only slightly.

"Now say the alphabet backward."

Her face falls. "I couldn't do that drunk or sober!"

"Okay, fine, you're not drunk," I lament with a smile that I can feel all the way down to my toes.

"So . . ." she starts, her eyes glittering with teasing mirth as she bites her lip and looks up at me. "Show me what a real kiss from Luke Fletcher feels like, then. Better I find out now than on our wedding day in front of all our friends and family."

I hum a noise of discontent because that's exactly what I am. I am discontented at the idea of kissing her, because if I kiss her the way I want to kiss her, I won't want to stop.

But if I act like a good boy, like her friend, like the respectable man my mother raised me to be and walk into my room without tasting her lips when I had the chance . . .

I will regret it for the rest of my life.

"You want me to kiss you, Addison?" My voice is strained and husky, revealing just how badly I want this.

She closes her eyes, letting my words wash over her. A shiver trembles through her body before she blinks up at me and answers, "Yes."

Exhaling sharply, I grab the bill of my hat, turning it around so the brim is no longer in my way when I do what I've been wanting to do for the better part of our friendship.

In one fluid motion, I close the distance between us, backing her up as I press my arm against the wall above her head, caging her in.

All humor drains from her face as she looks at me like she's never seen me before. Her minty breath is labored as her eyes score my lips, anticipation heady as my other hand finds her waist, my fingers twitching along the inch of her hot skin exposed between the bottom of her sweater and her jeans.

This is it. I'm finally going to kiss my best friend.

My jaw aches with restraint as I whisper against her lips, "This is how our first kiss should have gone."

She inhales sharply as I crush my mouth to hers, her whole body tensing and then relaxing beneath me as I take in her essence like a starved fucking animal.

Her fingers dig into my sides as I spread her lips apart with my tongue, sweeping in to claim the inside of her. I want to taste her, consume her, savor her in every way possible. Leave no stone unturned in case this is the only time she'll ever let me do this. I've thought of this moment way too many times to hold back now.

She whimpers as her hands move to my back, pulling me in as her tongue plays with mine.

Fuck yes, she wants this just as much as I do.

She arches into me and I thrust my tongue deep in her mouth, my cock aching as it thickens inside my jeans. I marvel at the sensation of her soft pillowy lips gliding against mine, catching on my mustache in a way that lights my fucking skin on fire.

My mind reels with the reality of what's happening. I'm kissing my best friend. I've finally crossed that forbidden bridge I wasn't supposed to cross, and now that I'm here, my mind begs for more. I imagine her naked in my bed just ten feet away, my scent all over her, but instead of my tongue in her mouth it's my cock in her cunt and my name on her lips as she cries out her orgasm.

My kiss grows frenzied and erratic with my wandering thoughts, so I pull away to nip down her jaw, my tongue sliding against her throat, tasting the scent of her and burning it into memory.

"Luke," she cries out my name like she's making my dirty thoughts come to life. The tone of her voice has me digging in harder on her neck, sucking and biting her flesh, moving to the other side next, desperate to consume her whole fucking being.

I suddenly understand the psyche of vampires.

The urge to devour something so delectable, so tempting, so innocent and soft and hard in all the right places is a fucking head trip. I want every single part of her to be mine.

She moves her hand to my chin, forcing my head back up to her face. Her hooded eyes stare desperately at my lips, so I take my sexual deviance out on her mouth again, her tongue equally as feverish as mine.

We kiss like our lives depend on it. Like we both are aware of what we've been missing out on, day after day, night after night in all the years we've been friends. To have had something that feels this good right at our fingertips all this time and not have given in is an exercise in saintlike restraint.

When we finally come apart for air, I press my forehead to hers, refusing to let even an inch of space come between us, savoring the aftershocks of this reality, inhaling in her scent, her breaths, her heart and her soul.

My cock thumps against her heat, letting her know exactly what this kiss did to me.

All of me.

She's fucking perfect.

She's my wife.

And I want nothing more than to fuck her up against this wall right here and right now.

But irritating reality pinpricks my mind, and I realize that if I want this to be more . . . I need to take this slow. She's not here with me yet, but I can see glimmers of her getting there. And I know that if I push her too hard and too fast, she's going to run.

This is a marathon, not a sprint. My feelings have been alive and well for a while now, but this is all new to Roe. She isn't there yet and I need to give her time because *fuck* do I want her to be here with me.

I pull back, my cock weeping against my zipper as I stare at her slackened body shoved up against the wall like my own personal plaything.

"What are you doing?" she asks, out of breath.

I swallow the knot in my throat. "I gave you my first kiss . . . and now I'm going to bed."

"You're what?" she gasps, her lips and neck raw from my whiskers. God I love that look on her.

I lick my lips and point to her door. "You should be a good girl and go to bed too."

She huffs out a weak laugh, her brows pinched in confusion. "What if I don't want to be a good girl?"

I close my eyes and shake my head. "Go to bed, Addison."

She stares at me for a long, heavy moment. I don't often use her first name with her, so she knows I mean business and she doesn't seem to like it. Shoving a hand through her hair, she pries herself off the wall and turns unsteadily, gripping her doorframe for a moment before peering back over her shoulder at me.

"Good night, husband." She stares back at me, daring me to

come after her. Daring me to change my mind and eliminate the space between us and take her in her fucking bed.

But I am the patron saint of idiots, so I stay exactly where I am. "Good night, wife."

With a soft sigh, she closes the door and disappears from my sight, and I thump my head back against the wall behind me, hating myself more than I ever have in my entire life.

Chapter 22

FACT OR FICTION?
My vibrator is judging me.

Addison

"*Luke*," I whisper-sigh into my pillow as I hover over top of my vibrator and thrust into it, wishing it was a dildo for the first time in my life.

Normally, I'm a clitoral stimulation girlie through and through, so vibrators are my jam. But right now, all I want is to feel Luke Fletcher inside of me, hard and punishing as he rocks into me over and over as he grips my neck and calls me a good girl for taking his big, aching cock so deep.

"Luke, don't stop," I squeak quietly into the softness of my pillow as I feel another orgasm crest. It's wild how just saying his name out loud makes me even hornier. "Luke, I'm going to—"

I gasp when my vibrator cuts out and I ram it against my flesh in the hope it'll somehow be revived by my impending orgasm. Unfortunately, my climax isn't some sort of mythical power source, so I pull it out from under me to confirm what I fear.

It's completely dead.

With a frustrated growl, I toss it onto my nightstand and wince when it bounces against the lamp and drops to the floor, sending an ear-piercing crack echoing through the room.

"Shit." I lean over the bed, my hair dusting the floor as I scoop up the loose batteries. I attempt to slide them back in, but notice the back is cracked and now the damn thing won't stay closed.

"Motherfucker," I growl again, chucking the whole damn thing at the wall in frustration, only for it to break into even more pieces all over the floor.

I flop back and cover my face in shame. "Breaking vibrators? You are embarrassing yourself, Addison May Monroe." I roll over onto my stomach, burying myself in my pillow.

I've lost track of how many times I've used that godforsaken thing in the past eight hours. It was at least three times throughout the night. And another three times this morning.

And the sun has barely risen.

I swear even Rufus was judging me because he crowed longer today than he usually does, and I think it's because he knew what I was doing in here like a wanton little hussy.

Ugh. I'm gross.

But no matter how many orgasms I have, I can't scratch the itch. The ache. I can't find the spot that gives me the release I need to feel like I can breathe normally again.

If only I could stop replaying that kiss. Where the hell has that Luke Fletcher been hiding all these years? All this time he could kiss like that and just . . . didn't?

I suppose he did. He kissed other girls. Girls that were not me. Girls whose faces I want to fucking claw at just the notion of him giving them what he just gave me. Looking at them the way he looked at me. Fuck those fucking bitches.

But this is nonsensical. I can't be jealous of Luke's past. I can't lay claim to Luke any further than I already have. I've already asked him to marry me and give up a year of his life for Chrissake.

Now I'm considering the idea of letting him kiss me anywhere he wants.

My thighs squeeze together as an image of Luke's face between my legs plays for the twentieth time in the past eight hours. I roll my hips into my mattress, thrusting my aching clit into the bed as I imagine my fingers slicing through Luke's shaggy locks, squeezing at the roots. Riding his face bareback like he's my own personal stallion.

Jesus fucking Christ, I'm doomed.

And sleep? Forget about it. I'm used to rarely sleeping but last night was bad even for me. I maybe dozed for an hour?

I would have got up to make bread to do something more productive than overuse my broken-ass vibrator, but I was too terrified of running into Luke. How am I going to look him in the eye after knowing I defiled myself all night long picturing him. My friend.

My best friend.

But he's also my husband, which is what I told myself over and over again when I came. And came. And came. There are worse things to do than masturbate to your husband, right?

Only, I shouldn't keep thinking of Luke as my husband. He's my roommate. You can't take advantage of your roommate just because he makes you extremely horny, right? Not to mention he's already giving me so much by guaranteeing my future with the lumberyard.

I have to get control of myself.

I groan into my pillow as my bladder screams for relief. I'm embarrassed to admit that I considered peeing in my trash can just to avoid him. But that's ridiculous. And disgusting. I have to be an adult about this.

I stare at myself in the mirror, swiping half-heartedly at my smeared makeup. "Go pee, Addison. You can handle yourself in front of Luke. Just march out there and if you see him, act like nothing happened. Because obviously if Luke had feelings for you, like real feelings, he would have told you years ago. That's why he stopped the kiss last night. He doesn't like you like that.

"Not to mention you don't like him like that either! You aren't a relationship girlie. You aren't a marriage or babies girlie.

You are a lumberyard-owning badass who knows her emotional limits and you're not about to ruin the relationship you have with your best friend just to get your fucking rocks off on his cute little mustache."

Steeling myself, I take a deep breath in and swing my door open, ready to seize the day. When I step out to a quiet cabin, I can't help but look around, wondering where he is.

Still sleeping maybe. He is a normal human who sleeps normal hours. Of course he's asleep. It's not even seven in the morning on a Sunday. He's getting some well-earned rest.

So, I pad across the hardwood floor, my heart racing until I close myself into my bathroom and drop down onto the toilet to take care of business. I rake a hand through my hair and exhale heavily. "One week of marriage down, only fifty-one more to go."

How many new vibrators I'm going to need to get through that many weeks is TBD.

Chapter 23

FACT OR FICTION?
Babies are good husband blockers.

Addison

"Here, can you hold her for a second?" Trista asks, thrusting Stevie into my arms while I sit at Wyatt and Trista's dining room table on Thanksgiving Day. "Jo . . . can you come check the turkey with me? I don't know what the hell I'm doing."

"On my way!" Jo says, rushing into the kitchen from the living room where she was watching football with her sons.

"I can check the turkey," I call out, holding the baby awkwardly in my hands, but I'm completely ignored.

It's been three weeks of living on Fletcher Mountain, and this is the first time I've held Stevie. I've been doing the kind of nose-to-the-grind work-mode thing the past couple of weeks and haven't really seen the ladies much since our dress fitting night out. Admittedly, I've been avoiding them and my husband because things just sort of started to feel way too real, way too fast.

But now I'm plunked right in the middle of a Fletcher family holiday and since my dad is still in Florida, I didn't really have any good excuse to avoid everyone.

I shoot a pleading look over to Dakota, who's sitting across from me at the table. "Do I look weird? I'm not sure I'm great with babies."

"You look great. Trust me, I'm not a baby person either but this baby is like freakishly easy." Dakota smiles and grips her glass of white wine.

Stevie nuzzles into my chest as she sucks on her pacifier, so I sit back, letting her get comfortable in my arms. I look down at her and can't help but smile. This isn't so bad. "Will she walk soon? Trista said she'll be one at Christmas, right? When do babies usually walk?"

"The grown-ups in this family have to put her down long enough to figure it out I suppose," Dakota says with a knowing look to the men in the living room.

I laugh as I recall when we got here earlier, and the four Fletcher brothers all took turns passing Stevie around. And then literally all four of them stood around Ethan when he wanted a turn holding her. This little girl wants for nothing, that's for sure.

Dakota eyes me thoughtfully. "You're a natural."

My cheeks flush as I shake my head.

"I shouldn't have said that." Dakota holds her hands up. "I hate when a couple gets married, and people just assume you're having babies. Not everyone has to have babies to be happy in a relationship. I could see me and Calder just getting more cats."

"Yeah? You're a cat lover too?" I ask as I smile over at Calder. His tattooed, bearded, and rugged appearance is at complete odds with the man I see out for a walk with his tuxedo cat strapped to his chest.

"I mean, I don't know if I need to strap them to my chest . . . but yeah, I love cats."

I absorb her words, feeling mildly comforted by her confident thoughts behind children. There is just something so decent about this family. They're traditional and not. It feels . . . safe. Inclusive. Which is extraordinary in so many ways.

Dakota eyes me thoughtfully. "What about you? Kids, cats, or dogs? What's your poison?"

I lick my lips and shrug. "I'm not really sure, I guess. Is that bad?"

"God no," she replies with a flick of her wrist. "You have

time. My first born will always be my T-shirt Shop. I'm sure yours is your lumberyard. I get it. Running a company takes a lot of bandwidth, not much room for anything else."

"Yeah, that's so true," I confirm and squint my eyes as I glance down at Stevie, who's nuzzled into my arms now and doing long, slow blinks like she's just about to fall asleep. Her little mouth moves as she sucks on her pacifier.

Dakota lifts her empty wineglass and grabs mine at the same time. "But for now . . . more wine."

She heads into the kitchen to grab a new bottle, and I take a moment to gaze at the baby in my arms. A warmth spreads through me when her little hand moves up to rest on my chest. Her fingers clenched into a tiny little fist. I just want to nibble her fingers ever so gently. She stirs in my arms, fussing for just a second so I shush her and rock her and just like that . . . she's out again.

The sense of accomplishment I feel with that tiny act is overwhelming.

I look up, my eyes instantly finding Luke's across the room. He's staring back at me, so I smile and glance down at her and back to him. I want him to see what I've done. I want him to be proud of me for . . . doing this tiny little thing with this tiny little human.

Luke's expression turns pensive and full of something I can't quite decipher. It's the same one he's been giving me for the past two weeks. The same one I'm avoiding for fear of what I might do. If there wasn't a baby in my arms right now, I might just have to stand up and walk across the room to kiss the man I married. Hormones are fucking weird like that.

"Looking forward to tomorrow, sweetie?" Jo's voice rips me out of my inner musings.

"Huh?" I murmur, glancing down at Stevie and then back to Luke.

"The cake tasting," Jo says, finally pulling my attention away from her son. "It's at 11 a.m. sharp, don't forget."

I blow out a soft breath, trying to straighten my brain out a bit as I nod. "Oh yes, of course. I'll be there."

"Need me to take her?" Jo holds her hands out to Stevie but like a reflex, I pull her closer into me.

"I better keep hold of her," I murmur into her soft hair.

"Okay, dear." She hits me with a curious look before walking away.

I look down at Stevie's long lashes fanning her cheeks and try to count them to refocus my brain. At least if I'm holding this baby, I'm not trying anything with my husband, who really needs to stop looking at me like that.

The family buzzes around me as they set the table and get all the food laid out. I'm off the hook for helping as my arms are otherwise occupied, but I can't help but marvel over the chaotic team effort of everyone. Luke and Calder bicker over how to line up the silverware and Jo comes over and shows them the correct way to do it. Wyatt eats almost as much turkey as he cuts, sneaking some to Ethan, and Cozy snaps at both of them to wait to eat until everything is ready, with Max backing her up. It's sweet, really. Everyone has their place.

Dad never did much for the holidays. Thanksgiving was more about drinking and watching football, and Christmas just felt like another day of the week. I'll never forget the first Christmas we had after the accident when it was just me and him. It was the first year that there were no stockings and no visit from Santa on Christmas morning. Of course I hadn't believed in Santa, but the realization that Aaron still did before he died . . .

"What's this?" Ethan says, carrying the brown paper bag that I tucked my fresh sourdough loaf in this morning.

"Oh . . . that's my bread that I brought to go with the meal. Thanks for bringing it over."

Ethan's nose wrinkles.

"Do you have a problem with bread?" I ask, arching a brow at him as I shift Stevie in my arms.

He shrugs. "It's boring."

"Not my bread."

He eyes me skeptically. "What's so cool about your bread?"

"Why don't you get it out and see?" I smile as I watch him fumble with the bag and reach in to pull out my masterpiece that I hid from Luke this morning for this exact moment.

"It's a turkey!" Ethan squeals and everyone stops what they're doing to come over and see what all the fuss is about.

"Did you make that, Addison?" Jo gasps as she looks at the loaf that I made to resemble the shape of a cooked turkey. It has a rounded body, two wings and the appearance of two legs tucked underneath. I scored the loaf to give it a seasonal look along with a string wrapped around the two legs holding a sprig of rosemary as garnish.

"That is incredible," Max says, resting his hand on Ethan's shoulders. "Edible art, Ethan."

"Can we really eat it?" Ethan asks.

"Definitely! I have homemade tomato basil butter to go with it in the fridge."

"Yuck," Ethan exclaims and everyone laughs.

Trista sets the bread on a platter and places it in the center of the table with pride and I can't help but notice Ethan hurrying over to a seat right next to my loaf. A flash of my little brother causes my eyes to sting all over again and when I look away, I find Luke watching me thoughtfully.

"You good?" he asks, his eyes soft and tender, making that knot in my throat even bigger.

I nod and dip my head down to inhale the scent of the baby in my arms and the food around the table. "Yeah, Luke. I'm good." Maybe better than I have been in a long time.

Chapter 24

FACT OR FICTION?
Moist isn't always a gross word.

Luke

Cake tasting with your wife and mother sounds like a fairly innocent experience on the surface. Sitting in a cute little bakery in downtown Boulder. Light snow falling outside the picture window. Your mom prattling on and on about each cake's consistency, frosting texture, and the "moistness."

I always thought the word *moist* was disgusting, but hell if it isn't eliciting some indecent thoughts in me today. Was my wife moist the night we kissed? Is there a chance she could be moist now? How many times has she been moist since we locked lips? Am I a fucked-up deviant for contemplating these thoughts with my mother seated right beside me?

The answer is yes.

But fucking hell, I can't help it. Every time I watch Roe's lips wrap around the metal tongs of the fork, her tongue darting out to lick a dollop of frosting off the edge of her mouth and the way her cheeks flush when we make eye contact . . . *I realize that moist cake tasting might be the most erotic thing I've ever done.*

The past two weeks have been a mind fuck. Kissing my wife was quite possibly the worst and best thing I could have ever done. Best because it was life-changing. It confirmed everything I thought to be true about my best friend. We fucking work. The chemistry is there. The physical oneness is next level. The desire is goddamn mind-blowing.

However, it's the worst because we went from comfortable,

fun-loving friends who have dinner together every night to two ships passing in the night.

Roe is avoiding me and I'm in hell.

And the most frustrating part is she's not obviously avoiding me. She's doing that annoying customer service thing she does where she speaks to me like I'm a client instead of her best friend.

Her husband.

She still shoots me a text before she goes for a run in the trails behind our cabins. She still makes dinner and does all the normal things she did our first week together, but now she chooses to eat in her room without giving me any reason why. Just mentions it like it's totally normal for her to not eat with me, which fucking kills me. It feels like a form of rejection, like the kiss was bad or what I said to her afterward was too far.

Why did I have to call her a fucking good girl?

Because my penis had clearly taken over my fucking brain.

Roe isn't a woman who can be told what to do. She isn't a woman who takes orders. She's a woman who gets things done. Like finding a guy to marry her for a year so she can take over the family business. That's the kind of determined badass she is. And that's why she's here. That's the only reason she's here.

And I know Everly's big mastermind plan was to get my wife to fall in love with me, but that's going to be really hard when I can't even figure out how to get my wife to spend time with me.

"Which one is your favorite, Addison?" my mom asks from her seat plunked right between the two of us. She's got her binder spread out in front of her and has been taking notes through this entire tasting.

Addison yanks her eyes away from me and gives my mom her full attention. "I'm going to level with you, Jo. I love them all."

My mom laughs and I notice Roe's tense mood lightening just slightly. "You and me both. Gosh they don't make it easy, do they?" She makes a note and then pulls her pen to her mouth. "What do we think about cupcakes? The baker said most of these cakes can be made into cupcakes so we can do a variety that way."

"I love the cupcake idea." Roe smiles warmly, her hazel eyes striking against her silky black hair that's tied into a braid down one shoulder. My fingers itch to feel the nubs of that braid, to drag my coarse thumb over the strands, twist it around my fist and give it a little tug until she gasps in shock and submits to me. What I wouldn't do to see my powerful, irritating wife on her knees, naked, panting, and taking orders from me for once.

"Luke!" My mom's voice is loud, and I jerk my head to look at her, and the irritation on her face is obvious. "I asked what do you think of cupcakes?"

"Um . . . sure . . . whatever Roe wants." I frown and stare down at the cake sitting on my fork, my face hot with shame over where my thoughts were going right in front of my mother.

When I look up, Roe's eyes are tight on me, and I swear it's like she can read my fucking mind.

I have to get control of this situation.

After saying goodbye to my mother outside the bakery, Roe turns to head to her car and I follow, my heart hammering in my chest as I approach her from behind. "Hey, can we talk for a second?" I ask, falling into stride with her as her boots crunch over the snow-packed sidewalk.

"Sure, what's up?" she chirps in that irritating singsongy voice that she's been using.

"Are we okay?" I ask, pulling my hat off and facing it forward.

"Of course, why wouldn't we be?" She laughs and it grates on my nerves.

"Don't do that."

"Don't do what?" she chimes back, picking up pace.

"You know what." I stop walking and she keeps going until she realizes I'm not beside her and pivots to turn around and look at me.

We're silent for a few seconds before I lift my hands up. "I miss you, Roe."

Her brows furrow. "What do you mean?"

"I just . . ." I exhale heavily and grip the back of my neck. "I miss you. Things have been weird since I kissed you and I hate to think I fucked this all up for us."

"Things haven't been weird. I've just been busy! Things at the yard are crazy and my dad is coming back next week and has some meetings set up that I don't know anything about. It's just a lot. It's not you."

The polite smile on her face gives me a pit in my stomach. She has this fucking wall up that I hate. She usually never has this with me. I see her have it with her dad, with the guys at the yard, with my mother.

Never me.

I narrow my eyes and eliminate the space between us. "If we're good, then can we hang tonight?"

She shrugs her shoulders and says, "What do you mean, Luke? We live together."

"I know but can we just not do the thing where we both come home, eat by ourselves, and then hide out in our bedrooms?"

"That's not what—"

"Cut the shit, Roe. I miss my best friend."

Her cheeks flush and finally I see a glimpse of my old friend poking through the hard outer shell. Her throat contracts before she says with a sigh, "I miss you too."

"So let's hang out tonight. Watch a movie," I state firmly, tilting my head down to catch her downcast eyes. "I *promise* I won't kiss you."

Her cheeks flush and when she looks up at me, I swear I see disappointment flicker across her face. But she nods and says, "Okay, sure. Let's hang tonight."

"Good." I exhale a sigh of relief. "I'll bring home takeout. Any requests?"

She shakes her head. "Surprise me."

"You got it, babe." I make a move to brush her cheeks with my lips, but then think better of it. So, I step back and offer her a sideways smile instead. "See you tonight."

I turn on my heel as her voice calls back, "See you later, husband."

And that one word sends a flutter of need through my entire fucking body. Either she really is clueless about how I feel about her, or she knows exactly what she's doing.

"Ew, I can't handle the feel of his beak!" Roe squeals, dropping the walnuts out of her hand and back into a small glass bowl.

"I know," I reply with a laugh as I rejoin her on the sofa. "It's why I never hand-feed him. That sensation freaks me out too much."

"Like tiny little pinches," Roe confirms as she slides her hand down Rufus's back. He's standing on her lap as she sits on the couch. Our leftover sushi is on the coffee table, and we've been barely watching *Yellowstone* for almost two hours because we can't seem to stop talking long enough to listen.

It's been nice. Like the old days. The awkwardness from before seems well and truly gone, and I feel like I got my best friend back.

Roe yawns and stretches, the hem of her shirt riding up to reveal her soft stomach, which I would really like to touch like I did when we were kissing two weeks ago. She looks so good tonight in her baggy T-shirt and tiny shorts, her muscular legs hidden under the blanket that Rufus is now nuzzled into. If it were up to me, I would put that damn bird outside and get under that blanket with her.

But that's not what tonight is. We're not kissing. We're not touching. We're just . . . being friends.

Rufus jumps down off Addison's lap, which usually means he needs to go to the bathroom, so I pick him up and set him out front for the night.

When I walk back into the living room, I glance at the clock, surprised how late it is already. "I didn't realize what time it was. Do you want to go to bed yet?"

I pause when I realize how that sounded. It sounded like a husband asking his wife if she's ready for bed. It sounded like we'd go to the same room and sleep together. God, would I love that. I'd even love to just stay on this couch all night with her if it meant I got to remain near her, breathing in her sweet familiar scent.

She shrugs. "You can crash if you want. I'm good here."

I drop down on the sofa next to her again. "I've noticed your late-night bread baking is next level these past couple weeks."

She glances at the fresh loaves sitting on the counter all bagged and ready to go. "Well, since I got the new bread pan from the yard guys, I've been trying to get a fresh loaf to all of them as a thank-you for the gift. I'm just about done."

"That was really cool of them to give that to you," I reply, stretching my denim-clad legs out, and stare at the crackling fire. "They all must love you."

"Yeah, I guess, but I'm glad we got your mom to put 'no gifts please' on our wedding invitations. I feel super guilty accepting that pan from them considering this is all temporary."

I wince and look away, trying to hide the sting from that sentence and then go back to what she mentioned earlier. "Have you ever seen a doctor for your insomnia?" I ask, noting that some days the dark circles under her eyes are more obvious than others.

"Yes," she groans back and turns on her side to lay her head on the back of the sofa. "And I have meds that can help me sleep, but they make me feel awful the next day, so I try to only take them when I'm desperate."

"What happens exactly when you try to go to sleep?" I stretch my arm out behind her, my fingers itching to push the loose strand of hair off her cheek.

"My mind won't shut off." She turns to face me, crossing her legs under the blanket. "My body is tired but my head races with things I need to do or conversations I've had with people that embarrass me. I worry about the future and the past . . . especially the past."

"Like stuff about your brother?" I ask, my brows furrowed as I watch her body for cues that I'm going too far.

She nods woodenly. "It happened so many years ago, but I still can't stop remembering that jarring feeling of being woken up by my dad to say we have to go to the hospital because Mom and Aaron were in a car accident. It's like my body is constantly on edge, waiting for an emergency, which makes it impossible for me to fall sleep."

My jaw tightens as a similar memory floods my mind. "After my dad died, I couldn't stop counting the chest compressions I did on him every time I tried to go to sleep. One, two, three, four . . ."

Addison's head snaps to meet my eyes, her face full of shock and horror.

"Fuck, I'm sorry, I shouldn't have said that." I pull my arm out from behind her, shaking my head with irritation for even saying that out loud. She literally can't sleep because of her past trauma, and I just dumped my own on top of hers.

"No, please," she says, scooting closer to me and placing her hand on my leg. Her eyes are grave on mine. "I want to hear about this, Luke. I've wanted to ask about your dad for a long time but never felt like I had the right to after . . ."

After you barely responded to my texts when I told you he died.

After you didn't even show up for the funeral.

After your name wasn't even signed on a bouquet of flowers from the lumberyard that your dad's office assistant probably ordered.

Her not being there for me was cold and detached and hurt more than I've ever told her. And I never told her because I'm weak . . . and . . .

I love her.

You can forgive a lot when you love someone.

She swallows nervously, her entire body tense as she sits criss-cross, giving me her full attention. "What happened exactly? Can you tell me about it?"

I inhale a deep breath. I haven't spoken about this in the three years since we lost him. It's not exactly a fond memory to relive and I find that talking about it just resets my grief.

But looking at Addison, my best friend, my wife . . . I feel like I need her to know this part of me. I need the woman I'm in love with to know the hurt that I've endured in order for her to see me. All of me. And even then, she still may not want me or love me back.

I swallow the knot in my throat and close my eyes. "We were here on Fletcher Mountain . . . just me and Dad. He was helping me adjust my cabin's solar panels because a storm had screwed up their alignment. I ran to go get a tool from his truck, only to come back and find him collapsed—his lips already blue."

Addison inhales sharply, pressing her hand to her mouth. "Oh my God, Luke."

I wrinkle my nose and avoid eye contact with her. The look on her face too much for me to manage with all of the emotions swirling in me. "Being a volunteer firefighter for Jamestown prepared me medically for that situation. I knew CPR, so I got to work on him.

"But nothing prepared me for the emotional mind fuck that played through my head when I had to . . ." my voice cracks as the sensation roils through my body ". . . feel my own father's sternum break under my hands." I hold my hands up, looking at them like they're fucking monsters. Breaking a sternum during CPR is normal, but breaking my own father's? I am a fucking monster.

"And the part I've never told anyone because I'm so ashamed and disappointed in myself, is the unexpected gag reflex that happened to me when I had to blow air into his mouth. It's so fucked . . ."

I drop my elbows to my knees and bow my head, feeling the horror of that day all over me again. Like it was yesterday. CPR is not something anyone should have to do to their own father. It's why hospitals don't let doctors operate on family. It's not right to see a family member like that. It's fucking haunting.

"Oh, Luke," Addison croaks and I look up to see her eyes filled with tears, streams falling down her cheeks with every blink. "I'm so sorry."

"Yeah, me too," I grind out, my own eyes welling as the pain on her face matches the pain in my soul. "Especially because it was all for nothing. I tried to resuscitate him for eleven minutes and when he showed no signs of improvement, I made the decision to carry him to my truck and rush him to the hospital in Boulder. In my mind, I thought an ambulance would have taken way too long to get up the mountain and this was the smarter choice."

A flash of him slumped in my back seat hits me all over again. The man weighed more than me by at least twenty pounds, but I don't remember him feeling heavy. I was consumed with adrenaline. Panicked to be on this mountain alone with my dad, who was literally dying right in front of me.

"He was pronounced dead soon after they admitted him. Just like that."

Addison huffs out a noise of discontent. Her whole body curled up into a ball as she watches me through the tears in her eyes. "You did everything you could."

"I guess," I huff, yanking my hat off and tossing it on the coffee table. I run a hand through my hair, ruffling it off my head a bit. "But it took months for me to stop questioning every decision I made. Months for me to stop counting myself to sleep. It crushed my whole family obviously, but no one bore the burden of the memories I had. I was alone in that."

And I couldn't talk about it with any of them. With anyone.

Everyone was in shock.

Everyone was grieving.

Everyone was rallying around Mom, trying to comfort her in any way she needed. And I was so fucking alone.

Day after day.

Night after night.

And my best friend was nowhere to be seen.

I inhale deeply, staring at the embers sizzling in the hearth, hating that I have the memory of my dad's face in death. Slackened jaw, discolored lips. I don't want that memory. I want to remember him alive and well and yelling at me and my brothers to get our shit together.

"I always thought a heart attack would be the way to go. Quick and painless. But nothing about seeing my dad like that looked painless. I feel like I just hurt him for no goddamn reason."

"You were performing lifesaving measures, Luke," Addison says, her voice hoarse as she reaches out to grab my hand, her fingers trembling as she squeezes mine. "You would have had regrets if you did nothing too. And if you got a firefighter call and showed up to someone else's house, you would have done the same exact thing. Fact or fiction?"

I struggle to look into her eyes.

"Look at me," she states firmly, grabbing my chin and turning me to face her.

I blink slowly, my eyes hurting over the fact that the woman I love knows this darkness in me now. I liked being the light in Addison's life. I can tell she needs it. Craves it. Bringing this to her could have just set me back for all I know.

I breathe deeply and reply, "Fact."

"Then that's all you need to know." She wraps her hands around my arm and lays her head on my shoulder, the smell of her floral shampoo invading my nose and unexpectedly comforting me. "You should sleep well at night knowing you did everything you could."

"I just wish I could quiet the what-if questions. What if I'd called 911 to get an ambulance up there instead? What if I'd done CPR longer? What if my dad was showing symptoms earlier that day and helping me just made him worse?"

Addison's head moves on my arm as she nods her understanding. "What if my mom wouldn't have driven drunk? What if she would have opened up about not being sober and tried to get help? What if she would have attempted to have a relationship with me after jail? What if Aaron was still alive? It's fucking exhausting to live with the what-ifs."

"I know." I exhale heavily and wrap my arm around her, comforted by the feel of her weight on me. This is everything I wanted back then. "I just miss him. I miss his voice. He had this gruff sound to him that just . . . felt like home."

"Oh, I remember," Addison says, leaning back to smile up at me. "I took most of the orders at the building center back then and he was a talker on the phone."

I smile at that. I like that my dad knew Addison before he passed. It's comforting to me to know that he knew my wife.

Her brows knit together, and she chews her lip before reaching to the coffee table to retrieve her phone. "I have something for you actually."

I frown as she unlocks her phone to pull something up.

"I've been saving this, not sure what to do with it." She pulls up the voicemail app on her phone and I frown when she scrolls down and clicks Play, turning it on speaker as she does.

Suddenly, my dad is in the room with us.

"Hey, Addison, this is Steve Fletcher . . . say listen . . . we need to revise an order that my son placed with you for the Hope House before I gave him the go-ahead."

"Hey! You told me to do it!" Calder's voice shouts from somewhere in the distance.

"I didn't tell you to do it," my dad argues.

"Someone told me to do it. I bet it was Luke."

"Don't pin this on me," my voice says with a laugh.

"Then it was Wyatt. Ouch!" Calder yells. *"Dad! Wyatt just decked me. That's an HR violation. I want to file a report."*

The phone muffles and my dad's voice is loud and clear in the line again. *"Sorry you had to hear that, Addison. If you ever have sons who work for you at the lumberyard, I hope like hell you can manage them better than me, 'cause I'm fit to be tied with these knuckleheads. Anyways . . . call me back so we can get that order changed if it's not too late. Thanks."*

I frown at the phone, too stunned to speak and then hear a scuffle into the line. It's my dad's voice again.

"For the record though . . . I wouldn't change working with my sons for anything in this world. You would be lucky to have this life in your future. Talk to you later, kiddo."

Addison lowers the phone and turns to see that my eyes are flooded with tears. It was like I could close my eyes and none of the bad stuff happened. Suddenly, he was back on this earth, living with my mom. He was my boss and my dad again, giving me a pat on the back and I could pick up the phone to talk to him right fucking now. It's equal parts wonderful and dreadful and I'd listen to that message all over to feel this beautiful pain again.

"Why did you keep this?" I ask, staring at my best friend in wonder.

She blinks and errant tears fall down her face as well. "I didn't realize it was still on my phone until last year and I was too scared to share it with you then. It felt too personal. Like I didn't have a right to give it to you, especially after I was so awful when he died. I hope it's okay I played it for you now."

"It is. Good God, babe, it is more than okay." My chest swells with a pain that feels so bad and so good all at the same time as I pull my best friend into me and hug her with everything I have. "I think I needed that more than I realized."

She pulls back, her chin trembling wildly as her face fills with urgency. "Luke, when Steve died . . . you called me and said a lot of stuff about everything and I'm not proud, but it triggered me, and I shut down on you. I was suddenly twelve years old again and watching my dad bury my brother. I don't know when funerals will ever feel okay for me again. But I hate that I wasn't there for you. You have to know I was thinking of you constantly on that day and many days after. I still think of you constantly. You're on my mind like . . . all the time. When I can't sleep at night, I'm thinking about you as well." Her face flushes red as she shudders out a garbled breath and wipes aggressively at the tears on her face.

"I'm on your mind all the time?" My brain swims with confusion, wondering what I care more about. Her words or my dad's. Honestly, they're both giving me more than my heart can handle.

"Yes. Jesus," she croaks and sniffs loudly. "This is embarrassing. I don't know why I'm saying any of this."

"Hey, Roe. It's okay." I tip my hand under her chin, so she looks up at me.

"No, it's not," she snaps, pulling away. "I'm being weird. You just shared so much with me and I'm turning this into a me thing and it's not." She inhales deeply through her nose, her chin trembling slightly.

"Hey, Roe?"

"Yeah?"

"You're on my mind all the time too." My voice is deep and steady as I stare into the depths of her eyes, seeing glimmers of hope that I'm not sure I've ever seen before.

"I am?" She licks her lips and stares back at me with so much emotion, I want to kiss her pain away. She looks like she wants me to kiss the pain away.

I swallow the knot in my throat. "I like thinking about my wife."

She inhales a shaky breath and closes her eyes. "Is that fact or fiction?"

My lips thin as I gaze back at her. The woman who I would forgive for much worse because I guess that's what love is. Loving someone through their imperfect moments. "Fact."

But as she looks up at me all open and vulnerable and admitting how much I'm on her mind, I stop myself from kissing her. Because the next time I kiss her, I need it to be for forever. No more games. No more bullshit. I won't kiss Addison Monroe until I know she loves me back, because if she doesn't, there's no amount of CPR that will be able to heal my broken heart.

Chapter 25

FACT OR FICTION?
Blue is my favorite color.

Addison

The sound of Rufus crowing causes me to stir and, as I come to, I frown when I look down to see that I am not in my bed. I am still out in the living room, on the couch . . . with Luke.

And I'm not just on the couch with Luke.

I'm lying on the couch with Luke and he's . . . spooning me.

He's wrapped up around me, his warm heavy breath in my hair as his hand drapes over my belly like this is the most normal way to sleep. I glance at the clock, wondering when the hell I actually fell asleep. I remember laying my head on Luke's lap after our emotional confessions. One minute we were talking and the next thing I know, I'm waking up in his arms, feeling more rested than I've felt in ages.

For once I didn't watch every hour on the clock tick by and stress about how few hours I'm going to sleep. I just . . . slept. I slept with my best friend holding me. And Luke feels . . . incredible.

I guess a human heated blanket is all I needed to shut my brain off for a while. Or maybe it was me finally playing that voicemail. It was giving me anxiety knowing I had those words from Luke's dad and not passing them on to him, because he deserved to hear that. He deserved to hear the happiness in that man's voice, even while dealing with his sons giving him hell. And watching Luke break down while listening to it is something I will never forget. His dad was one of the good ones.

Mine is too for the most part. He made some mistakes to be sure, but he loves me, and he tries to do what's best for me, which is all I can ask of a man who was suddenly a single dad to a teenage daughter. He stuck around at least, which is more than I can say for my mom.

Luke makes a noise from behind me and my eyes fly wide when he shifts and wiggles into me closer.

Is that . . .

He moves again behind me, and I audibly gasp when I feel the very obvious, very recognizable, very *thick* sensation of his erection poking into my ass.

His hand that's draped over my waist moves downward and I chomp down on my lower lip when his fingers touch the waistband of my shorts, toying with the edge of them.

My knee-jerk reaction should be to push him off me. To grab his wrist and toss it back onto himself. But my body has other ideas. I find my hips tilting upward, ever so slightly, my body quaking with need that only gets worse when his rough hand brushes along my belly.

His hips pulse into my backside again and I slam my eyes shut when a spike of arousal lights off inside of me, sizzling from my core to my limbs, and electrifying me into a delirious, sleepy sort of dreamlike state.

Maybe I could just close my eyes and constrict my worldview to be just feelings. Just dark eyelids and heat and touch and racing pulses.

I feel his hand tighten on my belly.

Is he awake? He has to be awake. But his breaths are still so heavy—a warm, even cadence.

He thrusts into my back again and I feel myself squirming. But I'm not squirming away from him. I'm squirming into him. I'm wriggling and writhing with his movements, arching into him as butterflies swirl in my belly and heaviness pools between my legs.

So much heaviness.

It's like an empty aching that I've had since the moment I moved into this house. An itch I can't scratch. A yearning that refuses to be quieted.

I want Luke to fuck me.

Hard.

The morning sun pinpricks through the quiet darkness and my dreamy state drifts away, revealing just how awake I am and how not awake Luke is. I fixate on the particles floating in the air while my best friend grinds himself against me and I struggle to make sense of why this feels so damn good.

Luke pumps into me a few more times now, making no mistake what he's doing. He's . . . dry humping me. He's rubbing his insanely hard and, dare I say, sizable boner into my rear, rutting between my ass cheeks in a way that feels damn near animalistic.

I swivel and shift, feeling edged by his half-hearted movements. They start and stop in no discernable rhythm, stirring an ache in my groin that hasn't been touched by a man in far too long. Flashbacks of our kiss assault me and suddenly I'm back in my room putting my vibrator to use, only this time, I get to have the scent of Luke all over me while I fantasize.

Luke's breaths are heavy and warm on my neck, the essence of him driving me wild as he rubs himself all over me.

When his hand slips upward and his fingers brush the bottom of my bare breast, I turn my head into the pillow and silently scream as my goose bumps race over my flesh, my nipples becoming so hard they feel like razors against the fabric of my T-shirt.

What is going on right now? Are we doing this? Is this

happening? I need it to happen. I need something to happen. This is all too painful to endure for much longer.

And is he asleep? He can't be, right? No amount of vivid dreaming can allow you to slide your fingers along my ribs and—holy fuck he's just pinched my nipple. Now his whole hand is cupping my breast. I'm a small B cup at best so there's not exactly a lot for him to grab, but he's definitely got me in his grip and my skin feels like it's on fire beneath his big palm.

His fingers flex every time his ass does as he thrusts his erection hard into me again and again, turning me positively feral.

He lets out an odd, beastly sort of sound, like he's in pain. It's not a sex sound. It's the kind of sound you make when you're masturbating and not worried about what sounds you utter because no one can hear you.

He must be sleeping.

Which feels like the greatest tragedy of all time.

"Luke?" I whisper softly, wanting him to wake up but not wanting any of this to end.

He doesn't react, just continues thrusting into me, pulsing need through my whole body with every pump in an elemental, dirty way.

I moan softly as wetness pools in my panties. I'm so fucked up. My friend is sleep-fucking me and I'm . . . obsessed by it. Turned on by it. Consumed with it. I feel my entire body sliding into it, wanting more. I wonder briefly, if I pulled my shorts and panties down and arched my back, if he could just slide right into me. I'm sopping wet so I'm sure he could.

And I'd want him bare. I'd want his bare, silky hard cock to bury into me and possibly never come out.

His hands shift back down and skate right over the front of my shorts and I gasp as he cups my pussy firmly in his big, meaty palm. His fingers slide over the fabric covering my slit, and I groan and wriggle into him, egging his movements on as I greedily want more and more.

The dampness of my panties soaks through my shorts, probably coating his fingers, and the *idea* of that. The obscene image of my wetness on his big, thick fingers as he finger-fucks me through my shorts causes an ache to roil through me, and I let out a raspy cry.

I don't know how much more of this I can take. I need him to fuck me. I need to feel the pain of his size pushing inside me.

He has to be awake by now, right?

I spread my legs slightly to give him better access and he groans and grips my pussy hard, pulling me back into his cock. The hard ridge of him pressing through his sweats and into my hip as he grinds himself over me while still not saying a word is throwing me into a state of delirium.

When I feel his hot breath on my shoulder, I moan as warmth travels through my whole body. My limbs begin to tremble as he lazily fingers me through my shorts, and just as I feel myself on the brink of orgasm, he freezes and his whole body goes still beside me.

Heart racing, I close my eyes and pretend to be sleeping, trying to regulate my breathing as I hear him curse softly under his breath and yank his hand away from me.

I inwardly cry as his groin shifts away and he fumbles down low beside me as I continue to breathe long, slow breaths, feigning sleep. He pushes the blanket, putting it directly between us and I want to cry as I feel the warmth of him disappear while he attempts to extricate himself from his position as big "morning wood" spoon.

He's clearly not happy with himself and whatever was happening, whereas I was just letting him fuck me in his sleep apparently. I'm not sure who is more fucked up in this scenario. Probably me.

I hear another expletive come from his lips as he drapes the blanket over me and then the sound of his footsteps grow faint as he walks away. I lie still until I hear the click of his bedroom door and with a frustrated squeak, I throw the covers off me, my body heaving with my unfinished orgasm.

My nipples are rock-hard under my shirt, and I glance down and feel blanketed in shame over how wet I am. I debate shoving my hand down my shorts and finishing myself off right here on this couch. It wouldn't take long because I can still smell Luke beside me. The heat of him is still on the cushion. All I'd have to do is roll onto my belly, prop my ass up and do a few swift circles on my clit, and I could orgasm in less than a minute.

But it would feel hollow.

And if Luke came out and caught me, then he'll know that I let him defile me in his sleep. He'll know that I soaked through my panties and shorts as he touched me in his sleepy state of mind. And he'll know I liked it and wanted more.

I suck in a deep, cleansing breath and stand on shaky legs to make my way to my bathroom. I need a shower and an exorcism. And definitely a clean pair of underwear.

Luke

Ice-cold water sluices down my back as I press my head to the tile of the walk-in shower attached to my bedroom. My cock weeps under the assault, bobbing up at me like the unforgiving bastard I am.

But he deserves this pain. I deserve this pain. I am a sick fuck and I refuse to let myself come after the horror show that I just woke up to.

I was . . . defiling my wife in her sleep like a fucking creep. I don't deserve to climax. I don't deserve to have a boner ever again. I deserve to rot in hell because I am unwell.

Last night was groundbreaking for me and Roe. She let down her walls and apologized for abandoning me in my hour of need. I opened up to her more than I've ever opened up to anyone. We needed that. We needed to not only clear the air, but to drop the wall between us. Yes, we've shared a lot of ourselves with each other over the years, but if I'm honest, I know I've also held a lot back from her. In wanting to be her light, be everything she needs, I've kept parts of myself hidden. And if I really want Roe to love me, she needs to know all of me—especially the dark parts. And I need to know all of her, so she feels safe with me. That I won't abandon her either.

And my dumb ass had to fuck it all up by trying to sleep-fuck her.

I don't even know if that's a fucking thing. I probably belong in jail for even attempting it though.

I just hope to God she doesn't know what I did to her. If she does, she'll never be able to look at me the same again, let alone consider not divorcing me when this one-year marriage is up.

Fuck.

I get dressed and shove a baseball cap over my damp hair, pulling the bill down to hide my shame. I need to get out there and see what she knows. See if she can even look at me. One glance and I'll know if she thinks I'm a creep, so let's get this shit over with.

Steeling myself, I swing open my bedroom door and my eyes swing left when I see that she is standing in the bathroom doorway adjacent to me. Steam billows out from behind her and she's wrapped in an itty-bitty towel, her wet hair folded up into a towel, revealing her damn bare shoulders. My cock instantly perks up, still clearly putting in a good fight after that cold shower.

"Hey," she says, her eyes dancing from me to her bedroom door as she grips a wad of dirty clothes in her hands.

I clear my throat and give back a formal "Good morning."

She offers me a wobbly smile. "I was just . . . taking a shower."

"I see that." My eyes drop to her legs, glistening with humidity. "I was doing the same."

"Nice. Showering is good." She shoots me a bizarre smile and I can't tell if it's weird or normal, because my brain is just screaming at me to fuck her.

"I, um . . . you fell asleep on the couch last night," I stammer, pulling my hat down low because I feel like she can still see right through me.

"Yeah . . . I, um . . . don't think I've slept that good in a long time."

I smile at that, feeling happy that she got some good sleep despite my morning . . . pursuits.

"Did you, um . . . sleep on the couch with me?" Her cheeks flush red and I wince as my cock twitches.

"Yeah, um. I did sleep there with you." I frown, wondering if she's trying to tell me she knows. Either way, I can't lie to her. "Sorry about that but I didn't want to wake you so . . ."

Her eyes soften as she stares up at me, her lips parted, breaths coming in heavier. "You slept on the couch with me all night to not wake me?"

"Yeah," I state gruffly and my face flushes. It's hard to make eye contact with her when she looks at me like that. "Anyways."

With a deep inhale, I make a move to head down the hall, and Addison apparently has the same idea as she steps forward at the same time, bumping into me and twirling on her foot, dropping the ball of clothes in her hands.

"Shit, sorry." I bend over to help her pick them up and she shoves me away.

"It's fine, I got 'em." She grabs them all with one hand while holding her towel with the other and before I can say another word, she turns on her heel and hauls ass to her bedroom, slamming the door abruptly behind her as she goes.

She totally knows I tried to sleep-fuck her.

I lean on the doorway and cast my eyes downward as I shake my head, and my lips part when I catch sight of something.

Tiny pale blue underwear that look . . .

Moist.

There's that fucking word again.

I divert my eyes away, feeling like I'm invading her privacy by not only looking at her underwear but noticing how . . . damp they are. Are those what she had on last night? They sure look like it.

Was it what I was doing to her this morning that caused all that . . . moisture? Was she awake for all of that? My cock thickens in my jeans just at the idea of that. The idea that she wanted me to do what I did to her. That she encouraged it. Or that even in her sleep, she wanted me.

What happens next isn't something I'm proud of. In fact, it's something that puts my sleep fuckery game to shame.

Next thing I know, I bend over and pick them up, turning to go back into my bedroom, closing the door, and locking it behind me. My primitive, baseless, animalistic caveman comes out and like a man on fucking fire, I unbuckle my belt, ruck out of my jeans. I bring her panties to my nose like a ravenous beast, breathing in the damp scent of her, desperate to taste her arousal before wrapping the fabric around my cock and pumping my throbbing cock like I've never pumped it before.

"Fuuuck," I growl as I hunch over, gripping the dresser with my free hand, and grind the lacy blue fabric over my length in rapid speed.

"Fuck, fuck, fuck," I groan, dropping my chin to my chest, my abs clenching as I picture her wet pussy lips dripping with arousal.

For me.

She got herself soaking wet in these lacy blue panties.

For me.

"Oh God," I grunt, feeling my climax crest quicker than I ever imagined, and I hunch over and cover my tip with the fabric, blowing my hot load into it.

My body quakes and shivers, jerking every last drop from my raw unit. I hiss as I wipe the sensitive tip off before pulling my jeans back up and buckling myself back in.

I stare at the panties drenched with my semen and wonder what the fuck I'm going to do to hide this from my roommate.

My wife.

My stomach is a pit of right and wrong. What the fuck did I just do? Addison is not going to want to stay married to me if she knows I'm a goddamn sexual deviant.

With a huff, I stuff them into my jeans pocket and stomp out of my bedroom, grateful to see her door is still closed.

There are still embers on the fire in the living room, so I toss the panties onto them and lay fresh wood over top, stoking the fire and adding bits of kindling to get the flames going again.

As I brace myself on the mantel and stare at the lacy fabric turning black in the flames . . . I vow to myself to never tell a single soul what I've just done. And if my dad is watching from somewhere up above . . . well . . . all I can say is, "Forgive me, Father, I know not what I do."

Chapter 26

FACT OR FICTION?
I'm sleeping with my wife.

Luke

A dinging sound stirs me from my sleep, and I find myself blinking through the darkness of my bedroom while the moonlight streaming in through the blinds helps me get my bearings. I turn to glance at the clock and see that it's after midnight, and then I know exactly what woke me.

You'd think I'd be used to the sound of that oven timer after living with Roe for the past several weeks. But I still hear it nearly every night.

Most nights I just roll over and fall back asleep, but tonight, I feel the urge to check on her, just to make sure she's okay.

I crawl out of bed and adjust myself before padding barefoot down the hall in nothing but a loose pair of shorts. The warm yellow light pours down the hall from the kitchen, illuminating my path, and as I round the corner, my eyes land on a sight that has become all too familiar.

My wife.

Making sourdough at midnight.

Sounds like a country song.

I smile and cross my arms to lean on the wall and watch her for a moment, taking in every inch of flesh exposed between her baggy T-shirt and slouchy socks. Her legs are thick and muscular, tiny dimples dotting the backs of her thighs as she bends over to peek in the oven. Her hair is up high in a messy bun and her eyes appear dark with circles under them.

I know she loves making bread, but I hate seeing her like this. She's unsettled and tired, and dancing around the kitchen because she can't seem to let herself relax. It's like she needs someone in her life to give her permission to just . . . take a breath.

She pulls a large pan out of the oven and turns on her heel to set it on the cooling rack. It's been a few days since I jerked off into her underwear and I've been giving her space for fear of me opening my big mouth to confess the awful thing I did. We've still had our sunset dinners together and chatted about work and wedding plans. So, I think on the surface, we seem fine. But underneath, *I'm craving her like a drug.*

I want to touch her and hold her again. I want to feel the warmth of her body against mine like I did that night on the couch. The night when she finally was able to fall asleep.

"Oh my God," Roe squeals as she catches sight of me. She pulls her earbuds out and presses a hand to her chest. "You scared the shit out of me, Luke."

"Sorry," I reply, ruffling my hair self-consciously and flexing my stomach because . . . well . . . just because. "I was just enjoying the show."

She rolls her eyes, her gaze dropping down my chest in a nervous sort of way before she refocuses on the bread. "I just finished this loaf, so I'm done now. Sorry if I woke you."

I tilt my head and watch her carefully before saying exactly what's on my mind. "Why don't you sleep with me tonight?"

Her eyes snap to mine, wide and hollow with fatigue. "What?"

I inhale a deep breath and move closer, splaying my hands on the island as I stare at her. "Sleep with me, Roe."

"Luke . . . we don't . . ." Her cheeks flush as her eyes skate down my body again. If I didn't know any better, I'd say my wife is checking me out. *Have at it, babe. I'm all yours.*

"Just sleep," I clarify, and swear I see a flicker of disappointment cast over her face, but I shake it off because I'm a man on a mission. "You haven't slept well since the night you crashed with me on the sofa, and I have a theory that you could sleep better with me."

Her throat shifts as she swallows nervously, her fingers tapping lightly on the crusty slice she made along the top. "Wouldn't that be weird?"

"It's not weird for two people who are married to sleep together."

She peers up at me with a soft, tender look and I have the sudden urge to walk over and kiss her. Not in a dirty, all-consuming sexual way. I just want to feel that tenderness that she shows me from time to time. Taste it on my lips and commit it to memory.

It reminds me how tactile my dad was with my mom. He'd often walk up to her and kiss her forehead. She'd lean into him and seemed to love when he touched her. And that's what I want. I want those lazy touches just as much as I want everything else that comes with marriage.

"I don't know if that's a good idea," she murmurs, looking down.

Rolling my eyes, I stride over to the oven and shut it off before moving to stand behind my friend. I grip her by the waist, and she wiggles slightly as I begin to march her out of the kitchen and down the hall. "Just please listen to me for once. I think we should try this."

She groans but submits to my will, likely because she's too tired to fight with me. I watch affectionately from the hallway as she brushes her teeth at the bathroom sink and when she's done, she grips the door and pierces me with a glare. "Are you going to watch me pee too?"

I huff out a laugh and step back. "I'll be waiting in my bed for you."

Her cheeks flush and with an amused smirk, I head to my

room, giving myself a mental pep talk to keep my dirty thoughts in check. *We cannot have a repeat of the couch. You seemingly got out of that situation without getting caught so let's keep your panty-loving cock to yourself this time.*

I look up when I hear the bathroom door open and see Addison standing in my doorway, leaning up against the frame. Her foot slides up her calf and she's wringing her fingers nervously.

"Get your ass in here, wife," I command, flipping the covers back.

She rolls her eyes in the dark and then bounds into my bed, purposefully bumping her ass on me, as she settles into the little spoon position. I wrap my arm around her and am surprised when she grabs my hand and clutches it to her chest.

Heart racing, I nuzzle into her, breathing in her scent. "You smell like sourdough," I whisper in a deep, sexy voice.

She vibrates with silent laughter under my arm. "You smell like . . ." She pauses and pulls my hand to her cheek. "Like Luke."

My brows lift. "And what does that smell like?"

She inhales deeply, wriggling her ass on my cock in a way that feels so fucking good it hurts. "I don't know . . ." Her voice trails off. "Comfy."

Comfy.

I smell comfy.

It's not exactly the sexiest of smells, but I can hear the smile on her lips, so I'll take it.

"Feeling sleepy yet?"

"You're comfy but not that comfy, Fletcher."

I laugh and give her a playful squeeze. "You want me to tell you a bedtime story?"

"Sure."

I groan as I wrack my brain for a good story. Something light and playful, but still relaxing. "How about I tell you the story about the first time we met?"

She turns her head, frowning over her shoulder at me. "I was there. I already know that story."

"But do you know that day is why your dad hates me?" I ask her profile and see her lips part.

"What are you talking about?" she chirps and rolls over in my arms. I lean back, my stomach flexed as she drapes herself over my chest like it's the most normal thing in the world.

And I hate how normal it does feel.

I smile and slice my hand into my hair, pushing the strands off my forehead. "Well . . . your dad sort of . . . caught me checking you out."

"Shut up!" She pokes my chest, and I laugh, rubbing at the painful spot.

"In my defense, I didn't know you were his daughter. My dad always picked up our orders. It was literally my first time at Monroe Lumber. I didn't know anyone there."

"Yeah . . . okay, so what happened with you and my dad?" She props her chin on my chest and looks up at me with wide, excited eyes.

"You were helping these guys who were major assholes, and you ended up dumping the lumber on their truck causing all sorts of damage. It was a whole scene that I had front row seats to from outside the building center."

"I remember those fuckers," Addison drawls, rolling her eyes. "My dad was pissed at me over that because it caused our insurance rates to go up."

"Well . . . you did dump wood on their truck."

"Those fuckers deserved it!" she snaps back, fiery as ever.

I smile and shake my head. "Anyways, this guy walks up

beside me and starts watching the spectacle with me. I just assumed it was another customer, right?"

"But it was my dad." Addison winces knowingly.

"Sure was. Which means when I said to him, 'If I'd known someone who looked like that worked here, I would have offered to pick up my dad's orders years ago,' it did not go over well."

"Oh my God." Addison covers her face with her hands. "What did he do?"

"He looked me dead in the eye and smiled. I smiled back because I thought this was some random guy agreeing with me. And through his shit-eating grin he said without hesitation, 'If you ever talk about my daughter like that again, I will cut off your balls, hang them from the ceiling fan in my office and hold your body up to the fan so your own nuts can smack you in the face over and over and over again until they can knock some sense in you.'"

Addison's face falls in confusion, which isn't dissimilar to my own reaction at the time. It's just such a weirdly specific threat that evoked some very unpleasant imagery. I wasn't sure exactly how to take it. It didn't sound good, I know that. And the weird twinkle in his eye made me think he was the type of man who would actually do it.

"But . . . you still asked me to hang out." Addison frowns up at me.

I shrug. "I don't scare easy."

She bites her lip and looks down, her fingers moving over my pec as she shakes her head back and forth. "All this time, I thought you were one of the good ones, Luke Fletcher."

"Babe, I'm only human. And in my defense, I'd never seen a woman operate a forklift. I was turned-the-fuck-on."

She bursts out laughing, the sound something I could die

happy listening to. "So, does this mean you . . . liked me? All this time, I thought you didn't see me like that. Just as a friend."

I stare down at her, pressing my hand over where hers sits on my chest. She has to feel my heart racing right now. She has to know this has always felt deeper than friendship between us. Right?

My smile falls when I reply, "I saw you as someone I wasn't willing to lose, and with who I was back then, if I would have taken you to bed, I would have definitely lost you."

The lines between her brows deepen as she gazes up at me. "And who are you now?"

I inhale deeply and brush a piece of hair out of her face, fighting the urge to cup her cheek. "I'm your husband."

Her eyes glitter in the moonlight and the need I have to tell her that I'm in love with her is so strong, I can feel it on the tip of my tongue.

But I made a promise to myself. It has to be her that makes the first move. And if that means sleeping beside her every night and just sleeping until our wedding night . . . that's exactly what I'll do.

She's worth being patient for.

I lean forward and brush my lips over her forehead. "Get some sleep, wife."

She sighs and nuzzles into my chest, tucking herself under my chin like she's the absolute perfect fit. Because she is . . . even if she still doesn't see that yet.

Chapter 27

FACT OR FICTION?
This is my poker face.

Addison

"Good morning, daughter," my dad booms as he comes striding into my office bright and early on Friday.

"Dad?" I stand up from my desk, taking in his tall frame in the doorway. "What are you doing here?"

"I told you I was home," he replies gruffly, walking over to the coffee maker by the window and pouring himself a cup.

"I know but . . . I mean . . . what are you doing here-here?" I ask, pointing to the desk.

He holds the mug up to his mustache and blows on it as steam billows up around his face. "I have a couple meetings today and needed some files."

My brows crease at that because my dad hasn't really needed anything from the office in months. Not since he retired. "What meetings? What files? Can I help?"

"Don't you worry." He sets his mug down and walks over to the rusty filing cabinet, pulling it open and thumbing through some folders. "I can find what I need."

I join him at the filing cabinet and when I look at what he's sifting through, he turns his back on me, hiding what he's doing. "Dad, I'm running this place now so whatever meetings you're having that involve lumberyard files should probably involve me."

He turns his head to look at me, his bushy brows arched. "I'm still the owner, Addie May. I shouldn't need to remind you of that."

His tone is chastising, and I feel my throat tighten at the hard set of his jaw. I've seen my dad like this a lot throughout the years, but very rarely directed at me. He usually gets this way with mill workers during negotiations. But even if that was what his meetings were, why wouldn't he just tell me that?

I lick my lips and jut my chin upward. "Since I'm due to inherit this company, I think it'd be a good idea for me to know about what meetings you're still taking."

"Like a dog with a fucking bone." He exhales heavily and slams the cabinet drawer closed before propping his arm on top of it to glower down at me. "If you must know, I'm meeting with the people who wanted to buy the yard."

My jaw drops. "Are you meeting to tell them that I'm married now, and the deal is off?"

His lips twitch. "Perhaps."

"What the hell do you mean perhaps?" I grind through clenched teeth.

"Well, Addie May, a year is a long time away still. You and Luke Fletcher might not work out," he huffs, moving past me to go back to where he left his coffee mug.

I twirl on my heel to stare at the man who raised me. "Me and Luke will work out just fine."

"I'll be the judge of that." He eyes me harshly before taking a loud slurp of his coffee.

"What is that supposed to mean?" I march over and stand toe to toe with the old man, refusing to let him speak complete nonsense without backing it up.

"Oh, come on, Ads," he barks, waving his mug at me. "I know your marriage with Luke is bullshit."

"You don't know that," I exclaim, crossing my arms over my chest. "I'm living with him, aren't I?"

"And still paying rent at your apartment," he adds, taking another sip of coffee.

My lips part. "How do you know that?"

"Boulder ain't that big of a town, sweetheart. Word gets around."

He stares out the window at the guys all working in the yard, and I watch his body language closely, still not understanding why he's being like this. My dad can be an asshole, but he's usually a reasonable asshole. I don't understand this side to him.

"What are you doing, Dad?" I ask, walking over and trying to lower my voice to a softer level. "Why are you meeting with those people?"

His nostrils flare. "They want to present me with a new offer."

"A new offer? What kind of offer?"

"I don't know. That's why I'm meeting with them."

I blink rapidly, my mind swimming with this sudden new information. "But I got married to fulfill the stupid trust stipulation. I'm throwing a wedding because you asked me to. Why are you even entertaining these people?" I stare up at him, a knot forming in my throat because this feels personal now. "Why are you so determined for me not to run this lumberyard?"

"I'm not."

"You obviously are," I exclaim and fight back the tears welling in my eyes.

He scoffs and rolls his eyes dramatically. "Don't get all emotional. This is just business."

"This is my life and I should have a say in it!" A stray tear runs down my face and I swipe it away quickly, irritated that more seem to be following in its wake. Crying in front of my dad is never a good thing. In fact, it just adds fuel to this ridiculous fire he has over me not being able to handle the business on my own.

I really did think it had to do with me not being married. I thought that convoluted trust was legit, and marriage was the only thing preventing me from taking ownership. But now I can tell there's something else brewing here. Something my dad isn't saying.

His nose wrinkles as he looks at me. "This is why I think it's a bad idea for you to run this place on your own. You're too damn soft for all of this."

"I am what you made me," I growl, anger bubbling up in my veins. "I am you. I am your daughter. I've given my whole life to this place. Just because I don't have a dick and shed a tear every once in a while doesn't make me any less capable!"

"Now that's enough," Dad barks, setting his mug down to glare at me. He thrusts a finger in my face. "You're crying over nothing. It's just a meeting. Get your panties out of a wad and leave it be for Christ's sake."

Without another word, he stomps past me, out of the office, through the building center, and back into his car, stirring up a whole lot of insecurity and a whole lot of rage that I have no idea what to do with.

Luke

"So how goes it with the wifey?" Calder asks from across my brother Max's dining room table as he tosses some poker chips into the middle. "I haven't seen much of you two the past couple of weeks. Do I take it the honeymoon is going well?"

Calder waggles his brows at me, and I wince as I stare down at my cards, which have been cold all night. It's our monthly poker night, which usually consists of the four Fletcher brothers and a bunch of Max's guy friends from Boulder who have turned into our friends throughout the years. But tonight, it's just the four of us.

I hesitate with how to reply, chancing a glance at Max, who responds, "I know your marriage is total bullshit."

I drop my cards and glare at Wyatt and Calder. "This was supposed to be a fucking secret."

Wyatt points to Calder, who is pointing back at Wyatt.

"Everly told me," Max relents, his eyes tight as he tosses his own chips into the middle.

"Do the ladies all know too?" I ask, looking at my three brothers. "Cozy? Dakota? Trista? Mom?"

They all three shake their heads, so I sigh with relief. "Just keep it quiet, okay? The more people who know, the harder this is going to get for me."

"So, you guys aren't . . ." Wyatt doesn't finish his sentence because I can read his mind.

"No, we're not . . . together," I huff, tapping my cards on the table. "I mean . . . we're getting closer for sure." But I stop myself from revealing the sofa dry humping session and the fact that I got disgustingly close with her wet panties last week because they would taunt me mercilessly for that. And instead add, "But it's still . . . just friends."

"Jesus fuck, man, it's been damn near a month," Calder drawls, eyeing me with the most irritating wrinkled nose of judgment. "You're getting married in two weeks."

"I know," I growl and rake my hand through my hair. "But it needs to come from her. I kissed her a couple weeks ago and shit got super weird afterward and we're just still finding our way."

Max shakes his head, clearly judging me.

"Don't start, Max."

"I didn't say anything." He holds his hands up in surrender.

"You're giving me the dad look. Like I'm fucking fumbling this thing."

"Well, Everly said you need to close the deal before the wedding, so what is your plan exactly if you only have a couple more weeks?"

"I don't know anymore." I turn my hat backward, pushing down the top of it. "I'm just trying to show her how good we are. All week she's spent the night in my bed . . . just sleeping because she has issues with insomnia, and I swear she never sleeps as good as she does when she's with me. That feels like a big deal, right? Like she must be comfortable enough with me to do that, right? I mean hell, I fucked my shoulder up holding her every night because I don't want to move a muscle for fear of waking her up."

"That's really sweet, baby bro," Calder deadpans.

"Shut up."

"I'm being serious! That is sweet." He frowns thoughtfully at me. "But maybe that's the problem. You're being too sweet, and you need to be a little savage instead."

"That's what our kiss was. It was . . ." My voice trails off as the memory of it causes a shiver to run down my spine.

"Maybe you need to take her out," Max says, looking thoughtful and not judgmental for once in his life. "Get out of the cabin and take her somewhere that forces you to act like a couple."

"We could all go out together," Wyatt suggests, eyeing all of us. "You have to fake it in front of us, so . . . we can be your wingmen for the night."

I frown and nod at that suggestion. "I don't hate that idea."

"There's a band playing at the Mercantile tomorrow night," Calder says, eyes bright and excited. "Let's get all the ladies together and make it a couples night. Addison seemed to get along with them well last time they were all out."

Last time they were all out, I kissed the fuck out of my wife, and she liked it.

This is a good idea. Maybe even a great idea.

"Addison seemed stressed after work today, so I think this is exactly what she needs. I'll text her now."

My brothers resume the game while I pull my phone out to text my wife.

Me: My brothers and the ladies want to go out tomorrow night. You up for it?

Roe: Good God yes. I could use a drink after seeing my dad today.

Me: Everything okay?

Roe: I'll tell you about it when you get back.

Me: I'll be home soon.

Roe: Good. I'll be waiting in your bed.

I close my eyes as ache blooms in my chest. She has no idea what those words do to me. How much need they stir up in every cell of my body. When she crawls into my arms every night, when I smell her all over my sheets the next day . . . I'm in heaven and hell right now and just happy to be existing in any way with her.

My best friend.

My wife.

It will be good to go out tomorrow night with everyone and play the part of husband and wife. But right now, I just want to go home and cuddle with my best friend.

Chapter 28

FACT OR FICTION?
I love my best friend.

Addison

Luke's jaw is on the floor when I walk out of my bedroom for our big night out with his brothers and the ladies. I want to roll my eyes and laugh at his reaction, but I suppose he hasn't seen me dressed up since . . . well . . . since our wedding day. And even that was an outfit I just tossed on. I didn't have time to do my hair and makeup, so this is a bit of a glow-up moment for me.

I'm wearing a rust-colored cropped sweater with a black leather miniskirt and knee-high black boots. I've curled my long dark hair into loose waves, which is something I rarely make time for because I always end up tying it up anyways. And my makeup is dark and more dramatic than I usually wear it. I'm a tomboy for sure, usually choosing a pair of my well-worn Converse sneakers over a pair of heels, but after the fight I had with my dad yesterday, tonight I wanted to walk out of my bedroom and feel beautiful for my husband.

And Luke's reaction does not disappoint.

His eyes unabashedly move up and down my body as he gets a desperate, frantic look on his face like a person drowning and grasping at the surface for something, anything to hold on to. I've been seeing that expression on him more and more lately. He usually tries to hide it, but I clock it. It used to make me uncomfortable, but lately, I seek it out. Crave it. Feeling his eyes on me causes my entire body to hum with appreciation.

As desire settles in the pit of my belly, I bite my lip and look away from him. I need to remember this marriage isn't real. It's just convenient. Temporary. We're friends.

But sleeping with Luke every night this week has made that reality feel a bit less . . . real. And I'm still working through how I feel about that.

I push those anxious thoughts to the back of my mind and smile at my husband. "Did I overdo it for the Merc?"

He shakes his head and stutters out a labored breath. "Not at all. You look beautiful, babe."

There's that *babe* word again. He's using it more and more and I hate how much I love it. It shifts Luke from friend category into boyfriend category, which is weird because he's already in husband category. Things are getting complicated.

"Did you talk to your dad?" Luke asks, eyeing me thoughtfully.

I shrug. "I texted him and asked how the meeting went. He said fine. That was it."

My mood shifts with this change in topic. I was looking forward to a night of forgetting and now he's dredged it all back up again. But I love Luke for caring. It feels nice having someone to offload this stuff to.

Luke chucks me under the chin. "He's not going to make you go through the act of planning a whole wedding and sell it out from under you, Roe. He's not that big of a dick."

"You sure about that?" I ask, eyeing him warily.

He laughs and shakes his head. "Let's forget about it for tonight. That can be tomorrow's problem."

"And what will be tonight's problem?"

"My family," he replies with a grin, walking toward me, dressed in a green flannel and jeans, looking like some sort of sexy mountain man postcard. He's left his hat off for tonight, so his shaggy dirty blond hair is loose around his face and tucked haphazardly behind his ears. His beard has started to grow back the past couple of weeks, so it's finally just about caught up to the length of his mustache, but there's a tiny little spot on his chin where the hair won't grow because of his scar.

I fight the urge to reach out and touch it nearly every day.

"Roe . . . did you hear me?" he asks, and I blink rapidly and refocus on him.

"No, sorry, what did you say?" I look up at him, liking how these heels bring me a bit closer to his handsome face. His brown eyes look greener in that flannel.

"I said I might have to touch you a bit more tonight to really play this off in front of everyone. I mean . . . we're still in our honeymoon phase so my family will probably expect some level of affection between us."

I narrow my eyes at him. "I sleep in your arms every single night, Luke."

"This is true." He purses his lips, his eyes dropping to my mouth and I shiver when my nipples pebble at just that subtle shift in his gaze.

"I can handle a bit of touching." I wink at him and pat my hand on his chest, my palm staying there for a moment, noticing how fast his heart is racing.

"What about kissing?" he asks, his voice deep and gravelly.

"Kissing?" I whisper, feeling an ache bloom between my legs.

He shrugs as his eyes rake over my whole face. "We might have to kiss just a little."

I nod slowly, feeling drunk on his close proximity. "I can handle that."

He leans in close like he wants to test that theory and just before our lips touch, a horn honks from outside, drawing both of our attention to the door. Luke looks back at me, our faces dangerously close together. "You ready for this, wife?"

I lean my head up and press my lips to his cheek. "Very ready."

He hits me with a suspicious look, still not making a move. "Why do you look so nervous?"

He inhales a deep breath. "It's my brothers. There's always a reason to be nervous when it comes to going out with my brothers."

I laugh and grab his hand, threading my fingers through his and pulling him behind me toward the door, saying goodbye to Rufus on our way. Luke is worrying about nothing. His family is child's play compared to John Monroe. Plus, we're all adults. What's the worst that could happen?

One thing I've learned about myself after spending two hours in the local Jamestown bar with my husband and his family?

I like to play make-believe.

I might even love it.

I love the feel of Luke's hand on my lower back as he holds the door open for me and walks me inside.

I love the way he drapes his arm behind my chair all night, blanketing me in his body heat.

I love the way he leans in and I can feel his warm breath all over my neck when he asks me what I want to drink next.

I love the way he knows what food I want to order off the menu and then asks me what he should order so we can share.

I love the way his hands fold around mine every time the girls fire a million wedding questions at me, giving me that quiet sense of support that he knows I need.

I love the way he watches me when I get dragged onto the tiny dance floor with the girls.

I love the way he pushes a water toward me when I come back to the table.

I love the way he looks at me and doesn't look away when I catch him looking.

I . . . want him.

I want my best friend.

I want Luke.

And while I should probably be panicking about this quiet realization that I'm having smack-dab in the middle of a bar surrounded by his family . . . I feel . . . perfectly calm.

This is my best friend, and ever since that night we talked about grief—about losing his dad and the losses we've both experienced—we're different. More bonded and connected in a way that feels effortless.

Even sleeping with him feels completely normal. Like we've always done it. It's interesting because when I consider what marriage is, isn't it living with someone you like to spend time with? Being open and honest with someone who you trust won't let you down? Being attracted to the person you spend the most time with? Maybe marrying your friend can turn into something that's real?

All I know is tonight, I'm going to keep playing make-believe because it feels good. I'm going to enjoy this night out with his family in the large table we've commandeered in the corner and not stress about the future. I have a whole year to worry about what these newfound feelings mean.

"More Fireball!" Cozy cheers as she carries over a tray of shots to the table. Judy, the owner, eyes Cozy from her place behind the bar, and is clearly not happy about giving a tray of shots to the drunk girl from Boulder.

"Tastes like a chick drink," Wyatt says, wrinkling his nose after taking a sip.

"I love it." Calder shoots it back in one go.

"Calder, I was going to do a toast!" Cozy whacks her brother-in-law on the arm before she lifts her shot glass toward me. "To Addison and Luke. Welcome to the family, Addison!"

Everyone shoots back their drinks and suddenly I hear Calder yell, "Kiss, kiss, kiss, kiss!"

Everyone joins them and I can't help but laugh when I realize they're all looking at me and Luke, directing this chant to us.

"Guys, come on." Luke waves them off and turns his head to me with a frown, the scent of cinnamon on his breath wafting over my face and causing me to lick my lips.

They continue their chanting, the ladies joining in too and even Wyatt, the quiet one, is in on the game. If you can call it that. Luke glowers at his family, clearly not amused but all I can do is stare at Luke's mouth, my eyes zeroing in on that little scar again.

The scar he got trying to get me to marry him.

"Come on, Addison!" Dakota squeals, giving me a playful shove and shaking me out of my oral fixation on my husband. "Give that Fletcher brother a smooch!"

I turn to Luke, my lower lip sliding between my teeth as I fight the urges coursing through my body. He's just so big and cozy sitting there, all agitated with his family and smelling so . . . Luke-like.

He shakes his head and blinks a slow blink at me as he murmurs, "Just ignore them. They're a bunch of ass—"

I cut Luke off by crushing my mouth to his, locking our lips tight as I grip his face and shift off my chair to slide onto his lap for better leverage. I have to sit sideways on him because my skirt is too tight for me to spread my legs, but he doesn't seem to mind as his hands instantly come around me, grabbing my waist and thighs, holding me to him.

I move my hands back into his hair, my fingers raking through his tousled locks as I sweep my tongue into his mouth, swirling the cinnamon liquor lingering between us. His chest rumbles with a growl and he tightens his hold on me, his tongue meeting mine, dancing with it, fighting with it, claiming it with vigor that I've missed since our last embrace like this.

I've missed Luke's mouth. I've missed the warm, comforted feeling that rushes through me when we connect on this elemental level. I've missed the way he kisses harder than I ever would have expected. He doesn't kiss like a nice boy. He kisses like a man. A bad man who could do bad things to me if I let him.

And God do I want to let him.

I want to feel his mouth all over my body. I want to lick that tiny scar on his chin and wince at the sensation of his whiskers on my tongue. I want to know what it feels like to have his beard between my legs. I want to slice my fingers into his hair as he ravishes my core. I want to ravish his core. His length. God, I want him.

The sound of his family cheering us on feels distant and far away as I lose myself in this moment right here, right now. With my husband.

After what feels like seconds and an eternity, we pull apart, both panting, our eyes locked on one another, chests heaving with awareness that we did it again. And nothing about that kiss felt like make-believe.

Luke's rough palm reaches out and grips my neck, stealing my breath as he hauls me toward him to lock our lips one more time. His mouth is a fierce claiming as he devours my lips and then releases me just as quickly as he took me.

I'm wrecked.

I grip his shoulders for support as my fingers and toes tingle with shock, my nipples pebbling inside my bra as a heaviness swirls between my legs. I feel drunk, and I haven't even had that much to drink tonight.

"Holy fuck," Dakota deadpans.

"I'll second that," I hear Trista say from somewhere in the distance.

"I did not expect Luke to bust out the hand necklace!" Cozy exclaims, slapping her hand on the table. "We need to dance, ladies."

And before I know it, I'm being dragged out onto the dance floor on shaky legs that would much rather be wrapped around my husband.

Chapter 29

FACT OR FICTION?
A blast from the past is never good.

Luke

"I thought you said you weren't fucking her," Calder yells to me over the loud band.

"I'm not," I reply, not taking my eyes off my wife. She swivels her hips and holds her hands up, tossing her hair into her face. I feel desperate to walk out there and feel her body move against mine. Especially after that kiss.

"Could have fooled me." Calder clinks his beer bottle with mine and I glance at the time on my phone, wondering if it's too early to call it for the night. I need to get my wife in my bed and figure out what that kiss meant soon, or I am going to drive myself fucking nuts waiting.

She started that kiss, but I sure as fuck finished it. The confidence that surged through me knowing she clearly wanted it was too heady for me to ignore. I'd bet my life that my wife's panties are soaked right now, and all I want to do is go home and see if I can find out for myself.

"As I live and breathe, it's the Fletcher brothers," a shrill, familiar voice coos, causing all the hairs on the back of my neck to stand.

With a pit in my stomach, I turn my head and feel stunned speechless at the woman standing before us.

Robyn Whitaker . . . here from beyond the fucking grave. Standing next to her, about two inches shorter, is her husband, Matt. It is mind-blowing that these two are still together after all the fucked-up shit that happened over a decade ago. And why does she think she can simply waltz in and say hi as if we're all old friends?

All three of my brothers turn to stone as they stare up at the woman who nearly ripped our family apart. And she has the nerve to stand here with a cheery smile on her face, like she didn't fuck with all of us.

"I'll go find us a table and let you all catch up," Matt says, tipping his chin up to kiss Robyn on the cheek. The bizarre act has my lips curling.

The guy can't be right in the head. There's no fucking way I could stay in the same bar as the three men who fucked my wife while I was still married to her. Neither of these two are right in the head. And whatever marital shit they get off on is none of my business. I just want to know why the hell they're here.

Robyn darkened our doorstep a couple times throughout the years, but it's been ages now. I thought she'd moved on. Found some other set of dudes to torment. Or maybe turned things around to be a good mother to her kids. One can hope, right?

My eyes can't help but move over her body. Taking in her presence again after so many years is weird. She still has that same slender frame with the large tits she had before, but her face is thinner and more hollowed out. She's got to be almost forty by now, if memory serves. Admittedly, she looks good for a forty-year-old. But there's something in her heavily made-up eyes that has a beady, evil quality. I used to think her eyes were captivating.

Now . . . I see right through them.

Her straight brown hair hangs all the way down to her waist and shines in the lights from the band as she flips it over her shoulder and gestures up to the bar. "I was just passing through town and wanted to stop by to say hi to Judy. You guys remember I worked here for nearly six months."

"That's sure something to put on a résumé," Max drawls, looking completely uninterested. He met Robyn once and made it very clear after everything blew over that he didn't understand the appeal. I'm not sure I do either now.

Wyatt lifts his beer to his lips, looking completely disinterested. Calder, on the other hand, is shooting daggers at the woman, making no mistake she is not welcome here.

Me? I just feel uncomfortable.

My brothers have both moved on and are secure in their relationships. I, on the other hand, just got married and my relationship with Addison is tenuous at best. I don't want the biggest mistake of my life walking in and fucking that all up.

Especially one that I haven't told my best friend about.

God, we were fools back then.

How three men . . . three brothers . . . could all fall for the same woman still just seems like straight fiction.

And when I look back on that time in our lives, I don't really know why we all were so enraptured with her. She was the shiny new toy in town, and we were the guys building up on the mountain. She lived in the barn for a bit and exuded confidence and sex appeal and knew how to party. She really was like a siren, and we were her ships she called in every night.

It's disorienting because I look at her now and I don't know what I saw in her. She pales in comparison to Addison and I'm not referencing looks. Just . . . her overall being.

Addison emotes real, raw, honest spirit whereas Robyn gives calculated, contrived hollowness. Even now, I look at her and I feel nothing. How did I let this woman consume me for any length of time?

I shift left to look for Addison and when I don't see her on the dance floor, I scan the room and spot her at the bar with the girls. Thankfully, it looks like they haven't noticed Robyn, and I'd like to keep it that way. I don't want this part of my past to ever touch or taint what I have with Roe. She is too pure and good for the likes of this.

My chair scrapes loudly as I stand, preparing to extricate myself from this situation, but Robyn steps into my path, stopping me in my tracks.

Addison

"Judy, do you know who that woman is talking to the boys?" Trista asks, bracing her elbows on the bar as she glances over her shoulder and then back to the owner, who looks decidedly uncomfortable.

"Now, I don't want any trouble," Judy warns, splaying her hands out on the heavily lacquered wooden bar.

"Trouble? Why would there be trouble?" Dakota presses in closer so she can hear Judy.

"Maybe you should just go get your boys and head back up the peak, ladies." Judy grabs a rag and wipes down the counter. "You're such nice girls. You're good for those boys."

"But who is that?" I ask more firmly, because now I'm curious too.

Judy's lips purse, her wrinkles stacking on top of each other. "That's Robyn."

"Robyn?" Cozy, Trista, and Dakota all repeat the name in unison.

"Robyn Robyn?" Trista asks, her entire body going still.

Judy nods. "You better get the boys out of there before things escalate. Her husband is sitting right over there."

"Why would things escalate?" I ask, feeling like I'm the only asshole who doesn't know who this Robyn chick is.

"Everyone just needs to calm down," Cozy says, trying to be the voice of reason.

"Someone needs to tell me who the fuck Robyn is or I'm going to march over there and ask her myself."

Dakota and Trista cut each other knowing looks, so I grab their shoulders and force them to look at me. "Spill it."

Dakota sighs heavily. "She's a woman who used to live in the apartment above the barn years and years ago."

"Okay . . . and?"

Trista's nose wrinkles as she cuts a mean glare toward the guys before returning her vengeful face to me. "And she fucked all three of them."

Chills erupt over my skull as my lips part, my whole body feeling electrified with this sickening bit of information. "What do you mean 'fucked all three of them'? Like they shared her?"

Dakota makes a strange noise and says, "They didn't fuck her at the same time. It was all different times behind each other's backs after they'd made a bet over her. It's majorly fucked."

"And she ended up pregnant, right?" Cozy asks, and I swear to God my eyes are going to pop out of my face.

"Pregnant?" I press my hands to my temples, unable to comprehend all of this. I don't consider myself a prude. I grew up around lumberyard guys, but this story tops all of those by a mile.

"Yeah, it was a whole thing," Dakota answers like she's reading the daily weather report. "They didn't know who the father was, and all had to take a paternity test. Turned out the baby belonged to Robyn's husband back in Colorado Springs."

"She was married?" I screech, my voice thankfully drowned out by the loud band. I shake my head in denial as I turn to look at Luke. My sweet Luke. The guy whose shoulders ache every day because he lets me sleep on his chest every night.

He fucked a married woman . . . with his brothers?

My lips curl up in disgust, feeling like I don't know him at all. If that's the kind of shit he's into, no wonder he never made a move on me. I'm too boring for him. Too vanilla. Hell, he was mad at me for fucking a few lumberjacks, yet he failed to mention he fucked a married woman who was also fucking his brothers.

The fuck?

I look over at them and see that the woman is no longer standing where she was before. And neither is Luke. Jerking my head around, I find them in a corner, talking, just the two of them. My eyes drop down her body, noticing she has curves in all the right places. Not my tiny little nothing boobs or my dimply thighs or my stout, bottom-heavy frame. She's long and lean and has way more than a handful of tit. She's obviously beautiful.

Maybe she wants him back.

Maybe that's what they're discussing.

Clearly he must still have feelings for her or he would have told me about the fucked-up past he has with her and his brothers, because otherwise why would he hide it?

My God. What else is my supposed best friend hiding from me?

As I watch this Robyn chick move closer to Luke, a flash of possessiveness overcomes me. My chest heaves and my heart races while my hands turn to fists at my sides. Marriage of convenience or not, we are still fucking married, and it was my tongue shoved down his throat less than ten minutes ago. This simply will not do.

Luke

"Did I hear congratulations are in order, Lukey?" Robyn purrs, slithering up to me in the corner of the bar that she followed me to when I was trying to get the fuck away from her.

I eye my brothers, who are still at the table and doing nothing to help me out of this situation. They jerk their heads at me, clearly telling me to get the fuck away from her. I'm trying, damn it!

"Where did you hear that?" I shove a frustrated hand through my hair.

"Oh . . . around town. And Judy confirmed it of course."

"What are you even doing in town?" I can't help but ask.

Her shoulders lift. "Just had some meetings in Boulder. So? Married?" She shoots me a toothy smile that doesn't feel genuine.

I roll my eyes and shake my head. "Yeah, I'm married. Take care, Robyn."

I move to walk away from her, but her next words stop me dead in my tracks. "You married the daughter of John Monroe, right? Addison, is it?"

I turn slowly on my heel to eye the woman from my past who honestly never asks just an innocent question. My teeth clench as I tilt my head and shake a silent no at her. "Don't speak her name," I warn, my tone guttural.

"Testy, testy." Her tongue darts out to swipe across her ruby lips as her nose wrinkles. "It's interesting how protective you are of her considering the marriage is a total sham."

My jaw cracks as I clench my teeth so hard, my jaw aches. "What are you talking about?"

"Matt and I do business with John and had lunch with him yesterday. He told us this marriage you're in with his daughter isn't real. It's just so she can fulfill the trust requirement and the minute I laid eyes on her tonight, I knew he was telling the truth. She is *so* not your type."

"You don't even fucking know me anymore," I growl, my body vibrating with protectiveness over this woman I hate talking about the woman I love.

"Oh, I think I know you a little." Her gaze flashes down to my dick, causing me to jerk away from her. She snickers and I feel strangely violated.

"You don't know shit about me, Robyn. I'm a different man today than I was ten years ago. I've grown. You clearly haven't."

She loses all humor on her face and pins me with a curious look. "Come on, Lukey." She reaches out and drags her hand down my chest, causing my body to recoil. "Don't be like that. I've missed you the most. I know things got messy, but what you and I had was always different than what I had with Calder and Wyatt."

"What are you even saying to me right now?" I hook my thumb behind me. "You're here with your fucking husband."

"I know, but we're in an open marriage." She glances back to the table that her husband, Matt, is sitting at, and he's observing her like a goddamn cuckhold. "I like to play, and he likes to watch, and I'd *really* like to play with you again, Luke. You look so good."

"He's not interested," a shrill voice cuts in and I swerve my head to see my tiny wife standing near me with fire blazing in her eyes. She steps forward, backing Robyn into the wall, not even glancing at me as she adds, "Luke doesn't play, and he never will, so you can take your fucking toys, and your box-dyed hair, and get the fuck out of Jamestown, or I will go up that mountain and start an avalanche to bury your ass here."

Robyn looks mildly afraid before she sputters out a laugh. "Your wife must be a real firecracker in bed, Lukey."

"Leave, Robyn," I grind out through clenched teeth.

She wrinkles her nose as she looks down to Addison. "Does it bother you?"

"Does what bother me?" Addison asks, her eyes turn to slits as her jaw goes taut.

Robyn leans forward and whispers in her ear, "Does it bother you to know I had him first?"

A strange noise echoes from the woman beside me and before I realize it, Addison's hands are on Robyn's shirt, and she's yanked her down to the floor and is straddling her while she grips Robyn by the hair and yanks her around like a rag doll.

The sound of chairs scraping echoes in the room as Wyatt, Calder, and Max appear beside me watching the fight take place in complete awe.

"Should I stop it?" I ask, my heart racing at the sight of Addison going completely feral on a woman from my past.

"No!" Dakota and Trista both say in unison, appearing out of nowhere.

"Addison is killing her!" Dakota adds with a gleeful smile as Robyn grips Addison's wrists, screaming out for her to let go of her hair.

"What the hell?" Matt yells from across the bar and comes tearing over. The minute he presses his hand to Addison's shoulder and shoves her onto her back, I see red.

"Get your fucking hands off my wife!" I roar, lunging for him.

I grab him by the collar of his suit coat and haul his ass away from the two women on the floor. My body trembles with rage as I nearly lift him up off the ground and march him halfway across the room, his toes racing to keep up with my clipped pace.

"Touch her again and I will break both of your fucking arms," I grind, dropping him to his feet and pulling him close to my face so he can see how serious I am.

"She was attacking my wife!" Matt shouts back at me, his eyes wide with fear as I tower over him by several inches.

"Your wife started it," I grind out before launching him away from me, desperate to get some space between us before I pull my fist back and punch him like I've always wanted to.

He crashes into the barstools, falling on his ass in the process, which feels almost as good as a punch. This man has been a fucker ever since him and my dad were bidding on the same project years ago until we beat his price and won the job. We had no idea Robyn was married to him until everything blew up, and the fact that these two slimeballs are still together, existing and causing chaos, makes me fucking see red.

"Out!" Judy barks, standing in front of me, her bony finger pointing toward the door.

"Judy," I begin to argue, trying to soften my tone as I address her.

"Leave now!" she growls back and then points to something behind me. "And take her with you."

I look back and see Addison standing there, panting heavily. Her hair is a tousled mess and her chest heaves with labored breaths. With a curse, I close the distance between us, frantically inspecting her face and hands to make sure she's okay, but she refuses to look at me, jerking her hands from mine. My heart lurches when I see that her eyes are red-rimmed, and her chin is trembling. She's not just angry. She's hurt.

Fuck.

"You guys know the rules," Judy continues, clapping her hands and gesturing to the door. "No fighting, damn it. It will kill me if I have to permanently ban you all."

"She started it," Addison bites, her tone visceral.

"And I'm ending it," Judy snaps back. "Go outside and cool down."

I crack my neck and glance over to see Robyn crying while she picks her hair extensions up off the bar floor. With a heavy sigh, I wrap my arm around Addison to pull her toward the door with me. She shudders under my touch and jerks away to walk herself out of the bar.

As we reach the doorway, Robyn's voice screams out to us, "White trash cunt."

And in a flash, Addison turns on her heel and lunges back in Robyn's direction, but I manage to catch her at the waist, yanking her back against me as she fights with everything she has.

"Come outside with me," Addison screams, still lunging for Robyn.

"Cool it," I growl, grunting when her leg connects with my balls as she continues to try to squirm free. When she refuses to stop, I yank her around and bend over to toss her up over my shoulder as she's kicking and screaming the whole way.

The harsh December air is cold and biting as I crunch my boots over the snow to carry my flailing wife deep into the parking lot. The quietness of the outdoors must bring some semblance of reason back into her mind as she finally stops beating on my back. I lower her to the ground and shove my hair back out of my face to look at her.

"Are you okay, babe?"

"Don't you babe me!" Roe says, pressing the heels of her hand to my chest and giving me a hearty push. "Don't you dare babe me. Not now. Not *ever* after *that*."

"What are you so mad about?" I ask, glancing over my shoulder when I hear footsteps. Thankfully it's just my family all coming out to witness the shit show taking place.

"What am I so mad about?" Addison's eyes are wide as she barks out a hyenic laugh, looking damn near feral under the parking lot light. She glances around and notices we have an audience and hesitates before she replies, because this is an audience who doesn't know about our secret. An audience who thinks, by all account, this is my real wife.

Her face twists in pain and she begins walking backward away from me, pushing her hair out of her face as she goes.

I move toward her, holding my hand out. "Come on . . . let's get in the truck and we can talk about this at home."

"No," she croaks, a puff of cold air floating around her lips as her voice betrays her. It guts me to see her like this. She inhales deeply through her nose, her nostrils flaring with determination as she says, "I'm walking."

My jaw drops. "It's over two miles up the mountain. You're not fucking walking."

"I'm walking!" she screams, turning her back on me and making her way toward the highway, pausing as a semi goes squealing by.

"Damn it, Roe," I growl, wishing I had my hat on so I could rip it off and chuck it to the ground.

My brothers, Dakota, Trista, and Cozy all stare at her stocky frame as she jogs across the blacktop and turns onto the gravel lane that winds up the mountain toward our cabins.

Dakota hands me Roe's coat while Calder rests his hand on my shoulder. "Looks like you're walking, bro."

I sigh heavily and without a word, run across the highway to catch up to my wife.

Addison

My pulse rushes between my ears as I march up the snowy tire-worn path of Fletcher Mountain, the cold air biting the exposed flesh on my legs and my belly. My heart feels like it's going to beat out of my chest and my lungs burn as I pant out a puff of air in front of me.

Walk it off, Addison. You just need to walk it off.

But an evil voice echoes in my mind as I recall the way that woman looked at Luke. She looked at him like she could eat him alive. She looked at him like he belonged to her.

And the way he looked back at her? What the actual fuck? We're supposed to be exclusive through this arrangement. He shouldn't have been looking at her at all!

Footsteps crunch behind me as Luke calls my name, but I refuse to turn around. I'm too angry to look at him. He's going to hit me with that innocent puppy dog face that I will want to punch.

He finally catches up to me and drapes my coat over my shoulders. If I wasn't freezing my ass off, I would chuck it the ground and make him pick it up. But goddamn it, it's too cold for even my pride.

"Who the hell is Robyn?" I bite, my hands shaking with rage.

Luke makes a weird noise before replying, "She's no one."

"Bullshit no one," I spit, a white cloud of mist dancing on my lips. "You've obviously fucked her."

"So what," Luke huffs, stomping in stride beside me. "I don't know everyone that you've fucked."

"Do you want to know?"

"Fuck no."

"Good for you . . . but I want to know."

"Why?"

I stop in my track and thrust my finger at my friend. "Because when a woman has her claws all over you like you're open territory, it pisses me the fuck off. We're *married*, Luke." I flash my ring to him as proof. The ring that I love more than I can even admit to myself.

"I know that." He frowns back at me, his eyes looking soft and tender.

"So why lie to me?"

"Because I didn't want you to know about this part of my life," he roars, throwing his hands out wide. His face is stricken with fear and shame as his heavy exhales release plumes of vapor in front of him. His cheeks are red from the cold, and likely stress, as he grips the back of his neck and looks down at his feet. "Because it's embarrassing and fucked on so many twisted levels. And because it would kill me if you ever thought less of me."

"I wouldn't think less of you for that," I scoff, crossing my arms over my chest and shivering against the cold. "I'd think less of you for not being open with me though."

"That's rich coming from you." Luke shakes his head, his entire body radiating defensiveness.

"What does that mean?"

"You keep me at arm's length, Roe," he cries, the veins in his neck bulging as he hits me with an intense look that takes my breath away. "You let me in but not all the way. I don't feel safe with you because I don't ever know that you're not going to bolt. I mean, hell, I kissed you and you didn't look at me for two weeks. You're paying rent at your apartment in Boulder still because you need to make sure if you want to get away from me, you can. It's plain as fucking day that if I make one wrong move . . . we're done."

"That's how you see me?"

"Yes!" he roars, tossing his hands out wide, the snowy scenic background at odds with his tortured stance. "I'm fucking terrified of losing you all the time."

"But this is all fake," I exclaim and the devastated look on his face cuts straight through me.

His head drops and he begins walking up the hill again, trying to get away from me.

"Luke," I cry and run up to grab his arm.

He yanks it out of my hand. "Don't touch me."

"Why?"

"Because when you touch me, I can't think straight." His voice cracks as he stops in his tracks. "And it's not fair."

"What's not fair?"

"It's not fair that you get to touch me and hug me and kiss me in the bar and rock my whole fucking world and just continue living your life like—"

"Like what?"

"Like I mean nothing," he cries, his voice distraught. "Like it's just another day. Like I'm forgettable and meaningless and just a friend and that our marriage isn't fucking real."

My eyes swim with tears as I look up at him. There is so much to unpack in what he just said. He thinks he's forgettable? Meaningless? *He told me I'm his everything.* But what sticks the most is what he said about our marriage. He's angry our marriage isn't real? My voice is raw when I ask the question I'm terrified of hearing the answer to. "Do you want our marriage to be real?"

His lips thin and his nostrils flare as he glowers down at me. "The fact that you even have to ask just proves how big of a fucking wall you still have up between us."

Headlights suddenly illuminate the two of us and I spot Wyatt's truck pulling up. He comes to a stop beside us, his window down, everyone inside the car staring at us.

But Luke won't take his eyes off me. "Take Addison. I'll walk," he says softly and, without another word, he pushes past me, up the hill, and I stare at the back of him while Trista wraps her hands around me and ushers me into the back seat.

Squished into the vehicle, surrounded by Luke's family, I burst into tears and thank God for the Fletchers because they all say absolutely nothing.

Chapter 30

FACT OR FICTION?
You are my emergency contact.

Addison

It's dusk when I finally return to Fletcher Mountain from my run in the cemetery. I don't usually do a lot of running in the winter because the cold hurts my lungs, but after last night, I needed it more than I needed comfortable breathing.

However, even a jog and a visit with my brother did nothing to calm the anxiety still swirling in my belly. I haven't spoken to Luke since he walked away from me on the side of the mountaintop last night. I saw him briefly in the hallway this morning but then he closed himself off in his room and I never heard from him the rest of the day.

I'm not even sure who is supposed to be mad at who anymore. I'm mad at him for not being honest with me. He's mad at me for keeping him at a distance. I guess? But he doesn't realize I built this wall of mine brick by brick and it's not that easy for me to just knock it down, no matter how much I craved his arms last night.

I at least was open enough to send him a text to let him know I was going to Boulder for a run. I was rewarded with a curt thumbs-up emoji. Like I'm a roommate touching base, not the woman he poured his heart out to less than twenty-four hours ago.

I frown when I park in front of the cabin and notice Luke's truck isn't parked where it usually is. I check my phone and don't see a text from him, so I can't help but wonder where he went. As I hop out of the vehicle, I glance down the hill and see Dakota pacing on her front porch.

"Everything okay?" I call out as I walk toward her.

She shakes her head, crossing her arms over her chest. "I just hate these calls."

"What calls?" I ask as I reach the base of her steps.

"The fire department calls." She shakes out her arms and runs her hands through her hair, her feet loud on the wooden deck. "They don't come very often, but when they do, I can't sit down until Calder comes back home. And this one sounded bad—a barn fire with these kinds of winds? My mind is a dark place right now."

A lump forms in my throat, and I suddenly feel like I can't breathe, but manage to choak out, "Luke?"

"Did he not tell you?" Dakota pauses her pacing and looks at me with a frown.

Tears fill my eyes instantly. I don't even know they're coming, they just flood my vision, completely blinding me.

"Oh shit." Dakota rushes down the steps and opens her arms to wrap me in a hug, but I jerk back.

"It's fine." I hold my hand up to stop her from approaching again. "I just maybe missed the call."

But I know I didn't.

No missed calls. No texts. No nothing. My husband went out for an emergency fire call and never told me. I guess Luke is pretty good at putting walls up as well.

"Don't worry, Addison. Luke is going to be fine."

"I'm not worried." I wince and look down the mountain, like I'll be able to spot where the call is, but of course, I see nothing. Just the sleepy little community of Jamestown taunting me with its beauty when all that's going on in my mind is chaos.

"I'll see you later, Dakota." I turn and begin marching back up the hill.

"I'll text you if I hear from Calder," she calls after me.

"Don't bother!" I pick up pace, taking off into a run toward the cabin. Only I don't stop at the cabin, I keep going, choosing to jog the path that I've jogged countless times now even though I've already run three miles today.

The trail winds behind the three cabins that Luke pointed out to me shortly after I moved in. Apparently, Calder maintains the path so he can take his cat for walks year-round. Calder, the brother who knows how to inform his partner when he's going on a life-threatening call. They're not even married, and Dakota gets more information than I do.

Must be nice.

Rage simmers in my veins, the cold air shredding my lungs as fresh snow falls in fat, puffy flakes that soak my Carhartt coat. I push myself farther and farther up the mountain, going deeper into the forest than I have in all the other times I've run back here.

All too quickly, I run out of trail and begin trenching through the sometimes-knee-deep snow. My ankles freeze as my sneakers get soaked with each passing step, but eventually I can't feel them, which is nice. I don't want to feel anything. I especially don't want to feel this ache I have in my chest over the idea that Luke . . . the man I care about could not come home tonight.

He might not come home because he could die in that fucking fire, and I don't even know if I'm listed as his emergency contact to get the call.

Or . . . or! He might not come home by choice. He might choose to abandon me just like my own mother did.

"Hey, pumpkin. How's my baby girl today?" my mom asks from her spot at our kitchen table.

I stare at her for a moment to see what kind of mood she's in. She's been really tired lately because she's been out late so many nights. I heard her come home after midnight last night and Dad got mad 'cause she woke him up. If she's in one of her cranky moods, then I try to stay far far away from her usually. Maybe today she's better.*

"I'm fine, but Aaron ruined my school project about the ocean, and I was nearly finished," I groan. I like my little brother, most of the time, but days like today he really annoys me.

"That's family for you. Sometimes the ones we love the most disappoint us the most." She gives me one of her big hugs, the ones that always make me feel better.

God, I haven't thought about that conversation for years. Is that why this is upsetting me so much? Because Luke might choose that this is just too hard after all, that I'm not worth sticking around for? Just like my mom? Because God knows sometimes the ones we love the most can still manage to leave us without a backward glance and without a final hug goodbye.

Sometimes the ones we love the most disappoint us the most.

And would that crush me if Luke didn't come home because I love him? I mean, I know I love him like a friend. But do I *love* him, love him? That thought stops me dead in my tracks and a sob rips up my throat as I hold my stomach and try not to be sick.

Do you want our marriage to be real?

The fact that you even have to ask just proves how big of a fucking wall you still have up between us.

I fall to my knees in the snow, my hands burning in the powder as my face boils, steam billowing off me as I pant, fighting to catch my breath.

I wipe at the hot tears pouring out of me. I don't want Luke to be like my mom. I don't want Luke to be like my brother. I need Luke. I need him here, with me. I need him to call me. I need to stop pushing him away enough to let him call me. I have to be his emergency contact. He's been mine for years.

But I never even told him that.

I just did it without having the conversation with him,

because I didn't want to dig into what it meant when I did it. It meant that he matters to me. He is my lifeline, my comfort, my home. Somehow, he became irreplaceable to me, and now I'm at risk of losing him and it's too late for me to pull back to protect myself from this pain.

I unsteadily stand to my feet, my fleece-lined leggings soaked as a clamminess settles over me. Sweat and snow damp my skin as I glance around and struggle to find my bearings. I squint down into the bright white snow to use my footsteps to follow my path back to the trail. Back to home. I need to go home.

I've loved running back here. I haven't done it since it started snowing and I've missed the peace and serenity I feel when I'm out here in the middle of nowhere. Away from the urban sprawl of Boulder. Away from the voices in my head that don't shut up at night. But right now, this mountain isn't quieting anything in my mind.

Only Luke can do that.

He is my quiet. My calm. My mountain.

It's dark by the time I spot the cabin, and my face is swollen and numb, most likely covered in frozen tears and snot as I round the house, desperate to get out of these soggy shoes. I'm mentally preparing for how painful that hot shower is going to be when a gruff voice thunders, "Where the fuck have you been?"

I look up and see Luke. *My Luke.* He's standing on our front porch. *Our* front porch, wearing a white T-shirt covered in soot and firemen pants with reflective lines shining in the dark and suspenders up over his shoulders. The yellow porch light casts him in a silhouette as he stomps down the steps toward me, his face positively murderous when he steps out enough for me to see it.

"I've been calling you nonstop for an hour, ever since Dakota called to tell me you were upset."

I pull my phone out of my leggings pocket to see that it's dead and wet. "I didn't know my phone died. Sorry."

"Sorry?" he huffs out a laugh, his face a strange mix of sad and happy. "Jesus Christ. I've been worried sick and all you can say is sorry?"

"You're one to talk," I yell back, now that I know he's not fucking dead in a fiery barn. "I had to find out from Dakota that you got called away to a fire."

His jaw goes taut as he stares back at me, saying nothing.

"A fire, Luke!" My eyes fill with tears again and I swipe at them, annoyed that I still have any tears left to cry.

"I'm sorry," he says, noticing my obvious pain. "I was . . . angry."

"Angry." I shake my head and smile through my tears as pain bubbles up to the surface and erupts inside of me like a volcano. "I told you we needed to be good through this arrangement, Fletcher."

"I know that."

"I told you I couldn't lose you."

"I know that too."

"Then what the fuck are you doing?" I cry, my voice fraught with devastation. "What are you doing?"

"I don't know," he growls back, his face twisted in pain as his eyes score over my face.

I inhale a sharp breath and move closer to him, stabbing my finger into his chest. "Fact or fiction, Fletcher. You want me. Not as a friend but as something more."

Luke exhales heavily, his face long and sad as he holds his hands out in surrender. "Fact."

I nod slowly. "Now ask me."

"Roe, I can't—"

"Shut up and ask me."

His Adam's apple slides down his throat before he says, "Fact or fiction. You . . . want me."

I lick my lips, my chin quivering with fear because the answer to this feels big. Possibly bigger than I'm ready to admit, but I have to give him something. And I know as soon as I answer this question, we will never be the same. We can never go back to being just friends. But I'm not sure there's any going back at this point anyways. I'm too far gone.

"It's a fact, Luke. It was a fact before everything that happened last night and it's a fact after. I want you. As more than a friend."

His face turns fierce as he processes my words, having the ridiculous ability to look shocked. How could he not know? How is it not painfully obvious that I'm obsessed with this man?

In a flash, he eliminates the space between us and scoops me up into his arms. My feet dangle off the ground as he presses his forehead to mine, breathing me in as I breathe him in. He smells like smoke and sweat and musky clothes, but I love it. I want to wrap myself in this scent and remember this moment forever.

"Tell me again," he urges, his arms bound tight around my waist as he holds me to him. "Tell me you want me."

I shudder and grip his neck as I say, "I want you."

He groans, a guttural noise that sounds inhuman. "It's about fucking time." And then he drops me to my feet and his lips are on me, desperate and frenzied. His tongue urgent and unrelenting. My body melts into his as my frozen limbs thaw with every suck, nip, and lick. I fork my fingers through his hair, pulling him in as I arch into his kiss until a thought strikes me and our lips yank part with a hard shove to his chest.

"The next time you leave for a fire without telling me, I will kill you, Luke Fletcher. Do you hear me?" I pound my fist on his chest. "I'm your wife and you have to tell me where you're going."

"Okay," he replies with a drunken-looking smile while trying to pull me back in.

"I'm serious." I press my finger into his chest, not giving in quite yet. "You're my emergency contact and I better damn well be yours."

He pulls back and smirks at me like I'm some adorable puppy who needs a cuddle. "Okay, babe."

I swallow the knot in my throat, my brows still knit firmly together. "Okay."

He steps toward me again, cautiously, his eyebrows arched like he's waiting for me to wail on him one more time. "Okay?" he asks, as his hand snakes around my waist.

I nod. "Okay."

He dips down and brushes his lips softly over mine as he murmurs, "Okay."

"Okay," I repeat, feeling dizzy as I pull him closer, desperate to feel right again.

"Okay," he whispers one more time, and then my equilibrium is thwarted as my feet come out from under me because my husband has lifted me up to carry me over the threshold . . . into our home.

Well, okay.

Chapter 31

FACT OR FICTION?
So this is love.

Luke

My heart races as I stomp through my house, not bothering to kick off my snowy boots as the desperate urge to get this woman in my arms warmed up overwhelms me. And I don't mean warm her up with my lips. Yet.

Right now, Addison is soaked and shaking and needs out of these wet clothes before I can do any of the things I want to do to her.

I step into my bathroom and shift to flick on the lights as she shudders against me. "Fuck, I need to get you warmed up, babe," I growl, setting her down on her feet.

She looks up and nods, rubbing her hands together.

I step into her space and cup her hands with mine. "We gotta get you out of your wet clothes and into the shower. You okay with that?"

"Yy-yye-essss," she stutters, starting to peel her jacket off.

I have to bite my tongue as I help her shed the drenched clothes. The fact that she ran in this wet shit while it was snowing, only wearing sneakers and leggings, makes me fucking furious. I want to bend her over my knee and spank her for being so careless with the woman I'm fucking crazy about. The woman who is stubborn to her core.

But she did admit to wanting me.

That's progress.

And I'm embracing those words with everything I have.

She pulls her shoes off and I bend to remove her soaked socks, swearing under my breath when I see how red her toes are.

Standing, I rub her arms, trying to get the blood flowing back into her limbs. My breath hitches when she starts to pull her loose T-shirt up. Our eyes lock briefly with unspoken words as we prepare to step fully across our friendship barrier. Ready or not.

My fingers brush her ribs as I help bring her shirt up and toss it to the floor, fully intent on never going back to what we were before.

Inhaling deeply, I take a second to stare at her in nothing but her bra and leggings, but the moment is cut short when I see goose bumps pepper across her skin. "We need to get you naked and into the warm water, so you don't go hypothermic on me."

She lets out a laugh and smiles through her chattering teeth. "Sounds hot."

My nostrils flare at her little joke as I help her out of her sports bra next, my jaw going taut as her two tiny peaks point toward me with red, ruby nipples. She laughs and pushes me back, snapping me out of my stupor as she bends to push her tights off. I force myself to turn on the shower, making sure it's not too hot to shock her body even more.

"Get in and start warming up," I order a little too harshly, having a hard fucking time warring with my mind about not touching her yet and getting her warmed up first. "I'm coming in with you."

She quickly jumps and the moan that she utters as the water hits her skin has my dick swelling. I shuck off my fire repellent bibs so quick I almost fall over. Normally I leave this stuff at the station but when Dakota called me to tell me how upset Addison was when she found out about the fire, I couldn't take the time to stop on my way back. I had to get to her, especially when she didn't answer her damn phone. I was desperate to apologize for being such a fucking asshole. She'd texted me earlier today to tell me about her plans to go for a run and my response was cruel, petty, and fucking selfish.

I will never do that to her again.

To know she was so distraught, she ran through the snow fucking kills me. Her face when she came around the corner of my house looked like she'd been through war. And it was my fault. All of it.

Yes, I've been angry at her for holding back her feelings but leaving her at home to worry? It's unforgivable. And what I said to her last night in my anger? Fuck, I'm an asshole.

But seeing Robyn interact with Roe made my blood boil, and Roe's anger at me was justified. I hurt her, but I don't regret it because it woke us both up to see how important we are to each other. And it should have come as no shock to me that my wife, my Roe . . . is a fighter.

God that excites the ever-loving fuck out of me.

I'll fight with her forever if she'll have me.

I tug my jeans off and tear my shirt over my head. When I glance at the glass shower door, I find Addison watching me with her lip clamped tightly between her teeth. My dick jumps in my boxer briefs because I like her eyes on me. I've waited what feels like my whole fucking life to have her look at me like this, so I relish the moment I peel my boxers down and kick them out of the way.

Her hungry eyes are glued to my cock as I stalk toward her and swing the door open. She finally looks up, meeting my gaze, which makes me smile.

"Like what you see?" I ask, stepping into the shower and crowding into her space.

"Luke . . ." she says tentatively, reaching out to lay her hands on my chest, making me wince.

"Babe, your hands," I murmur, cupping them to my chest

and rubbing them aggressively as the water pours down over her, my own body standing outside the stream to not take any of the flow from her.

"I'm fine," she says, pulling her hands back and shaking them out. "They're tingling. That's good."

I reach around her to adjust the water temp a little warmer, now that she's been in here a few minutes. "What about your toes?" I ask, dropping to my knees, trying to ignore for a few seconds how close to me her delicious naked body is. Picking one foot up off the tile floor, she lets out a squeak as she regains her balance so I can rub them hard. They feel like ice.

She lets out another laugh when I massage my hands up her right calf and down over her ankle, gripping her toes until I finally start to feel them heat up. "The other one," I demand, repeating the motions with her other leg.

"They're burning like hell now, I think I'm good. We won't have to cut any toes off." She reaches down and tips my chin up to look at her. I squint through the splatter of the shower water and feel like I can finally breathe again, and when I do . . . I let myself take in what I have standing before me.

Addison's body glistens under the stream of water beading down her flesh. Her thick, muscular legs, round, supple hips, and soft, smooth belly are eye level with me. Begging to be touched. My gaze travels upward and I can't help feasting my eyes on her breasts. I've fantasized about having them bare to me every day she's been here. Imagining what was under those oversize T-shirts is nothing compared to this reality. Her nipples are hard and begging for my lips to be on them.

"Addison," I state, using her real name and not her nickname, because what I'm about to say is going to be very unfriendly.

Her stomach contracts with a deep breath. "Yes?"

I run my hands up her calves, leaning in to kiss her stomach, loving how she inhales deeply when I nip at her skin there. "I want to rub my hands all over you. Wash you. Worship you," I murmur, kissing at her naval. "I want to lick and suck every inch of your body."

She shudders with a labored breath and grabs my wet hair as I stroke my hands higher up her thighs, gripping her ass as I lick and kiss my way up her stomach. "Then I want to take you to my bed and fuck you to sleep."

Her breath comes out in quick pants as I gaze up at her, feeling my pulse racing beneath my skin. "How do you feel about all that?"

Her breath stutters as she shifts, pressing her back against the tile wall. She nods her head and lifts her foot to my shoulder, opening her legs to me. My mouth salivates as I take in her perfect pink pussy covered in a thin coat of hair. A beast awakens inside me as I hold myself back from attacking her like an animal who hasn't eaten in days.

"I want your answer, Addison." I smile and shake my head as I tsk at her. "I need to hear you say it, because once you say you want the same thing . . . once I get a taste of you . . ." I stand pulling her close to me, letting her feel how much I want her as my hard cock presses into her belly. "I won't want to stop."

She smiles a cheeky smile, looking like the spunky Roe I've grown to love. My best friend. Her voice is rich and virile when she cups her hands around my neck. "I feel like you better get started because lord knows I don't sleep well."

"You will when I'm done with you, babe," I warn before covering her body with mine as I seize her lips with a deep, guttural groan.

She meets my frantic wild kiss with her own. It's a kiss I've longed to share with her. One not weighed down by fear and insecurity. One that I can offer without abandon because I know she wants it. She wants me.

She might even love me even if she can't quite say it yet.

I press her against the tile, swallowing her gasp of shock as I reach down and pull her leg up to grind my cock into her as it grows even harder and seeks whatever friction it can find. She meets my needy thrusts with her own while she tries to pull me closer.

She tastes so fucking good, I think as I tear my lips from hers, kissing my way to her jaw . . . her neck . . . down her collarbone and over to the other side.

Pulling back, I stop to catch my breath before I get carried away. "I think I promised you I'd worship your body first." She lets out a frustrated noise that has me chuckling. I kiss her on the nose and pull back to grab my bodywash. "We have all night, babe. Let me do this for you."

I pop the top of the bottle. It's a mountain rain scent so it won't come close to smelling as good as she does, but I like the idea of her smelling like me. I want my scent and my cum all the fuck over her by the end of this night.

She's mine forever.

She scowls a little, watching me lather up my hands. I fucking love that she doesn't want me to stop kissing her, but I wasn't lying when I said I wanted to learn and touch every inch of her body. I run the suds up her arms, her chest rising and falling as she watches. Working the soap up around her neck and slowly sliding my hands down her chest to cup her perfect pert breasts, her hard nipples digging into my palms.

She moans softly when I roll her nipples between my thumb and forefinger, fighting back the urge I have to squeeze them until she screams.

When I get back down on my knees to wash her legs she inhales sharply as I stroke between her thighs. I can't help but growl when I feel how slick she is between her folds.

"Fuck, Addison," I say huskily, standing and removing my hands from her wet heat. She bites her lip, and I lean in to kiss her again. "Soon," I say, rubbing my hands over her breasts and pulling her into the full spray to wash the suds off her.

"My turn," she says, grabbing the soap herself. She squirts a healthy amount and brings it to my chest, swirling the suds over my light dusting of chest hair. Down my arms and back to my stomach. I relish in feeling her small hands on me as she explores my body. I've wanted this for so long.

Then her hands slide down my abs . . . and she strokes lower, fisting her hand over my cock. I hiss, pressing my forehead into her neck. I kiss and suck my way to her lips as she pumps me, making me see stars. When she cups my balls with her other hand, I grip her hair, tipping her head back to me with a groan as I devour her lips. She's too fucking good at that.

"I'm supposed to be washing you," I growl into the shell of her ear before nipping at her lobe.

She sighs with a small laugh on her lips as I pull my head back. "Friends don't let friends soap up alone."

My lips pull up into a smile and I can't help but kiss her again. It feels good to kiss her whenever I want. Whenever she amuses me or challenges me or pisses me off. I'm going to kiss her frequently and freely because she's finally mine.

I turn her around, making sure I soap every inch of her back and her fucking perfect ass. I pull her tight to me and grab the shampoo, then massage her head and hair as she presses back into me. I let her rinse out the suds and I quickly scrub my own hair and face, enjoying watching her raise her arms to stroke the suds out of her hair.

Pulling her to me again, I kiss her already swollen lips and turn her in my arms so her ass is pressed up against my throbbing cock. "Put your arms on the wall."

She does as she's asked, and I squeeze her breasts, lightly tugging her nipples in a way that has her ass pressing into my cock harder. I trail my hands lower and cup her sex, sliding a finger through her folds.

"I'm going to make you come on my fingers," I rasp, rubbing her clit as she arches back into me, moving her hips with me.

"Luke," she moans as I work her clit harder, feeling her legs tense against me.

"Fuck I love hearing you say my name like that." My jaw clenches as I work my two middle digits into her tight heat as she drops her head to watch me fuck her with my fingers.

Stroking in and out of her, I make sure my palm is rubbing her clit with every stroke as I kiss and suck her neck. Her body moves against mine as I feel her core begin to tighten.

"Luke . . . fuck . . . I'm going to come," she says breathily as her fingers splay out wide on the tile wall. She grinds into my movements with every thrust of my fingers. I fight back the urge to take myself into my own hand and come along with her, but I want her orgasm more than I want my own.

I palm her breast with my other hand, tweaking her nipples in time with my strokes. "Come on my fingers, babe, I want to feel it." I whisper heavily into her neck as her legs begin to shake. She reaches one hand down to mine. Not to stop me, but to press my hand into her harder. Letting me know she wants it harder and faster, and I give her what she wants.

"Luke," she pants out. "Luke!" Her breaths come out in quick, shallow gasps as she grips my hand that's fucking her. Her hips moving in rhythm to what I'm doing to her.

"I'm coming . . . I'm coming . . ." she cries out, standing on her tiptoes, and I feel her pussy pulsing around my fingers. Her whole body tenses against mine while I hold her as she rides the waves of her orgasm, her belly contracting under my arm.

Breathing just as hard as she is, she goes slack after a moment, and I withdraw my fingers from her while she still clutches my hand. I have to pull back and grip my cock hard to relieve some tension before I fucking cum all over her back.

Desperate, Roe turns on her heels and grabs my neck, kissing me fiercely. I grip the backs of her thighs and hoist her up around my waist, pressing her against the wall. We kiss and suck and nibble and moan and lick and devour each other for who knows how long. Long enough for the water to run cold.

I walk us out of the shower and wrap her in a towel while I grab my own, needing a minute to calm my racing heart and my cock. I'm not one to shy away from coming but I want to be inside her when I do it. Not spraying it on her back like a fucking neanderthal.

Roe watches me dry off with a hungry look that isn't helping. "Looking at me like that will only get you fucked." I tease her, watching her drop her towel as she stalks toward me.

"That better be a promise," she says, grabbing me by the waist of my towel and pulling me into my bedroom.

I shut the lights off, allowing the moonlight to be our guide as we slip into bed naked, clean, and warm. I crawl over my wife, kissing up her navel and taking one of her nipples into my mouth, sucking hard.

She delves her hands into my hair, crying out as I flick my tongue over the tight bud. I nudge a knee between her legs, and she opens them willingly for me. I move to kiss her lips, my fingers sliding between her thighs and finding her pussy still wet and waiting as I thrust a finger deep inside her.

She arches her back, breaking the kiss while I slowly work in and out of her, her wet hair draped over my pillow. "You're so fucking wet for me, babe." I'm so hard I know I'm leaving a trail of precum on her leg.

Nodding, she bites her lip as she thrusts her hips up. "Luke, I need you."

My head swims hearing her say that. "Fuck, I really want to

taste you, but I can save that for later. I need to be inside you or I'm going to lose it." I turn and rustle in my nightstand drawer, searching for a condom with hands shaking like it's my first time.

Grabbing one, I twist around, struggling to open it while Roe's warm hand stills on top of mine. "No condom."

My brows furrow as I look up at her, shifting my head so the moonlight illuminates her. I do a circuit of her face to ensure she's fully with it, and swallow hard when she grabs the condom from me and places it on the bed. "Are you sure?"

"I have an IUD and I want to feel you, Luke. All of you." She sits up and runs her hands up my chest.

My cock twitches and I glance down to see a bead of precum pulse out the tip like even he knows what she's just offered.

"When was the last time you slept with someone?" she asks, and her question carries weight in the silence of my bedroom.

My jaw muscle twitches as I look up at her and answer honestly. "It's been a couple years." It's sad but true. But also, not sad because I've been too busy pining for my best friend . . . which she does not need to know.

"Have you been tested since then?" she asks, clearly not judging me.

I nod. "Yes, and I used a condom."

She licks her lips and reaches down to grip my length. "It's been longer than that for me, and I was tested at my annual last year."

I let out a stuttered breath, pushing her down onto the bed while I hold myself above her. My mind spins thinking about the level of intimacy this means. "Are you positive? I don't mind using a condom."

"Yes, Luke," she practically begs, spreading her legs and letting a hand trail down her stomach between us. She dips two fingers into her sex as she reaches up with her other hand to pull me closer. "You're my husband and I want to feel all of you."

Blinking back the sting in my eyes at her words I let out a laugh and smile at her, because on the surface they're dirty and sexy. But underneath, I hear . . . mine . . . forever. *Mine. Mine. Mine.*

I pull her hand from between her legs and bring her fingers to my mouth sucking them off. I moan at the taste of her, my hips pulsing harshly between her as her scent elicits a carnal reaction in me.

"You're going to be the death of me," I growl, reaching down to grab my cock and run it along her glistening lips, feeling her scorching heat waiting for me. I push into her slowly. Her tight pussy struggling to take me in. I stare at her face as our mouths drop open at the same time. The pressure is too intense. The feelings too real. I pull back out and thrust harder, pushing through her tight muscles. I freeze at the fucking overwhelming sensation of feeling her bare.

"Oh God, Addison."

"Luke," she whispers, pulling me close to her so she can kiss me. Rolling her hips upward I feel myself sink even deeper.

"Fuck, you feel so good." I moan against her lips. Her pussy clenches around me and she rolls her hips again, making me grunt.

"I need you to fuck me, Luke. Fuck me. Please." She begs, moving her hips again as she wraps one leg around my back.

Her begging is music to my ears as I shift my arms and hold myself still, watching her struggle at my refusal to give her what she wants. Her eyes pop open and she looks up at me, confused.

"Tell me you want me," I command, my voice firm as my eyes score over every feature on her face, committing this moment to memory. I don't just want to fuck her right now. I want more. I want everything with this woman.

Her face softens and her hands move up to my cheeks, her finger sliding over the scar on my chin. "I want you."

Her words cause a chill to run up my spine because I know she's saying "want," but her eyes are saying more. I bite my lip and look away, savoring this moment like it could be my last. When I look back at her, she has a soft, secretive smile on her face, like she can read my mind. The one downfall of falling in love with your best friend . . . they can see right through you.

So, I reply with the only thing I can say. "I want you too."

And with a growl, I thrust hard into her, watching her expression shift in a flash from warm and fuzzy to shock and pain. It's the good kind of pain though. The kind of pain that comes from years of denying ourselves what we should have had all along.

Her lips part and her breath catches as she adjusts to the size of me, moaning and glancing down at where we're connected. Gripping my neck like a lifeline, she holds on as I rock into her again, and I love how her breasts brush my chest with the motion. She pulls me in for a kiss as I continue pumping into her, her channel stretching for me with each thrust. The sounds of our bodies connecting echo in the room along with our moans in-between frenzied kisses, and it's erotic as fuck.

She breaks the kiss and murmurs and groans "I want you, Luke" over and over like those words are the only thing to relieve her of this overwhelming feeling.

Warmth explodes in my chest that fights with the carnal urge I have going on below my waist as I lose myself inside of her. This must be what love is. The battle of heart and sex. Good versus evil. Feelings with desire. It's a heady sense of rightness and one I've never experienced before and one I never want to let go of. Ever.

Fuck, I'm so gone for her.

Her hand snakes down my neck as she lets her nails scratch my chest while she dips between us to rub her clit.

"Fuck," I growl, my voice guttural as I watch her hand move on her body. This is not helping stave off the release building at the base of my spine.

"Don't stop, I'm so close." She gasps with each word as I pound into her, our bodies slick with sweat, breath hot on each other's faces.

Her back arches as her core fists my dick so hard, barreling my release forward.

"Yes, Luke," she cries as her pussy clenches around me.

And it's my name on her lips that does me in.

My release surges through my shaft as her sex shudders around me, both of us coming at the same time. My vision is a kaleidoscope of nonsense constricting my world into hot moans and slick flesh and the smell of sex. It's not a bad place to live.

I pump into her several more times as the aftershocks ripple through me. When my vision finally returns, I can only smile down at my wife before I kiss her slowly, lazily, grunting when her pussy clenches one more time around me.

I will love you forever, Roe. And I'll wait until you're ready before I utter those words, because I know you're still unpacking things. So for now, I'm going to luxuriate in the bliss that is being inside my best friend.

Because this . . . is love.

Chapter 32

FACT OR FICTION?
We're snowed in.

Addison

"Oh my God." I gasp as I open the blinds to gaze out the window of Luke's bedroom, which overlooks the backside of the mountain. His entire back deck is covered in a snowdrift and it's halfway up his window, impeding my view.

Luke groans from the bed, his hand reaching out to where I was lying just minutes ago. "What are you doing?" he croaks, stretching his arms out as he arches his back into a long, lazy stretch. "Come back to bed."

The sheet slides down low, revealing the trail of hair that leads to what I now know is a spectacular-sized dick. Long, thick, and definitely leaving a lasting effect between my legs this morning.

Who knew Luke Fletcher has been packing all this time? I blush as I cover my mouth to hide my girlie smirk as he sports really obvious morning wood. I clear my throat. "We had to have gotten over a foot of snow in the night and it's still coming down out there. It never snows like this in Boulder this time of year."

"That's mountain life for you," Luke says, his sleepy brown eyes blinking at the bright daylight pouring in through the window. "Guess we won't be going anywhere for a while." He waggles his brows at me, and I can't help but smile.

"Are we really snowed in?" I can't hide the giddiness in my voice, and I should feel embarrassed but I just . . . don't.

He lifts his shoulders and nods. "If it keeps going, yeah. Does that scare you to be snowed in with me?" His eyes flash with wickedness as he looks me up and down, causing my nipples to pebble under the flannel blanket of his that I wrapped myself in before walking over to look outside.

I'm still just as naked as I was when I fell asleep with his cum inside me last night. I feel dirty and spent and stretched and all the things that make it impossible to wipe this smile off my face.

My cheeks flush at the heated, threatening look in his eyes. Am I scared to be snowed in with Luke Fletcher for who knows how long?

Hell yes, I'm scared.

I'm scared I'll screw myself into starvation because I haven't eaten anything in over twenty-four hours and all I want to devour is him.

My eyes flash to his cock as he reaches under the sheet and fists himself, watching me watch him. Need pools between my legs, and I clench my thighs together before my arousal drips out of me.

Then again, it could be Luke dripping out of me too.

Having him come in me last night was an experience unlike any I've ever had. So raw, so dirty, so intimate and elemental. I feel closer to him than I ever have, and I didn't even realize that was possible. I can't imagine what it would feel like to have his baby inside of me.

My head jerks back at that errant thought. Babies have never been an idea I've entertained, but suddenly, my body is intrigued by the idea of making a miniature Luke.

Jesus Christ, hormones are weird.

A rush of need stirs inside of me, and I wonder if I've ever felt this wet in my entire life. "Hey, have you seen my blue panties anywhere?" I ask, remembering the last time I was soaking wet. "I was too embarrassed to ask before but now that you've seen me naked . . ." My voice trails off when Luke's smile falls and his face twists with discomfort. "Oh my God, what?"

He shakes his head from side to side, struggling to make eye contact with me. "I don't want to do this."

"Do what?" I ask, my heart picking up speed as anxiety creeps into my aroused state of mind.

He blows out a long breath as he sits up to prop his back against the headboard, covering his erection by bending his legs under the sheets. "I don't want to lie to you, Roe."

"Lie to me?" I crawl over onto the bed and kneel at his feet, staring over at him, my brows tight on my forehead. "Why would you lie to me?"

He expels a strange, tortured noise from his chest and scrubs his face over his hands. "Fuck it. This is marriage . . . this is honesty . . . here we go." He looks up at me and winces slightly before saying, "I jerked off into your underwear the morning after we slept on the sofa together."

"You what?" I sputter, my body zapped with shock and then confusion.

He nods, looking solemn. Like a kid who just got caught with his hand in a cookie jar. "You dropped them in the hallway, and I took them to my room and fucking came all over them."

Silence hangs between us. The sound of blowing snow hitting the house breaks through the stillness between us.

And then . . . then . . . I burst out a strange noise, falling down on my side as I curl up in the fetal position.

"Don't laugh," Luke deadpans as I clutch my stomach, my eyes wet with tears.

"What am I supposed to do with that information?" I sputter, my words hard to say through the fits of giggles. "Should I give you a pat on the back and say, thanks for sharing that heavy truth with me. My God, you're sick in the head."

"I know." He presses a pillow over his face, his abs contracting in a really sexy way, totally at odds with the weird shit that just came out of his mouth. He murmurs into the fabric, "I was so embarrassed, I threw them in the fire afterward."

"Damn it, Luke! I loved those underwear!" I exclaim, sitting up to glare at him.

"I'm not proud, okay," he growls, dropping the pillow and giving it a fitful punch.

I fight back the smile on my face, watching him all tortured and humiliated over there while also looking like some sort of Greek god at the same time. It's an adorable combination.

How can someone so hot be so . . . bizarre?

Taking pity on him, I tilt my head and offer, "I broke my vibrator because of you."

His eyes snap to mine. "Come again?"

I bite my lip and shove a hand through my tangled hair. "It was after we kissed in the hallway. I got so mad that my vibrator wasn't getting the job done, I chucked it, and it broke."

He gets a naughty twinkle in his eye as he says, "Addison May Monroe, you little dirty slut."

"Don't you even." I pounce on him, straddling myself over his waist as I poke him hard in the chest. "At least I only damaged my own personal property."

"I'll buy you all the underwear you want, babe. I'll give you an underwear credit card if you like."

"Jesus, how often are you planning to jerk off into my underwear? Maybe I should get days of the week panties to make your selection process easier."

"You think you're funny?" He growls and grips me harshly on the waist, digging his fingers into my ticklish sides and causing me to squeal as he rolls us over, his body draped over top of me as he assaults my neck with his rough whiskers, biting and laughing and licking me until I'm dizzy.

I gasp when he reaches down and slides inside of me in one

fell swoop, giving me no warning, no prep work, just entering me like I'm ready and waiting for him.

Which, let's face it. I am.

I was soaked when I woke up, and watching him confess his sins with his abs and boner on display in his big cozy bed only got me more ready.

I moan and squirm against him as he snarls and dips his head to bite my nipple.

I grab his hair and yank him up to look at me. "Stop that."

He bites his lip and smirks, so I kiss him hard, his whiskers scraping over my lips causing a riot of goose bumps to erupt over my flesh. A fever takes over both of us as we make out and he pulls back and slams into me over and over, both of us swept up into the moment.

My head lifts off the bed when he rolls us back over so I'm riding on top of him, his hands pawing at my breasts as I grind down.

"You know the best way to spend a snow day?" he asks, his mouth open and panting, his brows furrowed as he watches me take him inside of me.

I shake my head, moving my hand to my clit, rubbing slow circles over myself and moaning greedily.

"I'm about to show you." He grips my hips and thrusts hard up inside of me, causing me to fold over and brace myself on the mattress by his face. My body is electrified by the sharp, white intrusion inside of me. His bare cock like a salve to my aching center.

"I'm going to fuck you so good, that by the time I'm done with you, you're going to miss the feel of me inside of you, you hear me?"

I press a lazy kiss to his lips and murmur, "Prove it, Fletcher."

Chapter 33

FACT OR FICTION?
Snowball fights with my wife are top-tier.

Luke

"Oh my God, this is fun!" Roe squeals with delight as she sits on my lap in the fully enclosed cab of the tractor, pushing snow into a pile at the top of the drive, just next to my cabin.

"Okay, now use the back blade and push that excess to the left."

"Here?" She points to the controller that shifts her into Reverse.

"Yeah, you got it." I smile and laugh, gripping her hips as she runs the tractor like a pro, picking up instructions easily with all her time spent on machinery at the lumberyard. Her hair is braided down one side and stuffed under a beanie, and she's dressed in a pair of my Carhartt overalls that are way too big on her, but she needed something better than what she had, so we made them work.

We have easily gotten two feet of snow in the past few days so Addison really got a taste of Fletcher Mountain snowstorms. The plow company finally called and said they're going to come do our road tomorrow morning, so I figured it was time to get outside and dig out our cabins so we're ready to get back to the real world in the morning.

But I would have much rather stayed snowed in with Roe. I've lost count of how many times we've fucked already this week, and miraculously I am in no way losing steam.

"You look good enough to eat in these overalls," I murmur,

snaking my hands inside and squeezing her tits. She ditched her coat in the heated cab and her little braid is driving me insane.

"After this, we're eating real food!" She gives me a playful shove away from her. "I swear you're trying to starve me."

"I think I fed you pretty well in the shower this morning," I state hungrily as I picture her lips wrapped around my cock again. God, she sucked me so good. Begged me to blow it down her throat as her fingers dug into my thighs and she swallowed every drop like the good little slut she's proving to be.

Fuck, she's even more perfect than my perverted dirty little heart could imagine.

It's no wonder I couldn't keep my hands off her a couple hours later when she was doing her precious "stretch and fold" process to her bread. Her hands were literally covered in sticky dough as I bent her over my kitchen counter and ate her out from behind. She screamed my name and pressed her face into the countertop so by the time I was done with her, she needed another shower.

My dick is raw from overuse and, still, I crave more. I can't get enough of her. And even though my girl is hungry, I know the feeling is mutual. That's why we forced ourselves to go outside just to get a break from the fucking pheromones floating around my small cabin. It's suffocating in the best possible way.

But once we're done pushing snow, I have every intention of stripping her out of her gear and taking her in this tractor to tell her what a good girl she was for working so hard. And then I'll feed her real food afterward as a thank-you.

Maybe.

However, when we finish, my plans are put on hold when we spy Calder, Dakota, Wyatt, Trista, and Stevie all bundled up and heading our way. The way they're looking at us, I can tell they're trying to gauge if we're okay. And the look of relief on their faces says it all.

Wyatt and Calder both have sleds in their hands and Calder has a dopey smile on his face . . . not too dissimilar to the dopey smile on my face.

Everyone loves some snow days.

"Hey," I say, hopping out of the tractor and turning around to help Addison down.

"Hey, you two," Trista calls out, shielding her eyes from the bright sun as she looks at the giant pile of snow we just created. It's the perfect snow for sledding, taking you right past all three cabins, down the driveway, and ending at the more flattened section in front of the barn.

"Baby's first sledding adventure." Trista cheers, holding Stevie's hand up, who looks completely unimpressed by the whiteout conditions all around her.

She's dressed in tiny pink Carhartt coveralls that match her mother's tan set. Her chestnut curls peek out under the matching pink Carhartt hat on her head, and I can't help but reach my hands out to take her in my arms. The cuteness of her is too overwhelming to stay away from. I hold her up to the sky and give her a little toss, causing her to giggle excitedly.

"We made a hill for you, Stevie baby!"

She babbles and slobbers down her chin as I hold her to my body, my chest full of a feeling of rightness that I've never experienced before. It's wild how my brothers and I swore off women just a few years ago and now we're all standing out here smiling with our ladies like one big happy family dressed for a Carhartt photoshoot.

Because we found the right women.

Except Wyatt, who doesn't look quite so happy. "She's too little for sledding."

"Stop being such an overprotective grump," Trista says, smacking him in the chest.

"Dakota and I will go first to make sure it's not too fast,"

Calder says, grabbing Dakota by the wrist and dragging her up the giant pile.

"Calder, I swear, if you crash us, I will kill you."

"Baby, you know I love to make you angry so that's not even a real threat."

They situate themselves at the top and Addison climbs up to help give them a push down. With a loud cheer, they skid past us, Dakota screaming and Calder laughing as they go soaring down toward the barn where the golden sun is just beginning to lower in the horizon.

It looks like fucking heaven.

Wyatt's goat Millie bleats from the pasture and he sighs. "I guess that doesn't look so bad."

"Stevie is going to love it," I confirm, giving him a pat on the back.

Wyatt turns to face me and then subtly cuts a glance up to Addison. "Are you two good?" He eyes me thoughtfully, clearly wanting to check in after all the drama the other night.

I bite my lip and feel a flush of heat crawl up my neck. "Oh yeah, we're good."

My grumpy fucking brother actually grins at me and pats me on the back, hitting me with a knowing wink. "You look good, baby bro."

"Thanks." I smile sheepishly.

And we spend the next two hours playing in the snow as six grown-ass adults all focus on the one baby on the mountain. Except for the moment when everyone else is down by the barn, and I push Addison up against a tree and kiss the life out of her.

A boner in snowpants is not a pleasant experience, but I'm way too happy to be bothered by it because I finally don't have to pretend in front of my family. I finally don't have to be the seventh wheel. I finally get to touch my best friend whenever I want.

After we end the day watching the sunset at our dad's bench, Addison and I stomp inside out of the fresh powder. We're cold and out of breath, but the crackling fire in the hearth and the smell of chili she threw together in the Crock-Pot before we went outside warms me instantly.

"I'm starving," Addison exclaims, her cheeks rosy as we undress each other in the doorway, smiling like a couple of lovesick puppies.

I grab her braid and pull her toward me. "I promise I'll let you eat food this time."

She presses a chase kiss to my lips before heading into the kitchen and prepping for our dinner. She begins cutting up a loaf of fresh bread and spreads her homemade cinnamon butter on it, offering it to me as an appetizer when I come to stand behind her. My hands skate around her hips as I pull her back into my groin.

Fuck, this is how we got in trouble last time.

I bite the toast out of her hand and groan my approval. Everything from this woman tastes like heaven, including her body. I press my lips to her shoulder and rest my chin on her, watching her slice a few more pieces.

"I'm going to text your family and tell them if they want to come grab some chili, they can. I made more than you and I will be able to eat in a week."

"Sounds good to me."

Smiling, she stops her work on the bread and shoots out a message in a group text that Trista started the night before the Mercantile. The Fletcher Mountain group chat has changed a lot these past couple of years as we've folded in the new women who have joined the peak. But it gives me a warm sense of rightness that we've included Addison in it now too. It's mostly jokes and memes, or images of Stevie trying to take her first steps, and Trista looking similar as she waddles down to the barn to do chores in all her winter gear. Calder just sends pictures of his fucking cat. God, he's obsessed.

"What do you think about bridesmaids and groomsmen?" Addison asks, licking a dollop of butter off her thumb.

"Huh?" I ask, turning to look at her and not the bread.

"And maybe a flower girl and ring bearer."

I shift over so I'm standing beside Addison instead of behind her and note those two worry lines are present between her eyebrows. "I feel like you were having a whole conversation in your head, and I need a bit of context before I can answer these questions."

She brushes crumbs off her hands before lifting her eyes to me, the setting sun casting a golden halo around her wild hair. "When you filled out that questionnaire from your mom, you put that we didn't want any bridesmaids and groomsmen."

"I figured that was for the best . . . all things considered."

"Right. But things have changed, no?"

My brows lift. We haven't really had the talk quite yet about what we are. I mean . . . we've admitting to caring about each other obviously, which felt like a huge accomplishment. I guess I was just waiting for the winds to die down before I hit her with another snowstorm. If it was up to me, we'd be walking through the sunset right now.

But it's not just up to me.

I swallow the knot in my throat, my muscles tightening as I ask the question, "This wedding we're having in a couple weeks . . . is it fact or fiction?"

She blinks back at me with a completely unreadable expression that makes me sweat. When will I feel secure with this woman? When will she be able to admit she doesn't just want me, but she loves me with her whole heart like I love her?

"I think," she starts, and I feel myself holding my breath, waiting for what she's about to say. "I think I still need more time."

Pain.

Deep, cutting, soul-crushing pain.

She notices my mood shift and closes the space between us, cupping my face with her hands. "Don't look like that."

"I'm not." I try to pull away, feeling like a fool.

"You look mad."

"I'm not mad."

She exhales out her nose as she waits for me to look her in the eyes. When I do, I hate what I see.

It's pity.

"Last week, I didn't want a relationship, a boyfriend, marriage, babies, anything. Now I'm watching you hold your niece on a sled in the snow and I can hardly contain myself."

My heart lurches at her words. Fuck, does this mean she's fantasizing about kids? With me? I would not have expected that. Love, yes . . . obviously.

Kids?

Holy shit.

Do I want kids? Honestly, I haven't really thought that far ahead. I've loved watching Wyatt's journey with Trista and Stevie, and Max is an amazing father to Everly and Ethan. But for the past several years, I've just wanted Addison. I think I'd be okay with kids or no kids as long as it was with her.

She purses her lips, and I watch her throat contract. "I need time to figure out what I'm feeling. Can you understand that?"

I close my eyes and feel like a total dick. I got so swept up in the snow days, and how good this all felt, and how perfectly we connected that I warped my mind into thinking she loved me. She said she wanted me. I heard she loved me.

This is a fucking *me* problem.

And I need to get my shit under control or I'm going to freak her out and she's going to bolt on me again.

I reach out and hook my thumb through the loop of her jeans, pulling her closer to me. "Of course I can understand that."

She rubs the pads of her thumbs along my jaw. "Thank you."

I lower my lips to kiss her, trying to hide the ache in my chest. I hate that it's there, but I'm only human. And I've been in love with her for a long-ass time.

She breaks the kiss and slides her hands down my chest. "Luckily you're stuck with me for a year, so we have time to figure this all out."

I wince at the deadline she just casually tossed out there, like it's the answer to our problems. It's not the answer. It's a fucking kill date and I hate that it exists. I hate even more that Addison is still thinking about it. I want our wedding day coming up to be forever, not for a year. If she can't see it by then, then I wonder if she'll ever see it.

Fuck.

Maybe my niece is right. Everly's right.

She has to fall in love with you before the wedding ceremony, Luke. Because the moment she walks down the aisle and sees the way you look at her . . . she'll know the truth anyways.

If Addison sees how much I love her on our wedding day, it could spook her and then she'll be looking for a way to divorce me early, lumberyard be damned.

I just have to hope that the next two weeks show her whatever she needs to see to feel safe enough to fall.

'Cause I'm ready to catch her.

"So where were you going with the bridesmaids question?" I ask, trying to let go of my inner thoughts and focus on the present.

She plays with the buttons of my flannel and shoots me a

thoughtful look. "I think you should have your brothers up there next to you at the wedding. I can see how close you guys are and I think it's important."

My heart thumps in my chest at that gesture from her. "But what about you?"

She bites her lip nervously. "I was thinking I'd ask Dakota, Trista, and Cozy if they want to stand up for me. I know we're not super close, but they feel like sisters already. No one needs to be in matching dresses or anything. Just whatever they planned on wearing to the wedding will be great. They've been so amazing to me since I moved up here. I want them to know how much that means to me."

My throat tightens as I realize the gravity of what she's considering. Putting herself out there like that to the girls is a big step for my best friend. She may not be ready to verbally say this wedding is real . . . but she's certainly making some real big decisions right now.

"And fact or fiction, Stevie would make the cutest little flower girl."

My eyes crinkle as I hit my wife with a heartfelt smile. "That's a fact."

"Maybe Ethan can be the ring bearer and help her down the aisle?"

My smile drops and I cut my wife an "are you out of your mind" look which she laughs at.

"We don't have to give him the real rings. Your brothers can hold those."

"Am I getting a ring?" My chest lurches with excitement over that thought and I stare down at my hand, liking the idea of a ring on my finger more than I have any business to.

"Don't you worry about it, Fletcher," she says coyly, turning away from me to resume her work. She nudges me with her elbow. "Why are you smiling at me?"

I inhale deeply through my nose. "I'm just . . . happy." *And scared but trying not to be.*

"This is your happy face?" She eyes me warily.

I nod. Damn this woman can see right through me.

"I thought this made you happy." She lowers her hand between us and strokes my cock, causing me to lean into her and expel a shaky breath, my body tightening with need as my balls begin to ache.

"Oh, it does. It really does."

She tilts her head and bites her lip. "So, lots of things make you happy?"

"No, not lots of things." I press a soft kiss to her lips. "Just you, babe." *And I could make you happy forever if you'd let me.*

Chapter 34

FACT OR FICTION?
My husband is a good dancer.

Addison

**Ladies of Fletcher Mountain
Group Chat Plus Cozy**

Me: Hey ladies . . . I've got sort of a big question for you and I'm doing it via text, so you have time to come up with an excuse to say no. I swear this is a no pressure situation and I don't want anyone to feel obligated to say yes.

Cozy: She wants more Fireball.

Dakota: She's going to tell us Luke has a micro-penis.

Trista: She wants to adopt one of my alpacas!

Me: LOL. No to all the above. I was wondering if you would all consider being my bridesmaids next weekend?

Cozy: OMG

Dakota: Fuck yes!

Trista: What do I have to wear?

Me: Haha. Wear whatever you planned to wear for the wedding. No matching horrific dresses, I promise.

Dakota: Thank God for that.

Trista: Can I wear my Carhartt coat?

Cozy: No farmer coats, Trista!

Me: I don't care what you all wear. I just would love to have you all with me if you're up for it. You ladies have welcomed me with open arms and healed something in me that has been broken for a long time. Not trying to get mushy but I just want you to know, this is legit, and I appreciate you all regardless of if you want to stand up there with me or not.

Cozy: 🥲 🥲 🥲

Dakota: I already said yes but now I'm crying and saying yes. Thanks for that, asshole.

Trista: You're the shit, Ads. It would be my honor.

Me: Thank you so much. And, Trista and Cozy . . . would Stevie and Ethan be our flower girl and ring bearer?

Cozy: Yikes.

Trista: YES! OMG, I HAVE THE PERFECT DRESS FOR HER ALREADY. YOU'RE GOING TO DIE.

Me: Cozy, is that a yes?

Cozy: On your own head it be.

Me: LOL. Duly noted. Thanks, ladies!

Dakota: You know Calder is going to ask for his cat to have a job now, right?

Me: LOL. I'll have to give that one more thought. Do you guys think Everly would walk Jo down the aisle? I don't want her to walk alone?

Trista: 🥲

Cozy: That is the perfect job for our Everly.

Dakota: This group chat needs more hilarious TikToks and less crying emojis. I'm at work for God's sake!

I swipe at my happy tears as I put my phone away and look up at Luke, standing in the middle of a dance studio with his mother and an instructor who's in the process of teaching them how to waltz.

Johanna set up this dance lesson for us, but Luke told me that Jo always wanted Steven to learn how to waltz and they never got around to it, so he asked if he could include his mom in the lesson as well.

I said a thousand times yes and have been sitting here with the dopiest smile on my face watching them work through the choreography. Leave it to my husband to make his mother's dream come true on his wedding day.

God, he really is one of the good ones.

I watch them in awe as they work together, laughing and teasing and figuring out the moves with more ease than I probably would have myself. It's an unusual thing watching Luke with his mom. There's such an effortless love between them, I can't help but wonder what gene my mom was missing. And would I be missing the same gene?

These are questions I've asked myself for years, and it's strange to me to be suddenly considering a relationship with Luke and doubting everything I thought I knew about myself. I guess that's what caring about someone does to you though. It gives you permission to dream again.

The music shifts into an old familiar song, "Feels like Home," and I see Luke lean in and whisper something to his mom. She nods and steps back, holding her hands over her mouth as she whispers something to the dance instructor.

I frown as Luke stalks toward me. He holds his hand out with a sexy smile, but I wave him off. "I'm okay. Keep dancing with your mom. You guys are so cute."

"She's ready for a break," he says with a smirk, bending over to grab my hand and pull me out onto the dance floor. "I missed you."

"Missed me? We literally live together, Fletcher." I laugh as he pulls me into him, moving us around the dance floor with ease, clearly picking up the dance moves much better than me.

He doesn't let my joking deter him as he folds our hands between our chests, his other sliding around my waist, resting unabashedly at the top of my ass. I tease my fingers through his hair as he presses his bearded cheek to me and hums the song in my ear, causing goose bumps to erupt all over my body. His warmth, his touch, his breath like the best kind of comfort.

I close my eyes and turn my face into his neck, breathing him in like a drug I can never get enough of. I lose myself to the movements, letting Luke take me wherever he wants. He could be leading me out into a street, and I wouldn't care. I'd go anywhere with this man.

"You're so sweet to your mom." I glance over to where Johanna stands watching us with a big tearful smile on her face.

"She makes it easy," he replies and then looks down at me with a frown. "Sorry, that was probably insensitive of me to say."

"No, it wasn't." I move my arm from his neck to his chest, tucking myself into his embrace. "It's nice. You should be proud of your mom. I'm proud of how you are with your mom."

Luke presses a kiss to my forehead and dips to whisper in my ear. "She'll love you to pieces if you let her."

My chest trembles as I let those words sink in. Johanna Fletcher is a woman who lost the love of her life and still has love to give. Luke too. He went through a horrific trauma with his dad, buried him, and still, he stands here comforting me.

How did I land myself smack-dab in the middle of such an incredible family?

"Your loss is so much more recent than mine," I say, glancing up at Luke. "How are you all so okay and I'm still such a mess?"

"We can't compare grief," he says firmly, tilting his head to look at me. "It's a sliding scale that everyone deals with differently. My mom has her good days and her bad days. As do I. We're all just doing the best we can."

His eyes are thoughtful, and kind, and I feel so damn lucky to be in his arms right now. I reach up and pull Luke's lips down to mine. Kissing the goodness right off him and hoping I can take some of it for myself. Maybe if I can, we have a shot of making this whole marriage fact and not fiction. If that's even what I want.

The sound of the studio door opens and we pull our lips apart as we turn our heads to see a tall blonde girl running in a dead sprint toward Luke's mom.

"Everly!" Jo squeals and opens her arms, catching her granddaughter in a big hug.

Everly has to crouch down for the hug, her tall, slender frame looking like a baby giraffe in that awkward pose. Luke and I pause our dancing, and I see him eyeing his niece with a knowing smirk.

"Who let you back in the country?" he drawls, narrowing his eyes playfully.

Everly turns to scowl at her uncle, her blue eyes bright and piercing as she props her hands on her hips. "Well, the party can't start until I arrive, so you better be thanking me for gracing you with my presence."

She curtsies dramatically and I can't help but laugh. The girl is as likable and sweet as she was when I hung out with her in Mexico.

She strides over to us as Luke wraps his arms around me from behind. "Everly, I'd like to introduce you to someone."

"I already know Addison, Uncle Luke." She rolls her eyes and smiles sweetly at me.

"Just let me say this, please?" He inhales a deep breath and says, "Everly, this is my wife, Addison."

Everly jumps up and down, squealing and clapping all the way over to me. She wraps me in a big hug and makes me laugh into submission. She pulls back and looks from me to Luke and back to me. "You did good, Luke. You did really good."

I frown at Everly's curious look, but our happy reunion is cut short when the instructor claps his hands, refocusing the group of us to continue the lesson. Everly stays to dance with her grandma. I get to dance with my husband. And it all feels not the least bit scary.

Chapter 35

FACT OR FICTION?

A mastermind and a saboteur walk into a bar.

Luke

"Well, aren't you a sight for sore eyes!" Judy bellows, shuffling over to me, my brothers, and Everly as we come striding into the Mercantile. We met up with Everly after work because she wanted to come up the peak and see all of Trista's critters before the wedding, and the four of us decided to stop at the Merc for some drinks first.

Judy pulls Everly into a big hug. "How's college, kiddo? You're in Scotland, is it?"

"Ireland, and it's great," Everly peals, a bit too excitedly. "I'm having the best time. A really transformative experience. Couldn't be happier over there."

Wyatt, Calder, and I all frown at each other. That answer seemed a bit over-the-top even for Everly.

"Well, it's good to have you back. These boys are animals without you around to keep them in check."

"What?" Everly shoots her wide blue eyes at all of us. "Don't the ladies do that job in my absence?"

Judy's eyes fly wide. "Maybe Trista and Dakota, but the new girl?" She points to me and trembles. "She's formidable. He's got his hands full with her."

I can't help the smile that spreads across my face. My wife is formidable in more ways than one. She was certainly formidable this morning when she woke me by rubbing her ass on my cock.

Judy barks at us to sit anywhere and that she'll bring us our usuals, so we find a spot by the fireplace to warm up. The snow is really coming down now and the mountain is looking pretty perfect for a wedding this weekend. And if I didn't know any better, I'd say Roe is excited for the big day too. She had to bring her wedding dress home yesterday from the bridal store and got all weird when I tried to peek inside the bag. That's definitely not someone acting like this wedding isn't real.

"I have to say, I'm impressed, boys," Everly exclaims, sitting back in her chair beside me and folding her hands behind her head. "You guys actually put in some good work in my absence."

Wyatt and Calder both cut me a knowing look, silently saying, *you asked for this* . . . and they would be right. I let my niece weave her wild web of matchmaking from the beginning and here I am . . . hopelessly in love.

Granted, the woman I'm in love with hasn't said it back yet, but we're better off than where we started.

"He and Addison didn't look so good the other night when we were all here as a group," Calder says with a laugh. "That's what has Judy so spooked."

I glare at him from across the table. "We had some things to work through, but we figured it out."

Wyatt clears his throat, looking doubtful.

"We're good," I argue, frowning back at them. "Pretty much."

"What does 'pretty much' mean?" Everly eyes me nervously.

I inhale a deep breath, not really wanting to spill all my relationship business to my family, but I alluded to some stuff with Wyatt the other day when Addison was down in the barn with Trista and Stevie, so I guess I might as well tell everyone that's in on this whole scheme. Everly will drag it out of me eventually.

"We've admitted that we care about each other, but Addison said she still needs more time to really figure out what that means for her."

Everly's face falls. "But the wedding is in four days!"

"I'm aware."

"Has she said she loves you?"

I wince and look away.

"This is a disaster," Everly barks dramatically.

"It's not a disaster," I growl, my shoulders tensing with irritation. "We're good. You don't need to worry about me and Roe."

"Luke, she's known you for years. If she can't admit that she loves you, then we need to fix this." Judy comes over just then, bringing three beers and a soda for Everly. As soon as she turns back to put in our food order, Everly dives into planning mode. "You need a grand gesture. An epic moment before the wedding. Look what we did for Calder and Dakota at poker night. You need something like that. Or the baby shower for Wyatt and Trista. The surprise meeting with Cozy and my dad? You need a moment where she can just surrender her whole heart to you."

"I don't know, Evs," I reply, taking a big drink of beer because this all feels overwhelming. "I think I just want to let things land where they are. I don't want to pressure her."

"This isn't pressure, Luke! This is love. Sometimes we have to help it along." She ties her blond hair back into a clip like she's preparing for battle. "You start brainstorming your big move with Calder and Wyatt. I need to go check on my special projects."

"What special projects?"

"Luke," Everly snaps, losing all humor on her face. "Do you really think I sat over in Ireland and did nothing to help with this wedding?"

I blink back at her. "Um . . . kind of?"

She rolls her eyes. "I swear you three would be lost without me."

"Hey!" Calder barks defensively. "I'm not lost at all. I have a growing new business and a girlfriend who tells me she loves me and my cat all the time. I'm in fucking heaven."

Calder arches a cocky eyebrow that drops the second Everly asks, "When are you going to put a ring on it?"

All humor drains from his face as he broods into his beer. "Dakota needs more time. She just got divorced. Our circumstances are way different than Luke's."

Everly eyes Calder warily. "I'll be watching you two closely over this holiday break. You better not be screwing this up. And you . . ." Everly swerves her head to stare at Wyatt sitting beside Calder. "Mr. Quiet Wyatt. What's your status?"

My brother stares back at Everly, not saying a word.

"Baby number two?" she chirps, lifting her brows expectantly.

Wyatt closes his eyes and shakes his head. "I promised Trista we'd get the rescue center built before we discussed more babies."

"Well, chop, chop! A woman's fertility doesn't last forever. Get that center built and get me another cousin or maybe I'll find Trista a surrogate sperm donor." She frowns and shakes her head. "I don't . . . you know what . . . forget I said that. Just get to work on the rescue center, okay? I'll be right back. I need to go make a call."

She jumps up and marches out of the bar, muttering obscenities under her breath the whole way.

"Ireland has made her even more fucking terrifying," Calder deadpans.

Wyatt and I nod in agreement.

And as I watch her tapping into her phone outside, I can't help but frown. Everly's usually pretty passionate about stuff, but this feels different. It feels like she's choosing to fixate on our problems to avoid some of her own. And despite my own mess of a life, I'm going to get to the bottom of it before she heads back for school.

Judy comes over with a tray of food, eyeing Everly as she gesticulates wildly on her phone. "That girl ain't right."

We all nod in agreement as she begins setting our food down in front of us. She pauses when she's done, shooting us all an uncomfortable look. "Say, I wasn't sure I should say anything, but I feel like I won't be able to sleep at night if I don't."

Wyatt, Calder, and I all straighten in our seats, taking in the obvious shift in Judy's demeanor.

She puffs out a sharp breath and says, "Robyn told me when she was here last weekend that her and her husband are trying to buy Monroe Lumber."

Wyatt and Calder's jaws drop, and I close my eyes and pinch the bridge of my nose.

"Now, I know it's none of my business and you're all adults, but I just don't get a good feeling about their intentions with all of this. Her husband has always held a grudge against you boys even after all these years and I wouldn't be surprised if they're trying to buy it to make your lives miserable."

"Addison is going to lose her shit over this," I state through clenched teeth.

"Not to mention Monroe's is our primary lumber supplier," Wyatt adds, his voice deep and ominous. "If we have to outsource, it will fuck with our costs big-time. Our estimates won't be market competitive with the other builders around here."

"Are they planning to move to Boulder?" Calder asks, frowning up at Judy.

She grimaces. "It sounds like they might. I think Matt has burned some bridges in Colorado Springs with his construction company and they're trying to start over somewhere."

"Fucking hell," Wyatt grumbles under his breath.

"But John won't sell to them, right, Luke?" Calder asks,

looking at me intently. "That's the whole point of . . ." His voice trails off.

I clench my beer, my jaw taut with irritation. I don't honestly know if John would sell to them. He's certainly making Addison uncomfortable with the meetings he's been having with them. And with how intent John seems to be for Addison not to run the yard on her own, I wouldn't put it past him to undercut his own daughter.

How did I not realize this when I saw Robyn last week? I should have known right away she was up to something when she said she had lunch with John.

Fuck.

I don't want this for Addison. This feels personal now. Like it's my fault Robyn and Matt are even here. Of all the businesses those fuck-wits could buy, it has to be Monroe's? This is way too intentional.

Damn this fucking nightmare of my past that I can't seem to break free of.

Addison is just collateral damage in all of this, which she doesn't deserve. And God, she's been so happy this week. We're happy. We're getting married and on the path to figuring us out. This could totally fuck everything up.

And if John does sell to Robyn and Matt, then what does that mean for me and Addison? Would she ask me for a divorce sooner?

Fuck.

Fuck. Fuck. Fuck.

I drink down the contents of my beer and crack my neck. Looks like I have an errand to run before the wedding festivities begin.

I wonder where I can find a bulletproof vest.

Chapter 36

FACT OR FICTION?
I'm officially a lady of Fletcher Mountain.

Addison

"Hey, Old Man River." I answer a call on my car's Bluetooth as I drive straight from the lumberyard to Max and Cozy's house where I'm already late for a ladies' night Cozy is hosting. The female bonding thing is intense in this family, but I think I'm adapting well to the girl squad vibes, all things considered.

"Hello, my darling daughter," Dad says gruffly. "I was calling to make sure this wedding shindig is still happening this weekend."

My brows furrow. "Obviously, yes."

"Thank goodness for that." He coughs loudly into the phone. "Edith made me buy a new suit and I just wanted to make sure it wasn't for nothing."

I sigh, really not knowing what to say to that. "You wanted a wedding, Dad. We're giving you a wedding."

"Well, I hope you wanted a wedding too," he replies and waits for me to say something back.

"I mean . . . I was fine with the courthouse thing we did but . . . as a matter of fact . . . I'm kind of getting excited for this weekend."

"Really?" I can practically see my dad's bushy eyebrows lift. "My little yard girl is excited to put on a fancy dress?"

"Yes, I am," I reply firmly, happy to put him in his place. "And Luke's family has been really great with all the planning and prep work. And not that you've asked, but I actually love living on the mountain. It's beautiful and serene and quiets my mind. The wedding is going to be stunning up there. Things are going well, Dad, even though I know you had your doubts."

He pauses for a moment before saying, "I guess if that's all true then I'm happy for you, Addie May."

A knot forms in my throat at the surprising tenderness in his voice. It's felt like this game of chicken between me and my dad has distanced us since this whole will stipulation came up, and I guess I've missed just feeling like a daughter and not a problem he needs to manage.

And even though I told Luke I needed more time to figure out my feelings with him, things between us are getting realer and realer by the day. I think I might be falling for him.

Which is scary and overwhelming, and I don't know what it means for our future and that one-year mark when we hit it. But I like our situation, and I don't want to let it go.

"I appreciate you saying that, Dad," I reply, sniffing softly and then ask, "How did you know Mom was the one before you married her?"

The silence is deafening, and I slap my hand to my face when I realize what I so carelessly just asked my father. We don't talk about Mom. We never talk about Mom. Or Aaron, for that matter. I used to try to get Dad to come with me to the cemetery and he never would, always said he didn't have the heart for it. Dad and I exist in a monolith of just the two of us like that's all we ever were.

His voice is solemn and curt when he finally answers, "I don't think you should be taking any notes from me on marriage. I'll see you at the rehearsal dinner at your place tomorrow."

We hang up and tears fill my eyes at the overwhelming sadness that is my childhood. Even my own father has marriage issues, it's no wonder I've been so resistant. I have the greatest guy in the world, and I still feel myself inching away from him. I'm broken just like my old man.

I scrub my hand over my face, annoyed at myself for trying to open up to him of all people. The last thing I need to do is be poking the bear that is my father days before my wedding when he's still dangling the possibility of selling the lumberyard out from under me.

I just need to shut my mouth and not cause any waves until I get through this wedding. Then he can go back to Florida, and I can get back to running the yard without him just fine.

Which I can do with or without a husband.

Though I'm starting to understand why the trust wants the owner of the yard to have a spouse. It's been nice having someone to come home to at the end of a long day at work. Especially when that someone is Luke Fletcher.

I pull into Max and Cozy's driveway and try to shake the dark thoughts out of my head, mentally pep talking myself to keep my eye on the prize. Luckily, I know that if anyone can help lighten my mood, it's these Fletcher ladies.

I smile as I glance up at the giant house in front of me. I'm not surprised at how nice it is. I knew Max and Cozy were pretty well off since I was lucky enough to ride on that private jet to Mexico with the rest of the family last year. But I've yet to actually see their home, and I'm worried I should have maybe dressed a little nicer for whatever this ladies' night is going to look like inside.

Everly greets me at the door with a big hug. "Come in, come in! We're all in the garage."

"The garage?" I ask with a frown.

"Yeah, it's where Cozy set up the activity."

"What is the activity?" I glance down at my leggings and sweater that I changed in to at the yard before I came over.

Maybe I would have been better off staying in my work gear.

"Come on through the house and I'll show you!"

Everly drags me through their beautiful home to the door that leads out to their attached garage off the kitchen. It's there I find Johanna, Cozy, Dakota, and Trista stationed around a long table staining some sort of wood pieces.

"Welcome, Addison! We're making charcuterie boards," Cozy says excitedly.

"Oh, that's so cool." I narrow my eyes at the lumber on the table. "Where did you get the wood?"

Cozy stops what she's doing and looks up at me as I move to stand closer to her. "Oh my gosh, I bet we could have scored some great pieces from you!"

Cozy shakes her fists in frustration, and I laugh and wave her off. "I'm just kidding. This looks so great." I move over to Johanna across the table, whose gloved hands are currently wiping excess stain off her board with a rag.

"Hello, bride-to-be." She shoots me a wink and it warms my insides.

"Hi, Jo," I reply, realizing I feel a lot more comfortable around her than I did several weeks ago. In fact, I didn't even flinch that much when she hugged me goodbye after our dance lesson. It was nice. Comforting. Like Luke's hugs.

"Your board is down at the far end." Cozy gestures with her head while her hands are already engaged.

"Just be glad it's not shaped like a penis," Dakota mutters under her breath.

"Excuse me?" I stop in my tracks.

Cozy cuts Dakota a look. "I made phallic-shaped charcuterie boards for a romance novelist who lives in town. Mercedes Lee Loveletter. It was for a book box thing she was doing, and when she found out about my charcuterie board making hobby, it turned into a whole business thing between us. If you haven't read her, we will change that before the end of the year."

My brows lift. "Sounds interesting."

"Cozy is a superfan," Trista whispers loudly.

Everly giggles and drags me down to my spot, fitting me with an apron and gloves so I'm fully prepped to stain my board. It isn't until I get to my spot that I see that mine has a special personalization on it that no one else's does.

"What is this?" I ask, as I pick up the board to get a closer look.

"Call it a wedding present," Cozy replies with a smirk. "Yours is a cutting board, not a charcuterie board. They're different, trust me. I thought you'd like a cutting board better with all your bread making."

"We said no gifts," I state, glancing up at her in confusion.

Cozy buzzes her lips. "It's nothing."

I gaze down at the beautiful board in front of me and my fingers tremble as I trace over the engraving that says *Mr. & Mrs. Fletcher* with our upcoming wedding date carved below it. It's sweet and thoughtful and so personal. I can already see it sitting on the counter in Luke's cabin.

My cabin.

Our home.

It's crazy how easy that is for me to consider. That Luke's home is now my home. But somehow, my stuff just fits there so well. Even my damn KitchenAid mixer has its own cabinet. His shower already has all my toiletries in it. My wedding dress is hanging in his walk-in closet.

I've forgotten about all the things I left at my Boulder apartment, because somewhere along the way without even realizing it, I left my old life behind.

A droplet hits the raw wood, and I jerk my head, not even realizing tears are falling down my cheeks.

"Oh shit, I never even asked if you took Luke's name," Cozy

says, dropping her paintbrush and looking horrified, like my tears are because of the engraving.

"She probably didn't take his name because of the lumber business," Dakota offers, nudging Cozy with her elbow.

"That would make total sense," Everly chirps, putting her hand on my arm.

"I was all too happy to get rid of my last name," Trista adds with a harrumph.

"But we can fix this, I'm sure." Everly look to Cozy with urgency.

"Yes, I will totally make you a new board. It's what I do. I can do hyphenated or just keep it your name straight-up. I could do *Addison and Luke* with the date. But he always calls you 'Roe' so I wasn't sure. I'm so sorry, but don't worry about it. I do these engravings myself. I have a tool—"

"This is perfect," I reply, cutting her off as I hold the board to my chest. "I don't want anything changed."

All the women stare at me like I'm a time bomb waiting to go off, and I guess maybe I am. I've been so stuck in my ways, certain I knew exactly how my life was going to turn out and now . . . now everything has changed.

And I fucking love every bit of it.

"It's just hard to get used to because my whole life I only saw myself as a Monroe. I've been proud to be a Monroe," I say, staring at the table. "My family is messy, and my dad is tough, but I love him, you know? He did the best he could, and he taught me our family business and I'm proud of what we provide for the community, you know? I liked passing out those awards at the lumberjack competition and signing a check to our charity. It means a lot to share the last name of my brother too. Carrying on his legacy."

The ladies all nod, their eyes fixed on me as I work through something big in my head.

I look up and lock eyes with Johanna, my chest swelling with emotion. "But I guess I'm realizing that two things can be true at once because I would be equally as proud to be a Fletcher."

Johanna brings her hand up, covering a soft sob that escapes her lips. I feel guilty for hitting her with the feels out of nowhere but they're hitting me too and suddenly I'm a dam that's finally broken free, gushing all my feelings out all over the table.

"I'm really grateful to you, Jo," I croak, eyeing her with a pained smile. "I don't know most of the details of this wedding and I already know it's going to be one of the best days of my life."

"Oh, sweetie," she blubbers and pulls her gloves off before rushing around the table to pull me into a hug. "It was my pleasure. I would do anything for you. Anything."

I feel myself fight back a sob into her shoulder as her words repeat in my head. *I would do anything for you. Anything.*

It's a deep pain to know that my own mother couldn't, but this mother could. Some mothers do good. I could do good.

I swallow down the painful knot in my throat and when Jo releases me, she doesn't fully let go. She keeps rubbing my back and holding on to my arm, gazing at the engraved board with me. And I realize for once I'm not pulling away from her one bit. I'm leaning in and accepting it with everything I have in me.

Through watery eyes, I look at the ladies all standing around the table and offering me silent looks of support. "I'm glad you gals are going to be standing up there with me on Saturday because I'm going to be a mess, I fear," I say with a garbled laugh. "But girlfriends sure do make it all a lot less scary."

"We got you," Trista says, reaching out to hold my hand.

"The ladies of Fletcher Mountain are always here for you," Dakota adds with a smile.

Cozy lets out an angry growl. "Okay, we're seriously building a cabin up there. I can't take this shit anymore. Jo, we'll add a mother-in-law suite on our house."

"No Fletcher woman left behind," Everly adds with twinkling eyes.

Jo laughs and hugs me one more time and I grin over the fact that I too am in the Fletcher women club, and I don't think I ever want to leave.

Addison Monroe Fletcher.

Has a pretty good ring to it, I think.

Chapter 37

FACT OR FICTION?
A moving target is harder to hit.

Luke

When I pull up to John Monroe's property and get out of my truck, I duck behind my door when I hear a loud bang off in the distance. My eyes swerve around, trying to find the source of what sounds like gunshots, but when another bang sounds off, I realize it's coming from behind the house.

At least those shots aren't being fired at me . . . yet.

Wrapping my coat up tight around me, I crunch through the thick snow as I walk around back and spot John off in the distance. He's standing at a table with a long rifle propped on a bipod stand, which he's apparently using to shoot down a row of beer cans on a ledge that runs along the border of his wooded property.

He's clearly in the middle of target practice, which makes me feel a bit like I couldn't have picked a worse time to drop by unannounced.

But I'm here for my wife. The love of my life. And I'm not going to let her big bear of a father scare me away no matter how much ammunition he has. We must have the same end goal in sight. We want his daughter happy. And I feel well-informed on what will make her happy these days.

I pause as I watch him knock down another can, my nerves dancing in my belly with the loud boom. My dad was never a big hunter, so it wasn't something we all engaged in growing up. And even living in the rural mountains all these years, with the hope of being as sustainable as possible up on our peak, none of us has ever taken to hunting. We each have some protection rifles that rarely see the light of day, but for the most part, we are not killers. We respect it for the necessity of feeding a family and I can appreciate the sustainability of it, but to be the one to do the work to kill it . . . not for me. What can I say? I'm a lover not a fighter.

Something tells me John is a fighter.

"Mr. Monroe," I call out and step behind a tree in case he perceives me as a threat and aims his weapon right at me.

John removes his noise-canceling earmuffs and turns around, his brows furrowed as he squints in my direction. I offer a timid wave as I force myself to come out from behind the tree like a big boy.

"What the hell are you doing here?" John barks, turning to dismount his rifle from the holder.

I make my way over and see that he's removing the shells from the chamber.

That's a good start, I guess.

"I was hoping I could talk to you for a moment." I grip the back of my neck as I stand beside him at the table, squinting at the mangled beer cans off in the distance. Most people would probably be using a target to shoot on. Not John.

"Is now a good time?"

"Now is a great time!" John grips his gun and props it upward on the table, posing like he's ready for me to take his photo. All he needs is a dead animal carcass in his free hand to really complete the scene.

I pause, wondering if it's me he's picturing in the photo with him, playing the part of a carcass, and as if he can read my thoughts, he sighs heavily and lays the rifle back down.

"What can I do for you?" he asks with a deep, throaty voice.

My mouth goes dry instantly as I struggle with where to start.

I practiced what I was going to say to him on the drive over here, but now my mind is blank. A void of nothing. Robyn . . . something about Robyn. God, I hate saying her name.

Clearing my throat I mutter, "Um . . . it was made aware to me this week that the potential buyers for Monroe Lumber are Robyn and Matt Whitaker with Precision Construction?"

John wrinkles his nose at me. "Yeah . . . what of it?"

I nod now that he's confirmed it. "Well, I know them. Kind of. And I thought you should know that my family doesn't have the best history with them. It dates back to a beef between my father and Matt over a bidding war on a new development here in Boulder."

John twitches his gray mustache and waves me off. "Oh, that's just business."

"It gets worse," I state quickly, an edge to my voice over the fact that I know I'm going to have to share more than I wanted to with him in order to get him to fucking listen. "My brothers and I were . . . involved with Robyn."

John's face twists in confusion.

Can't blame the guy.

"It was over a decade ago, but it wasn't pretty. I'm not proud. In fact, I'm fucking ashamed, and I'd really not like to discuss the particulars. I hid this past from your daughter because of how disappointed in myself I am over it, but I'm here to tell you that if you sell Monroe's to the Whitakers, you are letting a world of darkness into your life."

"What are you talking about?" John shakes his hand in front of me, clearly not absorbing the gravity of what I'm saying.

"They're horrible people," I state firmly, refusing to let him slag me off. "They don't live by normal rules of society, and that's saying a lot when my brothers and I chose to live on a secluded mountain to get away from society."

John exhales harshly. "So, what are you saying? Their money

is no good? They doubled their offer to me. *Doubled.* Signed a letter of intent and showed proof of funds. Do you know how much money we're talking here?"

"I'm saying that if you sell to them, you will be without a doubt extricating your daughter from that business. She will not want to work for them and if she does, they will figure out a way to make her life miserable so she quits."

"What, ya still got the hots for his wife?" John huffs, wrinkling his nose.

"I love your daughter, sir," I state firmly, my eyes laser focused on the man I refuse to let make me feel small in this moment. "I love her with everything I have and I'm telling you that what you're doing is wrong."

"Now, listen here," John barks, stepping forward and forcing me to take a step back. His eyes are slits as his jaw works back and forth. "I know I came and helped you boys with some business when Steven passed, but that doesn't give you the right to come over and tell me how to run my business. You got it?"

"But—"

"This conversation is over." He turns around like he's going back to his target practice, and I can't help but step forward and place a hand on the barrel, forcing him to lower it and listen.

"You're selling your daughter short," I snap, and my eyes widen when John's face fills with rage. My teeth crack as I grind out, "And if you can't see that, then you don't deserve her."

"You think you deserve her?" he snarls, stabbing a finger into my chest. "From what it sounds like, you and your brothers are a bunch of perverts up on that mountain. How do I know you're not all fucking with my daughter in the same way?"

My lips thin as I look away. "We made bad choices, but we've learned from them. Have you learned from your mistakes?"

"What is that supposed to mean?" His eyes flare and I have

to swallow down the pit in my throat to stay strong. He'll never respect me if I back down now.

"I mean, unless you've been a perfect father and a perfect husband and a perfect business owner, maybe extend a bit of grace to someone before you judge them."

"Bullshit." He waves me off and turns away. "You should be happy about this deal. It means you guys no longer have to keep the charade up. My daughter will never have to work another day in her life."

"She likes to work!"

"I don't give a shit," he thunders, the veins in his temples bulging angrily. "I know what's best for my business and selling for this kind of life-changing money is what's best."

I shake my head and eye my supposed father-in-law harshly. He looks tired and old and, if I'm being honest, painfully insecure. He gives the illusion of control and confidence, but there's a hitch in his stance that reveals a weak spot.

My voice is grave when I ask, "Why don't you believe in her?"

"I do believe in her," he snaps, his eyes wide and urgent.

"Then why not let her have this?"

"'Cause she's all I fucking got left!" he roars, his face twisting in pain. He coughs loudly and turns away, agitated and trembling as he props his hands on his hips and stares out into the trees. He runs his fingers through his thinning hair and sighs as if in pain. "Until you know the horror of losing a child, don't you tell me you'd know what you'd do in my situation."

I stare at the man standing before me and, weirdly, I see a lot of Addison in him. Both of them scared and pushing away the good things in their life because they're too afraid of what might happen if it all goes away. It's a coward's game and they're playing to win.

But my dad taught me different.

"I may not have lost a child, but I lost my dad," I state, my voice tight and showing more emotion than I want to in front of this old bear. "I literally had him die in my fucking arms, so I'm no stranger to pain." I inhale a breath, steeling myself to continue. "But one thing my dad would never do . . . is not believe in me with something I was passionate about. And your daughter is passionate about that yard and the people who work there. Hell, they gave her a bread pan as a wedding present, and she spent weeks making fresh loaves every night until she was able to give one to every single employee. Did you ever do anything like that? Has anyone on this earth ever done anything like that?" I lift my shoulders and feel my chest ache with love and adoration. "Most people would just write a fucking thank-you card."

John stares back at me with a scowl as he crosses his arms over his chest, clearly not as impressed by that story as I thought he should be.

Damn him.

Damn him for not seeing her.

She's all I see.

I realize with grave disappointment that this was a fool's errand. Guys like John don't change their minds. They're too old and too set in their ways. My dad had his stubborn streaks too.

But my dad wouldn't do this. He's one of the good ones.

The jury is still out on John.

I zip my coat up because I've said all that I need to say. Today wasn't just about informing him of Robyn and Matt. It was about informing him of his daughter. And if he doesn't see how wonderful Addison is by now, he never will. But I'll make it my life's mission to make sure she knows for as long as she'll have me.

"Anyways, I came here to warn you about the Whitakers. They aren't good people. It would be a huge mistake to sell to them. Robyn has made it very clear how she feels about your daughter, so if you do sell to them, you'll be dropping Roe in the middle of an impossible situation that will destroy her because the lumberyard is her life. No amount of money will change that fact or buy back the respect you'll lose from your only child. I'll see you at the rehearsal."

I turn to leave and then pause to add one more thing. "The marriage is real for me, by the way. I don't want out. It's real and it always has been for me." I turn on my heel to look him in the eyes. "I don't think it's the same for your daughter, but I'll be whatever she needs me to be because that's how much I love her . . . for whatever that's worth to you."

He nods as his eyes move up and down my body, assessing me like he's seeing me for the first time. "You know it was Aaron who started the whole fact-or-fiction thing."

A chill runs down my spine and I forget the second part of the sentence and because I'm so focused on the first part. Addison said her father never talks about Aaron. Doesn't even speak his name, so I'm shocked at him uttering it so casually just now.

"I've heard you and Addison say that phrase to each other before and I didn't know if you ever knew it came from Aaron." John's cheeks stretch into something resembling a smirk. "He was learning the definition of nonfiction books in school just before he died, and he got real obsessed with it. He'd constantly ask Addie if stuff was fact or fiction on the television. It was their thing."

My chest aches with that information and who I learned it from. "I'm really grateful you told me that."

He coughs loudly and loses all affection on his face. "She loves you back." John nods, his jaw taut. "Even if she don't say it. It's still a fact."

Chapter 38

FACT OR FICTION?
Hot girls wear their guys' hats.

Addison

I have one thing on my mind as I make the drive from Boulder to Fletcher Mountain, following closely behind Dakota and Trista in the vehicle ahead.

I'm excited to get home.

I'm practically giddy as I wind my SUV up the dark, snowy lane, feeling my ears pop as the elevation climbs. A grin spreads across my face as I drive by Wyatt's and Calder's cabins, both lit up and showing signs of life inside as smoke plumes out the chimneys. I wave to the girls as I park in front of Luke's and look up to see he left the front step light on, clearly waiting for me to come home. It's crazy how much that tiny act warms me up inside.

"You're home late," Luke says as I walk in the front door and shuck my coat. The fire is crackling, and his computer is open on the coffee table like he's been working but as I walk around the sofa, I find him cuddling his cock.

Rufus that is.

"Hey, babe." Luke hits me with a soft smile that makes me feel drunk on something nonalcoholic. He frowns curiously as I bend to pick up his cock . . . rooster. Without a word, I take Rufus to the front door and set him outside, not feeling the least bit bad. It's my turn to cuddle the cock daddy.

"What's going on?" Luke asks as I return, kicking my shoes off and crawling onto his lap to straddle him. "You good?"

"I'm great." I grab his hat and turn it backward so I can lean in and murmur against his lips, "I just missed you."

His brows furrow as his hands slide up my back, his warm palms sending goose bumps to my core. "Was my family that bad?"

I shake my head and pull back to slowly undo the buttons of his flannel. "They were wonderful. I had a really nice night."

"That's good to hear." His exposed abs contract with a confused laugh as I skate my nails over his flesh, feasting on this person that I get to sleep with every night. He stills my hands on his chest and hits me with his sexy brown eyes. "Hey, I wanted to talk to you about something."

"Can it wait?" I stand up off his lap and remove my sweater, watching his eyes widen as I lean over and pull his hat off, placing it on my head, bill forward.

"Oh fuck," Luke growls, pressing his fist to his mouth like he's wrecked. "Not the hat."

I smile and pull the brim down low over my face, my dark hair loose over my shoulders as I shoot him a sexy smirk. "You like me in your hat?"

He blinks back at me, his neck and cheeks flushed with color. "I stop existing when you wear my fucking hat."

I laugh at that dramatic response before bending over to slide my leggings off. His cheeks puff out as he yanks his shirt off completely, sitting before me in nothing but his jeans, mussed golden hair, and the firelight licking his skin in the most delicious way. He points to his lap and shoots me a serious look. "Get your ass back over here."

His command is deep and sexy and causes my stomach to squeeze, but I feel myself taking a step back instead.

He shakes his head and quirks a brow—a look of absolute warning. "Don't you come in here all cute and smiley and putting my hat on and then play hard to get. That's not how this marriage is going to work."

"Oh no?" I cross my arms and nibble the tip of my thumb. "Why don't you show me how it'll work?"

With a frustrated growl, Luke jumps up from the couch and stomps toward me. I squeal and try to run away but his hands catch me around my waist, spinning me into his chest before manhandling me onto the couch. His warm body lies over mine, his lips diving into my neck as I hold his hat on my head, pulling the bill down to lose myself to the darkness of his whiskers and hard muscles and warm flesh gliding over top of me.

He slides down, yanking the cups of my bra low to drag his tongue across each of my nipples, sucking hard, his noises desperate and frustrated against my skin. Wearing his hat was either a really good idea or a really bad idea and I have a feeling I'm going to like either answer.

He continues his descent until his bearded face is between my legs and he nips at my inner thighs with a growl, while holding me in place. "I'll make you pay for teasing me," he rumbles before sliding the fabric of my panties to the side and groaning when he sees the state of me. Pink, soaked, and throbbing to be touched. By him.

A rush of heat flows over my skin as he looks at my center and bites his lip, edging me with that unmanned expression of his as I pulse my hips up, desperate to be touched. I need him to touch me so fucking bad.

"I really like you in my hat," he says once more, glancing at me before swiping his tongue long and slow over my slit.

I hiss at the direct contact and buck against his whiskered face when he pays extra attention to my clit. He squeezes my legs tight as he holds me in place and licks and tongues my sex, driving me wild as I comb my fingers into his shaggy hair, gripping it by the roots as he devours me whole.

He brings a finger up and pushes it inside of me, groaning over how soaked I am as he fucks me with it in and out, in and out.

"So goddamn wet," he murmurs as he spreads my juices over my lips and crushes his mouth to mine again like he can't get enough of me.

I moan loudly, one hand in his hair and the other gripping the back of the couch like I'm going to topple over any minute as I writhe against his assault on my sex. My mind reels as I wonder if any man ever made me feel this good? The answer is categorically no.

And I feel weirdly grateful for that. Grateful for not only the sexual pleasure Luke gives me but the emotional kind too. He's given me a family with his brothers, their better halves, his nieces, nephew, and even his mom. They care for me unconditionally even if they've only known me for a short time. I hadn't realized how empty my life was until Luke brought me further into his life.

He's my person and I . . . I love him.

I feel the words on the tip of my tongue, desperate to come out of me like they've been trapped in a deep, dark dungeon for years and starved nearly to death. Words that I've never allowed myself to say to anyone in my whole life. Not even my dad.

My orgasm crests, distracting me from my thoughts. Luke must sense it because he grips my thighs harshly and tilts his head to nibble his teeth along my clit and light bursts behind my eyelids.

"Fuck, Luke," I scream as I grip his hair way too fucking hard, but I can't help it. I am unwell.

Pleasure vibrates through my whole body and I yank the hat down over my face, screaming obscenities into it as the combination of my orgasm and the scent of Luke's hat drives me absolutely feral.

My hips ache and I look down to see that I've wrapped my legs around Luke's face and yanked him into me so deep, I'm not sure he can breathe. I huff out a noise and relax to spread my legs and release the man causing me to lose control of my faculties.

Luke pulls back, gasping for air with a big goofy smile on his face, looking like the cat that got the cream, the weirdo.

"I need you inside me," I beg, my body warring with the feeling in my heart and my body.

Luke takes my command and sits up on his knees, both of our hands trembling as I slip out of my underwear and he shoves his jeans down to his thighs, not taking the time to push them all the way off.

I grab his thick velvety cock, rubbing my fingers over his hard length, my thumb brushing his slit as I pull him down on top of me, centering him before he thrusts hard and fast into me, stilling for an impossibly long moment.

Our breaths synchronize, my hands finding his backside as he buries his face in my neck, his breath hot on my skin. And it's there in front of the roaring fire in our home together that we both find oblivion together and a feeling I can't bring myself to say out loud yet, but I really hope he feels it too.

Chapter 39

FACT OR FICTION?
The Fletchers get shit done.

Luke

It's wedding prep madness on Fletcher Mountain as my brothers and I assist the rental crew who are here to set up the large outdoor tent for the reception tomorrow night. The tent comes equipped with ceiling heaters and clear sides that zip closed to keep the warmth in without impeding the view of Fletcher Mountain. It'll feel like we're in one of those clear igloos I see at restaurants in Denver. But here we're in the middle of the mountain. It's spectacular.

My mom and Everly are buzzing all over the place, literally wearing matching headsets as they transform the space into a winter wonderland of garland, pine cones, wood accents. They bark orders at Dakota, Trista, and Cozy, who all took the day off to help prep for the big day tomorrow. Even John's girlfriend Edith showed up to help with all the decorating. For a small wedding, this is looking like quite the production.

Wyatt walks out from behind his house, carrying a large box of twelve-inch logs sliced into cookies, similar to the pieces I cut off for the lumberjack competition.

"What the hell are those for?" I ask as he sets them down on the nearest table.

"Those are the wedding favors for guests!" Everly exclaims, walking over to us with her own box in hand. She sets it down and pulls out a mason jar with a white LED tea light candle inside. The jar is wrapped with a piece of twine that holds a sprig of eucalyptus and baby's breath around it. She sets it on top of the round wooden slab and smiles. "They're the table centerpieces and everyone gets to take one home at the end of the night."

"Eucalyptus was marked as her favorite green filler plant on the quiz," my mom says, rushing by with a box just like Everly's. "Think Addison will like them?"

I smile and nod even though I don't really know for sure if eucalyptus is her favorite plant. I just knew that was the scent on the lotion she wears every day, and it was an option in the multiple choices, so I marked it.

I watch as Everly and my mom begin placing the centerpieces along the long wooden tables that are covered with deep green velvet runners down the center.

A bar is stationed in the corner with a hot cocoa sign that's written out in calligraphy on a chalkboard. There are twinkling fairy lights running up the beams that support the tent casting the space in cozy, yellow lighting.

"Another truck is coming!" Ethan yells from the pasture where he's chasing Trista's alpacas around like a wild man. Rufus is MIA, likely fearing for his life.

A loud beep sounds on Everly's headset. "Grandma, the chair rental guy is here. I'm going to go meet him and tell them where to set them for the service."

"By the bench, dear."

"Copy," Everly says and marches off.

Calder calls out to Everly. "Do you want me to bring out my—"

"Shhhh!" Everly hisses at Calder. "No, we're not revealing that until later tonight after the dinner."

"Got it, boss." Calder salutes.

I cut him a look. "She's even got you in on this shit?"

Calder waggles his brows. "Oh yeah . . . I'm all in, bro. Speaking of which, I need to go check on the car service guys your wifey had us book for everyone tonight. They're doing pickups at Judy's, and I need to make sure those guys have four-wheel drive. Better go find my phone."

He takes off to resume his work and I look around, seeing that everyone seems to have a job, except me. Glancing at my cabin, I decide that maybe my wife could use some help inside, so I make my way out of the tent to head up the hill.

It was Addison's idea to host the rehearsal dinner at our place and do all the cooking even though I said we could have the Mercantile do the food. They're already catering tomorrow night, so it would have been very easy to add to their list, but my wife would not be deterred.

As I walk into the house, my nose is filled with the scent of savory meat and smoked spices that makes my stomach growl. Addison opted for a cowboy-style dinner of brisket, short ribs, corn on the cob, and some kind of twice-baked potatoes that she made me taste test earlier in the week. And of course, she worked her ass off late last night making fresh sourdough bread rolls and cinnamon butter to go with everything.

My wife is an overachiever.

Which is only confirmed when I find her in the kitchen wrapped in nothing but a bath towel as she bends over the oven to temperature check her meat.

I'd like to temp check her right now.

She turns her head when she hears me coming. "How's it going out there?" she asks, closing the oven and shooting me a nervous expression.

"It's total chaos," I reply, stifling down my dirty thoughts.

Her face falls. "Shit . . . I should go out and help."

"No, you shouldn't," I bark firmly, glancing at the windows to see the curtains are all still closed. "Everly and my mom insisted this all stay a surprise and that's what we're doing. No peeking."

She groans and grips the towel wrapped around her head. "I shouldn't have let them do all the planning. They're probably going overboard."

"Oh, they're definitely going overboard," I confirm and laugh at my wife's panicked expression.

She spins to walk away, but I capture her in my hands, pulling her back to me. "Relax, they love this shit."

She shakes her head. "I just . . . I'm starting to feel guilty about everything."

"Don't," I rasp, pressing a kiss to her lips. "They love doing this. They love you."

"They do?" Her brows lift and she looks up at me timidly, like it's even in question.

"Of course they love you. You're . . ." my chest contracts with the emotion swelling inside of me ". . . easy to love."

Her lower lip disappears between her teeth as she stares at my chest, mulling something over. What I wouldn't give to have the power to reach inside her mind and hear what she's thinking.

Just say it, Addison. Say you love me. You look at me like you do. You touch me like you do. Why can't you just say it?

"How much hair did you get cut this morning when you went to town?" she asks, changing the subject as she pulls my hat off and musses my locks.

"A decent amount. I thought it would look better for the pictures." I drag my hand through my freshly trimmed beard as well. "Do you hate it?"

She shakes her head. "No, I like it. I . . . love it."

My brows pop. "Love it?"

"Yeah." She combs her fingers through my tresses, scoring her nails on my scalp as I melt into her like I always do when she touches me. "I . . . love it," she confirms, making it very clear she's capable of using that word. I stare deeply into her eyes, willing her to say more, but she inhales sharply and looks away.

"It's getting late, and my dad is going to be here soon, so I better get ready. You too, Fletcher."

She pushes me away playfully and I struggle to hide the disappointment on my face. We're so close . . . and yet . . . so far away.

Addison

My heart races as I hold a glass of wine to my lips and glance around the dining room table consisting of my dad and Edith, Luke's mom, his three brothers and the ladies, plus Everly, Ethan, and Stevie.

I smile as I watch Stevie at the far end of the table struggle against Trista's attempts to wipe barbecue sauce off her cherubic little cheeks. Wyatt is grumbling next to them while dabbing at a barbecue sauce stain that Stevie managed to smear all over his white button-down and a strange premonition hits me.

I swear I can see me and Luke in a similar scenario. The two of us at this table with a little one of our own. Arguing over whose fault it is. What would the baby look like? Me or Luke?

My heart races with that imagery because it doesn't make me panic. It makes me happy. It makes me feel excited about the future.

I twine my fingers through Luke's on top of the table, and he turns to smile at me, pulling my hand up to press his lips to my knuckle. He laughs at something Ethan said, looking away as his eyes crinkle in the most delicious way. His new haircut and trimmed beard give me butterflies as he sits there in a dark green dress shirt that brings out his eyes. What a husband he makes.

When I finally pry my attention away from him, I catch Everly grinning at me from across the table. I shift in my seat, adjusting the turtleneck of my cream sweater dress self-consciously because I swear, I've caught that girl looking at me all night. I'd be developing a complex if she didn't seem so happy.

Everyone is happy.

I am happy.

I am in love.

I push back from the table, needing some air because no matter how many times I say that in my head, it still sends me into a mini panic. "I'm going to get the dessert."

"Can you wait a second on that, Addison?" Johanna asks from her place at the end of the table. She stands up from her seat between Trista and Edith and holds her glass up. "I feel like I'm doing a lot of toasts these days." She eyes Trista and Wyatt, rubbing her hand on Trista's back affectionately. "I don't love doing them, but I know Steven would if he could so . . ."

Everyone's smiles twitch as she sighs heavily, staring into her wineglass. "It's an accomplishment to fall in love with another person. To open your heart and decide to let someone in. It puts you at great risk of being hurt because, well . . . your heart is open. It's more vulnerable and that can feel scary."

Her hand trembles so she brings her other up to steady it. "Luckily, you two kids started off as friends, so your hearts opened to each other slowly over time. You always knew it was in safe hands. Which is why none of us were really that shocked to find out you got married on a whim without telling anyone first."

The table laughs and Luke squeezes my hand, kissing it again. God, this all feels real.

"But I'm real glad to have tomorrow to celebrate the two of you," Johanna continues. "This wedding has given me the opportunity to get to know you more, Addison, and it is painfully obvious why it was so easy for my Luke to fall in love with you. You are salt-of-the-earth goodness, honey, and I'm thankful you see in my son what I've always seen. His big, open heart. To Addison and Luke."

"To Addison and Luke!" Everyone cheers and clinks glasses.

My dad holds his drink up to me, catching my eyes for a long moment before I feel Luke's hand on my cheek as he turns me toward him.

He presses his lips to mine in a sweet, soulful kiss that I lean into, prolonging the contact because in some strange way, it feels like the first real kiss I've had with him. My heart is open too now. It's as vulnerable as Johanna said. And somewhere along the way, I've given it to him completely and I hope he's given me his in return.

"Okay, guys!" Everly claps her hands, ripping us from our moment. "The officiant texted and she's on her way up the mountain so we can head outside to do the rehearsal now. Bundle up, it's going to be cold."

I move to glance out the window and Everly sidesteps to block my view. "Not yet! I need a ten-minute head start so, Luke . . . control your woman."

Luke laughs as Everly throws on her coat and runs outside with Jo to greet the person in charge of the service tomorrow.

"Quite the ordeal," my dad murmurs under his breath as he slips his work coat on and zips it up to his chin.

"They all mean well." I glance over to Luke, who's waiting at the front door for me.

"I'm not saying it like it's a bad thing. This is all very nice." He offers me a crooked smile as he helps Edith with her coat. "I'm happy for you, Addie."

"Me too, sweetie," Edith confirms as she wraps her arm around my dad and smiles warmly at me.

I stare at the two of them holding each other, finding each other even later in life than I'm sure they wanted. But they just work. It's plain as day and I'm happy for them. I'm happy they have each other. Edith is good for my dad, and he deserves it after all the pain he's suffered. His suffering has been greater than mine in many ways. He lost a wife, a son, and became a single father all in one horrific night. It's a wonder he's even allowed himself to find love again at all.

Without thinking too much about it, I attack them both with a hug that clearly shocks them as they harrumph in stereo into my ears. Their bodies tense with surprise, but Edith catches up to the moment quickly as she squeezes me back, her sniffles echoing in my ears while my dad begrudgingly accepts the forced affection. It's not the most elegant of embraces, but if my old man can soften up enough to accept love, then surely I can too.

"Alright, alright. Don't get all soft on me." He huffs out an awkward noise and wiggles himself free.

Edith's smile is grateful, and I feel excited about the future of our relationship now. So much has changed, and I hope this means only good things to come for our family.

My dad nods toward the door, ignoring my tears. "Let's go see what all the fuss is about. They probably flew in fucking penguins or some crazy shit."

I can't wipe the smile off my face as I hold Luke's arm, and we shuffle out into the cold, boots crunching over the snow-packed driveway toward the yellow lights shining just past the tent that's all closed and dark. According to Everly, I don't get to see that space until tomorrow. The girl seems to be running the show now that she's here and I wonder what we'd do without her.

"Whoa," Luke says, stopping us in our tracks. "This is beautiful."

I inhale sharply as I take in the sight of where our ceremony is happening tomorrow, positioned directly in front of the memorial bench of Luke's father like we'd planned. It's the perfect lookout point on Fletcher Mountain, and it feels as if it was meant for exactly this kind of setup. And what a setup it is.

Yellow twinkle lights illuminate several white chairs lined up neatly in the snow with an aisle down the middle framed with garlands and glowing lanterns. The city of Jamestown glows at the base of the canyon walls, just below the captivating view of the starlit winter sky.

Everly and Johanna appear before us, smiling ear to ear. "Everything is lit with LED lights because Uncle Wyatt is a freak about open flames up here," Everly says, nudging her uncle.

"Eighty-five percent of forest fires start because of careless humans," Wyatt grouses.

"Yeah, yeah, we got it," Everly murmurs, side-eyeing me.

"Do you guy like it?" Jo asks, turning around to stand beside me and take it in from my vantage point.

"I love it," I reply, moving toward her to give her a hug. "You knocked it out of the park, Jo . . . and Everly, I suspect."

Everly squeals excitedly and claps her hands.

"Where did that pergola come from?" Luke asks, frowning back at my mom. "Was that from the rental company?"

Calder steps forward with a sheepish smile on his face.

"You made that?" Luke asks, his face slack with shock.

He shrugs and waves his hand casually. "Yeah, you know, I had some extra wood lying around."

"Jeez, man." Luke shakes his head in disbelief.

"It's stunning," I offer, stepping closer to admire the wooden pergola draped with Edison bulbs, asymmetrical evergreen garlands, white roses, and hunter-green velvet ribbons.

"I thought we could put it over Dad's bench after the wedding stuff is over. Give us a little shade when we sit there."

"It's too much," Luke says, stepping closer to Calder and pulling him into a hug. "That was too fucking much."

They clap each other on the back, not saying anything, and we all watch as they share a quiet brotherly moment together, Johanna fighting back tears.

"Wait until you see inside the tent tomorrow," Everly whispers to me.

"I'm already blown away," I state, still taking it all in.

"Are we all ready?" a woman dressed in a tan one-piece snowsuit asks, walking up to us with a binder in her hand. "I'm Sharon and I'll be doing your service tomorrow. I know it's cold, so I'll make this rehearsal quick and easy so we can all go home and . . ." The woman's voice trails off as she looks up into the night sky. "Oh my, it's snowing!"

Everyone's heads lift as large, puffy snowflakes begin to float and swirl all around us, illuminated by the moon's silvery glow. It's beautiful and feels like some sort of magical gift. Luke's eyes find mine and we smile at each other as the flakes cling to our lashes and hair.

"Well, this wasn't in the forecast but will certainly make for some beautiful pictures tomorrow," Sharon says with a bright smile. "Let's begin, shall we?"

Luke moves toward me, taking my hand in his and leading me down the snow-kissed aisle. I never thought this would be my life. I'd been determined to miss out on this, if I'm honest. And now I understand Luke's annoyance that I'd planned to marry a logger. Nothing about the wedding would have been real or special. And despite the fact that I've never dreamed about getting married, Everly and Jo have somehow made this a wedding of my dreams.

Fact: I'm about to marry my best friend . . . and I've never been happier.

Chapter 40

FACT OR FICTION?

Seven Brides for Seven Brothers is fucked up.

Luke

Snow sparkles over everything as I struggle to focus on the walk-through of the service tomorrow, my mind swimming with thoughts that I can't quiet no matter how hard I try. My head tips up as I look at the pergola Addison and I are standing under. It looks even more beautiful with the fresh flakes clinging to the greenery and a weighted pressure hits me in the chest. I can't believe my brother made this. He must have spent hours on it. Days. Weeks. When did he start it? As soon as he heard about the wedding? Fuck. This is a big thing for him, to dedicate time to a wedding that's not even real. He already pretty much works two jobs between his own furniture stuff and the family business. Why did he go to all this trouble?

Addison smiles at me, looking stunning as white flakes cling to her glossy black hair. She looks like a damn princess up here as she listens to the officiant rambling about the readings she selected for tomorrow. I release Addison's hands to wipe the sweat off my palms, my throat feeling tight like I'm having an allergic reaction to something, but I'm not allergic to something.

Except maybe lying.

I glance at my mom, who keeps peeking inside her binder like she's forgetting something. The lines on her forehead are creased like she's stressed. I didn't want her to be stressed. Everly keeps adjusting the chairs, moving them an inch one way or another so they're all in a perfect line.

Max and Cozy are bribing Ethan with candy to get him to pull Stevie down the aisle in a wagon instead of doing snow angels like he wants to.

It's all . . . a lot.

Earlier today, I loved it. Now it's like I've finally taken off my rose-colored glasses and I'm seeing what I've done to lead up to this moment.

It's all too much. Too much kindness, too much pressure, too much trust that this thing between me and Addison will work out. She could still walk away from me at the end of this, especially when she finds out John is going to sell the lumberyard. She won't want to stay married to me then. She might not even want to stay in Boulder. She'll be devastated and rich and can do whatever the fuck she wants with her life. That is if her dad gives her some of the sale money. Who knows what he might do?

And fuck, my mom's toast tonight? Jesus Christ. If I tell her I'm getting a divorce after all of this, it will kill her. She's been through enough. What was I thinking?

I was so focused on Addison and how much I wanted her, how much I wanted her to be happy, that I somehow missed the fact that I'm being a selfish prick to my entire family who have grown attached to this magnificent woman beside me.

My eyes land on John, who's been giving me looks all night long. Looks I can't even decipher. He probably thinks I'm a lying asshole too because I obviously haven't told his daughter about his plans to sell the yard. I am disgusting. I hid the truth from my best friend because I wanted to trick her into marrying me and falling in love with me.

It's like I'm doing CPR but our relationship is DOA . . . dead on arrival.

Blood rushes in my ears as the officiant ends the rehearsal and I say my goodbyes to everyone on some sort of detached autopilot. I watch all the cars leave the mountain, waving cheerily like this is the best weekend ever, but my mind is battling with this overwhelming sense of impending doom.

Addison kisses me on the cheek and says something about going back to our house with Dakota and Trista to discuss plans for hair and makeup tomorrow. My mom takes Stevie back to Wyatt's to put her to bed, opting to spend the night in their spare room so she doesn't have to make the drive up the mountain roads again tomorrow.

I nod and watch everyone go their separate ways when suddenly I feel my feet carrying me backward, away from my cabin, and as far away from this wedding setup as I can get. Part of me wants to disappear into the woods, but it's cold as fuck and the night air nips at my neck, so I pull my coat collar up and beeline to the barn. I just need a moment to collect my thoughts. Just a breather. Today was a lot and I need to touch some fucking ground and get my shit together.

Millie bleats as soon as I enter the barn and start pacing down the alleyway, completely ignoring Trista's pig, Sir Reginald, and the weird fucking tongue-hanging horse Handsome and the alpacas. Shit, what were their names again? Like band instruments? Trombone? Fuck knows. Three black-headed sheep are asleep in the corner stall, and I didn't even know we had sheep. Plus, the highland cow that looks like a toy is sharing a stall with Millie.

It's a damn petting zoo in here and it's overflowing. I need to get Trista's rescue center estimate sent to her. I've been sitting on it for too long. Distracted by . . . my best friend . . .

Who doesn't love me.

"Hey, what are you doing out here?" Calder asks, stepping through the Dutch barn doors with Wyatt close behind.

"You good?" Wyatt asks, staring at me with concern that looks just like dad.

Fuck I hate that look. It makes me feel panicky inside.

"This is all too much, you guys. This was a bad idea. The whole thing."

"What are you talking about?" Wyatt folds his arms over his chest and furrows his brow at me.

"The lying, the manipulating. It's bad enough that *I* did it, but I dragged you all down with me and that makes this all ten times worse."

I rake my hands through my hair and kick Reggie's stall, stirring him from his sleep under his fucking blanket on his own personal mattress.

"You need to take a breath," Calder says, holding his hands out to me like he's going to corral me into a pen next.

"I need to confess everything to Addison before the wedding. I can't let her walk down the aisle tomorrow and be faking it for all of you. This wedding Mom and Everly threw together is beautiful. I don't want it to be fake. I want it to be real."

"I think it is real," Wyatt says, his eyes urgent on me. "She loves you. It's clear as day."

"It's not real if she doesn't know everything we did," I exclaim, my heart pounding. "Jesus Christ, Everly roped you guys into helping me train for weeks for that lumberjack competition just so I could get her to marry me and fall in love with me. That is so fucked. Then the night out at the Merc when you made us kiss."

"Luke, I think this is just prewedding nerves," Calder says with a tense shrug.

"It's deeper than that, damn it," I snap back, my tone visceral. "I don't want her love if the only way I got it was through lying and manipulating. I want to be enough for her."

"You are enough, Luke," Wyatt states, eyeing me harshly. "It's obvious you've just been trying to impress her all this time. What's the real harm in that?"

"The harm is that it was all for nothing because her dad is going to sell the yard to Robyn and her husband anyways, which means Addison doesn't need me and she never did," I add, my mind flashing back to my conversation with John. "Her whole life is going to be turned upside down when she finds out, and as her friend, I should be the one person she can lean on through it all, but I've been too busy lying to her for weeks just like her father. This is all too much. I have to come clean."

"You just did." Addison's voice cuts into my mental warfare and I turn around to see her stepping into the barn, and the expression on her face . . . is completely devastating.

Addison

"Babe . . . listen," Luke rushes out, trying to approach me but I hold my hand up, stopping him in his tracks.

"I heard all I needed to hear." I frown and lick my lips, pulling my coat tight around me, refusing to show a spec of emotion on my face. I squint over to Luke and his brothers as they stand in the barn with their fucking dicks in their hands talking about me behind my back. How many times have they all done that? How many times have they plotted and schemed together about me?

Me.

Like I'm so damn important.

I focus on the most important thing first. "My dad is selling the yard to your ex?"

Luke's face is hollow and slack as he nods. "I think so."

"That should be a fun transition." I bark out a dry laugh as I sniff and stare at the floor, dragging my feet through the straw scattered beneath my boots. "And on top of that, everyone on this mountain knew our marriage was a lie? Did I hear right?"

"Not everyone knew," Luke offers, shoving a hand through his hair.

"Who didn't know, Luke? The fucking goat?" I bite, my tone acidic as I hang on to my sanity by a thread.

As if on cue, Millie bleats and I want to scream.

"I feel like such an idiot." I laugh and shake my head, my stomach twisted in knots. "I thought this was real between you and me, but it wasn't. I thought I was becoming a part of your family, but I've been an unknowing participant to some weird manipulative game you're all playing to get me."

My mind reels as I replay the last several weeks with this Fletcher family. All the women in that bridal store with me, gushing over my gowns, taking me out for drinks. The Fletcher Mountain group chat. The engraved cutting board. Luke's mom being so sweet with all the wedding planning. All those kind, tender looks. They were all just . . . playing their part? No wonder Everly was watching me all night long. She was just waiting to see if their big, grand scheme worked.

I thought these people were my friends, but they were just playing make-believe as well. This is humiliating.

"And Robyn?" I ask, hating to even utter her name. "You knew your ex was trying to buy the lumberyard out from under me and you didn't tell me? How fucking easy is it for you to lie to me, Luke?"

"I found out two days ago and went straight to your dad."

"Oh cool, so you plotted with him about me as well. Wonderful! I'm surrounded by liars." I blow out a deep breath, feeling my head start to spin. "You know, maybe you can run the yard with Robyn. The way you were looking at her a couple weeks ago, it's clear there's nothing fake between the two of you. Maybe that's been your plan all along."

"Don't do this," Luke says, his face sad and resolute. "Don't make shit up just to villainize me further. You know that's not who I am."

"I don't know you at all!" I scream, my voice hoarse and dense in the quiet barn. "How long have you had feelings for me?"

Luke's jaw clenches as his lips twitch. "A while."

"How long?"

He closes his eyes and says in a breath, "Years."

"And you didn't think maybe you should just grow a pair of balls and tell me?"

"No, Addison, I didn't because I know you and you would have never given me a fucking chance."

"Now we'll never know!"

He exhales harshly out his nose. "You are looking for reasons to push me away because you're scared about what's building between us because it's not the future you planned for yourself. But this is real. You know it's real."

"Our marriage is a mountain of lies. It's fiction!"

"It was never fiction for me," Luke says, and I feel my whole head spin.

"Well, it doesn't matter because now not only do I have to divorce my best friend. I have to divorce the man I'm in love with because he's a fucking liar."

I turn on my heel, ignoring the devastated look on Luke's face over my declaration as I storm out of the barn and away from the man who sounds like a complete stranger. That is not my best friend. That is not the person I let hold me in bed every night. The man who I thought I fell in love with. Love? What a joke. I clearly have no clue what love even feels like if I fell for all of this.

And my God, the Robyn stuff. What the actual fuck? My dad is going to sell anyways? To her? How? How did she get her hands into him of all people? That girl better pray she never crosses paths with me again or I will end up in jail just like my mother.

I stumble in the snow-packed lane as a deep, soul-crushing pain slices through me with that dark thought. My fear of turning out like my mother is exactly why I never wanted to fall in love or get married. I'm not built for this. I'm too raw, too troubled, too fucked-up. My genetics are horrific.

The sound of footsteps echoes behind me, so I pick up my pace, pushing my dark thoughts away. I dig into my coat pocket for my car keys ready to get as far away from Luke as possible.

"What are you doing?" Luke asks, out of breath as a cloud of air puffs in front of his lips.

"I'm going to leave this fucking mountain."

"Don't do that."

"Why?"

"Because it's snowing."

"I've got four-wheel drive, Luke. I'll be fine."

"You're upset. You shouldn't drive."

"Why would I be upset? I'd have to care about you to be upset."

"You just told me you love me, Addison."

"I loved who I thought you were! Not this person in front of me who lies just like everyone else in my life." I get to my car and grab my door handle, jumping in shock when Luke reaches out to take my keys. "Give those back."

"No."

"Luke!"

"I'm not going to let you drive away like this," he roars, his face red with anger. "We're married and you're going to stay and work this out with me. You don't leave. This is real now. No more fact or fiction question. You are my wife. I am your husband. We signed those papers together. And I fucking love you, Addison. I love you so much that I will trap you up on this mountain until you can admit you still love me."

"Of course I love you," I cry, my voice hoarse. "I love you, Luke, but you lied to me."

The sounds of more footsteps approach and I swerve my head to see Luke's brothers closing in, herding me like I'm one of Trista's livestock animals. They even have the nerve to stand in front of my car with their arms crossed like they won't let me go. "What are you guys going to do? Hold me hostage?"

"What's going on?" Trista's voice calls from Luke's front deck as she steps outside with Dakota.

"These Fletcher brothers have trapped me up on this mountain!"

Trista and Dakota stare back at us in confusion.

"The jig is up," I snarl at their perplexed expressions. "I know you guys all know that my marriage to Luke was bullshit. You can all quit acting like you like me or like I'm one of the family. Just give me my keys so I can go home and get away from you all. Please." I fight back the tears at how utterly alone I feel in this moment. I don't have Luke. I don't have the ladies. I don't even have Luke's mom. Probably the fucking rooster even hates me.

Dakota steps down the front steps walking straight toward me. "Addison, on my life, I have no idea what you're talking about."

"Me neither," Trista adds, following close behind.

I swerve my eyes to Luke, who nods to confirm. "They didn't know. It's only me, Calder, and Wyatt who know. And Max I guess."

"And Everly," Calder adds, looking wildly uncomfortable. "She was kind of in charge."

"Oh, is that all?" I groan and shove a hand through my hair.

"What are you guys talking about?" Trista asks, turning to her husband.

Wyatt winces but it's Calder who fills in the blanks. "Luke

HONEYMOON PHASE

and Addison got married to help Addison inherit the lumberyard and we were sort of helping Luke figure out a way to get her to . . . fall in love with him." Calder lifts his hands, looking sheepish.

"Why would you do that? She obviously already loves him," Trista says and somehow those words cut deeper than they should.

"Wait, so you knew these two weren't married for real and you just lied to me?" Dakota asks, stepping past me to stare at Calder accusingly.

"Give her the keys," Trista growls, turning her attention to Luke.

"No." Luke steps back with a stubborn set to his jaw.

"Give them to her!" Dakota yells at Luke, who has the nerve to look at least moderately afraid.

Luke turns his eyes to me with a pleading look. "It's not safe."

Trista turns her fury to her husband. "Fine, then we're going to *Seven Brides for Seven Brothers* this shit."

"What?" Dakota and I both ask, frowning at Trista.

"*Seven Brides for Seven Brothers* . . . the 1950s musical about seven brothers who all live on a mountain and go to town and basically human traffic women to be their brides?"

Everyone continues staring back in confusion, but I hear Wyatt murmur something under his breath.

"They abduct them and take them up to their mountain and an avalanche blocks the roadway preventing the townspeople from riding up to save them. Anyways, Milly, the only ridiculous female up there by choice, gets mad at the brothers and kicks them all out to the barn, so yeah . . . you boys are all sleeping in the barn."

"Wait a minute," Calder says, taking a step forward.

"You're all sleeping in the barn," Trista screeches, leaving no room for argument.

Wyatt grumbles under his breath as he and Calder both stare back at the girls before turning on their heels and sulking all the way back to the barn.

Luke steps toward me. "Addison, please. Can we just talk?"

"You talked plenty with your brothers," I croak, my voice raw in my throat. "It's too late for you to want to talk to me now."

Luke exhales heavily and when he turns to walk down the hill toward the barn, my chin trembles as tears fill my eyes. Instantly, Trista and Dakota wrap me up in their arms and walk me into the house . . . that doesn't feel a bit like home anymore. It feels like a stranger's house.

Chapter 41

FACT OR FICTION?
We didn't rehearse this.

Addison

It's three in the morning and I'm at the kitchen island, stretching and folding my sourdough way more than I need to, giving the dough a harsh punch every once in a while, just for good measure.

I've not slept a wink, my mind doing what it always does and fixating on everything that's fucked-up in my life.

It took two hours to get Trista and Dakota to leave. They forced me to sit here and talk through everything with them. They assured me they knew nothing, and they were honored when I asked them to be a part of my wedding. They told me if I wanted to call off the wedding, they would have my back.

But they also asked me if it really was the worst thing in the world for Luke's biggest lie to be that he loved me.

"I totally understand why you're angry, Addison. I'm fucking fuming that we were all being lied to," Trista says. "But I'm struggling with why you're so angry at Luke. Wasn't it obvious how much he loved you?"

"We all saw how determined he was to become a lumberjack," Dakota adds. "That was for you, Ads. Because he loves you. I've never seen Luke so passionate about something in the years that I've known him. He may have been hiding his feelings, but it clearly wasn't a game."

"But the whole Robyn thing?" I ask. "He knew who my dad was selling the lumberyard to—"

"But, Ads, that's on your dad," Trista corrects firmly. "It's your dad who's selling you out of your job. Not Luke. The fact that he went to your dad on your behalf shows how much he cares."

"So, is the main issue that Luke loves you but didn't tell you?"

And I feel fundamentally broken for feeling like that is the biggest issue. I feel duped, just like I did with my mom. No part of me ever expected her to not come back home. Yes, it was awful what we all went through, but I thought family worked through stuff. I thought family stuck together through hard times.

And the worst part is . . . just a few hours ago, I was walking around thinking I had found a family that would do that. A husband, a home, a new family who loved me enough to be a part of our special day.

I was ready to make my wedding with Luke real tomorrow and planned on telling him my feelings tonight. I was going to let him hold me in bed and tell him that I loved him. He was going to say it back and we were going to make love whispering it onto each other's lips.

Tomorrow was set to be the best day of my life.

Now it's like someone has woken me up from a dream I've been stuck in and they're pointing at all the things I was ignoring in my time here on Fletcher Mountain. Everyone is capable of lying. Everyone is capable of leaving me.

It's so laughable of me to think I could have a normal relationship with a man. I have an alcoholic, dangerous, absentee mother and an overbearing, narcissistic, misogynistic father. To think I was dreaming about having kids.

I am clearly not thinking straight.

I am not equipped for that life. No child should be subjected to the likes of me and my baggage. I'm too much to handle. I'm overreactive and emotional and clearly incompetent in relationships. Which is why Luke didn't trust me to open my heart to him. And I'm obviously incompetent in business too because my dad doesn't trust me to inherit the lumberyard.

I'm a mess!

It's no wonder my mother left us after prison. I'd probably leave me too.

It's nearly 4 a.m. by the time I force myself to go lie in the spare bed. I hate that it doesn't smell like Luke. I hate that he taught me what a good night of sleep felt like because now I'm conditioned to need it. Before him, I was fine only getting a few hours of sleep at night. Now I feel literally ill when I can't get my brain to shut off.

With a frustrated growl, I do something really fucking bad. I grab my phone and fire off a text.

Luke

I stare at the barn ceiling from my place on the sofa, my mind spinning with the events of the past several hours. How I let it go this far without just telling Addison how I felt is something I need to really reflect on. My brothers tried to talk to me after we retreated like whipped puppies to the barn, but I didn't want to hear it. I didn't need a pep talk from them. Or Everly. Or anyone. I know where my fear comes from. It's a fear that has lived in me for the past three years.

To hold someone in their last moments on this earth and not be able to save them is a fucking sobering experience. The death of my father changed me and unfortunately, I'm experiencing the consequences of that change now.

Will I ever be able to let someone fully in without fear that I'll never be enough for them? That I'll ever have the ability to keep them alive if something terrible happens? Maybe that's why I never made a move on Roe after I started developing feelings for her. It wasn't just a silly anti-relationship pact I had with my brothers. I'm fucking terrified to fall in love and then lose someone. Roe's question about how we keep loving the other struck a chord. She's easy to love, and I'll probably love her for the rest of my life. But clearly, it's not enough for her. She doesn't want me in my fucked-up, manipulative state.

I glance over at my brothers, who are passed out on the bed that still sits up here since Trista moved out. The apartment above the barn has become a bit of a dumping ground the past few months, but at least we have a place to crash for the night.

Not that I'm getting any sleep anyways.

My phone buzzes from the end table beside me and I inhale sharply, my heart pounding in my chest when I pick it up and see three words from Roe.

I need you.

I type back a quick response, letting her know I'm on my way and jump off the couch to stuff my feet back into my boots, abandoning my snoring brothers as I run my fucking ass out of the barn and up the hill. I've been texting her all night with no replies, staring out the window and seeing the lights on in our place. My pulse races with every step that brings me closer to her. My wife. My best friend. Please let this be a good sign.

As I walk up to my front porch, the smell of sourdough hits me, and I spot Addison through the window pacing in the kitchen. A fresh loaf of bread is cooling on a rack and she's chewing her nails, looking completely exhausted.

I hesitate to walk in, not knowing if I should, so I lift my hand and knock, holding my breath as I prepare myself to see her face-to-face again.

When she opens the door, the minute her eyes lift to mine, her face twists in pain as she covers her face and starts to cry.

"Fuck," I growl and move toward her to take her in my arms, but she presses her hands to my chest and stops me.

"I don't want to be touched," she says firmly, wiping at her running nose.

"Okay." My hands flex at my sides as I fight every urge in my body to comfort my wife. I've never seen her like this and it's gutting me.

"I can't sleep," she croaks, looking so young and innocent.

"Me neither," I offer because I don't know what else to say.

She nods woodenly, wiping the tears out of her eyes. "We're going to lie in your bed and we're not going to touch. We're just going to sleep. I don't know what tomorrow will bring yet. I haven't decided. But I need to sleep and damn you, Fletcher, I can't do it without you anymore."

I wince, fighting back my own tears because it's maybe the best thing I've ever heard in my life. I want her to need me the way I need her, but I know she hates me for it all the same.

I follow her to the bedroom, and we crawl under the covers fully clothed. I lie on my side facing her, stupidly hoping she'll curl into me, but she doesn't. She lies on her side facing away from me, the silvery moon illuminating her body in a way that stabs straight through my heart. It's weird not touching her.

We lie silently for a moment before she asks, "When did you know you were in love with me? Like truly know?"

"I think it was after my dad died," I answer with a heavy sigh. "When I couldn't hold your hand or get a hug from the one person I wanted one the most from. When I forgave you for not showing up and we started hanging out again, I realized that's what love is. It's tolerating things you might not like from someone you care about because you know their essence. You know them at their best and their worst and you love them through it."

She sniffs loudly and I feel the bed shake so I shift closer, my hand hovering over her frame, wanting so much to pull her into my arms, but I stop myself.

"I'm terrified that loving you could ruin me," she croaks, her voice thick with emotion.

"How could it ruin you?" I ask, squeezing the pillow under my head.

She rolls over to face me, hitting me with the devastating emotion on her face. "Because what if something happens to you? I was a wreck that day you went out on that fire call. A complete mess."

I take a risk and touch her arm, and in one breath, she shifts closer to me, allowing me to pull her into my chest and it feels so goddamn good that tears prick the backs of my eyes.

"I know it's hard to be vulnerable, babe," I say softly and run my fingers through her hair. "But this is a good thing."

"No, it's not," she argues, her voice trembling. "I want to be independent. I can't let you be my world, Luke."

"Why not?"

"Because it will hurt too much if we don't work."

"It's going to hurt no matter what at this point, just look at us now," I argue, my teary eyes finding hers in the darkness. "We're better together. You're in this with me and it's going to hurt if you lose me now or if you lose me fifty years from now when we're old and gray and sitting on my front porch looking at our grandkids and marveling over the life we made. And if it's all the same to you, I'd like option two."

She sobs into my shoulder, and I tense, wondering if I've pushed her too far. But then again, not pushing her is how I got to where we are in the first place. I can't hold back anymore. I want her to know what I see for us. *I see everything for us.*

"The truth is, Addison, I love you so much I would have just been your friend through all of this if that's truly all you ever wanted from me. But the past couple weeks have proven we are more. We can be everything to each other if you just allow yourself to love me back."

She shakes her head against my chest. "I don't think I can ever trust you again. You lied to me, Luke. Just like my mom lied to my dad about being sober."

My chest feels like it's caving in. "That is so fucking different, Roe."

"I don't think it is. A lie is a lie."

Silence grows between us as I bite my lip and struggle with what to say next. How could I have got this all so wrong? How could I let myself get so deep I can't dig myself out?

Hell. I'm in fucking hell.

I'm holding the woman of my dreams in my arms, and I can feel her slipping through my fingers.

"I just think we go back to being friends," she says quietly against my chest. "I can move back to my place in Boulder, and we just go back to being what we were before. Can you handle that?"

I close my eyes in the darkness, wishing I could figure out a way to have this mattress swallow me whole. This. This is why I never told her how I felt. I know my friend. I know her all too well. And now my greatest fear is coming true.

She's pushing me away.

I press my lips into her hair, inhaling her scent one last time because I don't know when I'll ever get to hold her like this again. The ache in my chest is so intense, I struggle through my reply that rips my very soul to shreds, "I'd rather have you as a friend than nothing at all."

She nods against me, breathing out one long sigh of relief that feels as if it's sucked all the oxygen from my lungs. "Tomorrow, I think we should go through the motions of the wedding. Your mom worked so hard on all of this, and I don't want to break her heart yet. We can work out our divorce plan later."

My jaw aches at the finality in her words as I close my eyes and fight back my tears. "Whatever you say, Roe."

Chapter 42

FACT OR FICTION?
No one is a mastermind.

Luke

I'm on autopilot the next day, going through the motions of getting everything ready. Taking orders from Everly and my mom. Managing my brothers with their sympathetic looks and my crazy nephew, Ethan, who keeps asking how long until the wedding starts.

It's my wedding day but, somehow, I feel like I'm preparing for a funeral.

When I woke up this morning, the bed was empty, and Addison's car was gone. I wondered if she was going to leave me hanging at the altar, but when I checked my phone, I saw a text from her letting me know she was going for a run.

I stare at the wedding band I bought for her today, wondering if she's going to give it back to me when this is all done and hating that idea. I'd rather she keep it. Even if we are over. I want her to want to keep it. I want her to keep at least a piece of these last couple of months we had together, even if they didn't mean to her what they meant to me.

At one point I feed Stevie a bottle and it's the first time I feel good all day long. I hold my niece to my chest, and press a kiss into her chestnut curls, aching inside because I know I'll never have this. If I don't have this with Roe, I don't want it with anybody. I'm trying to come to terms with the idea that I'll always be the single uncle.

"You look great, Luke!" Everly says excitedly as she bounds

into Calder's living room where I'm slipping on my hunter-green wool blazer that I picked out weeks ago. I turn on my heel and eye Everly's navy velvet gown. Under normal circumstances, I would remark on how lovely she looks. How grown-up and mature she's become. But these aren't normal circumstances.

I'm miserable.

"Thanks," I reply flatly and force a smile I don't feel.

"What's wrong?" she asks, tipping her head to look at me closer.

"Nothing."

"Not nothing. I can tell something's up. What is it?"

I sigh heavily, knowing she's going to get it out of me eventually, so I might as well tell her now. "Your mastermind plan is a bust, kid."

"What do you mean?"

I shrug half-heartedly. "Addison found out everything we've been doing last night, and she told me she just wants to be friends."

Everly's lips part. "What the hell?"

"We're done. We're doing the wedding to keep the peace with everyone, but after this Addison is moving back to Boulder. Doesn't sound like she's inheriting the lumberyard anymore, so she doesn't really need me anymore."

"No, Luke," Everly exclaims, her blue eyes wide with horror. "This can't be the end. We can fix this. You just haven't done your grand gesture yet. Let's think. There's still time. We could—"

"Enough, Everly," I growl, my tone harsh. "We're done plotting. No more games."

"But—"

"But nothing," I snap, cutting her off. "It was stupid for me to take advice from you anyways. You've never even been in love. You know nothing. You're just a kid."

Silence spreads in the room like a fucking wildfire and I look up to see hurt and pain all over Everly's face.

"Fuck," I murmur, pushing a hand through my hair. "I'm sorry, Everly, I didn't mean it."

"No, you're right. I don't know anything about love." She steps back and tightens the brown fur shawl around her shoulders. "I'm just gonna go check on Grandma."

"Everly," I call out, but she ignores me, rushing out the door and making her way down the hill to Wyatt's place where the ladies are all camped out for the day.

"Way to go, Luke," I murmur to myself as I stare out the window at the snowcapped pines and the beautiful wedding setup. "Now when you tell your mother you're getting divorced in a few weeks, you will have made every woman in your life hate you."

Chapter 43

FACT OR FICTION?
I've always been a daddy's girl.

Addison

"My God, Addie May. You really do look like a princess," my dad says as I step out of the spare bedroom at Luke's to find him standing in my kitchen nibbling on a piece of bread.

I force a wobbly smile as I look down at my dress. It's a simple satin long-sleeve gown that's a mermaid fit so it's tight around my hips and bottom. It has a boat neckline and a long row of silver buttons down the backside all the way through the train. It's simple and I remember the day I tried it on, feeling like I'd never felt more beautiful in my life.

Today, I feel ambivalent about it.

I thought my run at the cemetery this morning would help me collect my thoughts, but it didn't. I feel just as wretched about my plan now as I did last night when I presented it to Luke. Not even a conversation with my brother, Aaron, could help bring me any sense of peace over all of this.

"Thanks, Dad," I mumble back, unable to look him in the eyes because I know if I do, I'm going to start a fight with him. I'm going to scream at him for letting me believe that getting married and having a big, traditional wedding was how I'd get the lumberyard handed over to me when all along, he had buyers lined up to take it over.

This is just another betrayal.

He has no faith in me, and he clearly never has. So why the

fuck did he suggest I marry someone for something he's taking away from me anyway?

I'm so fucking sick of losing in life. I'm so fucking sick of the people who are supposed to love me in my life doing nothing but hurt me.

"That blonde girl popped in and gave me a ten-minute warning so . . ."

I nod and stare at the bouquet of white roses and eucalyptus. It's modern and unlike anything I've ever seen before and under normal circumstances, I would be so excited about it.

These aren't normal circumstances.

"Let's head out and see if we can start early," I say, making my way to the door.

"Hey," my dad calls out, but I ignore him. "Hey," he barks more forcefully. "What is your problem? This is your wedding day, and you look like you're going to a funeral."

I bark out a dry laugh at the audacity of that statement. But in many ways, I feel like I am going to a funeral. My own. "Let's just get this over with."

"This is not how a blushing bride should be on her wedding day," Dad says, running a finger over his mustache. "If you don't want to get married, you shouldn't be walking down that aisle."

"You're pushing me down that aisle," I bite back.

"The hell I am." His face is the picture of offended.

"You're right actually," I reply with a laugh. "This has nothing to do with you anymore because I already know you're going to do what you want with the yard regardless of whether I get married today or not."

"So, he told you, then?" my dad huffs back and shakes his head. "That boy's timing needs some work." He frowns curiously back at me. "If you already know I'm selling the yard, then why are you going through all this?"

"I'm doing this for Luke's mom and everyone else sitting

out there who worked so hard to make me feel loved and included . . . and worthy—" My voice cracks as I clutch my belly, trying to control my emotions. "Some of those people haven't spent months lying to me, so I'm not about to let them down. Let's please just get on with this."

"Ads," my dad barks.

"What?" I snarl back, turning my head to look at the man who raised me.

His eyes swim with pain before he shrugs and say, "I'm sorry."

"Sorry for what?" I ask, watching him closely.

He works his jaw from side to side and then whispers, "I'm sorry for being scared."

The words are so simple and childlike, they sound strange coming from my dad. "What are you scared of?"

"Of losing you of course." He harrumphs and walks around the island to sit down on a barstool. "I'm scared the yard could be too much for you. It was too much for me and that's why your mom left. I wasn't around enough. Didn't help enough. The stress made me stay out drinking too much." He splays his hand on the counter and stares down at the ground. "I never told a single person this, but your mom called me for a ride home the night of the accident and I didn't come. I was at the bar with Chuck. I just . . . ignored her call and then . . . we lost Aaron." His voice cracks as his face crumples, his body going slack as he struggles to stay upright in his chair.

I stand stock-still, watching my dad lose it. I've never seen him lose it in my whole life. Not even at Aaron's funeral.

Like a volcano erupting uncontrollably now, he continues, "And then she went to prison, and I just kept at it like an ass. Drinking and driving with you in the car. Jesus Christ, Ads. We donate money to that charity every year, and every year I have to look those people in the eye and know what I did with you even after losing my son."

My chin wobbles as I watch my dad unload years of guilt and bad decision-making. Things we never talk about, never acknowledge. Just exist knowing they happened.

"I don't want you running the damn yard because I want better for you," he croaks, his red eyes fierce on me. "I want you to have a life outside of that dusty old place."

"Dad." I move over to stand in front of him, squatting so I can look up into his tortured downturned face. "I still can have a life. And I'll also never do what you and Mom did either. I refuse to be like that. I'm ridiculously disciplined when it comes to my alcohol intake and my driving decisions afterward."

"But what if you're not?" he cries, his large frame slumped toward me. "What if the stress becomes too much?"

"Then I have Luke," I reply, and gasp when I realize what just came out of my mouth so easily. So freely. So automatically. Like a reflex.

I have Luke.

My best friend.

The man I love with every fiber of my being.

Except I don't have him.

I pushed him away.

Because I'm afraid.

Just like my dad.

"Luke loves me," I say the words out loud, knowing they're true. "He'll do anything to help me. Even marry me for a year so I can inherit a business."

He huffs out a laugh and shakes his head. "I knew it was all bullshit."

I sniff loudly. "Except at some point, it stopped being bullshit. At some point . . . it became real." My eyes well with tears. "I love him, Daddy."

Pain crawls up my throat at that realization. Something that felt impossible to say yesterday. But I look at my dad, a hard, broken man, and I don't want to be like him. I want to be like Luke. Loving and willing to do crazy shit for the people he loves.

"He's one of the good ones," I offer tearfully, my hands trembling as I grip my dad's hands on his lap.

"You might be right." He wrinkles his nose and shakes his head. "I don't like to admit that, but I think it's true."

I garble out a laugh. "I'm afraid it's one of those things that's just true. Even when he screws up, he still somehow manages to do it with good intentions."

I stare down at the ground, hating that I've fumbled all of this so badly. We were good, happy, in love. We were perfect and I let my own insecurities and fears push him away.

Sort of like how my dad is trying to push me away from the yard.

Like father, like daughter.

"Dad, I will admit you made some mistakes when I was growing up. But can I tell you one thing? I never doubted that you loved me."

His shoulders shake as he absorbs that statement. "Really?" he asks with a loud sniff.

"Yeah, it's why I was taking this yard issue so hard. I can see now that you were coming from a good place, but you went about it the wrong way."

"I've been wrong once before." His face splits open into a big, teasing smile.

I laugh with him and then sigh. "I've been wrong once before too." I wipe at the tears falling down my face and swallow deeply.

I've been wrong to use the lumberyard as my hiding place from the world. I made it my whole identity because the words my mother said to me as a child have stuck with me for far too long . . .

Sometimes the ones we love the most disappoint us the most.

It's wrong of me to put those toxic words on Luke, who has done nothing to deserve them. If lying about loving me is the worst that man could do, I should be so lucky.

I want to be better than my parents. I don't want to live in fear of disappointment. And maybe it's naive of me, but I don't see how Luke could ever disappoint me enough to change how I feel about him.

I love him too much.

"You do what you have to do with the lumberyard," I state firmly to my dad, wiping at my tears and knowing I'm going to have to touch up my makeup. "I'll be fine either way."

"You sure about that?" my dad asks, and I glance outside to see the bridal party is starting to line up.

I nod firmly because at the end of the day, I can manage anything as long as I have my best friend beside me.

I shoot my dad a watery smile. "I'll be fine as long as you get me down that aisle."

My dad grabs my hands and stands up. "I got you, Addie May."

Chapter 44

FACT OR FICTION?
This marriage is fiction.

Luke

I watch my niece Everly walk my mom down the snow-covered aisle, forcing a smile I know she doesn't feel. My mom, on the other hand, feels every bit of her happiness as she takes her seat and gives me a wave and a hearty thumbs-up, completely oblivious to the absolute pain shredding through my heart right now.

I have to marry the woman I love today . . .

Who is planning to divorce me tomorrow.

Life is a fucking bitch.

I glance out at the guests all covered in blankets and wearing their winter coats. Crisp, mountain air dances in front of their lips as they speak quietly to each other. The snow-dusted evergreens all around us are beautiful, but I can't appreciate them like I normally do. In fact, every beautiful snowy image today feels like an extra stab through my frozen heart.

I glance over at my three brothers standing beside me. They're outfitted in their Sunday best as they watch their ladies walk down the aisle one by one. They all gaze at their person with love and adoration even though two of them were in the doghouse—or the barn—with me last night.

But they still love each other.

They worked through it.

And they found forgiveness.

If only I could have been so lucky.

Ethan is next and he's looking sharp in his dark green suit

while pulling Stevie in a wagon covered in fluffy tulle. Stevie has my heart ready to burst as she smiles big and toothless in her blue-and-yellow flannel dress with a matching stocking cap on top.

Ethan pulls the wagon up to my mom, running over her foot in the process. Everly jumps up to help get them settled beside her and then Sharon, the officiant, tells everyone to rise.

The music shifts to the song "Can't Help Falling in Love" sung by Kina Grannis, which I handpicked for today when I thought this was going to be the happiest day of my life. Now it's taunting me with a love story that doesn't have a happy ending.

When Addison and her father round the corner, my heart stops, and the world disappears. All I see is her gliding toward me, looking like fresh snow against the wintery landscape. Her dark hair is swept over to one side, curled and loose down one shoulder. Her long lashes fan her rosy cheeks, and her shoulders peek out above the white fur shawl wrapped around her arms. White Converse sneakers peek out under her skirt, and I'd laugh . . . if only I wasn't crying.

Calder taps me on the shoulder and hands me a handkerchief, which I use. I'm crying about so many things. I'm crying because she's the most beautiful woman in the world. I'm crying because she's my best friend and I'm lucky to know her. And I'm crying because I'll never have her in the way I want, but at least I'll have her as my friend.

I would take Addison Monroe as a friend over nothing at all. And if that's all she's willing to give me, I'll hang on to it with everything in my heart. I will grow comfortable with this sense of longing. It will be my constant companion and that's okay. I would rather this throb of yearning live inside me if it allows me to keep her in my life. She's worth it for me.

Sharon welcomes everyone to the service and tells us all why we're gathered here before asking, "Who gives this woman in marriage?"

"I do," John says firmly and then surprises me when he steps toward me and holds his hand out.

I stab my fingers into my eyes to see more clearly as I shake his hand, not expecting that gesture from him. He pats me on the back and gives me a small smile.

Addison and I turn to face each other, and I struggle to make eye contact with her, knowing that looking her in the eyes will only make repeating the vows the officiant wants us to repeat even more difficult.

When it's finally time to say our vows, Sharons asks us to take each other's hands. Addison passes her bouquet back to Dakota and when Sharon says, "Addison, repeat after me," Addison holds her hand up.

"Actually, can we do our own vows?"

My eyes snap up as I look at my friend, who's staring nervously at the officiant.

Sharon looks to me and then back to Addison. "Of course, dear. This is your day."

Addison turns to face me and it's the first time I realize that she's crying too. Her eyes are red-rimmed, and a tear streak is frozen on her cheek. She licks her lips and exhales a trembling breath, reaching out to grip my hands firmly.

"Fact or fiction. I'm a fool."

My head jerks back as I frown and force out a laugh I don't feel as I look out at the guests who are all sort of laughing but sort of not. They're just as confused as I am, so I quickly shake my head and answer, "Fiction."

Addison cocks her head and glares at me. "Don't do that. Answer it honestly. You know we only ever ask each other questions we know are fact."

I rub my lips together, trying to figure out how the hell to get out of this weird line of questioning she's forcing on me. "You're not a fool, Addison."

"I'm going to ask again, and I need you to be honest, Luke. Come on now."

I shake my head adamantly refusing to be set up to fail like this. "No, don't ask me—"

"Fact or fiction. I love you."

Chills erupt over my shoulders, my chest, my arms, legs, and toes. I feel them all over as my body language transforms from tense and defensiveness to pure, undiluted longing.

I circuit her face, taking in every inch of her expression and I see something there that I didn't see before.

Hope.

I swallow the knot in my throat. "Please let it be a fact."

She expels a noise and shrugs. "You know it is. It's a fact. I love you. I don't know when it happened, Luke, but somewhere along the way, I stopped being able to exist without you and that is utterly terrifying because you are the only person I've let in since . . . since . . ." Her voice cuts off as she shakes violently.

"Aaron," I finish her sentence, letting his name exist in the space between us. He's an important part of her life and I want her to know I see that. I've always seen that.

Her face bends with emotion as her chin quivers. She nods as fresh tears fall down her cheeks. "I love you so much, and I'm sorry for not letting that be enough last night. But I love you, Luke. I don't want to be afraid. I want to be brave. You're my home and I want to build a life with you."

I close my eyes and feel her words wrap around me like a heated blanket in this snowy wonderland we're standing in. "My turn?"

"For what?" she asks, frowning at me.

"For my vows."

"Oh . . ." She looks to Sharon, who nods, seeming enraptured by our little change in format.

I blow out a breath, trying to pull myself together. "Fact or fiction, I love you, babe."

She smiles wobbly back at me. "Fact."

"It is a fact. And it's a fact that I want to take care of you. I want to wipe your tears after a hard day and eat your bread until I'm fat. I want to lie on the couch with you until you fall asleep. And if the weight of my arm is what you need to stay asleep, it's yours. Forever my arms are yours, Addison, because I will love you forever. You're my home and I want to build a life with you too."

"I love you so much," she says and falls into my arms, her hands wrapping around my neck as she kisses me with abandon. Kisses me with every single part of her soul. And I give her mine in return.

"Um . . . guys . . ." Sharon's voice cuts into our moment. "We have some other things to do before that part."

"Oh." Addison laughs and pulls away. Her cheeks are flush, and her smile lights up her whole face as it heals the hurt inside of me.

She loves me.

She fucking loves me.

"Rings?" Sharon asks and Addison turns her attention to her dad, who stands up and pulls a ring box out of his pocket.

He gives me a half smile that feels important as he opens the box and sets the band on the officiant's open book. Calder steps forward and adds the ring I got, and Addison and I both look at what we bought and smile.

They're the matching Cartier love wedding bands. They're both white gold and feature a flat head screw design motif on them, but the one I selected for Addison also has three round brilliant-cut diamonds evenly spaced around the band between the screwhead cuts.

"You did it again," she says, her voice hoarse as she shakes her head and looks at the ring in shock.

"You like surprises," I remind my girl and feel my insides melt over that thought.

She's my girl.

Sharon has us take our rings and repeat after her. We actually listen this time and do as she says, and the moment I slide Roe's wedding band onto her finger alongside her nail design ring, I feel something inside my body click into place. A rightness in the world.

This wedding is fact. Not fiction.

Nothing like coming down to the fucking wire.

"Without further ado, Luke, you may now kiss your bride . . . again!" Sharon exclaims excitedly.

Our eyes lock before we meet each other in the middle, our foreheads gently touching for a moment as we hold each other's face and smile softly knowing this is finally it. There's no going back now.

I slip my hand down below her jaw and pull her into me, fusing our lips together as the whole world disappears and for a few precious seconds, we're just us again. Luke and Addison. Two friends who met in a lumberyard and fell in love.

The distant cheering of our friends and family pulls us apart as Sharon introduces us as Mr. and Mrs. Luke and Addison Monroe Fletcher.

It's about damn time.

Chapter 45

FACT OR FICTION?
This reception is lit with LED.

Addison

"Fact or fiction, this hot cocoa is amazing," I say, bending over next to Ethan, who's currently slurping down what has to be his third cup of the night. He has a chocolate mustache and hot chocolate splatters all over his crisp white shirt.

"Total fact." He slurps down more, and I tear up when I see a glimpse of my little brother in him.

"Hey, Ethan." I drop down into the seat next to him. "Do you want to have a sleepover at our house sometime?"

"Are you kidding me? Duh! Yes. I am available tonight."

I laugh and shake my head. "Um, tonight maybe doesn't work the best but like maybe next weekend?"

"Okay, sure. Just ask my mom, she knows my schedule."

"I like your style, kid." I ruffle his hair, and he frowns and straightens it out.

"I don't like your dress."

"No?" I look down at it and frown. "What don't you like about it?"

"White is boring. You should have tie-dyed it."

I purse my lips thoughtfully. "You know, I think you're right."

"You want me to spill hot cocoa on it to give it some color?" He looks at me dead-ass serious.

"I'm gonna say no to that one."

"You sure?" He holds the cup up toward me and I quickly grab his wrist and push him gently away.

"Yeah, I'm good. Thanks though."

"You're welcome."

"Ethan," Max barks, staring daggers at his son. "That is your second shirt of the night. We only have one more left."

Ethan shrugs. "I'm just going to ruin that one too."

Max sighs and shakes his head before looking at me. "You feeling good?"

I smile and find my husband across the room staring at me. "I'm feeling great."

Max squints his eyes and nods. "It's always harder for one person."

I gaze up at him. "What do you mean?"

"It always takes one person a bit longer to come to their senses than the other."

I tilt my head curiously. "Who held out between you and Cozy?"

"Oh, that's a very long story." He waggles his brows and then turns to glance at Luke. "Take care of my baby brother, alright?"

I lick my lips and feel butterflies in my belly. "I intend to."

Max gestures for Ethan to follow him to go change. Ethan takes off in a sprint in the opposite direction with his dad hot on his heels.

I can't help but laugh at the older brother speech because Jo said something similar earlier.

"He's all yours, beautiful girl. Thank you for saying yes to him today," Jo says, holding me close. Today's hug is the best one yet, and I love that she's holding me as if I'm precious to her. "If I may, I want to share some wisdom on marriage as I learned a thing or two in the thirty-eight years Steven and I were married. Love isn't always easy, but life can be even harder. It's about saying yes to the man you married. Yes, to the hard things when it would be easier to walk away. Yes, to forgiving him when he screws up, because he will." I laugh. "And it's a yes that you say every day to loving him with everything you have."

And for the first time, I initiated a Jo Fletcher hug, and it was me who held on tighter and longer than her for once. "Thank you for showing me the most beautiful kind of motherhood."

I smile through my tears, hoping I can be just like her to one of my own children someday, and the fact that that thought alone doesn't scare the absolute shit out of me just shows how far I've come up here on Fletcher Mountain.

"Addison, can I talk to you for a second?" Everly asks, walking over to me and ripping me out of my family building fantasy.

"Of course, Evs. What's up?"

"I just have to say I'm so sorry for the part I played in the fight you guys had last night. I only wanted the best for my uncle, and I knew you were the best, but it was wrong of us to lie to you. And it was wrong of me to pressure Luke into all of this and I really hope you can forgive me."

I pin the adorable blonde with a "get the fuck out of here" look before I wrap her in my arms and hug the shit out of her, murmuring into her shoulder, "Everly Fletcher, look around here."

Everly's blue eyes scan the room that looks like a winter wonderland fairy tale. The dance floor is hopping with lumberyard friends and Edith has barely let my dad sit down all night. It's the best surprise of my life . . . other than finding out my best friend was in love with me, of course.

"You make magic happen," I state firmly to my new niece. "Please don't ever change."

"You really mean it?"

"Yes." I reach over and hold her face in my hands. "Keep pushing, keep micromanaging, keep not taking no for an answer. And don't ever let anyone dull your shine. Got it?"

She gets a funny look on her face before she nods, and when the music shifts to a girlie pop anthem, I jump up to my feet and pull my niece onto the dance floor to twirl the night away.

By the end of the night, I find myself in my husband's arms swaying on the dance floor.

"Can we get married a third time?" Luke murmurs into my neck before lifting his head to look down at me. "I'd like to know what a wedding would feel like without being miserable for every moment leading up to it. Maybe we could get married every year."

I stand up on my toes to kiss his lips. "I think we can just celebrate an anniversary, can't we?"

"I guess so." He pulls me in close. "As long as we get to have a wedding night each year."

"I'm hoping for a lot more than once a year, fella." I poke him in the chest.

"Oh, you can count on it, wife. Just let me know whenever I need to fulfill my husbandly duties."

"You were doing a pretty good job of it the last couple of weeks, so just . . . more of that."

"Done."

I giggle and sigh, realizing the future isn't all that scary anymore because we've lived it together already. It's just going to be more of what we already know works, except this time I get to tell him I love him anytime I want.

"Mind if I cut in?" a deep voice interrupts our dance, and Luke and I turn to see my father standing there in all his tall, mustache-wearing, overbearing glory.

Luke smiles and glances down at me for approval and I nod before he holds my hand out to my dad and respectfully steps away, shooting me an encouraging wink as he goes.

My dad smells like that familiar scent in the bathroom after he'd shower growing up. Clean bar soap and shaving cream. It's comforting in an odd way. As dysfunctional as he is as a father, I still love him. He's my dad.

"Nice to see you looking happy, kiddo," he rumbles, looking around the dance floor. "Hoping when I tell you I just made a call and turned down the offer from the Whitakers, it'll make you even more happy."

My lips part as I look up at him in shock. "Seriously?"

He nods, looking somber. "They were a bit too fancy to take over the yard. Bullhead would have been so uncomfortable."

"Oh well, we can't have Bullhead being uncomfortable." I glance over where Bullhead is sitting at a table with Chuck and some yard guys and there are piles of beer cans stacked up all around them.

Dad harrumphs. "Really smart of you to line up sober drivers for everyone tonight."

I shrug and smile. "I'm a smart girl, Dad."

He nods and exhales heavily. "I know that, Ads." He tilts his head and looks down at me. "Which is why I'm going to let you take over the yard, on one condition."

"If you tell me there's another stipulation in this trust that says I need to give you a certain number of grandchildren, I am going to scream."

His head jerks back. "That's not in the will, but it's maybe not a bad idea to add something—"

"Dad!" I exclaim, ready to pounce on him, but his face twists up into a devilish grin.

"I'm messing with you, Addie May." He sighs, the crinkles in his eyes appearing thoughtful. "I just want you to promise that if the yard gets to be too much, you bring Chuck up to manage more of it. Even if it means you take a pay cut."

"I don't care about the money, Dad."

"I know but I just need to hear you say it."

I stare up at him with a serious expression. "I promise that if it starts to become too much, I will ask for help."

He offers me a wobbly smile. "Chuck says you run it better than I ever did anyhow."

"Obviously," I snort, and my dad just scowls down at me.

His gaze turns to find Luke, who's now dancing with his mom. "I guess he isn't the worst guy you could have picked."

"I'm afraid he's a keeper." *And I fear he will make an excellent father if we decide that's what we want someday.*

My dad eyes me warily. "I take it those vows mean you will be keeping him, then? That was all a fact?"

"It was a fact."

He nods. "Aaron would have liked him too, I think."

My eyes sting with that and I feel myself sniffing. "Hey, Dad. Would you . . . maybe want to bring some of these wedding flowers to the cemetery with me tomorrow?"

His lips turn down as he nods. "I could do that, kid."

And with that, I lay my cheek on my dad's chest and let him spin me around the dance floor, feeling more like a daddy's girl than I have in a very long time.

Chapter 46

FACT OR FICTION?

Getting down on one knee is overrated.

Luke

I stand on the front porch with my wife as we watch the car service take the last of the guests down the mountain and back to their homes. I move to stand behind my wife, wrapping my hands around her waist, my fingers digging into the satin of her dress as I kiss her neck, which is chilled from the night air.

"You better have that fire going inside, Fletcher," she says, leaning back and combing her fingers through my hair.

"My fire is always burning for you, babe."

She laughs and turns to grab my hand and pull me inside, but I plant my feet and stop her movement.

She looks back with a frown. "What are you doing? Let's go inside. It's freezing out here."

"I have one more thing I want to do." I inhale a deep breath and drop down to one knee. "Addison May Monroe, will you make me the happiest man on Fletcher Mountain and marry me and be my wife for life and not for a year?"

She laughs and props her free hand on her hip. "I think we've already done this a couple times, haven't we?"

I shrug and smile up at her. "I didn't get to kneel."

Her eyes soften as she reaches out and caresses my face, her cool fingers warming up my entire soul. "Yes, I'll marry you, Luke Fletcher. You're kind of my best friend."

My brows lift. "I'm a lot more than that now, hot stuff." I hop up to my feet, tucking my shoulder into her waist as I toss her over my back like a beautiful bridal sack of concrete mix.

"What are you doing?" she asks, pounding her tiny fists into my rear.

"I'm carrying you over the threshold obviously," I deadpan.

"Um . . . I think there's a more elegant way to do that."

I smack her ass firmly. "Yeah, but I know my wife, and this is much more her style."

She giggles when I give her bottom a cheeky squeeze and I carry her into our house, which has never felt more like home than it has in this moment right now.

And that . . . is a fact.

Chapter 47

FACT OR FICTION?
Grief can bring people together.

Luke

Addison lays her bridal bouquet in front of the gravestone at her brother's plot and I stand back to give her space as she traces her fingers over the etching on the stone. She told me on our way out here that all the times she goes for a run in town, this is where she goes.

She runs in the cemetery.

It's unusual and something I feel like I should have known about the woman I've called my friend for many years, but I can understand why she kept it to herself. People process grief in any number of ways. I know my mom visits our dad's plot quite often, but my brothers and I have the bench on the peak. That's where we feel closest to him. That's where we can talk to him or reflect on him. Remember him and thank him for the beautiful life he's given us. I even sat out there and replayed that voicemail Addison sent me and cried like a damn baby.

I glance up to the sky, having my own sort of moment with my dad. I have a feeling he'd be smiling big-time and not at all surprised that it was Addison I ended up with after all. He probably saw it coming the moment I started volunteering to pick up the lumber orders.

Damn, I miss him.

And I had years with him, unlike Addison, who only had her brother for eight. I can't imagine how hard it was for them to lose Aaron so young. I'm glad she comes out here to run. Whatever she needs, I want her to feel supported.

"I talk to him a lot when I come out here. Is that going to freak you out?" Addison asks, turning her head to look back at me.

"Only if he talks back." I cringe at the probably awful joke that this is really not the time or place for, but luckily, my wife laughs.

"I just wanted to officially introduce two of the men I've loved the most in my life." She blinks up at me and I feel my heart swell in my chest.

Our wedding night was one for the books. Full of passion and confessions. Confessing all the feelings we've both been hiding from each other and ourselves. The buildup of Addison and I was painful in more ways than one, but the satisfying conclusion is something I'll cherish forever. I fought for her. For us. I was patient. I was present. And she found me. She loves me. And introducing me to her brother is probably the best way she could tell me.

A loud throat-clearing sound echoes from behind us and we swerve around to see Addison's dad standing before us. "So I take it I'm third on your list of men you love?"

Addison stands up and smiles, moving over beside me. "Naw, you're fifth."

"Fifth." John rolls his eyes. "After Chuck and Bullhead?"

Addison giggles and I wrap my arms around her and press my lips into her hair.

John sobers as he glances down at the gravestone. "Been a long time since I came out here."

"Flowers look good, don't they?" Addison asks, her eyes soft on her father.

John nods and makes his way past us to stand a little closer. We watch him stand silently for a moment before he shakes his head. "You two will do better than me and her."

My brows furrow as I feel Addison tense beneath my arm.

"What do you mean?" Addison asks, her voice soft.

John turns and looks back at us. "You two will make better parents than me and your mom. Though in fairness, we set the bar pretty low." John crosses his arms and harrumphs. "Maybe I'll get a second chance as a grandpa."

"Dad, it's a little soon to be talking about kids." Addison shoots me a coy look that I would really love to kiss off her face, because she has come so far, and I feel honored to be a small part of her healing.

"Fine, let's share some memories of Aaron instead," he says, shoving his hands into his pockets. "Where should we start?"

"Oh, I love this idea," Addison laughs and the two of them begin ruminating over which story to tell first while I sit back and enjoy my father-in-law not looking at me like he wants to kill me . . . for once.

And my best friend looking at me like she loves me . . . forever.

Chapter 48

FACT OR FICTION?
Emma Woodhouse finds her Mr. Knightley.

Everly

My stomach swirls with anxiety as my plane begins its initial decent into Dublin. Christmas and my winter break went by way too fast and now it's back to the reality of my own life instead of my family's, which kind of sucks because my family is a wonderful distraction.

But Luke's words have been on repeat in my mind since the moment he said them before the wedding.

You've never even been in love. You know nothing. You're just a kid.

We had a long talk after the wedding on the lookout bench and Luke told me he didn't mean what he said, he was just hurting, but you know those jokes that people make that are just a little too close to home?

That was in Luke's words.

There was a sliver of truth to them. I have never been in love. I had a boyfriend for two years in high school and was still never able to say the words. Which is just wild because my love cup runneth over in every other part of my life. My moms, my dad, Cozy, my uncles, my brother, my niece. My grandma. My God, I am the most loved, most blessed young adult that ever existed.

The only hardship in my life thus far was losing my grandpa. Which was absolutely brutal. And it seems like ever since then, I can't seem to shake this feeling of needing to do right by him.

Needing to make sure everyone is good for him. I want to take care of everyone all the time. Anything to avoid looking at my own life and my own experiences, because if I really looked at my life in Ireland . . .

It's kind of pathetic.

Sure I go to parties, but it's almost like I'm just checking a box, not genuinely letting myself go.

And even my classes are a struggle. I'm barely scraping by and the coursework is only getting harder. I'm studying, but it's not sticking. I don't know what's wrong with me. I just . . . want to be present in my own damn life.

My phone pings with a text and I swipe the screen to see a message from Luke.

Luke: Don't forget about what I said.

Everly: What did you say again? Refresh my memory please because it's been a long flight.

Luke: I said you need to LIVE a little, kid. It's your turn to experience life for yourself and not worry about anyone else. Be selfish. We're all good back here. Your masterminding worked and we're happy and in love. Now you need to go find your own great love story. Even if it's not the love of your life. It's time you experience something just for you . . . and not for all of us. And if you don't report back with something interesting, your uncles will fly their asses over there and force you into it. Got it?

My lips curl up into a smile as I picture my three uncles in Dublin. Somehow, I think they'd find a way to fit right in.

Everly: Got it.

Luke: Love ya, Evie-bear. Keep me posted, okay?

Everly: Will do. Give a big hug to Addison for me. And go enjoy your honeymoon! Love you both.

I close my phone and sit back in my seat to glance out my window. Ireland is about to get a taste of the real Everly Fletcher.

Epilogue

FACT OR FICTION?
Compound living is peak mountain life.

Luke

A Couple Years Later

I stand on the mountain staring at the beautiful image in front of me. It's summertime on the peak and my wife is sitting on my father's memorial bench, which is now nestled under the pergola Calder made. There are purple flowers vining up the boards that my mom planted last summer and they're in full bloom right now. Just like my wife.

She sits there a lot these days, talking to her brother. I surprised Addison on her brother's birthday last year by adding a memorial plaque to the pergola that says:

Fact or Fiction: Little brothers make the best guardian angels.

And well, there were definite tears.

We put Aaron's name on it along with his birth and death date, and while I know my wife still goes to the cemetery for her runs, these past few weeks, the bench has been a better place for her.

I make my way over to join her at the bench, glancing down the hill at the goings-on. Fletcher Mountain is bustling with life this Saturday summer afternoon. Wyatt and Trista are down by the barn with Stevie prancing around in her little cowboy boots that match her mother's. Calder's saw can be heard echoing down the canyon as he works on furniture in his shop, and Dakota appears to be reading a book on their front porch with their new cat curled up on her lap. They just got back from their honeymoon and their cats missed them something fierce. I know because we had to take care of them while they were gone.

Down the mountain a ways Trista has a couple of employees busy at her new rescue center that creates more traffic than this mountain has ever seen. We're working on developing another drive to give it its own entrance. Opening her rescue center to visitors creates more opportunity for donations. So while a few years ago, Fletcher Mountain was a sleepy little peak consisting of a few bachelors who caused ruckus in town every once in a while, it's now a fully functioning, sustainable compound.

Hell, even Max's new house is in the process of going up. We forced him to scale it back to half its original size because Wyatt refused to let his brother build something obnoxious up here, but it's coming along. Even includes a mother-in-law suite for our mom that we're all excited about. Her and Max and his family up here will make Fletcher Mountain feel fully complete. No more new construction projects.

Unless my wife decides we need to add on more space for our very near future.

I smile when I see the side view of her and make my way over to the bench to sit next to her. I can't help but stretch my hand out and rest it on her belly.

"Doing okay, babe?" I ask as I rake my eyes over her face.

She clutches my hand to her round bump that's the size of a basketball. "He's kicking like crazy in there, which is wild because there's not much room left so I don't know how he's moving at all."

I press my lips to her shoulder and murmur, "Any day now."

"I'm ready," she sighs and glances down at her swollen stomach. "I'm going to be the best mom."

"I know you are," I reply automatically.

She says this a lot lately. I think that fear of turning out like her parents is still alive and well. Which is why she's already trained Chuck at the yard to take over so she can have a full three months of maternity leave. And she lined my mom up to take the baby when she goes back to work part time. She's signed up for mommy and me classes already and our coffee table is covered with pregnancy and parenting books. She's dedicated to being the best working mom that ever existed, and I hate that she's putting so much pressure on herself because she has no idea how much love she gives just by existing.

But if this is what she needs to feel good in this decision we made to have a child, then I'm going to support her no matter what.

We miscarried our first baby at eight weeks, and I thought she'd never want to try again. I held her and we grieved, and our home was flooded with my family, who supported us through every painful day in their own unique ways.

But it wasn't until my mom told Addison that our baby was with Aaron now that I felt like my wife found some sense of hope to try again.

Now here we are. Thirty-eight weeks and holding our breath that this is it. I have a good feeling.

"Incoming!" Trista yells from down at the barn and I turn around to see Stevie barreling toward us with a big smile on her face.

"I got her," I call back and watch my three-year-old niece run like the perfect girl she is all the way over to us.

She pants loudly as she moves around the bench to crawl up

next to Addison. Her hands instantly wrap around Roe's belly, and she lays her ear on top of the bump and gasps. "I hear him!"

"You do?" Addison laughs and runs her fingers through Stevie's chestnut curls.

"He says he's hungry."

"Does he now?"

"He says he wants bread," Stevie says, blinking her big eyes up at my wife.

Addison's jaw drops. "He's hungry again?"

Stevie nods with vigor, so I hold my hand out to help my wife up off the bench. I'm afraid our niece has learned the deliciousness that is Addison's bread and uses her incoming cousin as an excuse to get snacks. Often.

I watch in awe as my wife waddles back to our cabin with one hand on her lower back and the other holding Stevie's as she skips beside her.

"Hey, fucker," Calder says, dropping down on the bench beside me with a six-pack of beers. He hands one over to me before opening one for himself.

I hear the sounds of footsteps and find Wyatt walking over to join us as well. I pass him a beer and hook my thumb back to Addison. "Your daughter is pawning more snacks off of us."

"Put it on my tab," Wyatt harrumphs and takes a drink of his beer.

The three of us share a beer in silence for a moment, taking in the breathtaking view that never gets old. Rolling pine trees stacked amongst the rugged cliffs. Long grass swaying in the breeze below them all bathed in the warm colors of an incoming sunset twinkling above Jamestown.

"Remember when Calder stood right here and said, 'No woman is better than this'?" I state with a laugh as I jab my elbow into him.

Calder frowns. "I'm eating my words for sure, but I believe

it was you who came up with the pact that we all live up here alone, so you're no less foolish than me."

Wyatt shakes his head and glances behind us. "I think Dad was looking out for us."

"You can say that again," Calder confirms with a nod.

"New pact?" I ask, quirking a brow them.

They stare at me curiously.

"Let's vow to be just as good at life as Dad was." My throat tightens as I look over at both of them. "Whether that's in business, in parenting, with our partners. We live our lives to keep making him proud and the rest will fall into place."

Wyatt quirks a smile. "I'll drink to that."

Calder holds his beer up. "We're not here for a long time . . ."

"We're here for a good time," I finish, and we clink our bottles together and drink for the man who taught us that life is indeed a good time . . . even through the hard times.

★ ★ ★ ★ ★

If you liked reading about the Fletcher brothers, keep an eye out for the final book in the Mountain Men Matchmaker *series, featuring the beloved mastermind matchmaker Everly, out in May 2026!*

You can also check out Everly's origin story in Last on the List *featuring her father, CEO and single dad Max Fletcher, and her nanny-turned-stepmom Cozy, available now in all formats!*

Read on for excerpts from the first book in the Mountain Men Matchmaker series, Nine Month Contract, *and* Last on the List, *both available now from Amy Daws and Canary Street Press.*

Excerpt from Nine Month Contract

Wyatt

Help Wanted: Grumpy Mountain Man seeks baby momma to grow his seed. Uterus a must. Ovaries negotiable. Boobs not required but a nice bonus. Job is an incubator position only. No parenting allowed. Surrogate must be impervious to grunting in the form of communication and impartial to goat droppings. Rustic mountain range housing available upon request. Interested parties can text 555–5456. Murderers need not apply. Expect sizable payment and signed legal contracts before insemination commences. Also, must be cool with brotherly neighbors . . . and no, that isn't code for Why Choose.

Pet Goats: 1
Annoying Brothers: 3

"You fucking fuckers!" I roar as I slam my foot on the brakes in front of my brother's cabin, sending a dust storm of gravel swirling around my truck. Jumping out of the driver's seat, I charge up the steps toward my two siblings sitting on Calder's front porch and come to a stop between them. I glare at their relaxed frames stretched out on a couple of wooden rocking chairs with tin cups of coffee in hand.

Like it's just a normal Saturday fucking morning.

I hold up the piece of paper in my hand. "Which one of you posted this at the bar?"

"Easy there, Wyatt . . . you don't want to hit your daily word quota all before lunch." Calder laughs and sets his cup down on the end table beside him and snaps his fingers. "Although I guess 'fuck' was redundant, so you have a few more words to burn."

Without warning, I reach out and grab his collar, yanking him out of his chair. I knew it was Calder. It's always fucking Calder. "Is my life some kind of joke to you?" I seethe, feeling every muscle in my arms flex as I hold my six-foot-three brother up on his tiptoes. I'm only an inch taller than him, so it's no easy task.

"How do you know it was me?" Calder's eyes dance with mirth. Mirth that I am two seconds away from punching off his smug face.

I glance over at Luke, the youngest of us, who seems perfectly at ease as he scratches his short beard and enjoys the show. I slant my gaze back to the most typical middle child on the face of this earth—never mind the fucker is thirty-five now. He was a pain in the ass when we were young, and he's a pain in the ass now. The only difference now is he has more disposable income and more "inspired" ideas for his shenanigans.

My voice is growly as I crumple the sheet between us. "'Impervious' was your word of the day last week, and you used it incorrectly for hours."

The corner of Calder's mouth tips up. "Pretty sure I got it right in that ad though, didn't I, Papa Bear?"

Rage spikes in my veins now that he's confirmed his guilt. "I'm going to throw you off this mountain and burn your cabin down."

I drag Calder's floundering body down the front steps of his porch toward the lookout point in front of my cabin, ignoring his raucous laughter that echoes off the foothills. I spent weeks clearing trees from this mountain vista when I bought this land to create this view before I even built my home. I wanted a place to quiet my thoughts and bring me peace.

This is the opposite of peace.

"Whoa, whoa, whoa," Luke calls out, his boots crunching on the gravel as he jogs past me to press a hand to my chest. "It's way too early in the day for manslaughter and arson threats."

"No shit," Calder scoffs, extricating himself from my grip. He steps back and straightens his flannel, concealing the ink scrawled across his chest. "This violent behavior will make finding you a Momma Bear very difficult, Papa Bear."

"Stop calling me Papa Bear," I hiss, ruing the day I ever thought it'd be a good idea to have my brothers build on this secluded mountain with me.

I fist the ridiculous ad in my hand and glance up the hill at the three cabins we all built together almost ten years ago. Three brothers living on a mountaintop I bought in rural Colorado sounded like a dream back then. We all worked side by side to develop this stretch of land and build self-sustaining cabins to survive up here on minimal energy resources. Even in the snowiest of winters, we have everything we need to survive for days without contact from the outside world. Weeks even.

Sounds like fucking heaven.

Or it did . . . until something started to feel different for me. *As though something was missing.*

"This isn't a fucking joke," I grumble, running my hand over my short hair.

Calder's expression shifts from cocky to damn near somber as he pins me with a serious look. "I didn't make that ad as a joke, Wyatt. I made it because you're a damn fool for going back to that agency in Denver that's going to charge you six figures for a surrogate when there are decent women right here in Jamestown who will grow your baby for a fraction of the price."

"It's not about the cost, Calder," I boom for the hundredth

time. "I'll pay whatever it takes to become a . . ." I hesitate to say the word out loud, my voice getting caught in my throat as the weight of it presses down on me.

Dad.

When will that word ever stop being difficult for me to say out loud? My eyes move over to the memorial bench Calder built and placed at the lookout point two years ago after our father passed unexpectedly. Our dad's favorite saying is inscribed on it: *We're not here for a long time, we're here for a good time.*

Dad was the salt of the earth—hardworking, protective, and challenging in all the best ways. I can close my eyes and still feel his presence all around me—his signature scent of Brut cologne, his chastising tone when my brothers and I were late to a jobsite, his bark of a laugh, or the way he never sneezed just once. It was always an attack of eight sneezes in a row. Fuck, I miss him.

And let's not even think about how hard it's been for my mom, who was just about to celebrate their forty-fifth wedding anniversary before he passed. Now she's a widow who still cries at family events.

Dad was the definition of *patriarch*, and when we lost him, we lost our guide, our anchor, our voice of reason. The world got a little darker.

Now, I want to bring some light back into our lives. I want to see my mom hold my kid for once instead of my niece or nephew. I'm proud of what my brothers and I have built on this mountain, and I want to share that with a child of my own.

And I'll be damned if I let Calder fuck with my plan.

Nine Month Contract is available now in all formats from Amy Daws and Canary Street Press wherever books are sold!

Excerpt from Last on the List

Max Fletcher

A light knock on my door has me straightening in my desk chair. Everly doesn't knock, so I can only assume it's the nanny. I smooth down my new tie for the day and attempt to look busy as I call out, "Come in."

Cassandra walks into my bedroom, dressed in a long tie-dyed T-shirt and a pair of black leggings. She glances briefly at my bed and then forces her eyes on me.

"Can I have a word with you, Mr. Fletcher?" she asks, her hands playing with the hem of her shirt as she approaches my desk.

"Yes, of course. Where's Everly?"

"She's reading upstairs," she replies quickly, tucking her damp hair behind her ears.

The smell of coconut invades the room, and I wonder if she's just gotten out of the shower. Not that I should be thinking of my nanny in the fucking shower.

"I was wondering if maybe we could tell Everly I quit?" Cassandra quips, her tone sharp and contained.

My heart rate increases as I repeat her words in my head before I can mutter them out loud. "Quit?"

"Yeah . . ." she responds, her eyes staring down at the floor. "I'd rather she think I quit than blame herself for getting me fired. She keeps apologizing about the accident today, and I know it's breaking her little heart that she hurt me. If she thinks you let me go because of the pool incident, she'll never forgive herself."

I sit back in my chair, processing everything Cassandra has just said to me. She's known my kid for one freaking day, and she's willing to take the fall for her? I'm rarely speechless, but this situation makes forming a coherent sentence difficult.

I clear my throat. "Do you want to quit?"

"Not at all." Cassandra's round eyes lift to meet mine. The sunlight pouring in the windows behind me makes her eyes look greener than ever. "But I know that what happened today was terrifying for you and Everly. We were lucky you were here. I mean, I don't think I was going to drown. I was getting up to the top of the water before you jumped in. But I fully admit that it wasn't safe. Yes, it's true I'm not a great swimmer. I mean, I think I can save my own life, but if something like this happened to Everly, I'd be terrified of what that could look like. And with how much time you want us to spend in the pool this summer, I realize this makes me unqualified for the job I accepted. Therefore, I take full responsibility and will tender my resignation, Mr. Fletcher."

My head jerks back. *Tender her resignation?* That's pretty official language for someone whose past employer involved making footlong subs. I inhale a deep breath and stand, propping myself on the edge of the desk. "Let's take a breath here, Cassandra," I say, crossing my arms over my chest.

She nods and tucks her hands behind her back, her chest jutting out toward me. I flinch as I recall the feel of her extremely full breasts in my hands. How is it possible to be completely fucking terrified and half hard at the same time? That's really something I should talk to a therapist about someday. But not Josh's wife, Lynsey. Patient confidentiality or not, I don't need my best friend's wife to think I'm lusting after my kid's nanny.

"The truth is, Everly is an excellent swimmer," I continue,

refocusing on the task at hand. "An incident like this never should have happened. Everly feels awful because she knows what she did was wrong. She usually has better impulse control than that, but I think she's really excited about hanging out with you this summer, and she got carried away."

"Hey, I've been there," Cassandra huffs with a laugh, her hand pushing into her dark hair as she gazes out the sliders behind me. "I remember pushing my sister off the dock at the lake once. She whacked her ankle on the boat hoist and screamed bloody murder for hours. Even had to get stitches."

I fight back a smile at that very random overshare. "Ouch."

"Yeah . . . the whole lake heard her battle cry. It was Awkward City. I immediately regretted my life choice that day."

I cringe knowingly, thankful for the turn in the conversation as the tension relaxes. "Kind of like your new boss regretting accidentally grabbing your chest as he attempted to save your life?" My shoulders lift with embarrassment.

"I mean, I was a kid, and you are a full-grown man, but I guess you can still relate." She lets out a soft giggle, and the tension eases between us as I watch her with downcast eyes.

"Awkward what?" I frown and watch her curiously, wanting to know more about her.

"City. Awkward City." The teasing smirk on her face makes it hard to keep scowling.

I click my tongue and sigh, trying to figure out the best way to resolve this. Giving up, I gesture toward her chest, trying hard not to look at it. "Well . . . I am sorry about that."

"It's fine. My tits get in the way a lot." She closes her eyes and shakes her head. "I shouldn't have said that. Can we stop talking about my breasts now?"

"Please," I agree because now I can't stop looking at them and recalling how the weight of them felt in my hands. Fucking hell . . . Awkward City indeed.

"Okay then." She pulls her shirt away from her chest as if she's trying to conceal her completely unconcealable breasts. "So are you saying I'm not fired?"

> Last on the List *is available now wherever books are sold! The trade paperback from Amy Daws and Canary Street Press includes exclusive bonus material!*